UNTIL TONIGHT

He smiled. "You're sure I'll win. You've planned everything."

"I'm betting on it, Rowdy Darnell."

"And if I don't?" He had to know what would remain between them if tonight didn't go as planned.

"Then I'll go home as if nothing has changed and pick up the bag when I'm in town alone." Laurel's blue eyes met his. "It may take me a few hours, but I'll meet you under the cottonwood before midnight."

He knew what she meant. What was going to happen between them would happen. At the hotel, or beneath the stars. It would happen.

He stood. "Until tonight," he said as he kissed her.

from "Silent Partner" by Jodi Thomas

BOOK YOUR PLACE ON OUR WEBSITE AND MAKE THE READING CONNECTION!

We've created a customized website just for our very special readers, where you can get the inside scoop on everything that's going on with Zebra, Pinnacle and Kensington books.

When you come online, you'll have the exciting opportunity to:

- View covers of upcoming books
- Read sample chapters
- Learn about our future publishing schedule (listed by publication month *and author*)
- Find out when your favorite authors will be visiting a city near you
- Search for and order backlist books from our online catalog
- Check out author bios and background information
- Send e-mail to your favorite authors
- Meet the Kensington staff online
- Join us in weekly chats with authors, readers and other guests
- Get writing guidelines
- AND MUCH MORE!

**Visit our website at
http://www.kensingtonbooks.com**

JODI THOMAS
DeWANNA PACE
LINDA BRODAY
PHYLISS MIRANDA

GIVE ME A
COWBOY

ZEBRA BOOKS
Kensington Publishing Corp.
http://www.kensingtonbooks.com

ZEBRA BOOKS are published by

Kensington Publishing Corp.
850 Third Avenue
New York, NY 10022

All Kensington titles, imprints, and distributed lines are available
at special quantity discounts for bulk purchases for sales promotion,
premiums, fund-raising, educational, or institutional use.

Special book excerpts or customized printings can also be created
to fit specific needs. For details, write or phone the office of the
Kensington Special Sales Manager: Attn. Special Sales Department.
Kensington Publishing Corp., 850 Third Avenue, New York, NY
10022. Phone: 1-800-221-2647.

Zebra and the Z logo Reg. U.S. Pat. & TM Off.

ISBN-13: 978-1-4201-0371-7
ISBN-10: 1-4201-0371-7

First Zebra Mass Market Printing: February 2009
10 9 8 7 6 5 4 3 2 1

Printed in the United States of America

Contents

SILENT PARTNER

PARTNER

JODI THOMAS

Chapter 1

Dust circled around Rowdy Darnell's worn boots as he stepped from the noon train. The reddish brown dirt whirled, trying to wipe his footprints away before they were even planted in this nothing of a town called Kasota Springs, which suited him fine. If he could, he'd erase every trace of him ever having lived here.

Beneath the shadow of his hat, Rowdy looked around, fearing he'd see someone he knew. Someone who remembered him.

But only strangers hurried past and most didn't bother to look in his direction. Not that they'd recognize him now. Prison had hardened the boy they'd sent away into a man, tall, lean and unforgiving.

Rowdy pulled his saddle from among the luggage, balanced it over one shoulder and walked off the platform toward Main Street. In the five years since he'd been gone, the place had changed, more than doubling in size, thanks mostly, he guessed, to the railhead. New storefronts and businesses framed a town square in huddled progress. To the north a line of two story roofs stood behind the bank and hardware store. One end of Main was braced by the railroad, but on the other end houses and barns scattered out for half a mile, uneven veins leading into the heart of town.

Rowdy was glad for Kasota Springs' growth. Maybe he'd be able to sell the nothing of a ranch his father had left him and be on his way. He had a hundred places he wanted to see and five years of catching up to do. The sooner he got out of this part of Texas and away from memories, the better.

He walked straight to the livery and picked out a horse to rent. All the corral stock looked better than any horse he'd worked with in years. Prison horses were either broken down or wild and crazy-eyed. A guard once told him horses too tough to eat were sold to the prisons. Rowdy almost laughed. The stock reminded him of the prisoners, he decided, wondering which category he fit into.

"You here for the rodeo?" the blacksmith asked a few minutes later when he pulled the bay Rowdy had pointed out from the herd.

"No," Rowdy answered without looking at the man.

"I'm surprised. You look like you could rodeo. Got the build for it."

Rowdy didn't answer. He'd spent too many years avoiding conversation to jump in.

The man didn't seem to notice. "If I were younger, I'd give it a try. All the ranchers have gone together and donated cattle. They say the all-around winner will walk away with a couple hundred head. Imagine that. Biggest prize I ever heard of. We're expecting cowboys from three states to be riding and the cattle are in the far pen, ready."

Rowdy moved to the horse's head, introducing himself with a touch before he looked back at the blacksmith. "You mind if I brush him down and check his hooves before I saddle up?"

The barrel-chested man shook his head, accepted the dollar for the rental, and turned his attention to the next customers riding in.

Rowdy picked up a brush and began working some of the mud out of the horse's hide. The familiar action relaxed him. One thing he'd learned in prison was that animals were a great deal more predictable than humans. Treat them right and they tend to return the favor.

As he worked, he watched a fancy red surrey pull up to the livery with three girls inside and one cowboy, dressed in his best, handling the rig. Another cowhand rode beside the buggy as if on guard.

"Sam!" the driver yelled. "Can you check this rigging? I'd hate to tell the Captain I risked an accident with this precious cargo of sisters." He turned back and winked at the two girls sitting on the second seat.

They giggled in harmony.

Rowdy noticed that the third girl sat alone on the backseat looking out of place. She didn't laugh, or even look like she was paying attention. Her dress was far plainer than her sisters', and her bonnet held no ribbon but the one that tied just below her chin. A stubborn chin, he thought. Sticking out as if daring anyone to take a swing at it.

"Give me an hour," Sam yelled as he crossed into the barn. "I'll oil the wheels and have it checked."

The driver tied off the reins and jumped down. The silver on his spurs chimed as he moved. "Ladies, how about lunch at the hotel?" He offered his hand to the first giggly girl, a petite blonde with apple cheeks, while the other cowhand climbed from his saddle and did the same to the second one, a slightly plumper version of her sister.

When the first girl started to step down, the driver moved closer. "We can't have you getting that pretty dress dirty. How about I carry you to the walk?"

Rowdy watched as the cowboys each lifted a laughing bundle of lace and ribbons. It took him a minute to realize the silent one in the back had been forgotten. She sat, stiff and straight as if saying to the world she didn't care. When she raised her chin slightly with pride, Rowdy saw her face beneath the simple bonnet.

Plain, he thought. As plain as the flat land and endless sky of this country. She didn't look all that old, but she had "old maid" written all over her. She'd be the one to stay with the parents long after the other two had married. She'd age alone, or worse, be forced to live from midlife to old age with one of the sisters and her family.

He glanced at the others, their voices drifting lower as they strolled toward the hotel. Rowdy wondered how often this third sister had been left behind, forgotten.

He moved around his horse and tossed the brush he'd been using in a bucket. For once in his life he wished he had clean Sunday-go-to-meeting clothes. He'd been an outsider enough to recognize another. The least he could do was offer her a way out of her awkward situation.

"Miss," he said, shoving his hat back so she could see his face. "May I help you down?"

She looked at him with a flash of surprise, as if she thought herself alone in the world.

For a moment he figured she'd tell him to mind his own business, but then he saw it . . . a smile that lifted the corner of her mouth. A pretty mouth, he thought, in a plain face.

"Thank you," she whispered and took his hand as he helped her down.

The surrey shifted slightly and he placed his free hand on her waist to steady her. Though she stood taller than his shoulder, she felt soft, almost fragile. He didn't offer to carry her. He had a feeling that would have embarrassed them both, but when she reached the ground, he tucked her gloved hand into his elbow and walked across the road to a boardwalk made from mostly green planks.

Once she stepped on the boards, he touched his hat and turned to leave.

"Thank you, Rowdy Darnell," she whispered.

He froze. Without facing her, he asked, "You know who I am?"

"Of course. We were in sixth grade together the year you

and your father moved here." Her soft voice changed slightly. "The year before I was sent away to school."

Shifting, he wished she'd look up so he could see her face again. After his mother died, his father only sent him to school when he wanted an undisturbed day of drinking. Rowdy was there barely long enough to learn the other kids' names. Not that it mattered much. They weren't interested in being friends with the town drunk's boy.

"Laurel," Rowdy said slowly as the memory of a thin, shy girl drifted across his mind. "Laurel Hayes." He remembered liking the way her name sounded.

She looked up. The tiny smile was back. "I'm glad you're home," she said in a voice as gentle as wind chimes whispering on a midnight breeze. "I ride by your father's place once in a while. Part of the roof on the cabin fell in last winter, but the barn still stands."

He nodded, suddenly not wanting to leave her. "I figured that. The sheriff wrote me when my dad died. Sheriff Barnett said he sold off the last of the stock to pay debts." Rowdy liked the way she looked him in the eye, silently telling him that she had no fear of him. He'd expected to see fear or even hatred in folks when he returned. "But, Miss, I'm not coming back. Just passing through. Thought I'd sell the place and move on."

Understanding showed in her eyes along with a sadness that surprised him. "The water's good on your place. You could make a living running cattle."

He didn't want to tell her that he had less than twelve dollars in his pocket. Not enough to buy even a calf. If he remembered right, she was the oldest daughter of one of the richest ranchers around. She probably shouldn't even be talking to the likes of him.

"Well . . ." He wished he knew more about what to say, but for five years most of the language he'd heard hadn't been something a lady like her should ever hear. "I'd best be going."

To his surprise, the sadness brushed across her pale blue

eyes once more. She offered her gloved hand. "Good day, Mr. Darnell. I wish you luck."

He hesitated, then gently took her hand in his. Touching someone was another thing he'd almost forgotten how to do.

When he didn't say anything, or let go of her hand, she added, "I have to go. The registration for the rodeo events ends in an hour and my father wants me to make sure all our cowhands are signed up for at least one event. For a ten dollar entry fee, each event pays fifty. The best all-around wins cattle. My father says even if his men don't win, it will work some of the orneriness out of them."

"I heard about the cattle prize." Rowdy let go of her hand thinking that if he entered one event he could walk away with fifty dollars, enough to keep him in food until the ranch sold.

She hesitated another moment, but neither could think of anything else to say. Rowdy watched her walk toward the post office where a banner flew announcing the rodeo.

He fingered the ten dollar bill in his pocket. If he signed up and lost, he'd starve until he could sell his land and no one in town would likely offer him a job to tide him over. In fact, Laurel Hayes was probably the only person who would talk to him, and she wouldn't be allowed after her bear of a father found out who he was. After all, at fifteen, they said he killed a man. The facts hadn't mattered to the town when he'd been fifteen and they wouldn't matter now.

Rowdy thought of the past five years and how he'd been in the saddle from dawn to dark most days. He'd loved working the prison herd and hated each night when they took him back to his cell. He knew he was good at roping and riding. If he entered the rodeo, he wouldn't be just riding for the fun of it. He'd be riding to survive. He'd pick the category with the fewest entries, give it his all and collect his winnings.

Walking across to the post office he made up his mind that three days from now he'd be fifty dollars richer no matter what he had to do.

When he reached the registration table on the porch, several cowhands were standing around, but none seemed in line. He walked up and forced himself to stand tall.

"How can I help you, mister?" a man, who looked like a banker, said around a cigar.

"I'd like to enter one event." Rowdy scanned the choices. Calf roping, bull dogging, tying down for branding, horse racing, saddle bronc riding, steer wrestling.

"Ten dollars for one event, but you can enter all you want for twenty. Then you'd have a chance at the grand prize. A whole herd of cattle." The banker pulled out his cigar and pointed it at Rowdy. "Now that would make a cowboy a cattleman." He laughed and waited.

Rowdy stepped away to think. Ten dollars more didn't seem like much. Maybe he could find something to sell on the old ranch. His father used to have a box of tools in the barn. All together they might be worth ten dollars. But he'd never make it to the ranch and back in time, much less make the sale. The only thing he had of value was his saddle and if he sold that he'd have no way of winning any event.

Turning the corner of the building, he bumped into Laurel in the shadows. His hand shot out to steady her. "Sorry, miss." With his fingers curved at her waist, he realized he would have known the feel of her even if the shadows had been black as night.

She looked embarrassed that they'd been so close, but she managed to nod her acceptance of his apology.

He relaxed. "Hiding out?"

She nodded again.

Her plan was painfully obvious. She hadn't been invited to lunch. It was too early to go back to the surrey, and she couldn't just wander the streets. The small alley between the bank and the post office offered refuge.

He tried to think of something to say. "I'm thinking of entering the rodeo."

She managed to look up, her cheeks still spotted with embarrassment. "Best all-around?"

"No, it's too expensive." Now it was his turn to look down. He shouldn't have told her that. The town idiot could figure out that he had more than ten and less than twenty dollars to his name.

They stood, silent for a while. He was too tall to see her face unless she looked up, but he felt good just standing near her. He'd been more boy than man when he'd been sent to prison. The smell of a woman had almost been forgotten.

Finally, he found words. "I thought I'd go take a look at the stock being brought in. They were starting to unload them when I got off the train. Would you like to walk over with me?"

"Yes . . . I'd like that, Mr. Darnell." She didn't look up.

He thought of telling her that he liked her voice, but offered his arm in silence for fear she'd change her mind if he talked too much.

She hesitated, then laid her gloved hand lightly atop his elbow.

"Call me Rowdy, Laurel," he finally stammered. "After all, we've known each other since the sixth grade." In his memory he could almost see her sitting in the back of the classroom, curled around a book, looking at no one.

She nodded and said in a very practical voice, "You're right. We've known each other for years."

They sliced between the buildings and circled to the corrals beside the railroad. Chuckwagons from the big ranches were already setting up camp at the far end. Rows and rows of pens and shoots framed a small arena. He found himself far more interested in her than the stock as they discussed the horses and cattle. To his surprise, she knew livestock, pointing out things he wouldn't have noticed about the animals.

They walked, stopping now and then. She'd lean into the fence, getting closer to study the wild horses as carefully as a buyer might. But when she finished, she'd turn and place her hand on his arm as if it were the most natural thing.

When they were at the back fence, she finally faced him. She looked up, letting the sun shine on her face. He saw tiny freckles across her nose and tears sparkling in her eyes. Watery blue eyes, he thought, like a rainy morning sunrise.

"You may think me insane, Mr. Dar—I mean Rowdy, but I've something to ask you." She looked like she was mustering every drop of courage inside her.

"Ask." He studied her, half wishing she'd pull off her bonnet so he could see the color of her hair. Brown, he thought he remembered, light brown. "I've already decided you must be crazy to be walking with the likes of me. So I doubt I'll be surprised by anything you say."

She grinned, her smile almost crossing her mouth. "All right." She raised her hand and opened it palm up. Lying atop her glove was a ten dollar gold piece. "If I pay half your fee, will you ride for best all-around? Will you ride for the cattle?"

Rowdy frowned. "Why would you loan me money? If I win, I might be beating one of the Captain's cowhands. Your father, like most ranchers, want men riding for their brand to win these things. I don't ride for any brand."

"Exactly," she said. "And I'm not loaning you the money. I'm buying into a partnership. If you win, you keep any prize money for any individual entries, but I get half the cattle."

"But—"

"No questions. All I ask is that I'm your silent partner. No one can know of our bargain."

"You've never even seen me ride."

She didn't answer, but pressed her lips together as if debating crying. He realized this meant a great deal to her. "I've never seen those wild horses buck, but I can tell you which will give you the winning ride."

He raised one eyebrow studying her. He knew nothing about women, but he had a feeling this one was one of a kind.

"Are we partners or not?" She bit into her bottom lip and waited. "You've very little time left to register."

He took the money. Her reasons were none of his business. "Silent partners, if that's the way you want it, lady."

"That's the way I want it."

Then the shy Miss Laurel did something he never expected.

She stood on her toes and kissed him lightly on the cheek. Before he could react, she turned and ran. Her bonnet tumbled to her back as she ran.

"Brown," he said, as if she were near enough to hear. "I knew your hair would still be light brown."

He walked back slowly, turning the gold coin over and over in his hand. He'd ride and do his best. Not just for his start, but he had a feeling for hers as well.

Chapter 2

Laurel ran all the way back to her corner between the buildings and tried to slow her heart while she waited. From the
shadows, she watched.

A few minutes passed before Rowdy Darnell stepped in
front of the table and tossed down ten dollars in bills and her
ten dollar gold piece. The boy she remembered was gone,
replaced by a man, hard and lean.

She smiled remembering how kind he'd been to her, helping her down from the surrey and asking her to take a walk.
Something no other man in town had ever done. He might
look like a man most would fear to cross, but somewhere in
the man still lived the boy this town had sacrificed so that
none of their sons would go to jail.

Laurel waited for one of the men to recognize him, but none
seemed to. Too many families had moved in and out in these
parts.

Jeffery Filmore, one of the town's junior bankers, fingered
the money. "Mighty lot of money to toss away if you're no
good."

"I'm good," Rowdy answered without a hint of brag in
his tone.

The banker snuffed. "Might be, might not be. That's what

we're here to find out." He shoved a chart toward Rowdy. "List your name and check every event you're planning on entering. You got to enter at least three of the four to have a shot at the big prize."

Rowdy wrote his name and drew a line across all the squares.

The banker raised an eyebrow. "You planning on trying them all."

"I am."

Filmore shook his head. "Most cowhands sit out one or two that they don't think they can place in. It'll give you time to rest and lessen the chances you get busted up on something you don't have a chance of winning."

Rowdy took the number off the top of the pile. "I've spent enough time resting and I figure I got a chance at them all. You got an objection?"

Filmore stared at him a moment, then backed down. "No, none at all."

Rowdy turned and walked back toward the livery. He never glanced at the alley shadows, but Laurel had a feeling he knew she was watching him.

She let out a long held breath. He was registered. She'd been waiting for two years for this chance. If he won, she'd have enough money to run.

When she'd finished school she'd had offers to go to work in Houston and Austin, but her father had insisted she come home to straighten out his books. Three months later, when she had them in good order, she found her small inheritance from her mother had vanished. Her father made sure she had no money to leave. He wanted her to work for him and remain home under his control. Now, after two years, she saw a way out.

Feeling brave, she stepped out of the shadows and walked into the hotel lobby before Jeffery Filmore had time to notice her. The banker had a habit of looking at her the way he looked at his meal when he came to dinner with her father.

She was something he planned to have, maybe even enjoy. He hadn't even asked her yet, but Jeffery Filmore was already talking to her father about setting a date for their wedding. He wanted his ring on her finger and her working in his bank before fall.

Her father's only hesitation seemed to be that he needed her to do his bookkeeping until after roundup. Neither of the men had ever considered what she wanted. With no funds of her own, her father knew she wasn't going anywhere and Jeffery knew no other man in town bothered to speak to her. So, to their way of thinking, she was just something to pass from one to the other when the time was right.

Laurel almost laughed as she crossed the empty hotel lobby and entered the small parlor where ladies could have lunch or tea without being exposed to the noisy bar area near the back.

She wasn't surprised the room was empty. Her sisters would love the thrill and the audience in the back room. It was more a café than a saloon, but Laurel knew her father wouldn't approve of his darlings sitting among the cowhands. She also knew she'd never tell him because if she did, he'd either laugh or tease her little sisters about how bold they were, or blame Laurel for allowing them to go into such a place.

Sitting by the window, Laurel folded her hands in her lap and waited. The room smelled of pipe smoke. Dust reflected off the furniture as thick as fur in places. The innkeeper obviously saw the room as a bother, but probably kept it to promote the appearance of respectability. He made far more money off the drinks and food in the back.

"Sorry, miss"—a young maid, with hair the color of rust, leaned in the door—"I didn't know you was there. Would you like something?"

Laurel swallowed hard. "No, thank you. I'd like to just wait here if I may."

The girl disappeared without a word.

Laurel closed her eyes. She was the daughter of Captain Hayes and his first wife. Her father was very likely the richest man in the county. She could walk into any store in town and buy whatever she liked on account.

But, Laurel almost said aloud, she didn't have enough cash to buy a cup of tea.

The ten dollar gold piece had been a gift from the headmaster when she'd graduated. Laurel had kept it with her for two years, hoping one day she'd be brave enough to buy a train ticket for as far as ten dollars would take her. Once she'd asked if she could have the salary her father paid the last bookkeeper. Her father had laughed and told her she was lucky to have a roof over her head and food to eat.

"Miss?" The young maid stood at the doorway with a wicker tray the size of a plate. "A lady upstairs ordered this tea, then said she didn't want it. You'd be doing me a favor if you'd take it."

"But I haven't—"

"There ain't no charge for it." She set the tray on the table next to Laurel.

"Thank you." Laurel smiled. "You're very kind."

Rusty curls tossed about her shoulders. "We all do what we can, Miss, to help each other."

Laurel felt humbled by the maid. She offered her hand. "I'm Laurel Hayes."

"I'm Bonnie Lynn." The maid laughed nervously. "Pleased to meet you, I am." Now it was the maid's turn to be uncomfortable. "I got to go."

"I hope to see you again," Laurel said. "Thanks for the tea."

Bonnie Lynn nodded and hurried out of the room.

Laurel leaned back and sipped her tea. She'd let go of her ten dollars on a hope. A hope that if it paid off would allow her to go all the way to Kansas City, or Houston, or maybe even Santa Fe. She'd have enough money for the train and then a few months at a boarding house. She'd look for a job at a bank or as a bookkeeper. She was good at what she did. Her father's books had never been off a penny since she'd started managing them.

Lost in her daydreams and plans, Laurel didn't hear Jeffery Filmore come into the hotel until he was at the door to the parlor. He always reminded her of a bear someone had dressed up and trained to act proper. When he removed his hat, his hair wiggled across his balding head like thin wrinkled wool and his complexion always appeared sunburned.

"There you are," he bellowed. "I saw your sisters come in and guessed you'd be about."

Laurel didn't answer. She never answered his ramblings for Jeffery talked only to hear himself.

She expected him to storm off, but he barged into the room and stuck out a piece of paper. "Your father wanted a list of the names of those who entered for best all-around in the rodeo. You can take it out and save me a trip. I know it's not as many as he'd hoped would enter, but after seeing some of the rough stock a few of the men backed out. They say one of the steers turned on a roper and killed him in El Paso last month. Some of the bucking horses look like they're too mean to be worth the bullet it'd take to kill them."

"Isn't that the kind of stock a rodeo needs?" she asked.

"Yeah, it makes for wild rides and a man who puts much value on his life would be wise to stay in the stands and watch."

She lowered her head, hoping he'd leave.

Like a nervous elephant, he shifted from foot to foot.

Finally, she looked up.

He didn't wait for her to ask any questions. "I've come to terms with your father, Laurel. We'll marry the end of August. No frills, just a small ceremony after Sunday services so I can teach you what you don't know that afternoon. My bank records require a higher standard than your father's ranch accounts."

"But . . ."

He rushed on as if he already knew what she might ask.

"You're to have a new dress, of course, for the wedding, but nothing too fancy. I see no need for parties, or a honeymoon. I've already had that with my first wife, and your father agrees with me that such things are just a waste of money."

Laurel stared openmouthed at his ramblings. She wanted to shout that she'd never been asked to marry him and, if she had been, she would have said no.

Jeffery didn't stop. "You'll work with me at the bank Monday through Thursday, then I'll drive you out and you can do your father's books Friday and Saturday. Your father said you could ride out alone. You've been making the trip between there and town for years, but I see no need to have to board a horse in town. I'll take you and pick you up."

He paused as if allowing questions in his lecture.

A hundred screams log-piled in her mind, but all she managed to say was, "I'll have Sundays off?"

He huffed again. "Of course. A banker and his family are expected to be in church every week. It adds stability to his name. After church, we'll want to invite your father and sisters to dinner. It's only proper if they make the drive into town. He assures me you're a passable cook. Once they're gone, you'll need time to do the laundry."

Her head felt like mice were eating away inside it. All rational thought left her. "Family. What family?" she started before he interrupted her.

"Don't be an idiot. You're far too old for it to be cute to play dumb." He frowned at her as if he found her only mildly tolerable. "I'm not a young man, Laurel. We'll have a baby before we're married a year. I prefer a son, but if it doesn't happen, we'll try again until I have an heir who can eventually take over the bank."

He stared at her. "You are a virgin? I told your father I'd have nothing less."

As she reddened, he laughed. "Of course you are. You know little of these things, but I know my seed is strong. My first wife was pregnant within a month of our marriage, but she wasn't healthy enough to stay alive to deliver full term." He stared at her. "Don't worry, your father says you ride every day. Such exercise makes you strong and hardy." He grinned to himself. "My seed will grow in you. You're like rich dirt, from strong stock and ready to be made use of. Lots of children will round that thin frame out nicely in time."

Laurel was too horrified to answer. She lowered her head and focused on the piece of paper Jeffery had given her. Rowdy Darnell's name stood out.

He had to win, her mind whispered. He had to.

The banker heard her sisters and hurried to pay his respects without another word to her. He was all smiles and pats with them. Like her father, Jeffery seemed to think every senseless thing they said was funny. She could imagine what his Sunday dinners would be like.

She almost laughed aloud. They'd be pretty much like they were now. Sunday was the housekeeper's day off. So Laurel cooked and cleaned up while everyone else complained that none of the food was good enough, hot enough or served fast enough.

Laurel closed her eyes and blocked out all the noise coming from the others. She focused on the way Rowdy had touched her waist so gently when he'd helped her down from the surrey and again in the shadows when he'd bumped into her.

She smiled. He'd touched her as if she mattered.

Chapter 3

The sun bore down on Rowdy as he rode toward his father's farm. He'd always hated the place and July was the worst month, hot and dry. But he looked forward to being alone. When he'd first gone to prison at fifteen, he thought he'd go mad with the loneliness, but finally he grew to prefer it. There were so many people in town for the rodeo that he felt like the air had thinned just so it would last. He rode hard until town was well out of sight and land, more prairie than farm, stretched before him.

His father had sold their farm in East Texas and moved here after Rowdy's mom died. He could get almost ten times the acreage for the same money. The old man had planned to get away from the memories of her death, but West Texas hadn't been far enough. He'd continued the journey into a bottle.

Rowdy remembered his father being drunk when they'd pulled up to the place and as far as he knew the old man had never sobered up enough to care where he was. They'd brought fifty head of cattle with them. His dad sold them off one by one. After three years he didn't have enough cows left to sell to pay for a lawyer for his son. The horses he'd bred with pride a few years ago had withered into nags.

Reaching the gate, Rowdy was surprised it had been closed.

Sheriff Barnett had written twice over the last five years. Once to tell Rowdy that his father had died, and once to tell him the place was still his. Rowdy guessed the sheriff wanted him to know that he had a home; he couldn't have known how little the place meant to Rowdy. It was just something to sell so he could make a fresh start where no one knew him.

As he saw the shack of a house and the barn, he thought of burning the place down, but he knew memories would shift through even the ashes. His father hadn't been a bad man, only a weak one. He'd loved one woman and when she'd died he couldn't seem to find his footing, not even to finish raising his only son.

When the sheriff and some men came to get Rowdy before dawn five years ago, his father's only words had been, "I'm sorry." Not, "I'll help." Or "I don't believe you could shoot anyone." Just, "I'm sorry."

The night before there had been a gang of boys drinking and firing off guns down by the creek bordering Darnell land. One was shot. With no one to stand beside Rowdy, the drunk's son was an easy target. Everyone wanted to lay the blame somewhere.

Rowdy shoved the memory aside as he rode up to the house. He wasn't surprised to find the sheriff waited on the porch. Barnett had put on a few pounds in five years and his hair looked whiter, but he still had the same sad eyes that seemed to say he'd seen too much in this world.

"Darnell." He nodded in greeting.

Rowdy swung down. He owed the lawman. If it hadn't been for Barnett, the judge wouldn't have considered his age at the sentencing and Rowdy would have drawn far more than five years. The sheriff had also rounded up a few strays his father hadn't taken the trouble to chase and sold them, along with the corral stock, to pay the taxes on this place for five years.

"I figured you'd be looking me up," Rowdy said as he offered his hand.

Barnett gripped his hand. "Just stopped by to say hello, son."

Rowdy waited. Barnett had been the only man in town who hadn't wanted to string him up five years ago. "I want to thank you for—"

"You don't owe me nothing, but I would like to give you one last piece of advice. If I were you, I'd keep low and just stay long enough to sell the place and move on. No sense looking for trouble."

Rowdy nodded. "I agree. This place has never been home. If I could make a few bucks, I plan to head south. There's a man down near the border who said he'd give me a job breaking horses when I got out. I figured I'd look him up. Maybe buy a little spread down there in time."

The sheriff moved toward his horse. "I'll get the word out that you're looking for a buyer. With the rodeo in town, it should get around fast. I wouldn't be surprised if you don't have an offer within a week. Captain Hayes to the north will probably make you a fair one. He's gobbling up land as fast as he can lately. You'd think he had sons and not daughters."

"That would be fine with me. I don't much care who takes it off my hands."

Barnett shoved his hat back and seemed to pick his words carefully. "You know, son, you were mighty angry when you left."

Rowdy almost said he'd had a right to be, but he knew nothing would change the past. "I still fire up now and then before I think," he admitted, remembering the fights he'd had in prison. "But all I want to do is sell this place and move on now. I'm not looking for any trouble."

The sheriff smiled. "I'm glad to hear that. I'm getting too old for any new worries."

Rowdy watched the sheriff climb on his horse and ride away with only a wave. He wasn't sure he had a friend in Barnett, but at least the man seemed fair and at this point in Rowdy's life that was about the best he could hope for.

He checked the barn, then decided to unsaddle his horse and let her graze on wild grass growing in the corral. Walking through the house, he found it just as he'd left it, filthy. It had to be his imagination, but the smell of whiskey seemed to linger in the air. More to use up energy than out of any need to clean the place, Rowdy opened all the doors and windows and swept a layer of top soil out of the house.

At sunset he pulled his bedroll from behind his saddle, deciding to sleep on the porch. It was too hot to build a fire. Besides, he didn't even have coffee to boil anyway. The jerky and hard tack in his saddlebags wasn't worth eating.

He fell asleep listening to the sounds of freedom around him. Tomorrow he'd ride into town and win the first event. He hadn't even checked to see what came first. He didn't care.

Just after dawn he woke to the smell of blueberry muffins. He hadn't tasted one since his mother died, but he'd never forget the aroma. He opened his eyes. Laurel Hayes sat three feet away on the steps.

Rising, he raked his hair back and mumbled, "What are you doing here?"

She smiled. "Watching you sleep."

"I don't think that's proper," he said.

"Probably not," she agreed. "I don't think I've ever done anything that wasn't proper. I might as well start with you."

He growled at her and to his surprise, she laughed. It seemed to him that if she had any sense, she'd be afraid of him.

He studied her, all prim and proper in her white blouse and navy riding skirt. She didn't look quite so "old maid" today. He had a feeling her rich daddy would shoot him on sight if the old man thought he was even talking to Laurel.

When he frowned, she added, "I brought you a good horse."

He stood, dusting off his clothes. "I don't think the Captain would like me riding one of his horses."

"It's not his, but if you don't want the mare, I'll just take my muffins and go."

"Wait." Rowdy shook sleep from his head. "How about I think about the offer while I test the muffins?"

"All right." She pushed back her wide brimmed hat and studied him with the same look she'd given most of the stock in the corral yesterday. "You want to wash up and make coffee first before you eat?"

"No," he said, then backtracked when he saw her frown. "I can't make coffee. No supplies around here. All my father left was the pot, but I could wash up."

She watched as he went to the well and drew up water. "I'm surprised the rope and bucket are still here," he mumbled as he washed.

"I put them there last year," she said. "I ride this way often and I like to stop to water my horse. Hope you don't mind."

It hadn't occurred to him to mind. "You happen to bring a towel too?"

She laughed and tossed him the towel she'd spread over the basket of muffins.

He dried and placed the towel on the nail by the well. "Great, I got the towel wet so now I guess I'll have to eat all the muffins." He took the first one from her hand and asked, "Now tell me how come you own this horse?" If she had horses and maybe even cattle, she'd have no use for half the herd they might win.

They walked toward her mount. A lead rope had been tied to the saddle horn. A chestnut mare was at the other end of the rope. At first glance it appeared ordinary, but Rowdy didn't miss the look in the animal's eyes. Intelligent, he thought. He downed another muffin while he circled the horse.

"I don't own him," she said when he returned to her side. "You do."

When he showed no sign of believing her, she added, "When the sheriff came to get the stock after your father died, she was only a colt limping around the corral. The sheriff didn't figure she'd last to town so he turned her loose." Laurel brushed the roan's neck. "I found her the next day and knew she'd be coyote dinner if I didn't put her in the barn for a few weeks."

The horse pushed her with its nose as if playing.

"I checked on her every day until she was big enough to run the land. Whenever I was home from school, I rode by to check on her. The wound on her leg healed with a little help from the whiskey I found in the cabin and she began to grow. I was afraid someone might ride by and see her, so I moved her down to the little canyon by the stream. There's water and grass there year-round along with plenty of shallow caves to get out of the worst weather."

Rowdy ran his hand along the horse's withers and back, feeling strong muscles. "Looks like she'd have had the sense to run."

"I thought that too, but every time I came back, she was somewhere on your place." Laurel pulled an apple from her pocket. "I taught her to come when I whistle." She offered the apple to Rowdy. "Here, you feed her. She's yours."

"No." Just because the horse survived here didn't make the mare his.

"You need a better horse than one of the livery mounts. Cinnamon can be that horse."

"Cinnamon? Don't tell me you named her?" He'd called a few horses names over the years, but nothing he'd want to repeat in her company.

She laughed at the face he made, then handed him the basket and moved away. "You two share breakfast and get acquainted. I have to get back."

He set the basket down and followed her to her horse. He offered her a step up, but she didn't take it. She hadn't needed it. Her long legs flew over the saddle with ease.

"Good luck tonight."

"Thanks," he said, realizing he didn't want her to leave. "When will I see you again?"

"I'll be around. My father insists we all go every night. He goes for the rodeo and my sisters go for the dance afterward."

"And why do you go?" he asked as he took the lead rope from her hand.

She looked down at him. "I'll go to watch my partner win." Kicking her horse, she was gone before he had time to answer.

He watched her ride away. With her height and lean form, she rode like a man, one with the horse, not bumping along like most women he'd seen ride. He decided she probably wouldn't think that a compliment, even though he meant it as such.

He tossed the apple in the air and caught it, proud of the way he'd handled himself. He'd managed to talk to her, even made her laugh. It was only a guess, but he thought that Laurel laughed very little in her life. She'd been different this morning, but he couldn't put his finger on why. Maybe it had something to do with the fact that they were alone, out of sight of any prying eyes or ears.

Winning this rodeo might prove great fun with her as his partner.

Walking back to the mare, Rowdy swore when he realized the horse had eaten the basket of muffins and left him with the apple.

Laughing, he patted the horse's neck. "Well, Cinnamon, since you've had my breakfast it looks like we'd better go to work. I got about ten hours to turn you into a cow horse."

Chapter 4

The rodeo started with little more than an hour until sunset. Men drew for events and nights. Since the celebration lasted four nights, one fourth of the men did each event each night. That way anyone coming only to one night got to see all the rodeo had to offer even if he got to watch only one out of four of the men compete for any one event.

Laurel checked the charts. Rowdy had drawn saddleback riding the first night. Good. That would give him at least one more day to work with the horse on steer roping. She was so excited she couldn't wait for the buggy, so she'd insisted on riding in with her father. He didn't talk to her, but it didn't matter. In four days, she would have the money to leave.

Deep down she hoped that if she had the means to leave, he might tell her he wanted her to stay. She knew she was only fooling herself. Since the day he'd married Rosy when Laurel had been four, the Captain had always tried to make his oldest daughter disappear. Leftover children never mattered much when the new batch came along. Laurel had a feeling that when she left the ranch Sunday night after Rowdy won, her father would be more angry about losing a free bookkeeper than a daughter.

When they arrived at the rodeo, she stood just behind him

listening to the men talk and hoping to learn something that might help Rowdy. As usual, no one noticed her.

After an hour, Laurel moved behind the row of wagons and buggies pulled in a circle. She'd sat quietly waiting for her chance. Finally, her father had stepped into a crowd of men who were placing bets on a horse race to be run in the morning and passing around a bottle. Her sisters were flirting with half a dozen cowhands who'd stopped by for a cool drink from the pitcher of lemonade in the back of their rig. No one would miss her.

She found Rowdy off by himself in the shadows of a barn. Since he'd drawn bronc riding as his first challenge, he'd be part of the last group to compete.

Without a word, she moved beside him, leaned her back on the barn only a few inches from his arm and handed him a canteen. She could feel the tension in his body.

"A fellow named Dan O'Brien offered to ride drag for me during the calf roping."

"He's all right, I guess," she said without looking at Rowdy. "He owns a little farm to the south of here." She hesitated, then added, "I'm not sure he's much of a cowhand. I think he raises mostly hogs at his place."

"I've already told him I'd trade the favor off for him. He only entered calf roping, so he must feel like he can handle his own."

Laurel nodded once. "All right." She could have suggested a few others who might have been better, but he hadn't asked.

While he drank, she decided to tell him what she knew before he made another mistake, "I've been watching the black you drew for tonight. He goes to his left more than his right and fires up easy even in the pen. I think you should—"

"I know how to ride," he snapped as if resenting her advice. "I'm no greenhorn."

Silence hung still and heavy between them.

"Fine. Good luck." She planted a quick, hard kiss on his cheek and walked away.

She thought he might catch up to her and say he was sorry, but he didn't. A tiny part of her knew she'd done it wrong. She could have said something to him first, maybe let him tell her what he thought. But Laurel would never be like her sisters. She couldn't have conversations that made no sense. She couldn't giggle at nothing and bat her lashes. It wasn't her. It never would be.

"Where you been, girl?" Her father's voice made her jump.

"Looking at the stock," she said in a whisper. She didn't mention that she'd met a cattle buyer from Fort Worth who told her to pass the word along that he'd be willing to buy off the winner's cattle if the all-around cowboy wanted cash.

"That's better than hiding in some corner, I guess." Her father took her elbow in a tight grip. "You remind me more of your mother every day."

Laurel knew better than to think that was a compliment. Her father had often told her that his first wife was a mouse of a woman, plain and boring. Laurel knew he'd married her for money, he'd even joked once that he'd talked her father into paying more just to get her out of the house.

Her father let go of her arm and climbed on the wagon bench. "I'm going home after the saddle bronc riders. You stay and see that your sisters get home in the wagon after the dance."

"But I rode in," she protested. "One of the men will be happy to."

He looked at her with his usual bothered expression. "All right, see that James or Phil drives the girls home. You can ride back alone, but try to stay for at least one dance. You never know, someone might actually ask you to dance."

Laurel knew he didn't care what she did. He probably didn't care if she danced, he just wanted her to stay behind long enough so that she didn't ride back with him. If he hadn't needed her to do the books, he probably would have left her at school until she was thirty. She was a reminder of a time in his life when he'd settled for something far less than what he'd wanted.

She stood silently and watched the competition. The first rider fell off his horse coming out of the shoot. The second rode, but his horse didn't buck enough to earn many points. The third and fourth started well but didn't make the clock. Rowdy's horse came out fighting with all his might to get the saddle and the man off his back.

The crowd rose to their feet. Several people cheered as the animal kicked dust every time Rowdy's spurs brushed his hide.

Laurel watched, mentally taking each jolt with Rowdy. His back bowed back and forth, but his left hand stayed in the air.

When the ride ended, he jumped from the black horse and landed on his feet. The crowd went crazy, yelling and clapping. Laurel only smiled, knowing she'd invested her ten dollar gold piece wisely.

Her father cussed and demanded to know who number forty was. Five minutes later, when his men gathered round him, he said that Rowdy Darnell was the man to beat in this rodeo and there would be an extra month's pay to the man who topped his final score.

Laurel felt proud. She stood and watched the young people move to the dance floor as the last light of the day disappeared. Her father and a few of his men rode off toward the saloon talking of plans for tomorrow. Every night the rodeo would end with saddle bronc riding and they planned to have the Captain's men shatter Darnell's score.

When she knew no one was watching, she climbed on her horse and rode into the darkness. She didn't need much light, for she knew the trail by heart. In fact, she knew the land for miles around. For as long as she could remember, she'd saddled up before dawn and rode out to watch the sunrise, crisscrossing the land before anyone else was up and about.

When she was in sight of her home, she remembered what her father had said about staying long enough to dance. If he got home and found her already there, he'd probably yell at her.

Laurel turned toward the cottonwoods along the creek that separated the Captain's land from the Darnell place. She rode through the shallow water until she reached a spot where cliff walls on either side of the creek were high enough to act as fence. There, twenty feet into the walled area, she found the slice in the rocks just big enough for a horse to climb up out of the water and through. No one watching from either ranch could have seen her, but one minute she was on Hayes' land and the next on Rowdy's property.

She knew he'd still be at the rodeo grounds. Everyone would want to shake his hand. She'd even heard several say that his ride was the best they'd ever seen.

As the land spread out before her, Laurel gave her mount his head and they began to run over the open pasture. Rowdy's place had always been so beautiful to her. The way the ground sloped gently between outcroppings of rock colored like different shades of brick lined up. The landscape made her feel like every detail had been planned by God. Almost as if He'd designed the perfect ranch. Rich earth and good water. Then, He had set it down so gently in the middle of the prairie that no one had even noticed it.

She rode close enough to the ranch house to see that no light shone, then decided to turn toward home.

At the creek's edge, she thought she heard another horse. Laurel slipped down and walked between the trees until she saw a man standing shoulder deep in the middle of the stream.

Her first thought was that she might have been followed. But most of the men who worked for her father were at the dance and someone following wouldn't be a quarter mile away from the pass-through wading in the deepest part of the stream.

She stood perfectly still in the shadows and listened. The sound of a horse came again not far from her. As her eyes adjusted, she spotted Cinnamon standing under a cottonwood with branches so long they almost touched the water.

Rowdy had to be the man in the water.

Laurel wanted to vanish completely. She couldn't get to her land, he stood in between her and the passage. If she moved he might spot her, or worse, shoot her as a trespasser for she *was* on his property.

Closing her eyes, she played a game she'd played when she was a child. If I can't see him, he can't see me, she thought.

"Laurel?" His low voice was little more than a whisper. "Is that you?"

She opened one eye. He'd walked close enough to her that the water now only came to his waist. His powerful body sparkled with water. "It's me," she admitted, trying not to look directly at him because there was no doubt that he was nude. "I was . . . I was . . ."

"Turn around," he ordered.

"But . . ."

He took a step closer. "I don't plan to come out until you turn around."

She nodded and whirled. "I didn't mean to interrupt you. I swear. I was just riding and I thought you'd be at the dance, so you wouldn't be home and I could ride on your land without anyone bothering me." She was rambling, but she couldn't seem to stop. She didn't want him to think that she was looking for him, or worse, spying on him. "I know I'm trespassing, but you've been gone so long I didn't think about anyone being on the place."

"Laurel." He barely whispered her name, but he was so near she jumped. "You can turn around now."

Squaring her shoulders, she faced him. He'd pulled on his jeans and had a towel wrapped around the back of his neck. The same towel she'd given him that morning. She couldn't say another word. She could only stare. Until this moment she'd thought she saw the boy she remembered from school when she looked at Rowdy, but no boy stood before her.

"I'm glad you came." He shoved his wet hair back. "I looked for you after the rodeo. I wanted to say I was sorry I snapped at you. I was nervous about the ride and didn't feel much like talking."

"You were right. You did know what you were doing. That ride was magnificent."

He didn't seem to hear her as he continued. "I'm not used to much conversation, but you had a right. We're partners after all." He smiled at her and she swore he could see her blush. "If you ride by here often, I might want to change my bathing habits."

"I'm sorry . . ."

He reached behind her and grabbed his shirt off the cottonwood. "How about we stop apologizing to each other and relax? Deal, partner?"

"Deal," she managed. "Why aren't you at the dance?"

"Why aren't you?" he countered as he buttoned his shirt.

"I . . . I . . ." She could think of no answer but the truth and she didn't want to tell him that. He could figure it out for himself. She wasn't the kind of girl anyone asked to dance. First, she was taller than half the men. Second, she was so shy she couldn't talk to them and, third, everyone knew she was the Captain's plain daughter. The old maid.

"I can't dance either," he said.

She smiled. He'd given her a way out.

Without a word, he took her hand and led her to a spot of moonlight shining near the water's edge. She sat on a log and he stretched out in the grass as if they were old friends settling down for a long visit.

Somehow the shadows made it easier to talk. She told him everything she'd heard about the stock and the other riders. He said he'd drawn calf roping for tomorrow. She mentioned all the extra things going on around the rodeo. Besides the dance, there was a box supper one night and a horse race, as well as a sharpshooting contest.

When they talked of the competition, she told him of her dreams of working in a bank and maybe buying her own little house one day on a quiet street. With the money they'd get if he won, she might have enough for a down payment. Though she planned to put most of the money away for a rainy day. A woman alone has to prepare for that.

He told her of living on a ranch, a busy, productive one, not a dead one like his father's place. She had the feeling as he talked of what he wanted to do that he was voicing a boy's dreams he'd tucked away at fifteen and hadn't brought out again until tonight.

They settled into an easy silence, listening to the sounds around them. Finally, he said, "I talked with Dan O'Brien after I rode. He said he'd heard I'd been in prison and wanted to know if it was true."

"What did you say?" She knew it wouldn't be a secret for long, but she thought they might make it through the rodeo without everyone knowing.

"I said I had." Rowdy stared up at her. "No matter what folks say I've done, I'm not in the habit of lying, Laurel. Not now, not ever."

Even when she looked at the water she could still feel his dark eyes watching her. "What did Dan say?"

"He said it didn't matter to him, he was in the habit of judging a man for himself, not by what he heard, but he wanted to know from me if the rumors were true."

She'd never given the farmer a glance, but the next time she passed Dan O'Brien on the street she planned to nod politely, maybe even say good morning to the man.

"From the morning I heard about the shooting, I didn't believe you did it," she said, almost to herself.

"You were the only one," he answered.

She agreed. "I went away to school before the trial, but I kept up with it in the papers. No one wanted to believe it might have been a stray bullet, but after you went to prison all the boys who'd been on the creek that night found reasons to leave town. I think they felt sorry for what they'd done."

"Not sorry enough to drop me a note." Rowdy stood and walked to the water's edge. "You have any idea what prison's like when you're fifteen? I spent the first year mad at the world and the second wishing I was dead. No one would have cared, one way or the other."

"I would have," she answered, then hurried on when he glared back at her as if he was about to call her a liar. "I know it couldn't have been as bad as prison, but the school my father sent me to was dark and hard. Most of the girls were two or three years older than me and offered no friendship. I had no one to talk to and my family never wrote. On Sundays, we had to go to chapel and pray." She straightened. "I prayed you were safe."

All the anger melted away from Rowdy. He walked back to her and knelt down beside her. "Why?"

She shook her head. "Maybe because you were the only person I knew who had also been sent away to hell."

She stood, embarrassed by her own honesty, and straightened her skirts as if they'd been having tea in her parlor. "I'd better get back."

He held the reins of her horse. "Let me help you up," he said from behind her as she reached for the saddle horn.

She almost said that she'd been climbing on a horse by herself since she was six. Instead, she nodded. She felt the warmth of his body only an inch away from hers.

Hesitantly, his hands went around her waist. He lifted her up. Laurel closed her eyes and imagined that he was really touching her out of caring and not politeness.

His hands remained at her waist for a moment. "I haven't been around a woman in a long time," he said. "I've forgotten how they feel. I know you're strong, but I'm afraid I'll break you if I hold too tight."

She almost said that she'd never been touched with such care. He'd lifted her as if she were a treasure.

He moved his hand over hers. "I like the way you feel, Laurel. I'll be careful helping you up if you allow me to when we're alone."

When he started to move his hand away, she caught his fingers in hers and held on tightly. She might not be able to tell him how she felt, but she had to show him.

He finally pulled his hand away and whispered, "It's all right, Laurel. I think I understand."

When she took the reins, he stepped back and watched her leave. Neither said a word.

She rode back through the passage and straight home, her thoughts full of the way he'd touched her.

When she walked down the hall, she wasn't surprised to see her father's study light still on. The man never went to bed if he could walk straight.

"There you are, girl," he yelled in a slurred voice watered down by a dozen drinks. "I'm glad to see you stayed awhile at the dance. Filmore mentioned that he worried about you being so shy. A banker needs a wife who can be part of society, not a mouse running to the corner every time someone talks to her."

"Jeffery Filmore never talks to me, only at me." Laurel voiced her thoughts for once.

Her father laughed. "That doesn't matter, girl. I never did have a conversation longer than a minute with my Rosy and we got along just fine."

Rosy had been his second wife. She'd died ten years ago, but he still mourned her, especially around bedtime.

Laurel tried again. "What if I don't want to marry Jeffery?"

The Captain gave most of his attention to refilling his drink. "You won't get a better offer. Best take this one. His being twenty years older is a great advantage. He'll die and leave you comfortable." He looked up at her through blood-shot eyes. "In the meantime, he'll make a woman out of you. You're stiffening up, drying on the vine, girl. You need a man to fill your belly with his seed so you'll ripen." He looked down at her blouse. "You look more like a boy than a woman. Most men aren't interested in a woman like that."

She stood silent and took his abuse. All her life she'd never been right, she'd never passed muster. She'd been too thin, too tall, too flat, too shy, too ordinary. But tonight, his cutting ways didn't hurt so badly because Rowdy had touched her if only for a moment and he didn't seem to find her lacking.

She went up to her room, changed into her cotton gown and stood in front of the mirror for a long while. For the first time she saw herself through another man's eyes besides her father's and she liked what she saw.

Chapter 5

Rowdy was up and shaving when he heard Laurel drive a wagon into the front yard. He wiped the last of the soap off and went to meet her. She'd been on his mind so thick all night he didn't feel like they'd been apart.

"I have news," she said as if she thought she needed a reason to visit him. "And breakfast."

"For me or Cinnamon?" He smiled when he noticed she'd left her bonnet at home.

"Both."

She handed him a basket and a campfire coffeepot, still steaming. "I hope it's still hot."

"Looks grand," he said, but he was staring at her, not the breakfast. Something was different about her. She seemed more confident, happier.

They ate on the porch steps laughing about how she'd managed to fix breakfast, even coffee, without waking anyone up. "In my father's younger days he would be in the saddle by dawn, but after twenty years of drinking late, he's decided the sun could come up without him. Since my sisters never rise before nine, the cook doesn't bother to ride over until full daylight."

"And you?"

She looked surprised that he asked. "Me? I like to get up

early and ride. Before I hear anyone else out of bed I've usually finished half a pot of coffee and worked on the books for an hour or more."

"With the size of your father's spread, it must be a job to keep up with the paperwork. You like managing the books?" Rowdy shifted to face her. His knee was almost touching her shoulder. He wondered if she was half as aware of him as he was of her.

She shook her head. "It's what I was trained in school to do." She stared down at her hands and added, "My father thought I'd never marry so, 'a girl like me needs a skill,' he said."

Rowdy watched her closely. He'd heard the rumors about her and the banker yesterday and wanted to know if they were true. "Do you plan to marry, Laurel?"

She shrugged. "My father told the banker I'd marry him by fall."

"But you don't want to?" he guessed.

Her eyes were filled with a thousand unshed tears when she looked up. "But I don't want to," she repeated.

Rowdy saw it all then. He knew without asking why she needed the money. Her father thought he could control her. "You plan to leave as soon as I win."

She nodded. "My father thinks room and board are enough pay, so I've never been able to think of a way out. When you win, I know where we can get a good price for the herd. You'll have enough to go somewhere and start a new life and so will I."

She was as much of a prisoner as he'd been. "Then we'd better win." He grinned, wishing he felt half as confident as he sounded. "How soon can we change the cattle into money?"

"An hour after the rodeo. They are already in the pens by the station," she answered. "I plan to make the Monday morning train. Once my father learns we're partners, there will be no going home. I can spend the night in the hotel and be ready to leave at dawn."

"That sounds like a great plan, partner. I might catch it and ride along until a place looks right."

"What are you looking for?"

He shrugged. "Any place but here where the land is cheap and the people scarce. How about you?"

"A city. I've always wanted to work in a big bank."

"Too many people." He shook his head.

"If my father hears about our deal, he'll try to stop me by stopping you."

"He won't hear about it." Rowdy stood and offered her a hand. "But maybe it would be a good idea if you didn't come around me at the rodeo tonight. Someone might notice."

She nodded and placed her hand in his. "All right. I brought you a few things you can use around here. When you leave, you can give back or leave them for the next owner."

He wouldn't have taken anything from her but a loan didn't seem wrong. She handed him blankets, towels, coffee and a lantern. "They won't be missed. I took them from the chuck wagon that's stored in the barn until roundup."

He set the supplies down on the porch and unloaded a bale of hay and some oats for Cinnamon. "Thanks," he said when the wagon was empty.

"It's only fair. You seem to be doing all the work in this partnership." She picked a piece of straw off his shoulder and then looked embarrassed at her boldness.

She turned to climb in the wagon, but his hand stopped her with a touch.

"No kiss for luck?" he asked as his fingers rested at her waist.

When she leaned to kiss his cheek, he shifted and their lips touched. He felt her jerk like a colt about to run, but she didn't back away.

For a moment they stood in the morning sun, their bodies

an inch apart, their lips barely touching. He wanted to pull her against him, but he figured he'd frighten her to death if he did.

He pulled away and stared down into her pretty blue eyes. She looked a little surprised, maybe bewildered, but not afraid, he thought. Then he smiled, thinking that if she could read his mind she'd probably run like hell.

"Good luck," she whispered.

"Kiss me again," he answered back without moving. "I can't believe it felt so good."

She hesitated, then closed the distance between them. Her lips touched his lightly once more.

He moved his mouth in a gentle caress over hers this time and her body leaned into him in response. Her lips were the softest thing he'd ever touched and he couldn't resist tugging one into his mouth for a taste.

He felt her shock, then smiled when she didn't jump away or slap him for being so forward.

"You like that?" he whispered against her cheek as his hand moved around her waist.

She made a little sound of pleasure.

"Then open your mouth just a little, Laurel, and I'll show you something you might like even more."

He could feel her heart pounding against his chest as he moved his lips over her mouth, now soft and full. This time when he tugged on her bottom lip, she melted against him. Before he changed his mind, he kissed her fully, taking her breath along with her small cry of joy before he straightened.

Her forehead rested against his cheek for a moment while she breathed. He drew the smell of her deep into his lungs, and with each rise and fall of his chest, he felt her body against his . . . and she felt so good. Nothing in his life had ever felt so right.

When she finally pulled away, neither said a word, but his touch lingered at her waist as she climbed into the wagon.

Without looking at him, she said, "I'll be watching you tonight."

"I like your hair down." His brushed his hand gently over a curl.

He couldn't think of any more to say as he watched her drive away. Every nerve in his body was fighting to keep from riding after her, grabbing her and teaching her what a kiss was all about. He'd kissed a few girls before he went to prison and a few others when he'd gone with the warden to pick up horses in Mexico. Those saloon girls wanted money he didn't have and were willing to kiss him to show what they had to offer.

But not one of them felt like Laurel in his arms.

Rowdy turned to the barn. Most men at twenty knew all about women. Most had probably had a half dozen or more. Most wouldn't get all worked up over one kiss that hadn't gone deep enough to taste passion.

He worked his frustration off cleaning the barn. If Laurel Hayes had a drop of sense, she wouldn't be having anything to do with the likes of him. He had nothing to offer her. Even his friendship would hurt her reputation if anyone knew. She'd be wise to marry the banker and live in a fine house. But, he reasoned, the banker would never kiss her as he had and she'd never let him. That was what surprised him the most, she'd let him.

By the time the barn was clean, he'd reached one conclusion. He'd win this rodeo and split the money with her. Then, when she was free of her father and on her own, he'd see if she still wanted to be friends. If not, he'd understand. But if she did, she'd need to know that he wanted more than just a partnership. He wanted her.

He worked with Cinnamon the rest of the morning, then rode in and ate supper at one of the chuck wagons that invited any man riding to eat.

Cinnamon was bright and quick, but in the calf roping

event, Rowdy only took second for the night. It was little comfort that none of the bronc riders came close to his score from the night before. With another two nights left, he'd be lucky if he placed in calf roping. He figured he could afford to miss one event. Most riding for all-around weren't scheduled in all events. They usually sat out bronc riding or bareback riding because those were the two that had the greatest chance of causing injury. He'd heard two men had dropped out after seeing his ride, figuring they couldn't beat it.

He saw Laurel sitting near her father when he stood directly across the arena and watched the last few events. She didn't look happy, but he had to smile when he noticed she'd worn her hair down with only a small ribbon holding it in place at the back.

One kiss and he'd ached for her all day long.

After the rodeo ended, Dan talked him into walking over to the dance. It was little more than a floor of boards surrounded by poles of lanterns and hay bales to act as benches. The band sat in the grass a few feet away from the dancers. Half the time he couldn't tell if they were playing the same song.

Dan rocked back and forth on his boots. "I'm thinking I should ask a pretty girl to dance."

"I'll watch," Rowdy answered, but he was looking at Laurel standing across the floor from him. She had the banker on one side and her father on the other. Neither man was talking to her, but he had a feeling they'd be none too happy if he walked over and asked her to dance.

If he could dance, he thought, and then he studied the cowhands bumping into each other to the music. None of them looked like they could dance and most of the women seemed more interested in keeping their feet out of harm's way than holding on to the fellow they were with.

"There sure are a lot of pretty girls," Dan sounded in awe.

"How about one of the Captain's daughters?" Rowdy suggested.

They both looked over at the two blondes surrounded by cowhands.

Dan shook his head. "I set my standards a little higher than them two. They ain't got a full brain between them."

"I'm impressed with your wisdom, Dan." Rowdy slapped his new friend on the back. "How about the other daughter? The one there by her father."

Dan stared at Laurel. "Not that one. She's the opposite of her sisters. They say she went away to school for years. Say she can figure in her head faster than most folks can on paper. She'd think I was as dumb as a box of rocks."

"You could give it a try."

Dan let out a long breath as if he'd accepted a challenge. "I guess so."

He walked across the floor and stepped right up to Laurel. Rowdy couldn't hear what he said, but he did see both the Captain and the banker frown and shake their heads. Laurel, to everyone's surprise, raised her hand and stepped onto the floor with Dan O'Brien.

Rowdy frowned. He wasn't sure he liked the idea of Dan dancing with her. Not one bit. In fact, the idiot who suggested it should be whipped. He stared at Dan's hand resting lightly on her back and knew just how it felt.

His only satisfaction was that neither of them seemed to have any idea how to dance. They stepped first one way and then the other. Dan looked like an ox tromping in mud and she seemed like a feather being blown in the wind. When the music ended, they both looked relieved.

They stepped off the floor a few feet from Rowdy.

"Miss Hayes," Dan said politely. "Thank you for the dance."

"You're welcome," she managed shyly.

Dan smiled at Rowdy. "I'd like to introduce my friend Rowdy Darnell to you if you'll let me."

Laurel offered her hand and Rowdy held it. Neither said a word.

She looked around as if afraid to meet Rowdy's stare. Afraid she might give away too much, or he would if they looked at each other.

Pulling away, she stepped into the crowd. Both men stood watching her go and wondering if they'd offended her.

Before either could comment, she reappeared with a petite, redheaded girl at her side. "Gentlemen," Laurel said, "I'd like you to meet a friend of mine. Bonnie Lynn, this is Dan O'Brien and Rowdy Darnell."

"Pleased to meet you," Dan said as if practicing what he'd been taught.

Bonnie Lynn smiled and offered him a curtsy. "I'm glad to meet you too. I've seen you in town, Dan O'Brien, and I'm thinking you are the biggest Irishman I've ever seen."

They all laughed.

"Would you like to dance?" Dan offered.

She looked down at his big boots and said, "I'm afraid you'd step on me, Dan O'Brien, but I'd still like to dance with you."

When he took her in his arms, she pulled away far enough to see her feet and stepped onto the toes of his boots.

He laughed and began to move across the floor.

Rowdy smiled at Laurel. "It appears you lost your partner."

"I'm not sure I would have survived another round."

He saw the banker coming toward them and knew he had little time. Turning his back to the banker, he said low and urgent, "Meet me by the cottonwoods tonight."

"I don't know how long I'll be."

"It doesn't matter. I'll wait."

She didn't have time to answer. Rowdy could feel the banker standing behind him and he didn't like the fear he saw in Laurel's eyes.

Chapter 6

Laurel listened to her father rant all the way home. Her sisters had danced with half the cowboys at the rodeo and he hadn't said a word. She'd danced with one and now he swore she would be marked as a tramp. "Why'd you have to pick the pig farmer? One of my men would have asked you eventually."

Laurel didn't answer and her father never gave her long enough to even if she had wanted to.

By the time they reached the ranch, he'd decided that she would attend no more dances until she was married and no longer his problem. When Laurel asked if it were the dance or the man she danced with that made him so angry, the Captain said the man, of course.

"I have nothing against Dan O'Brien, but you are engaged. You should only be seen with Jeffery Filmore. He's a fine man and one of the most powerful figures in town. In ten years I wouldn't be surprised if he owns half the land around here and I plan to have the other half. Marrying him would be smart, girl."

"But he's never asked me to marry him," she tried to reason. How could she be engaged if she'd never been asked?

"He asked me," her father announced. "And that is enough. A man like him doesn't have time to waste."

That wasn't enough by a long shot, she thought, but didn't bother to argue. Once her father made up his mind about something, hell or high water couldn't change him. He was still set on building his spread when most men his age were looking for a rocking chair.

"I always thought if I married it would be for love."

"Don't be a fool. You're not the type men marry for love."

When they reached the house, the Captain stormed to his study and slammed the door.

Laurel walked through the house and closed the back door softly as she left for the barn. She saddled her own horse and rode out toward the creek, knowing that once her father started drinking he'd forget all about her.

As she rode, she remembered how Jeffery Filmore had gripped her arm just like her father did when he wanted her to follow orders. The banker had walked her all the way to the buggy and hadn't said a word to her. She couldn't tell if he were angry or simply wanted to get her out of the way so he could enjoy the dance with the other older men who sat about drinking and talking without really watching the dancing.

When they'd reached the buggy, he'd pressed her against it before she'd had time to climb in. "Good night," he said and kissed her hard on the mouth. So hard she'd felt his teeth beneath his thin lip.

She'd shoved away, but it took her a few seconds to push his mass off her.

He'd tried to use his weight to hold her between him and the buggy. He fought her for a moment before letting her slip away. She hated the kiss and the feeling. It was as if he was proving something to her.

Filmore had said good night to her father and walked away without ever saying one word to her. She was a thing to him, nothing more.

When she reached the creek, she splashed across suddenly in a hurry to get away from her life and from the memory of

Filmore's kiss. She wished she could erase the feel of him from her mind. His body had been heavy and shifting like a huge flour sack pressing against her.

When the cottonwoods blocked the moon, she saw Rowdy waiting for her. His arms went up to gently help her down.

"I didn't know if you'd come," he said as he lowered her beside him.

For once in her life, Laurel didn't think. She knew what she needed and wanted.

"I'm glad—" he got out before she rose to her toes and kissed him.

It took a few seconds for Rowdy to react. Then, as if he'd also been hungry for another kiss, he pulled her against him and gave her what she wanted. A long, sweet kiss that made her forget to breathe.

When he finally straightened and pulled away, she could see his gaze still staring at her mouth. She'd shocked him.

Laughing, she pretended to pout. "Sorry I forced myself on you."

A slow smile spread across his lips. "You're not sorry at all and neither am I."

"Good." She closed the distance between them. Her words brushed against his mouth. "Then would you mind kissing me again?"

"How do you want to be kissed, gentle Laurel?" he answered.

"Completely," she whispered, leaving her mouth slightly open in invitation.

He met her challenge. With his body pressing like a wall against hers, he kissed her, widening her mouth until he'd tasted all he wanted, then teasing her until she answered in kind. He tugged the ribbon from her hair and wrapped his fingers in the softness.

When she pulled away to breathe, he whispered, "I love your hair. The warmth of it, the softness of it. The way I feel with my hands wrapped in it."

"I could cut it off and give you a few strands." She laughed.

He kissed her quick and hard. "No thanks. I prefer it attached to you. There are a few other parts of you I'm growing fond of having near. This partnership has some very interesting side benefits."

"Like what?" She knew she was fishing, but she needed to hear something other than she was smart and practical.

He hesitated, brushing her cheek with his knuckles. "I like how your mouth fits against mine. I like watching your thoughts sparkle in the pale sunrise blue of your eyes."

"And?"

"Are you sure you want the list?"

She nodded.

He tugged her a little tighter to him. "I like the feel of your body against me."

She buried her face in his shoulder.

His fingers moved gently along her back. "You asked," he whispered against her ear. "And you didn't pull away so I'm guessing you like it too."

He held her for a while, playing with her hair, caressing her gently, then he held her at arm's length. "Want to tell me what's wrong?"

"Nothing," she lied.

"You rode in here like the devil was chasing you, Laurel. Something happened."

He was right. She couldn't believe she was so easy to read. She'd wanted to wash the feel of Jeffery from her and she'd used Rowdy to do just that. Maybe she'd needed affection that had never come from her father. Maybe she wanted to feel like a woman for once and not a thing. Maybe she wanted to prove her father wrong, that she was desirable.

If she told Rowdy any of those reasons he'd think he was being used and she didn't want to make him feel that way.

She couldn't lie to him and she wouldn't tell him the truth. "If I don't tell you, will you still kiss me again?"

He grinned. "Sure. I kind of like communicating without words. Talking is overrated anyway." He kissed her nose. "When I was waiting for you, I was wondering if you'd let me kiss you again. I wasn't prepared for you to attack me."

She started to argue, then reconsidered. She liked the way this conversation was going. "That's me. I look all shy but underneath I'm a wild woman."

He raised an eyebrow. "How many people know about this secret of yours?"

She rubbed her cheek against his and whispered in his ear. "You're the first so far."

He caught her jaw and kissed her playfully, then whispered, "If I give you what you want, maybe this secret can stay between us."

"I want lots of kisses," she announced. "I can be very demanding."

"I think I can handle that, darling."

She felt like she was melting. Locking her arms around his neck, she let him lift her off the ground and whirl her around. When they were both laughing, he said, "Laurel Hayes, you are a wonder in this world."

They stood in the moonlight staring at each other. She brushed his hair off his forehead. He tucked a wild strand of hers behind her ear. When their lips touched, it was as if they had a lifetime to finish one kiss.

When he finally broke the kiss, she sighed and moved away. "Thank you," she said.

He still held her hand. "For what?"

"For making me feel good all the way to my toes."

He raised a wicked eyebrow. "I wouldn't mind testing to see if that's true. From what I've touched so far, I'd guess you do feel good all the way to your toes. You're tall and slim, but you seem to fit against me in all the right places."

She blushed and turned to her horse. "I have to go. It's late."

He stepped behind her as she reached for the saddle horn.

His hand glided from her shoulder to her waist. She leaned against the saddle, loving the feel of his fingers moving down her back. His hands spread wide and made a slow journey along her sides. She caught her breath when the tips of his fingers moved around her enough to brush the sides of her breasts.

"Rowdy," she whispered.

He was so close she could feel his breath brushing her hair at the back of her neck. "Do you want me to apologize?"

She tried to control her breathing, her knuckles white as they gripped the saddle. "No," she finally answered.

His hands moved once more along her sides, only this time, when he reached her breasts, he slowed, tenderly feeling the sides, pressing gently as he tested the softness beneath her blouse.

She was glad he couldn't see her face for she felt like it was on fire. No one had ever touched her as he was now.

He leaned down and kissed the side of her throat. "You feel like heaven come to earth, woman. I could spend all night doing this."

"Then do it once more before I go." She couldn't believe her own words. "So I'll remember exactly how it feels."

With the same gentleness, he moved his hand up from her waist, only this time his fingers covered her breasts, cupping each. As she gulped for air, she pressed into his palms and his grip tightened.

Neither said a word as he held her in his tender grip. As her breathing calmed, she felt his fingers gently brushing against her breasts.

Finally, he pulled his hands away. When he turned her to face him, she rested her head on his shoulder and they simply held each other. What they'd done hadn't been a casual or an accidental touch. She had a feeling they'd both remember it all their lives.

"I'm not sure . . ." He took a deep breath. "I haven't been around many women. I . . ."

She moved so that he could feel her smile against his skin. "I think you did it just right," she whispered and felt him relax against her.

His lips brushed her cheek. "If you get another urge to let that wild woman inside of you come out, you know where to find me. I'll always be there if you need me."

She couldn't believe she'd been so honest with him. In the clear sober light of day she wasn't sure she could face him. But now, right now, she didn't regret anything.

Putting her foot in the stirrup, she felt his hands tighten around her as he lifted her up. "Thank you," she whispered. "For making me feel like a woman."

"You're welcome," he said as if he didn't understand exactly what she was thanking him for. "And believe me, Laurel, you feel very much like a woman."

Leaning down, she brushed his mouth one last time. "Good luck tomorrow."

"Will I see you at the dance?"

"No." She didn't want a repeat of the lecture her father had given her. "I'll meet you here if I can."

He stood on the edge of the creek and watched her ride away. When she looked back, he was still there.

Part of her wondered how she could be so free and wild with him. Then, slowly, she understood what all women come to know. A woman is a different woman in each man's arms. She'd never be like she was tonight with Jeffery Filmore, not if they married and lived together for forty years.

This Laurel born tonight would only live in the circle of Rowdy Darnell's embrace.

Chapter 7

Clouds blocked any sunrise, but Rowdy was up and dressed by the time the first watery light managed to show along the horizon. He'd cleaned the cabin up enough to make it livable but the place was still depressing. Despite the chill of rain, he opened the doors and welcomed the damp air.

Today he would compete in steer roping. Dan O'Brien would try for his only event, calf roping. Both had agreed to help the other. His lead in saddle bronc riding from the first night had held two days and his second place from last night's event had a good chance of making it. The best all-around cowboy didn't have to win every event. When all the events were over, each man competing for best all-around got three points for first, two for second, and one for third. It was possible for a rider not to place in one round and still win best overall. No man's ranking was safe until the last entry rode.

Rowdy worked with Cinnamon all morning. He swore the horse was so smart Cinnamon would be teaching him soon.

Around noon he noticed a basket sitting on his front porch. Laurel was nowhere in sight, but he knew she'd brought it. By the time he brushed the horse down and made it to the porch he saw Dan riding up.

"Join me for lunch," Rowdy offered, knowing Laurel would have packed more than he could eat.

Dan smiled and moved into the shade.

Rowdy set out fried chicken, mashed potatoes and corn on the cob. Dan's eyes were bulging. The quart of buttermilk made his mouth drop open.

Rowdy offered him the best plate he had and one of the two forks he owned.

Dan frowned. "Either you were raised in the kitchen and travel with a coop of chickens and a cow, or you didn't make all this." He looked around. "I don't see any fire going."

"I didn't make this." Rowdy laughed. "I can't roast a rabbit fit to eat." He took a bite and smiled. "And," he added when he could speak, "I'm not telling you where it came from. So eat, not knowing, or watch me. It's up to you."

"I'll eat." Dan dove into the food.

Rowdy had a feeling the man hadn't eaten all morning. They devoured the food. When they found an apple pie at the bottom of the basket, they split it in half.

Finally, Dan leaned back on the porch and stretched his long legs. "I ain't asking no questions," he yawned, "but if food like this falls from heaven again, would you invite me over?"

Rowdy laughed. "Sure." He liked the big man. Dan didn't ask too many questions.

They spent the afternoon practicing and then rode into town. Dan's calf roping came first. His one event. His chance to win fifty dollars. Tonight was the last ride for this event because the organizers needed time to hand out awards tomorrow.

Dan was the next to the last to ride. Rain had been splattering the dirt for several minutes when they shot out after the calf. Rowdy did his part and Dan had the calf tossed and tied with smooth skill. A few minutes later, the last contestant failed to loop the calf.

Rowdy smiled, knowing he'd just moved to third place and

Dan had won first. He looked for Laurel but the rain curtained the other end of the arena from sight.

Fifteen minutes later, he roped a steer almost by the time he cleared the gate and rolled in the mud to twist the horns until the animal tumbled, splattering water and dirt all over him.

Rowdy stood, waved his hat and walked to the gate knowing he'd just taken the lead in steer roping. He stepped behind the pens looking for Dan but the rain was driving so hard he couldn't see more than the dark outline of the barn. He guessed most of the hands sleeping around chuck wagons would be in the dry hay tonight.

Slashing through the mud, he headed toward the barn hoping to find Dan and congratulate him. When he stepped out of the rain at the side of the corral, he heard someone coming up fast behind him.

He swung around expecting Dan, but a fist caught him so hard in the stomach he folded over. All he saw were three men in oil slickers, boots and dark rain-drenched hats. The next blow knocked him against the side of the barn and he thought he heard the chime of silver spurs.

Rowdy shook his ringing head and came up fighting. He knew he hit one man hard enough on the jaw to knock him down and felt another's nose crack beneath his knuckles, but their fists rained down worse than the storm. Finally, when he twisted to avoid one blow, a man behind him hit him hard in the back of the head with what felt like an anvil.

Rowdy crumbled and the dark night turned black. Vaguely, from far away, he thought he felt a few kicks to his ribs and then nothing.

Chapter 8

"Miss Hayes. Laurel?"

Laurel shifted in her chair by the window and looked around the café. Everyone from the rodeo seemed to have moved into the hotel out of the rain. Most of the cowboys were in the bar in the back, but her father had insisted she stay in the parlor surrounded by nursing mothers and whining children ready to go home.

She'd heard rumors that even though the dance tonight had be cancelled, there were still games the men called "outlawed events" going on. There the betting was heavy. Those not out in the rain participating were inside awaiting the outcome.

She had no idea where her sisters were, but her father had gone upstairs with several men to drink and play poker until the rain let up enough to head for home.

Staring out the window she decided that might never be.

"Laurel?" The whisper came again as if it were drifting in the wind.

She studied the people around her. No one was even looking in her direction.

"Laurel," the voice whispered again.

This time she had a direction to follow. Three feet away she saw Bonnie Lynn serving tea to one of the older women.

"Yes," Laurel took a chance and answered.

Bonnie Lynn only spared her a quick glance as she straightened. "Follow me."

Laurel didn't ask questions. She stood slowly, looked around and followed several feet behind Bonnie Lynn as they left the room and moved into a hallway to the kitchen that served both the parlor and the café.

"What is it?" she asked as soon as Bonnie Lynn turned around in the quiet passage.

"Dan's at the kitchen door. He says he has to talk to you."

If it had been anyone but Dan O'Brien, Laurel would have thought it was some kind of joke her sisters were playing on her.

"From the look on his face, I think you'd better hurry," Bonnie Lynn said as she slipped into the kitchen.

Laurel tried not to look at the rotting food and dirty dishes scattered around. The place was so busy it looked as if it hadn't been cleaned in weeks.

Just outside the back door, Dan stood in the rain. Bonnie Lynn was at her side as they stepped onto the tiny back porch. "What is it?" Laurel yelled over the rain and the kitchen noises behind her.

"It's Darnell, miss. He's hurt. I don't know what to do for him."

Bonnie Lynn's hand caught Laurel's arm before she could step into the downpour. "Wait, miss. Take my cape."

It took all her control to stand still as the maid wrapped a cape over her shoulders. She pulled the hood up and Dan offered his arm.

"Where is he?" Laurel asked as she matched the big man's stride.

"In the old barn down by the corrals."

"What happened?"

"One of the men who work the stock said he saw three cowhands kicking something in the mud. He didn't know it was a man until he almost fell over him when the cowhands walked away. We got him in the barn, but he's bleeding, Miss, and I wasn't sure what to do."

"What about the doctor?"

"Rowdy wouldn't hear of us getting him. He says they'd disqualify him if they knew he was hurt."

Laurel could barely speak. Fear blocked her words. "Did he tell you to come find me?"

"No, miss. He's going to be madder than hell when he figures out I come to get you, but I'm hoping you can talk some sense into him."

"But why me?"

Dan smiled. "I seen the way you looked at him that night at the dance and the way he looked at me when I was holding you. I didn't think it was nothing much until I saw that basket of food this morning on his porch. A man don't pack a basket with lace napkins, and the food was too hot to have come all the way from town." He helped her over a mud hole and added, "It made sense it came from the Captain's place, and I knew if it was one of your sisters he liked that'd make my friend dumber than a warm cow patty."

She looked away so he wouldn't see her smile.

"Meaning no disrespect against your sisters."

They stepped into the sudden silence of the barn.

"If you won't take offense," Dan said as he pointed to the loft, "I'll swing you up."

She nodded and she was lifted up like a child.

For a moment she saw nothing but hay, then, in the corner, a tiny light flickered.

"Bring another lantern," she called down to Dan and ran toward Rowdy.

He moaned as she tugged his shoulder and turned him onto his back. Blood and mud were everywhere.

"Laurel," he whispered, then tried to push her away.

"Stop it." She shoved back. "Be still. I need to see where you're hurt."

"Pretty much all over," he mumbled.

"Then let me look."

She wasn't sure if he passed out or just decided to follow orders for once. He crumbled like a rag doll.

The light wasn't good enough to see, but she could feel. Laurel tugged off her cape and pressed her hand against his heart. It beat solid and strong. She took a deep breath and began to move over him, feeling the strong muscles of his body beneath his soaked clothes.

When she touched his left side, he jerked in pain but didn't cry out. None of his limbs seemed broken but warm blood dripped from his bottom lip and nose. A cut sliced across his forehead close to his hairline and a knot as big as an egg stood out on the back of his skull. By the time Dan arrived with the lantern, she felt safe in believing Rowdy wasn't going to die.

When Rowdy opened his eyes, she said, "You need to see a doctor."

"No," he answered.

"But . . ."

"No," he repeated.

Dan knelt on one knee. "I figure whoever did this was trying to take Rowdy out of the competition. I don't think it was anything personal. If we take him to a doc, he'll be out no matter how it happened."

"But he can't ride tomorrow like this."

"He has to. I heard one of the judges say if he places even third tomorrow, he'll win best all-around."

"No. His ribs could be broken." She pulled his shirt away and saw the dark bruises already forming.

"Stop talking about me like I'm not in my right mind." Rowdy swore as he forced himself to sit up. "I'm riding tomorrow. End of discussion."

"I say no. It's not worth risking your life."

He stared at her. "If I don't ride, I'll be risking both our lives. I'm not willing to do that." He closed his bruised hand over hers. "I've been hurt far worse than this. I can ride tomorrow."

Laurel shoved the tear off her cheek. "Dan, can you get him home?"

"I'll borrow a wagon and have him there in an hour."

"Good. Stay with him until I get there. I'll bring bandages and all the medicine I can find."

If the big man thought it strange that Laurel Hayes was crying over Rowdy, he didn't say a word. He helped her get him downstairs to a wagon. She pulled all the blankets from her buggy and packed them around him.

When Dan brought his horse and Cinnamon to the back of the wagon, she whispered her thanks.

"Ain't nothing he wouldn't do for me," Dan answered, then hesitated before adding, "He's a good man, Miss Laurel."

"I know," she answered. "I'll be there as soon as I can."

She watched the wagon move into the rain and then walked back to the hotel.

Bonnie Lynn met her at the kitchen door. "Your father is looking for you."

She handed Bonnie Lynn back her cape and stepped into the hallway. She could hear her father yelling.

He'd lost at poker and was too drunk to notice the mud on her clothes. All he wanted to do was go home. When they reached the barn, he borrowed one of his men's horses and had two of the cowhands ride with the women.

Her sisters complained about the lack of blankets until the men offered an arm around them. Laurel sat in the back too worried to be cold. She ordered the man driving to go faster, but he was in no hurry to get home. The road seemed endless.

When they finally made it, she ran in the house and up the stairs. Minutes later she was dressed in her wool riding clothes and leather jacket. Tossing all the supplies she could find in a bag, she started out of the house.

At the front door she almost collided with her father and one of his men.

"Where do you think you are going?"

Laurel knew better than to tell him the truth. She might be twenty, but he'd think he was well within his rights to lock her in her room if he thought she was leaving. "I'm going to check on my mare."

"At this hour?" He wasn't sober enough to figure out why her story made little sense.

"I couldn't sleep. I think the mare might have hurt her leg." She lifted the bag as if to prove what she was doing.

The cowhand laughed. "The horse isn't the only one hurting tonight."

To her shock, her father laughed and seemed to forget about Laurel. "We need a drink." He put his arm around the cowhand. "You've put in a long day."

Laurel disappeared the minute they turned the corner. She didn't like the feeling gnawing away inside her. Despite all her father was, until now she never would have believed he would have done something so unfair. He wanted his men to win tomorrow and he seemed to be covering his bet with a beating.

She shot out of the barn and rode full out into the rain. Once she reached the water, she had to slow because the banks were slippery. She would do Rowdy no good if she broke her neck getting to him.

Ten minutes later, she stepped into the cabin.

Dan had built a fire and laid down straw to soften the bedroll. The rain had washed most of the mud off them both, but Rowdy was still bleeding.

Without a word, she set to work. Dan watched, fetched water when she needed more and kept the fire going, but he was helpless in doctoring.

"He started talking out of his head about halfway home." Dan paced as he mumbled. "Kept wanting to know where you were and if you were all right. He thought you might get yourself in big trouble for coming to the barn." Dan stopped and watched her for a while. "You care about him, don't you, Miss? That's why you came even knowing it might not set well with your old man."

"I do care," she answered.

"Does your father know?"

"I have a feeling he might know something about Rowdy being hurt, but not about us." She could only guess how angry her father would be. "If he did, they might have killed Rowdy tonight."

Dan nodded, understanding. "I'm going to take care of the horses and then, if you don't mind, I think I'll sleep with my rifle on that porch. You just call me if you need me."

"Thanks," she said, as he lifted Rowdy enough so she could circle a bandage around his ribs. "I'll give him enough medicine to ease the pain. Maybe if he can sleep, he'll feel better tomorrow morning."

Dan left, closing the door. Laurel worked for another hour cleaning every cut until the bleeding stopped and keeping a cool rag on the back of Rowdy's head. She knew no one would miss her until breakfast so she could stay until sunup and have plenty of time to get back.

Finally, exhausted, she curled next to him, placed her hand over his heart and fell asleep.

Chapter 9

Rowdy woke feeling warm in the calm darkness. He moved and felt pain rattle through his body.

He smiled, remembering how worried Laurel had looked. She couldn't have known that he'd taken far worse in prison.

Silently, he took inventory. He was hurt but nothing was broken. In prison he'd been in fights where he wasn't sure he'd ever stand much less walk again. This seemed mild in comparison.

He moved his hand over his ribs and encountered Laurel's long slender fingers resting over his chest.

His head ached as he shifted just enough to see her sleeping beside him. She was so beautiful in the firelight, an angel dropped down to watch over him. He remembered how she'd said she prayed for him. He'd thought no one cared and she'd been kneeling in a chapel somewhere saying his name. The image warmed a heart he'd thought long dead.

As if she felt him watching her, she opened sleepy eyes.

"How are you?" she asked, worry wrinkling her brow.

"A little sore, but healing," he answered. "Did you sleep here next to me all night?"

"Yes." She smiled and sat up so she could check each of his wounds. Only the break in skin at his forehead looked like it had bled a little during the night. "I didn't want to leave you alone."

"You were right here next to me and I slept through it. What a shame."

Giggling, she said, "You were in no shape to do anything about it."

"I'd have died trying." He winked and then winced at his cracked lip.

"Shut up and take a deep breath. I want to listen to your lungs."

When she leaned her head against his chest, he took a deep breath and tangled his fingers in her hair. "I'm all right, Laurel. I swear."

She looked up, firelight sparkling in her tears. "I was so worried about you. I don't care if we win. I'll find another way to get free of my father. It doesn't matter. I just didn't want to lose you."

He tugged her against him and held her for a while. "We'll find a way," he finally whispered. "I plan on winning, but if I don't, we'll find a way. I'll stand with you win or lose."

"But you can't ride. You might fall."

"I don't think about how I'm going to fall when I ride. I just think about staying on." He laughed, then groaned. "I don't have to make the best showing tonight, all I have to do is stay on and draw third place. None of the bareback rides have been that good."

He knew she wanted to argue with him. He swore he could almost hear her mind working. But she didn't say a word. They just lay close, listening to the fire and waiting for sunrise. This was the last day. Tonight it would all be over. She'd stay at the hotel and by dawn tomorrow she'd be on the first train. She'd be off to start her new life in some big town and he'd have money in his pocket until the place sold.

By first light, Rowdy had fallen back asleep. She slipped

from his side and put on a pot of coffee to boil, then dug in the bag for bread she'd brought the day before.

When she took Dan a cup of hot coffee, he was hooking up the wagon. "I'm sorry I have no breakfast to offer you but bread. I was in too much of a hurry to think about what we'd eat with it."

"No problem. How's Rowdy?"

"Much better. He's asleep now, but earlier he said he plans to ride."

Dan nodded. "Tell him to sleep as much as he can today. I'll be around when he comes into town and make sure nothing happens to him before the rodeo."

"Thanks." She glanced up at the sun. "I'll try to stay until he wakes, then I have to get back before my family wakes and realizes I've been out all night. You headed home?"

Dan shook his head. "I'm thinking of riding into town and having breakfast at the hotel."

Laurel smiled. "I hear it's good, especially when served by Bonnie Lynn."

He grinned. "I have no understanding of women, but I think she likes me. She told me last night that I make her laugh and I figure that's a start."

"I think she likes you, Dan, even if you don't understand why."

He climbed into the wagon. "And as smart as everyone knows you are, Miss, you still like that busted up cowboy in there, don't you?"

"I do, but we're just friends. Have been since we were kids."

"Sure you are," he said without looking at her.

He waved as he drove away. Laurel sat on the porch and drank the coffee she'd meant for Dan. When she went back inside, Rowdy was awake and sitting up.

She knelt beside him. "How are you feeling?"

"Better." He rubbed his slightly swollen lip with his first knuckle. "I think I could take a little of that coffee."

She poured a fresh cup and shared with him.

When it was empty, he set the cup aside. "Lie back down beside me," he said. "I don't want you to go just yet."

She didn't hesitate as she spread out beside him. They lay in silence for a while, then he said, "I heard what you told Dan."

"That I like you?"

"Yes. And that we're just friends."

He rolled to his side and placed his hand on her middle. "I don't think it's true," he whispered. "I think you feel about me the way I feel about you. Neither of us is looking for love, but we've learned to trust each other. And there is something between us, pulling us closer."

"Maybe," she protested. "I do like being near you."

"No," he answered. "I think it's more than that even if neither of us wants to admit it. We went beyond just partners the first time you kissed me. What I feel for you is deeper than like."

"I don't think so," she whispered. She couldn't admit more, not after only three days. Not when she'd be leaving tomorrow and she might never see him again. "When you win tonight, we'll split the money and go our separate ways. All we can be is partners, Rowdy."

"No, we're already more," he answered as his fingers brushed lightly over the cotton of her blouse. "If your feelings aren't running deep right now with me touching you, then move away. We may not feel love, but I'm definitely attracted to you."

He wasn't holding her, only touching her. His hand slid up between her breasts and began unbuttoning her blouse. "Because if you don't run, Laurel, I'm going to touch you as no one else has ever touched you. If I don't, I'll regret it the rest of my life." He leaned down and brushed his lips over hers.

"There is no time," she mumbled as she answered his kiss with one of her own.

The kiss was so tender she wanted to cry. She felt the first button give way to his fingers.

"Make love with me, Laurel," he whispered against her ear.

She was too shy to say the words, but her kiss answered his question. As they kissed she felt him pulling buttons free, then tugging her blouse from the band of her riding skirt.

When he felt the layer of her camisole, he raised his head. "How many layers do you have on?"

She laughed. "Only one more."

"Good." He frowned. "I'd really like to see what I touched last night."

She turned her head away from him, too embarrassed to look at him. "I'm not—" She couldn't even say the words. Her body curled away from him.

Forgetting about the camisole, he gripped her shoulder and pulled her back. "Not what?" he asked.

"I'm not the kind of woman men want. I'm smart. I can keep books, but that's about all."

He swore and she felt his anger, not at her, but at what she believed. Finally, he calmed down and tugged her chin so that she had to look at him. "Look, Laurel, I don't care if you can count and, as for being smart, I've begun to question that since you started hanging around with the likes of me. And about being the kind of woman men want, I can't speak for all men, but you are exactly what I want."

"You do? How?"

He sat up and shoved his hair back, then winced at the pain. He took a long breath and said, "I thought you would have figured it out by now, but I'll explain so that there will be no misunderstanding between us." He met her gaze and held it. "I want you in my arms. I want you in my bed. I want to be so close that we share air and so deep inside you I forget there is a world other than with you."

"Oh," she said, sitting up to face him.

He laughed. "You know for a smart girl, you surprise me.

Or maybe I've had too little practice to get my feelings across. I don't suppose you want the same thing?"

She raised her chin. "I might. What did you have in mind?"

He glanced at the sun coming in the open door. "I would say we do everything right here, right now, but your father will be sending a hunting party for you any minute. How about we start now and finish tonight at the hotel? I don't want to be interrupted."

"All right." She could feel her nerves jumping. "What do we do first?"

"Unbutton that undergarment," he said, smiling a dare. "I think we could call that a start."

She sat perfectly straight and unbuttoned her camisole. Her gaze never left his eyes.

"Now pull it apart, darling, if you don't mind." His voice was lower.

She tugged the thin layer of cotton open an inch at a time and saw only pleasure in his dark gaze.

"You're beautiful," he whispered. "Beautiful."

She closed her eyes as he raised his hand and covered one breast. His other hand slid to the back of her neck as he gently laid her down on the straw bed. When his fingers closed around her and tightened, she let out a cry of joy. He lowered his mouth over hers and caught her next moan of pleasure.

"This is how we'll start tonight," he whispered. "Only the door will be locked and we'll have all night. I don't want to hurry loving you. We need to take our time getting to know each other." He kissed his way down her throat without turning loose of her breast.

When all thought but what he was doing to her had left her mind, she felt him move away and she protested.

"It's begun, darling. There's only one way this is going to end and I plan to make sure you enjoy each step." He stared at her as if she were a work of art. "We'd better stop now while I can. When I ride tonight I won't be thinking of the pain. All that I'll be dreaming of is having you all alone."

He leaned and kissed the tip of her breast, then pulled the cotton back in place. "You surprise me, Laurel."

"How?"

"I didn't think you'd love a man's touch."

"I don't. I love your touch and it is quite possible I may never find another's of any interest."

He grinned, satisfied with her answer.

She sat up and buttoned her clothes.

Watching her hands, he thought about how fine and beautiful they were. He liked her hands. Hell, he almost said aloud, he liked everything about her.

Lost in his thoughts he realized she'd been talking. He only hoped he hadn't missed something important.

"I'll pack and leave my trunk at the hotel. Bonnie Lynn will watch it for me and tell no one. As soon as you ride, I'll find the buyer and have him meet us at the hotel. He said he could bring ten percent in cash and have the rest deposited wherever we like."

He smiled. "You're sure I'll win. You've planned everything."

"I'm betting on it."

"And if I don't?" He had to know what would remain between them if tonight didn't go as planned.

"Then I'll go home as if nothing has changed and pick up the bag when I'm in town alone." Her blue eyes met his. "It may take me a few hours, but I'll meet you under the cottonwoods before midnight."

He knew what she meant. What was going to happen between them would happen. At the hotel, or beneath the stars. It would happen.

He stood. "Until tonight," he said as he kissed her. The need to whisper that he thought he loved her built inside him, but he couldn't—wouldn't love her. Love had killed his father and he'd never allow himself to crumble. Better never to love than to let it eat you away inside if love is lost.

At the door, he stopped her one step before the sun reached their faces. "Tell me you need me," he whispered against her ear.

"I need you," she answered.

He brushed a kiss into her hair. "Tonight, wait for me. I'll be there in time for a late supper."

He waited for her to answer, then smiled, guessing she wouldn't say the word until he did and as long as he didn't use the word love he could walk away if that was still the way she wanted it after their night together.

Chapter 10

Laurel sat in her tiny office and sharpened each of her pencils to a fine point, then lined them up neatly. If Rowdy won tonight, she wouldn't be coming back. For as long as she could remember this house had been her home. They'd moved here the summer before her father went to New Orleans and brought back a new wife. It had always been a cold house. Her stepmother's mood swings and her father's temper made it impossible for any housekeeper to stay more than a few seasons.

All she'd ever felt in this place was alone. She knew she wouldn't spend one day of her life to come missing it.

"You about ready to go?" her father said from the doorway.

"More than ready." She stood. "All is in order and up to date."

"Good." He smiled. "That schooling of yours was worth the money."

She didn't answer his almost-compliment as they walked to the parlor to wait for her sisters.

"You know that place over the creek, the Darnell Ranch?" he asked as if making conversation.

The attempt was so rare, it surprised Laurel. "Yes, I ride over there now and then."

He nodded, only half listening. "The sheriff tells me it's up for sale. I'm thinking of making Darnell's son a rock-bottom price. He's been gone so long he'll have no idea what it's worth and once I offer I'd be surprised if anyone tried to top me."

"How much is it worth?" Laurel tried to keep her tone bland as if simply making conversation.

"A small fortune, I'm guessing. They say the water's good. In the right hands, it could be a great addition to my holdings." He shrugged. "Since the young Darnell didn't win best all-around, I'm thinking he'll be needing money to move on and will take my first offer no matter how low I make it."

Laurel fought to swallow. "How do you know he won't win?"

"I heard he was hurt last night."

She couldn't say a word without giving away far more than she wanted her father to know.

He patted her pale cheek, seeing only her frailty. "Don't worry, Laurel. When I buy the place you can still ride over there if you like. I might even have a gate cut in the fence so you could cross through." Then as if he'd rationed out all his kindness for the day, he walked away yelling for his other daughters to get downstairs immediately.

A few minutes later, she silently climbed into the wagon. Her father rode his horse, making one of the men handle the surrey's team. Laurel sat alone on the backseat trying to figure out how her father had known Rowdy was hurt. Of course it was possible his men saw Dan carry him into the barn. Maybe the man who almost tumbled over Rowdy in the mud told someone, who told someone. Only they weren't in town that long after she'd visited the barn and, as far as she knew, both her father and his men had been working on the ranch all day.

She walked around and around the obvious answer, hoping to find another reason for her father knowing than that he somehow had ordered the attack.

When they reached the town square and her family hurried off to watch the children ride lambs and rope pigs, Laurel lay her coat over the small traveling bag she'd used when she went back and forth to school. With her head high, she walked directly to the hotel.

When she found Bonnie Lynn, she asked, "Do you have somewhere you can store this for me?"

Bonnie didn't ask questions, she just nodded and took the case.

"I may be needing a room later."

"We're full," Bonnie Lynn said, "but I wouldn't be surprised if some folks don't head home tonight after the rodeo's over. Don't you worry about your things. I'll put them in my room. They'll be safe there and I'll make sure you get the first room that comes open."

Laurel smiled, silently thanking the girl for asking no questions. "One more favor. Do you know where Rowdy is?

Bonnie winked. "That is no favor. He's sitting in the bar with my Dan having a piece of my pie."

Laurel took a breath. "I need to talk to him alone."

"I'll have him meet you in the parlor. It's always empty this time of day."

While the maid went to put up her case and tell Rowdy, Laurel stood in the front room and stared out dirty windows at the circus atmosphere outside. Everyone for a hundred miles around seemed to be in town. She watched as people walked only a few feet beyond the window and didn't notice her. That seemed to be how life in this town had always been for her, no one noticed her. She was invisible, or she had been to everyone but Rowdy.

Just as she saw Jeffery Filmore turn up the steps of the hotel, she heard Rowdy's voice.

"Good afternoon, Miss Laurel," he said. He stood politely with his hat in his hand, but she didn't miss the devil of a grin on his face.

When she nodded slightly, he added, "You're looking quite lovely this day."

She heard the front door open and knew within a few seconds Jeffery Filmore would be near enough to see them.

Shoving past Rowdy, she whispered, "Don't sell your ranch."

He'd raised his arms to hold her, but she was already in the doorway.

"Promise me!"

Jeffery's voice boomed. "I thought I'd find you here, Laurel."

Rowdy nodded and backed away so that the banker couldn't see him standing behind her.

"I'm not much for the nonsense on the streets," Jeffery complained. "In fact, I'll be glad when this whole thing is over and we can go back to normal." He was getting closer. "I thought I'd come in and have a cup of tea with you. Your father and I have been talking and there are a few plans you need to be working on."

"No." Laurel held up her hand, trying to think. "No tea. Not now. Since you're here I'm sure it would be all right for me to have tea in the café."

"It's more of a bar. No proper place for you."

Rowdy moved behind the door so that he wouldn't be seen until the banker was well into the room. And he couldn't step inside with Laurel blocking the door.

"I've heard," she said. "But I understand they serve pie in there and I'd love a piece, dear." The endearment tasted sour on her tongue, but she had to get him out of the way before he noticed Rowdy.

Filmore frowned at her as if he thought she had taken ill. "All right," he finally said, more in answer to the pie than her. "I might have a slice myself."

Laurel tugged the door closed as she followed the big man.

A moment before she let go, she felt Rowdy's fingers reach for hers, but she couldn't take the chance of ruining their dream now. He didn't know what was going on or how her father planned to cheat him, but she prayed he trusted her enough to follow her advice.

Chapter 11

Rowdy moved around the door frame in time to see Laurel disappear with the banker. Filmore laid his hand at the small of her back as if he had the right to touch her and wanted everyone to know it.

Anger washed over him as the scars of five years log-piled in his thoughts.

Who did he think he was kidding? Laurel Hayes was a rich man's daughter and he had one dollar to his name. She'd been sent away to school and he'd been sent to prison. The chance of her caring for him was about as likely as snow on a summer night.

He couldn't deny she was attracted to him. He'd felt the sparks fly whenever they were within touching distance. They both liked the game they'd played the past few days, but it was just a game to her. A pastime to make the rodeo more interesting maybe. She'd have no supper waiting for him in a hotel room tonight. There'd be no lovemaking.

She'd called the pig "dear." That one word kept sparking against his mind, sharpening anger with each memory. He would have thought five years of living with thieves and liars would have taught him not to believe anything anyone said.

He had no idea why she'd told him not to sell his land. Maybe that was part of the game she played also. She and Filmore were probably laughing about it right now over pie.

All he knew for sure was she left him and went with the banker. She could have told Filmore to wait a few minutes because she was busy talking to him. Or she could have introduced them as if they were equals. But she hadn't. She'd shoved him aside. She'd refused his touch. She kept him out of sight because he was her dirty little secret.

Rowdy hit the hotel door at a run. He stopped by the grounds and took his pick of among the last few wild horses left to ride, then found Dan near the barn.

"What's wrong?" the big Irishman asked the moment he saw Rowdy.

"Nothing."

Dan frowned. "I would have guessed that right off." He slapped Rowdy on the back. "You want to go down to pick out a mount? I'm thinking one of them might look sleepy or tired. That would be the one to ride. All you got to do is stay in the saddle, cowboy, and you'll win this thing."

Rowdy didn't answer or move toward the corral.

Dan watched him closely. "You don't look like a man who cares if he wins."

"I care," Rowdy answered as he checked Cinnamon's cinch, "but I'm not going for third. I plan to win this event."

Dan laughed. "Good way to think," he said. "Then with two first places you'll have a hundred dollars plus the cattle. That'd make you a fine start on that ranch of yours. You could use the money to rebuild the cabin and fatten up a few of the cattle to sell off this fall to get you through the winter. With two hundred head, you could have three hundred by this time next year."

"I'm selling all the cattle tonight, and as soon as I find a buyer for the ranch, I'm never coming back to this place."

Dan played along. "I can understand that. You got a good ranch with water most of us would fight you for and a woman who looks at you like you're about the grandest thing she's ever seen. If I was in your shoes, I'd run as hard and fast as I could as well."

Rowdy's swear died on his lips as he turned and saw Laurel's father and two of his men walking up the passage between the pens. The old man was headed straight for him.

He and Dan stood staring as if watching a storm moving in over open land. When the captain and his cowhands were within ten feet, Rowdy thought he heard the jangle of silver spurs. The bright day turned into a stormy night of memories, but he didn't move a muscle.

"Rowdy Darnell," Hayes began as if he wasn't sure which man was which.

"Yes." Rowdy didn't offer his hand.

The captain straightened, allowing his years of Army service to show. "I'm here, young man, with an offer I think you'll want to hear." He gave Dan a look that made it plain the conversation was only between them and the pig farmer should leave.

"We're listening," Rowdy said, silently letting everyone know that he wanted Dan to stay.

Dan looked like a bull shifting from one foot to the other. He, like everyone in town, knew the captain carried a great deal of weight, but Rowdy was one of Dan's few friends.

Rowdy ended his indecision by adding, "Dan, I'd like you to stay. I've developed a worry over being alone out here after last night."

Dan took the hint. He crossed his powerful arms and stood shoulder to shoulder with his friend.

Hayes, surprisingly, looked concerned. "Oh, why is that Mr. Darnell? Did something happen last night?"

Rowdy looked at the cowhand whose spurs sparkled in the sunshine. "Nothing that mattered." He lowered his voice. With the hint of a wild animal growling, he added, "Nothing that will ever happen again."

Hayes seemed bored and drew Rowdy back to him by saying, "I've come with an offer for your ranch. Now I know it's not worth much, never truly been built into anything, but out of respect for your father and my neighbor, I'm here to offer you a thousand dollars more than your father paid for it."

Rowdy knew Dan would react and he did. "That's not a fourth what it's worth, Mr. Hayes, and you know it."

"It's Captain Hayes," Laurel's father corrected.

Dan shook his head. "Changing your handle don't make any difference in what the ranch is worth."

The captain looked bothered. "All right." He smiled at Rowdy. "Your friend may be right. I haven't priced anything for a while. I'll up the offer by another two thousand but that is the best I can do. I don't think you'll find anyone around who'll make you a better price."

Dan huffed. "I would if I had the money."

"It doesn't matter," Rowdy finally spoke, "because the ranch is not for sale at any price."

"There's always a price," Hayes corrected.

"Not this time." As angry as he was at Laurel, her last words echoed in his thoughts, warning him. He couldn't make the pieces fit.

The captain didn't look defeated. "You think about it, Darnell. For most here, you're a stranger and it won't be easy making a go of it. For the rest, you're nothing but a jailbird. They'll remember and never trust you. You'd be better off to take the money and move on."

He started to leave, then turned back. "I just heard that you picked the wildest mount to ride today. Rumor is that horse has put more than one cowboy in a wheelchair."

"A great ride could mean a win," Rowdy said.

Hayes shook his head. "A good one would have made you the winner with a second or third place. But you picked the hardest to ride. I hear he can buck higher than the fence. If you can stay on, you're right, you'll win, but if you don't make the clock, you'll lose not only the event but the best all-around."

Rowdy stared as they turned and walked away. He'd already figured it out and knew the captain was right. If he drew no points in this event and the cowhand with the next best total placed first or second, Rowdy would lose.

Dan leaned close. "You up for it?"

"I can hardly wait," Rowdy answered.

Chapter 12

Laurel watched for Rowdy until the rodeo started, but she never saw him. She wished she'd had time to explain why she'd told him not to sell the ranch. But how could she tell him that her father was planning to cheat him.

She also felt bad about running off with the banker. She'd panicked and decided the hotel lobby had not been the place or time to cause trouble. There would be enough fireworks Monday morning when her father and Filmore figured out that she was gone. Since they both thought she had little money, they would spend a day, maybe two looking around town for her. Finally, someone was bound to check at the station. Her father would probably send men to bring her back, but she'd be a train ride ahead of them, maybe more. Once she stepped off in a big city, they'd never find her. She could let Rowdy know where to send the rest of her money.

With Rowdy staying in town for a while, no one would suspect him of having anything to do with her disappearance. She knew he'd never tell anyone that he passed half the profit from the sale of the cattle to her.

She wasn't brave enough to stand up to her father face-to-face. She never had been. The only way she could break free was to disappear completely.

The need to give Rowdy a good luck kiss weighed against the possibility of someone seeing them together. The kiss had always brought him luck, but if her father heard about it, he might look for her tonight or suspect Rowdy had something to do with her leaving. To keep him and their partnership safe, she had to be very careful. If that meant not seeing him until after the rodeo, then she could wait.

Her thoughts turned to what would happen when they were alone. It would be easy to tell her father she was riding home with her sisters, then tell her sisters she was going home early on horseback. Neither would check with the other. She would slip into the back of the hotel and Bonnie Lynn would, hopefully, have a room ready. She'd order supper and wait.

Laurel smiled. Women like her didn't have lovers, but tonight, for one night, she would. For one night she'd be desired even if he couldn't love her.

As the sun faded on the last night of the rodeo, Laurel couldn't sit still in the wagon. She had to pace. In a few minutes the rodeo would be over. She knew win or lose her life had changed. She'd never marry Filmore. If Rowdy lost tonight, she'd still be leaving her father's house, even if it took a little more planning.

For the first time she knew her own mind and would not live as a child any longer.

Something else had changed. She'd fallen hard for Rowdy. Not infatuation or a warm kind of cuddly loving feeling, but hard, fast, forever kind of love. For once in her life she'd found something—someone she couldn't resist. If he didn't feel the same, they'd walk away as friends tomorrow, but he'd never leave her heart. She'd have the memory of one night with him forever.

The first saddleback rider didn't make the clock. Three more to ride. Every nerve in her body felt like it was jumping.

Laurel paced. Her father was so wrapped up in what he was doing he hadn't even notice the changes in her over the past few days. But others did. She saw one of the cowhands who always followed after her sisters studying her as if seeing her for the first time. A stranger had smiled at her. One of the store clerks had gone out of his way to hold a door open for her. She almost felt like "been kissed" was written on her face. Maybe it was, her lips were swollen slightly from Rowdy's kisses and her cheeks burned each time she remembered the way he touched her.

She laughed suddenly, thinking that after tonight Filmore wouldn't want her anyway. She wouldn't be a virgin. She might spend the rest of her life a very proper old maid, but tonight she'd make a memory. One night with the man she loved was worth more than a lifetime of nights with one she could never give her heart to.

The second rider stayed on, but his horse looked half asleep. The mounts didn't seem as wild and fresh as they had the first night. No one had come close to Rowdy's saddle bronc ride the first night, but the scores for bareback riding were high.

She turned and watched as Rowdy came out of the shoot riding the one horse she'd thought no one would attempt. The animal bucked wildly as if in a death fight. Now Rowdy had no saddle to hang on to. She counted the seconds in her mind. One, two, three.

As she watched him being jerked back and forth she realized he was doing this for her. If she'd stayed out of it, he would have won one event and gone home a winner like Dan had. He wouldn't have put his body through four nights of torture. Her father's men wouldn't have beaten him.

He couldn't say he loved her, but he'd done this for her. He'd risked dying for her.

The crowd began to scream and she realized she'd lost count of the seconds. A moment after she heard a man yell time, Rowdy flew through the air and hit the ground hard. His whole body crumbled as if every bone and muscle liquefied.

Laurel thought of nothing but him. She jumped over the

barrier and ran across the field. A rodeo clown and one of the stock cowboys tried to stop her, but she shoved them aside. By the time they had the horse pulled away, she was kneeling at Rowdy's head, tears streaming down her face.

"Rowdy. Dear God, don't let him die! Rowdy." Her hand trembled as she brushed his dark hair aside. "Please don't die on me," she whispered. "Please."

He twisted slightly and rolled to one knee. "You praying over me again, Laurel?"

He'd scared her so badly, anger flashed along with relief. She swung at him, hitting him on the arm.

He stood slowly as if testing bones. Once standing, he offered her a hand. "How about waiting until I find out if I won before you kill me."

She realized everyone in town was watching them. Cheering as he stood. Seeing her cry.

Dan, near the judges' table, gave Rowdy a thumbs up.

"We won," he whispered. "We won." The joy she'd expected was missing from his tone. "You'll get your money."

She couldn't look up to see what was wrong with him. She'd never made a public scene in her life and she just made one in front of everyone.

When he turned to wave at the crowd, she bolted toward the side of the arena, wishing she could just disappear into the crowd. Trying to think of some way to explain away what she'd done, she moved toward the surrey. Her father looked furious and Filmore, beside him, had turned purple with anger.

"What in the hell were you doing!" Half the crowd heard her father yell when he spotted her coming toward him.

"I thought he was hurt," Laurel yelled. No one seemed to hear her.

He waited until she was five feet away before saying in his low, demeaning tone. "That was not proper behavior, Laurel. I'll be having a few words with you when we get home. I'll not tolerate such a show."

She could hear her sisters laughing and joking.

Laurel realized there would be no controlling the damage she'd done. But, for one moment, Rowdy was all she thought about, not the crowds or her father or the consequences of her action. She could bare her father's anger. She could ignore Filmore. But Rowdy's hard words echoed in her brain.

The crowd was still cheering. Laurel glanced toward the arena, hoping to catch sight of Rowdy. It wasn't hard. He was riding straight toward her at full gallop.

Everyone took a step back when Cinnamon pushed the barrier trying to stop. Laurel stood her ground, letting the horse's powerful shoulder brush against her.

Rowdy didn't look like he saw another person around but her. "I have to know," he said quick and angry. "Are you still my partner or was this all a game?"

She couldn't breathe. She saw hurt and confusion in his dark eyes.

Her father moved toward her, shoving people out of his way.

"I'm still your partner," she answered and lifted her chin.

Rowdy slid his boot out of the stirrup and offered his hand. "Then take the victory ride with me."

She gripped his fingers and stepped into the saddle as he shoved back to make room. A moment later, his arms were around her holding tight.

As her father's hand went out to grab her leg, Rowdy kicked Cinnamon into action. They shot out into the arena.

Laurel closed her eyes and leaned into his warmth. Nothing mattered but him, not the rodeo or the crowds or even her father. Only Rowdy.

As they circled, she whispered, "I'm sorry. I didn't mean to make a scene."

"That doesn't matter, but it took me a minute to figure out what you'd done. How unlike my shy Laurel to run to me." His fingers circled her waist. "God, I missed the feel of you all day, darling."

Everyone waved and yelled as they rounded the arena, but she didn't care. Rowdy and she had their own private world.

"Stop calling me darling," she said, laughing.

"Why, because you don't love me?"

"No, because *you* don't love me."

"You're wrong there, I do love you. I think I have since the sixth grade. I just didn't know it until that horse knocked the brains out of me."

Dan opened the side gate and Rowdy shot out of it away from the crowds and into the night. He rode for a while until the noise of town was only a whisper behind them, then he slowed.

She relaxed against him trying to let herself believe she'd just heard him say he loved her.

"It took me a while to figure out why you told me not to sell and why it was so important you acted like I wasn't in the room with you. I spent most of the day mad because you walked away, but then it hit me and you're right."

She started to ask about what, but he twisted her chin and kissed her hard.

"That wasn't my best," he said as he straightened. "But I'll work on it later."

She laughed and he kissed her again.

When he backed an inch away, he whispered against her cheek, "You do love me?"

"Yes." She smiled, watching the last hint of doubt disappear from his eyes.

"Good, then we go with your plan, but you got to promise never to call me dear."

"My plan? What plan?"

He nodded. "I keep the ranch and we don't sell the cattle. In a year we'll have a great place and who cares if no one in town will talk to us. Between the work and the nights together we won't notice."

"We'll be partners?" she said.

He smiled. "We'll be a lot more than that, darling."

Afterword

Rowdy Darnell and Laurel Hayes were married the last night of the 1890 Kasota Springs Rodeo. Within five years the RL Ranch became one of the most profitable spreads in West Texas.

They had three sons and a daughter.

In 1912, Laurel Darnell was elected mayor of Kasota Springs.

Rowdy never rode in another rodeo, but folks talked about his rides for years.

Rowdy and Laurel's partnership lasted fifty-seven years, until she died of a heart attack. Her headstone read, "Beloved wife, mother and partner."

Rowdy didn't mourn her death as his father had mourned his mother. Instead, he passed the ranch along to his children and spent the next two years teaching his eleven grandchildren to ride.

Two years to the day Laurel had died, he passed away in his sleep.

The children were surprised when they learned he'd already ordered his headstone. It was placed next to Laurel's in a small cemetery on their ranch.

His stone read, "Keep praying for me, darling, I'll be there by supper."

LUCK OF
THE DRAW
DeWanna Pace

Chapter 1

July 3, 1890

Speculation over who would win or lose rode ahead of Dally Angelo.

The betting started among his coworkers back at the bunkhouse two days ago when he and most of the Double D ranch hands had packed up their riggings and headed for Kasota Springs. It had continued for the forty-mile trek every time they met up with a wagonload of folks headed for the Fourth of July Cowboy Competition.

Dally was getting mighty tired of the wagering. Tired of everyone making his business theirs. Tired of being stopped when all he wanted to do was get there and make the draw.

"Bet you a slug of chaw they ask the same question." Slim, the cowpoke riding just ahead of Dally, slowed and waited for him to catch up.

Dally ignored his friend's teasing, as well as the wagon that approached from the south. Instead, he pulled his hat low over his eyes and nudged his roan into a trot. Plenty of cowboys heading for the competition had his lank and look of hard edges, but few could boast his banty height and ice blue eyes. He didn't much care that the way he sat short in the saddle made him odd-man out in a trace of tall Texans, as long as it gave him an advantage in riding Bone Buster. But Dally knew if the folks in the approaching wagon got a glimpse of his face, they'd see the Angelo eyes and wouldn't let him pass without some kind of comment on the ride he planned to make in Kasota Springs.

"Ho, the Double D!" shouted the man driving the brace of oxen toward them.

Dally moved to the edge and allowed the wagon to pull alongside him into the double-rutted path. He might not want to invite any real friendliness at the moment, but the woman who sat beside the man atop the bench demanded that he offer the better path to the wagon. Traveling across the prairie loam of the Texas Panhandle could jolt a soul's teeth out of their sockets even with the best of wheels. A rutted path, no matter how well traveled, always gave a bit of reprieve from the bone-jarring one across open plains.

"Y'all headed for the rodeo in Kasota?" the woman asked as a tow-headed boy in a cowboy hat suddenly appeared through the canvas that arched over the wagon. "Tie your bandanna around your nose if you're going to sit up here with us, Jory," she instructed. "The wind's kicking up dust."

"Did you say Double D, Mama?" the boy named Jory asked, his gaze scanning the line of riders first ahead of, then behind Dally. He ignored his mother's demand and instead focused on Dally. "Is 'zat you, Dally Angelo?" He pointed toward Dally. "Papa stop the wagon! It's gotta be him. I just know it is."

The wagon stopped and so did Dally. Of all the things he could ignore, a kid wasn't one of them. Best to get this over with so he could be on his way.

"That's him, kid." Slim confirmed Dally's identity, stopping alongside the roan. "All five feet six of bearing down and bailing out."

"See, I told ya so, Papa. I knew it was him. Just think . . .

being that little and riding a two thousand pound bull. Goshamightyjesus!"

"Dust that language off your tongue, Jory Johanson, or you won't have enough bottom to sit come sundown."

If Mrs. Johanson took on a bull at the moment, Dally would bet on her. The kid best watch his language.

The boy's cheeks turned crimson. "Sorry, Ma."

His father looked apologetically at Dally. "You'll have to excuse my son, Mr. Angelo. He heard about your ride up in Durango and that one in Canadian. When I told him you might be headed to Kasota, he nearly split his britches bragging to his friends that he was going to see you ride. You're quite the legend these days, you know."

"He's used to putting some feist in the little fellers, ain't you, Angelo?" Slim's mustache broadened to reveal a gap in his teeth. "Gives 'em somebody to look up to . . . a little ways, anyway."

If Dally didn't like his stringbean of a friend so much, he'd have already shucked him loose of a few more teeth. Being inches short of a well-dug grave didn't mean he couldn't hold his own if push came to shove. "Nothing more than a man bent on riding a particular bull, sir."

"You gonna ride Bone Buster, Mr. Angelo?" The awe in Jory's voice held reverence for the brindle. As well it should have. The two thousand pound bull had never been ridden for ten seconds and had killed a man.

A thousand emotions raced up to answer the boy, but only one found its voice. The one that had driven Dally to chase the bull across three states of competitions and for four years . . . *revenge*. "Depends on the luck of the draw."

"I saved a whole dollar so's I could bet on you, if you do." Jory pulled the dollar from his pocket and held it up for Dally to see.

Dally shook his head. "Put that money to better use, son. I'll ride the full ten when the time comes. Count on it."

Jory quickly stashed the money away and took off his hat, holding it over his heart. "I'm sure sorry to hear about your pa, Mr. Angelo. I'd ride old Bone Buster for ya myself if I could. I hope you draw him right out of the chute."

Of all the good wishes anyone had ever given him since that awful day in Pecos, Dally was most touched by Jory Johanson's simple act of respect. For the first time in a long time, Dally had more reason than revenge to ride the bull that had killed his father. He needed to prove to a little boy that betting on a done deal was useless.

"Come by the chute, if your ma and pa will let you, and I'll make sure you get to watch the draw. Maybe you're just the luck I need."

"Didja hear that?" Jory squealed and nearly jumped off the bench. "I get to watch the draw like with all the big fellows."

The wind whipped up reddish brown dirt and flung it into their faces. Jory coughed and sputtered. Dally realized the child had not followed his mother's advice. "Cowboys who mind their ma do."

When the boy immediately pulled up the bandanna, Mrs. Johanson offered a smile of gratitude. "We best let you get on your way. I hear the rodeo starts in less than two hours. We wouldn't want to make you late."

Slim shook his head. "The bull riding ain't part of the actual events. It don't take place till the dance starts later tonight. So's you can take all the time you want with him. Me and the other fellers, though, we got to hightail it or we're gonna miss out on getting our fees paid."

Dally glared at his friend, warning that he'd spoken out of turn. Slim knew they all needed to get to town and set up camp. "I'm sure you folks are just as anxious to get out of this wind as we are. Have a safe journey." He bid Jory farewell and spurred the roan into a lope.

After the Johansons and the rest of the Double D were long behind him, Dally discovered Slim had elected to give chase.

"Whoa, Angelo! Took me more'n fifteen minutes to catch up with ya. I rubbed a bunch of blisters on my butt while you ran our horses' hooves to the nubs."

"I don't remember inviting you to the race, friend."

"You might ought to practice up on some conviviality before you hit Kasota, hoss." Slim laughed. "Make it a little easier to shuffle a petticoat or two your direction if you do."

"I'm not going there to see the ladies, Slim."

"Heck, don't I know it. One bull. One lady. That's all you've ever had on your mind. Reckon Gus will be there?"

The mention of Augusta Garrison did what it had always done to Dally since Pecos. It turned his blood to ice water and set his jaw teeth to grinding. Old wounds might scar over but the memory of how they were inflicted remained raw and festering. "If Bone Buster's there, it's likely she could be too."

Slim had known Dally and Gus since childhood. Had been one of the first friends Dally told about his engagement to Augusta. Slim had been close friend enough to act as pallbearer at Flint Angelo's funeral. But of all the things Dally appreciated about his cohort was the fact that Slim had been wise enough never to ask why Augusta returned Dally's ring the same day of the funeral, took the killer bull and walked out of Dally's life. If Slim were smart, he wouldn't push the point now. Dally had spent four years hardening himself against Augusta and telling himself he didn't care whether he ever saw her again. It would be a shame to lose a good friend over her as well.

"How many ranches you reckon will be anteing up?"

Realizing Slim had changed the subject on purpose, Dally relaxed and slowed his gait. He was getting edgier the closer they came to Kasota Springs. Part of it was anticipation of the draw. Part was concern that Augusta might be there. He'd thought over countless times what he'd say to her when, and if, he ever saw her again. But finally facing the possibility shook him more than he thought it could.

Nothing was going to ruin his focus. Nothing or no one. Not even Augusta Garrison.

"Got dust in your craw," Slim asked, "or you just like to hear me rattle?"

Dally realized he'd never answered the man. Ranches. How many competing. "Boss said about twenty outfits are participating. Most from Texas, but some from Oklahoma. Even a few from Colorado."

"You gonna try for best all-around?"

"No. I'm here just for the bull riding. You?"

Slim reached into his pocket, flipped a gold coin into the air and caught it. "Whatever this here will let me enter. I figure I got as good a chance as any." His mustache lifted. "I could start my own place with the winnings and hire your rascally hide to ride herd for me."

Dally suspected Slim was more interested in the year's worth of bragging rights than he was in the hundred head of cattle to be given for "Best All-Around Cowboy." The string-bean preferred earning a payday than nursing the worry of making a payroll for others.

"Reckon the committee will ever make you guys official?"

"I don't see it happening anytime soon. They think we're too dangerous and an unnecessary risk." Dally crested the rise that bore the mark of the town's cemetery. It looked like someone had been cleaning the graves. Particularly the five that were separated by a wrought-iron fence. "They don't think bull riding's part of a ranch hand's regular duties."

"You don't sound too busted up over it." Slim slipped his coin back into his pocket.

"Outlaw event or authorized, makes no matter. I'm not riding for the money."

Below them, new storefronts and businesses framed a town square while double-storied roofs stood behind the hardware store and bank. The railhead bracketed one end of the main thoroughfare while houses and barns made up the other end of town. Tents and encampments sprawled across the edges of Kasota Springs, bursting the town at its seams.

"Hey, would you look at that!" Slim pointed toward the middle of town. "See that banner strung across Main Street?"

Dally focused on the wide swath of red, white and blue with huge letters that he could barely make out from this distance. "Yeah, what about it?"

"It says Rodeo." Slim squinted eyes that were already narrow from too many days spent staring into the western horizon. "Not Cowboy Competition but Rodeo, as that lady back there said."

The term was as old as the vaqueros who rode herd across the Spanish land grants of Texas, but it met with a lot of resistance from most folks.

"Bet the planning committee went a round or two over the wording of that one this year."

"I heard Tempest LeDoux is heading up the committee," Dally informed, knowing his friend would get a hoot out of that fact. The man had a soft spot in his heart for the lady who ran the town's weekly poker game. Too bad she was still in mourning last they'd heard. But Slim wouldn't have to wait too long, Dally supposed. The woman never let the grass green up on the grave before she set her hat for her next bridegroom.

"Well, that explains it." Pride filled Slim's tone. "She probably made 'em change it to Rodeo. Said she was going to last time I sat in on a game. I never known her to set her mind to something and not follow it through."

The sound of a gunshot drew their attention to a big crowd gathering in front of the mayor's house. "You best get on into town and put your money down. Looks like things are fixing to start. The mayor's called everyone together for the speech making."

"Sure wouldn't want to miss any of that, would we?" Slim laughed, spurring his horse into a lope.

Dally followed a bit more slowly, wanting to skirt as much of the crowd as possible so he could make his way over to the stock pens and find out if the Flying G had brought Bone Buster to the competition. The Garrisons had stocked the bull out to Prescott and bigger competitions but hadn't brought him this close to home in nearly four years now. Dally had chased the bull to every competition he could but never had the luck of the draw and gotten to ride the demon. Money ran out and he'd been forced to return home to work spring roundup before he could try again. When he'd heard that Augusta's parents might bring the bull home for the Fourth of July celebration, Dally thought his luck might have changed.

It had.

As he rode up to the chutes that normally held the stock waiting to be transferred by rail, there stood the beast. Two thousand pounds of massive horns, muscular body and suicide eyes blacker than hellsoot. His nose lifted, his nostrils flared, his eyes rolled wild as he breathed in Dally's presence.

"Remember me, mankiller," Dally whispered the threat low and full of reckoning. "I'm the smell of your defeat."

Hot steam rolled off the bull's back as it snorted and kicked the strains of its enclosure. A great bellow rumbled from deep within its throat, setting off a round of discontent from other stock frightened by the beast's disapproval.

"Tonight," Dally promised. "If I'm lucky, we'll have a go of it tonight. Just you and me and ten seconds."

"Hey look, everybody. It's Angelo and he's with Bone Buster," someone yelled. Men started to gather like tumbleweeds racing toward the pens.

Dally cursed under his breath and reined away, wanting

more time alone with the brindle but knowing it would never come now that he'd been noticed.

A sudden roar of the crowd reminded him that the festivities had already gotten under way and the best thing he could do was find the rest of the Double D and get busy. And, he had to make sure that he talked to whomever was handling the drawings and arrange a seat for the Johanson boy.

He headed toward the post office where he'd been told everyone should sign up for the events and pay entry fees. He supposed he could find out if the drawing for the outlaw event would be taking place there too. Though most didn't approve of the bull riding and didn't count it among the moneyed events, critics and gamblers alike appreciated the grit, skill and sheer bravado it took to ride the rank bulls, without the benefits of any purse or points toward best all-around. Knowing that Bone Buster was in town, they would be expecting Dally to show and ask for directions.

He made his way past the chutes and through a group of people watching a pair of rodeo tramps and a donkey. One of the tramps did a handstand, a flip, then hurdled over the donkey's bowed head like it was nothing more than a low rung on a hitching post. Something in the way the clown moved made Dally peer harder.

His heart thumped hard against his chest as he forgot to breathe. His jaw set so hard, Dally could have sworn it cracked like a whip. He wanted to move, to rein the roan into a ground-eating gallop away from the hip action he'd just recognized. Away from the body he'd known intimately. Away from these gut-wrenching feelings that threatened to destroy his fierce resolution to ignore them.

"Turn around," he heard himself whispering, damning his heart for taking voice. God, let him be mistaken about the clown's true identity.

The agile tramp turned. Curly red hair and eyes the color

of a clear Texas sky proved his suspicions true. There stood Augusta Garrison.

The woman who'd betrayed him.

The woman he'd never wanted to see again.

The woman he'd vowed would be his first and only love.

Chapter 2

Augusta Garrison thought she could handle seeing Dally again, but she was wrong. She knew what had brought him here. Knew that he could have no more resisted a potential ride on Bone Buster than she could resist the possibility of seeing him again . . . one last time.

Dally Angelo. The boy who had been sinfully good-looking at seventeen and broken her heart. The man who'd given that same heart its greatest pleasure.

A tingle of sensual awareness started in her belly and spread, shocking her as if she'd been kicked in the chest by the donkey. She couldn't breathe. Her head began to whirl. Her stomach felt as if it dropped to her knees, weakening them. She'd promised herself that if he came to Kasota Springs, if she saw him, she wouldn't let him affect her, wouldn't allow him to arouse any of the old feelings she'd spent years taming.

For an endless moment she could do no more than stare up at the man sitting atop the roan, aware only that her undeniable attraction to the man was just as alive and thriving as if she'd lain in his arms last night. Tame those feelings? Not hardly. At first sight of him, they were running wild and hell-bent through her bloodstream.

Could life have been more unkind, she thought, sucking in

air again. Did he have to have aged so well? The good-looking boy had developed into a lady-killer of a man. And, Heavens, what a man. Crow-black hair that made her fingers flex, remembering the feel of its thick curls as he deepened a kiss. The same ice blue gaze that swept over her so possessively that it left a rush of quivering gooseflesh in its wake. Five feet six of pure, hard male—the lean, lank sinews of a man skilled in harnessing power and passion.

A black leather vest and blue shirt stretched across his muscled chest and tapered to a flat abdomen and even muscular legs, wrapped in batwing chaps. Every bit the fantasy that haunted her dreams at night. Every ounce the man she'd hoped to call husband.

But at the thought of their failed engagement, the attraction that had heated her every pore evaporated into a shiver of fear. He would never forgive her. Never marry her. Not once he found out about the secret—no—*secrets* she'd hidden from him.

Augusta nearly forgot to dig in her heels and stop the momentum that kept her from tumbling headfirst into Joey, the other clown. She tapped her bulbous fake nose three times, the agreed-upon signal used to warn Joey, her fellow performer, that something was wrong with the routine and she needed a moment of recovery. Fortunately, the sad-faced clown was as quick thinking as he was agile. Joey lured the crowd's attention away by vaulting over the donkey backward, then completing a series of acrobatic maneuvers that would have made a team of clowns envious, much less one. If word got around about the *Charivari*, someone from Barnum & Bailey would come calling to see the unusual routine.

Dally removed his hat and brushed his forehead with his arm sleeve, nodding at her. "Gus," his mouth formed her name.

Though she couldn't hear it from where she stood, she remembered all too well the low resonance of that tantalizing voice. "Rusty the Tramp," she whispered back, then spurned his gaze.

She faced Joey and signaled for him to end their acrobatics. As boss clown, the tramp responsible for coordinating the routines and clown spots at the rodeo, she could decide to end or prolong the routine, depending on the crowd's enthusiasm. The crowd seemed pleased enough, according to its laughter and applause, but she needed to be done with the routine and now. She ran to her cohort, dug deep into his baggy pockets, lifted out an apple and offered the treat to the donkey. The donkey rose from its display of stubbornness and followed Augusta willingly out of the makeshift corral. Joey shook his head and held his palms up as if questioning why they hadn't thought of that before. The children in the crowd laughed loudest and the two tramps walked away with a hearty round of applause.

"Mind telling me what's going on, boss?" Joey asked, grabbing the lead rope from Augusta's hand. "It isn't like you to stop things when it's going so well. Folks were having a good time. Didn't have anything to do with that cowboy staring at you like you were fresh water after a drought, did it?"

"Just take care of the donkey, Joey," she said sharply.

Obviously surprised by her uncustomary curtness, Joey exaggerated his white-painted frown. "Well, sure, Gus. Didn't mean to make your frown any truer."

Feeling ashamed of her rudeness, Augusta apologized. "We'll talk about it later. I've got to get set up for the next routine, and I need a moment to collect things." *Myself mostly,* she added silently.

"Well, okay"—his lips lifted into a forgiving smile—"but I ought to warn you, you're being followed. Want me to run him off?"

"No." She had hoped to avoid Dally after the routine, but she should have known he would never let it alone. She hadn't given him the answer he wanted. If there was one thing she knew without a doubt, it was his bulldog persistence in not letting something go. That would never change. It was the reason they were apart. "I'll take care of it. I do know him. He's no threat to me."

At least no threat you can protect me from.

Augusta made her way down Clown Alley, the row of tents that had been set up to house their trunks with costumes and props. The tents were lined up so closely that there was only an alleyway to walk through. When she reached her own, she went inside and let the flap close behind her, hoping that he would not invite himself in.

That hope vanished as the flap drew back and he filled the tent with his presence. "I'd have recognized you anywhere." His voice held an edge of seduction in its tone, but his eyes lacked the warmth she had felt only a few minutes ago.

Four years since she'd seen him and he still could make her feel vulnerable. "I don't remember a padded clown suit and painted freckles being part of our past history together."

"I remember telling you once that no matter how you looked was beautiful to me."

She remembered that too. They'd started out fishing. The fishing had turned into wrestling in mud at the stream. The playful afternoon had ended in sweet ecstasy in a blanket of wildflowers near the bank.

She cast him a withering glance. "According to the Flying G hands, I'm told there are plenty of women who have come to see if you draw Bone Buster. Why don't you waste some of that charm on them?"

His smile came slow, sexy as hell. "So you think I've still got it?"

He had it all right. Enough to melt her into a pool inside her oversized boots. "It's never been whether you have it," she admitted, cursing herself for feeding his ego. But she wouldn't lie about that. The sooner they both focused on the truth between them, the sooner they might resolve the issues that separated them.

He had the good grace not to push the issue. If he walked over now . . . If he attempted to kiss her . . . she didn't know how or even, if, she would resist.

"How have you been, Gus?"

She was afraid to give him answers. Afraid she might slip up and say too much. Now was not the time. This was not the place. There was too much at stake. Maybe the best thing to do was just to remain silent. Let him get whatever he wanted said, said.

"I'd have known that hair and those eyes any—"

"Don't, Dally"—she warded off the compliment with her palm—"I'm not seventeen anymore. Trying to smooth talk me won't get you anywhere."

"You sure about that?"

No, she wasn't, but the sound of guitar and feisty fiddle playing reverberated through the tent, warning that the music competition had started. First place singers and pickers of everything from banjos to fiddles to French harps would provide the background music for the dance later tonight. She had to get out of this costume and into the next before Joey came back and grabbed up their drums to add to the melee of sound. She had to ignore the challenge in Dally's eyes. "Look, this has been a treat to see you again, but I have a job to do and not much time to do it."

He took a step toward her. "I could help you change. Make things a lot easier."

"You wish." She turned away from him and started to unbutton the back of her costume. "Stay back. I can do it myself."

Disregarding her command, he crossed the space that divided them and his hands immediately took over where hers were struggling. "Stubborn redhead."

Damn him, she could almost feel him smiling behind her.

Why did he have to call her his favorite nickname for her? She ought to turn around and belt him, but she wouldn't give him the satisfaction of knowing he could still provoke her. "That's one thing that hasn't changed for sure. Now why don't you get lost and leave me alone?"

"So you *do* want me to leave you alone." There was something more than teasing in his tone.

"I said it didn't I?"

"The point is, do you *mean* it?" He finished the last button, then spun her around. "Actually, Gus, I followed you in here for three reasons."

"One?"

"To hire a couple of tramps to ride herd on the rough stock during the bull riding event."

"You've got a lot of grit asking me to stand by and watch you ride that mankiller." Rage filled her and she was glad of it. Glad that it was so all-consuming that it immediately evaporated even the slightest heat of seduction still kindling inside her. "If you think for one minute that I'm going to—"

"I didn't say *you,* Augusta. I said a couple of tramps. Maybe one of them could be that donkey jumper who stared me down like he wanted to peel off my hide when I followed you here."

"Who, Joey?" Augusta laughed, though it pleased her that she thought she heard a tinge of jealousy in Dally's tone. "He looks out for me when I need him to."

"Yeah, he's just the tramp for the job I have in mind. See if he can somersault over old Bone Buster when he starts snorting and hooking, instead of some stubborn jackass that doesn't know sit from giddy-up."

"And two?" she asked, ignoring his barb about Joey. If any of her fellow clowns wanted to participate in the outlaw event, then that was up to them. Joey included. Dally would be damned lucky if Joey agreed to help. He was the most agile of all the clowns and had experience dealing with the bulls on occasion. That's why she'd hired him in the first place. If she was ever at the competition where Dally got the luck of the draw, then she wanted someone as adept as Joey to distract the bull, play bullfighter, if necessary. That is . . . if she ever allowed Dally to get a true draw.

"*Two?*" Dally looked puzzled.

"You said you had three reasons you followed me."

Dally's hands gripped her shoulders roughly at first, then softened. "Four years is a long time to make a man wait. I want to know why you won't answer the question I asked on the day you walked out on me. Do you ever plan to marry me?"

She willed her body stiff, trying to ignore the current sizzling from the simple contact of his fingers on her skin to every pulse ending in her bloodstream. But her flesh remembered the heat and leaned in to be warmed, challenging her mind's will to forget. It wasn't fair that so casual a touch could stir such longing within her.

"Don't touch me," she said, mustering enough sense to push him away. If this seduction of her senses didn't end soon, she might not be able to think clearly. Lord knew she'd never been able to resist him in the past. "And you know exactly why I never answered you. I said I wouldn't until the day you gave up on trying to ride that damned bull."

He didn't move back as she'd hoped. He stood there, looking eye to eye, waiting for her to do what? Tell him she still loved him. She did. Tell him that she could watch him possibly kill himself? She couldn't. Assure him that she would never marry another man? She loved only him.

But she couldn't tell him. Not until she was sure he never meant to ride that bull. Until she was sure that he would always be around and not so hell-bent to kill himself. Until she found the courage to admit the wrong she'd committed against him—a wrong that was the real reason behind his father's death.

Augusta knew she was overreacting, knew that seeing him again would throw her for a loop. But she couldn't be reasonable about the trepidation that hammered in her pulses like drums beating the deathsong of her dreams. Dally didn't know it, but once he learned the truth behind the secrets she'd kept from him, he had the power to tear her world apart more completely than he did when she'd left him.

The day he buried his father and said that he would ride Bone Buster or die trying.

The day she'd walked out of his life and vowed not to return until he gave up his deadly pursuit.

The day Augusta discovered her life would forever be tied to his.

"If I pull his name out of the hat, I'll make the ride."

The finality in Dally's tone was not a surprise to her. She knew what he'd say before he ever said it. She turned away. "Then we have nothing more to discuss."

He spun her around and lowered his lips to hers, stopping only a whisper away. "One more thing, Gus. You forgot number three."

"Three?" she croaked, unable to hide the fractured fragments of what was left of her senses.

"The third reason I followed you. To do this." His deep, seductive voice sent a shiver of anticipation through her as he took off his hat and threw it on a trunk. She gazed into his eyes and knew he was going to kiss her and she was going to let him. He took her into his arms and their bodies touched. Awareness, as old as the day she'd fallen in love with him, unlocked itself from her heart and rushed to trace the play of muscles in his back, the granite strength of his thighs rubbing against hers, the velvet perfection of breast against chest.

His lips touched hers in such slow, tender possession that she could not hold back the joyful moan that escaped her. Augusta closed her eyes and sank into the kiss, letting the sensations fill the emptiness that had become her life. She wanted more, demanded to remember it all. His tongue met hers, eager, enticing, erotic.

Her arms tightened around his neck as he deepened the kiss. This was no boy asking permission, but a man laying claim to what he knew was his.

Dally raised his head and they stared at each other for an endless moment, then he backed away. Clown makeup smeared his cheeks and nose, making him look comical, but his eyes were smoky with intent.

"That kiss just told me everything I need to know. You still love me. You might as well just say yes and marry me."

"Not if you're gonna ride that damned honker, I won't. Ever. Now get out!"

"I'll go for now, Augusta." He grabbed his hat and stopped at the flap that led outside. "But I'm coming back. After I ride that bull and when you have no more reason to put off marrying me."

Chapter 3

I must have lost my bull-busting mind, Dally decided as he left the tent and headed toward the post office. He'd only meant to follow Augusta inside the tent when he realized the other clown didn't intend to join her there. He'd thought a moment alone with her would give him time to easily settle the issues between them, then he could get his mind on making the draw for the night's bull riding. But no, it couldn't have been that simple.

He'd had to go and touch Augusta. *Kiss* her, for God's sake. And not just any kind of kiss, but a bend-one-knee-I-want-us-to-make-baby-cowboys-and-build-a-home-together kind of kiss. He'd wanted to feel nothing, planned that if he ever had the opportunity to kiss her again it would mean nothing more than putting an end to something left unfinished. Instead, the touch and taste of her had kindled old wants inside him. Had set fire to a white-hot blaze that promised new beginnings between them if he cowboy-upped and met her challenge.

Seeing her again had rattled Dally, though he'd tried his best not to show it. It stuck in his craw now having to admit it to himself. Those sky-blue eyes of hers had sizzled with challenge at first, and he'd almost let the anger he saw there intimidate him. But the memory of her lips on his encouraged Dally to be bold and accept the dare. He'd taken the lead, pressing his mouth against hers and demanding that she return the kiss. When she relented and gave in full measure, her lips sent something hotter, wilder than sin itself coursing through him. Feeling as if he'd been freight-trained, he finally let go and tried to regain his bearings.

He'd expected her anger, but not the bone-melting seduction of a woman full grown. Rekindling the old fire between them had definitely not been in his plans at all. He'd meant to ignore her, treat her like she never filled his thoughts when another woman happened to smile at him as she passed by. He meant to forget the countless midnights he woke up reaching for her and wondering where she was and whether she was safe. But if Dally had learned one thing in life it was like that old saying, "timing has a lot to do with the outcome of a rain dance." It was best that he remember now to grab leather and bail out before she left him bloody, beaten and without focus.

Seeing a long line at the post office, Dally decided to put off finding out where they would put the names in the hat for the draw. Instead, he decided to quench his thirst. No use standing in line and keeping others from paying their fee on time. A glance over at the Slats and Fats Saloon assured him that he'd made a good choice. It looked as if a bunch of the Double D hands had stopped in to shake some of the trail dust off before they joined in the festivities. Slim's horse was hitched among those wearing the Double D brand.

He found his friend bellied up to the bar and sitting next to the petite, glossy-skinned lady, Tempest LeDoux. The Cajun rancher was apparently husband hunting again. She had forgone her normal flare of colorful clothing and, instead, was wearing a white dress and resting a matching lace parasol at her side—surefire clues that her latest mourning garments had been laid to rest. She must have set her bonnet for some bootstrap in the room for she was looking primed and ready for courting. He hoped for his friend's sake that Slim was the target. The stringbean was one of the few folks in the Panhandle who saw no wrong with the woman and her ways, and Dally was one of the few men that Slim felt comfortable in sharing his feelings about her. Dally supposed it was because he didn't judge people's pasts. How she made a place here with folks was all that seemed accountable to him.

He sallied up to the bar and nudged Slim. Slim swung around and grinned. "What are you doing in here, Bull Buster? Thought you'd be out there giving that old brindle what-for."

"Done that." Slim knew him too well. "Looks like you're trying to rope one in yourself."

Slim shook his head. "Nah, she's got a bead on that shootist there. He's done spoiled a robbery over at Cattleman's Bank and captured ol' Cherokee Bill Bartlett, of all people. That's McKenna Smith, himself, they say. Passing through and promoting peace. They're even giving him a parade in his honor at noon. Can't compete with those kinds of odds, even with the best of the chances, can I? Guess I'm a reputation too late and a buncha muscles too thin." A deep sigh deflated his thin frame. "Maybe next time."

As far as he was concerned, it was Tempest LeDoux's loss if she didn't sit up and take notice of how much Slim cared for her. Dally took a look on the other side of the Cajun and noticed she was sort of leaning into the powerful-looking stranger standing next to her. When her hand flashed past the man's drink, Dally could've sworn he saw something move in the man's glass. The way the stranger was looking at her and she back at him, Dally was sure that Slim had faced his fate justifiably. The look those two were sharing would either stir up something like true love or lust everlasting. Dally could almost feel the sizzle from where he sat. Poor Slim, he never had a chance this time. Maybe any of the other five times, now that Dally thought about it some.

He started to call attention to the fact that there might be something live and kicking in Smith's glass when all of the sudden the bartender reminded Dally to remove his hat.

"No hats inside, Angelo. You know the rules."

Dally had been thinking so hard on Augusta when he'd entered the saloon that he'd forgotten to hang his hat at the door. He took it off and laid it on the counter. The bartender scowled, showing his disapproval. He guessed the hat would provide a barricade to beer mugs sliding their way down to the men just past him. Dally gauged the distance from bar to peg, grabbed the hat and let it sail. The Stetson hooked itself like a well-thrown horseshoe, instigating a howl of appreciation from several cowboys standing nearby.

"Crowd's easy to please this morning." Dally turned back to Slim and asked what he was drinking.

"Sarsparilla," Slim announced a bit loudly. "They're all in a festive mood because of their money being saved over at the bank."

Dally knew Tempest drank the same and figured his friend was trying to bring the point home to the husband hunter. "Fill his up," he told the bartender, "and I'll have some coffee."

"Figured you'd be drinking something stouter than bean juice today, considering you might be riding Bone Buster tonight." Slim found his good humor again and thanked him for the refill.

"Plan to be sober as a judge." Dally accepted the cup of coffee and took a drink of the bitter, hot liquid. Nothing like the taste of ground piñon beans to help a man shake off any sluggishness.

"You seen Augusta? A couple of the boys say she's playing boss tramp and following the competitions around with her folks."

Slim would have a lot to say if Dally chose to tell him that he'd seen her. Maybe he would. Maybe he wouldn't. He sure as hell wouldn't tell him that he'd kissed her. The stringbean would never let him hear the end of that. Dally decided not to lie to his friend, just not admit the truth. "Who would've figured she'd settle for that kind of life?"

Slim looked longingly at Tempest. "Some women are settling down kind of gals and some ain't. Some of 'em think they gotta ride all over kingdom come and back before they light somewhere with the right feller. Nothing like a woman who knows her mind and sets it to what she wants."

Dally didn't like the image Slim was conjuring. Augusta with other men. He'd thought it plenty of times and wondered how he'd react when he saw her on someone else's arm. Watching her just walk beside that other clown a while ago was enough to make him gnaw a jaw tooth loose. "She always said she was going to do something different with her life. I guess she meant it."

"You know, you were two shots short of a full trigger for giving anyone else a chance at courting her anyway." Slim gulped his refill in one swig.

Slim had disapproved of Dally telling Augusta that their wedding day would have to wait until he'd ridden Bone Buster, no matter how long it took. He'd been quite vocal about it every time the subject came up. "That's an old trail we don't need to go down again, friend."

He'd been grief stricken at the time and single-minded in purpose. He couldn't pretend that he cared about wedding preparations and planning a big to-do when all he could think about was riding the rank out of that mankiller who took his father's life. If Augusta couldn't understand that, then she didn't know him half as well as he thought she did.

"Easy on the trigger, hoss. Just stating facts." Slim's gaze focused on Dally's neck. "You still got the ring?"

Dally didn't know what he had expected Slim to say, but it wasn't anything concerning the ring that hung tied to a strap of rawhide around his neck and hidden beneath his shirt. It had hung there since the day Augusta had thrown it back at him and yelled that he needed to grow up before she would ever follow through on marrying him. The day she'd taken her father's bull and left the state. Slim had remarked about that fact one day when he'd caught Dally swimming in the creek without a shirt. Dally couldn't bring himself to admit that he never took the ring off. He'd just told his friend that it was easier to keep track of it that way and it was too valuable to lose.

"So what if I do?" Dally grumbled irritably, knowing that his anger wasn't at Slim but at himself for not being prepared for the sight of Augusta. That's all. Who would have imagined that she would look even more fetching than she had at seventeen and every bit the stubborn redhead that he remembered? No, not just fetching, but buck-a-cowboy-out-the-backdoor beautiful.

Even so, he shouldn't have had such a strong reaction to her, no matter how beautiful she'd become or how much he admitted he still wanted her. But the fact remained, seeing Augusta Garrison in the flesh had made his boots shake. That thought made him wish there was something a little stouter than piñon beans in his coffee.

"I say you find Gus and slap that ring on her finger," Slim said, his head turning as he watched the Cajun lead the stranger away from the bar and toward a room where others often went to have some privacy, "before it's too late and you're a broken old bronc buster full of what could have been. Want me to go fetch her for you?"

Dally gripped his friend's shoulder. "Nobody's fetching anybody. Come on, hoss, let's go do what we do best. We'll find out where they're making the draw and get camp set up. Let's leave those gals to cagier cowboys than us. What do ya say?"

"I say I'm lonely as hell and wishing you didn't make so damned much sense."

Dally wanted to laugh at the pitiful expression on his friend's face, but he couldn't. He knew exactly how Slim felt. He might act like he didn't care that his woman didn't belong to him, lock, stock and wedding-ring finger. But the truth was, it hurt like hell.

Chapter 4

"Is that him?" Joey asked as he deliberately bumped Augusta and made her look as if she were going to fall, just as they planned in order to set off a roar of laughter from the crowd who lined Main Street.

She ignored his question, focusing on dodging and darting between the pretty buckskins and paints that marched in the parade around them. Being a tramp was dangerous on every occasion that people and stock tried to dazzle a crowd. She always kept the old saying in the back of her mind to keep her aware of possible dangers. She'd found out on several occasions already that it wasn't a matter of *if* things will go wrong, but *when*.

Joey followed her and pointed to the blue-eyed cowboy who had just stepped out of the saloon and stood waiting for the parade to pass. "He and that skinny fellow standing next to him are staring holes through me. Is one of them Angelo?"

Augusta took up a position next to the wagon that carried some of the rodeo officials and was perturbed when Joey stepped up next to her instead of on the other side of the wagon as they'd rehearsed. She knew he wasn't going to let it alone. "You know it is. You saw him follow me to the tent."

"Honey, I'd be for shedding me some face paint and

putting on some prettier clothes if I had a looker like that following me."

She glanced up and realized that Tempest LeDoux, head of the rodeo committee, had overheard what she'd said and apparently had taken notice of Dally. Leave it to Mrs. LeDoux to spot a good-looking cowboy. She called the lady rancher and her daughter, Alaine, friends and had shared a little of her and Dally's history with them. But no one knew all of it. Not even Dally himself.

Tempest looked like a gypsy fortune-teller, all decked out in a fanciful off-the-shoulder white blouse and shimmering skirt. The wide gold belt around her waist was full of bangles that matched those at her wrist. Augusta pretended to be jealous of the woman's beauty, including her friend into the comic routine. She signaled to Joey to offer Tempest a sunflower from his clown's hat and, when he did, Augusta exaggerated her already sad face, acting jealous.

The crowd roared at her and Joey's antics, all their faces, except one, filled with approval. Ice blue eyes had turned their glare from Joey to her. Augusta realized that Dally was on the move, following the path the parade was taking up Main Street. If she didn't do something quick, he would meet up with her at the end of the livery. In no way was she ready for another face-to-face meeting with the man. The taste of him still lingered long after their kiss.

"Got to go, Mrs. LeDoux. I need to be over at the chutes when they draw for the rides. I'll see you over at the shooting competition."

"Then you are coming?" Tempest looked pleased.

"Wouldn't miss it for the world. Is Alaine ready?"

"About to split her britches." A grin stretched across Tempest's face as she accepted the sunflower and blew Joey a kiss.

"See you there." Augusta signaled to the tramps that it was time to end their part of the parade and give chase to Joey.

"Grab a bite to eat," she instructed as she ran alongside him, "then we'll meet up at the team roping."

"Then you can tell me more about this Angelo fellow." Joey just wouldn't let it go.

The clowns sliced through the crowd like they were bullets being sprayed in every direction. As they raced away, they reached into their baggy pockets and drew out strings of colorful beads, throwing them at the parade watchers. Oohs and ahhs of appreciation echoed all-around from those lucky enough to catch the gifts.

Fifteen minutes later, Augusta stood among the mob waiting for the shooting competition to commence. She should have been making sure everything was in order with the drawing, but she'd promised Alaine LeDoux she would watch her compete. Not many folks gave Alaine and her mother the time of day but, despite all the gossip and rumors, Augusta found them to be good-hearted, decent women. She meant to show her support, just as promised.

While Alaine strode to the shooting mark, her mother's feet braced as if she were facing a showdown. Tempest looked like she was praying, her hands clenched over her heart. Augusta prayed that her friend would show these people a thing or two. A well-aimed bullet today would go a long way in proving a point.

Alaine looked like she knew what she was doing. She'd certainly been practicing every day since Augusta had gotten off the train from St. Louis. The girl raised the 16-gauge Parker and drew a bead on the target. Blue smoke belched from the end of the firearm. Tempest jerked as if she'd been shot. Alaine's bullet went wide and seemed to make a rag doll out of her mother. For a moment, the crowd quit breathing and Augusta wondered if the bullet could have possibly struck the Cajun rancher. But Tempest stood slightly behind her daughter. No way a bullet could stray backward.

Finally, Mrs. LeDoux regained her high color and

sensibilities. "That's some mighty fancy shooting, honey," Tempest told her daughter as the girl stalked toward the nearest alley with her chin held high. "You'll do better tomorrow. I'm sure of it."

Augusta could read her friend's disappointment and knew Alaine would never give up till she got it right. And Tempest would never give up helping her get better. Whatever Alaine's dreams were her mother would champion.

Augusta respected that kind of loyalty even though she hadn't been able to give it to Dally. She couldn't champion his aim to ride Bone Buster.

Joey strode up beside her, munching on a delicious smelling beef rib. "Any particular reason you're avoiding this Angelo fellow and me anytime I ask you about him?"

"I thought I told you to take a break." Augusta moved away from the crowd and headed for the chutes out at the railhead.

"That's what I'm doing. Want a bite?" Joey offered her a rib as he walked with her. A couple of town mutts followed, waiting patiently for the clown to offer them a tidbit. "Don't know who I'm voting for, Cookie over at Burkburnett's camp or Sam from the Flying G. Both make some tasty beef, as far as I'm concerned."

"You don't have to vote for Sam just 'cause he works for my father." Augusta hadn't had a chance to sample any of the fare being offered by the cooks participating in the chuck-wagon cook-off. Seeing Dally had made her lose her appetite.

"I figure you haven't seen Angelo in about three, maybe four years until today, have you?" Joey finished off the rib and tossed the bone to one of the dogs. A fight ensued and Joey stopped it by giving the other dog a rib that still had meat on it.

Augusta's breath caught in her throat and she stopped to stare at the clown. "Why would you say that?"

"Oh, I'd say little Maddy's that old, give or take a few months."

Who else suspected the truth, Augusta wondered. "What makes you think he's her father?"

"I wasn't sure until I saw you with him today. He's her father, all right. Don't deny it." When she didn't, Joey continued. "He doesn't know, does he?"

"What was the point in telling him? Dally was so hell-bent on riding that bull I figured he'd go and get himself killed before she was ever born." Her hands knotted into fists as she took brisk strides toward the chutes. "I was seventeen and scared, Joey. He was grief stricken over his father's death and bent on revenge. I thought I was doing the right thing by not telling him. By leaving and taking that damn bull with me. I knew Dally was strapped for money and never dreamed he'd find a way to follow the brindle all over the southwest. But he followed anyway. Then I had to stay away from the reunions for a while until after the baby was born. I can't tell you the nights I prayed for him not to draw that brindle. The nights I prayed that, if he did, I wouldn't have to tell my daughter one day why she'd never met her father."

Augusta blinked back hot tears that threatened to brim in her eyes. "I knew there was only one thing I could do to make sure Dally lived. That's why I begged my folks to let me travel with them to the cowboy competitions. To let me hire on as one of the tramps who safeguard the men who ride the bulls. To make sure I was around anytime Dally showed up and had an opportunity to draw for the damned ride."

"Is that why you handle the hat?"

Joey was smarter than she'd given him credit for, but she wasn't about to admit to making sure Dally's name was never matched with Bone Buster's. "I handle the drawing because my father provides most of the stock."

"Then you're saying any Flying G hand could draw the names today?"

"Leave well enough alone, Joey, if you want to remain my friend."

"That's what I'm trying to be, Augusta—your friend. Let the man make his ride and tell him about his daughter."

"Make sure we're set up for the show just before the wild cow milking." She pulled rank and dismissed any further discussion about what she should and shouldn't do regarding Dally. She realized Joey was just trying to be helpful, but he couldn't possibly understand. "And Maddy's my business, understood?"

Joey saluted her and let her go on alone. She knew he would honor her demand. The clown was loyal and only meant the best for her. He'd proven it time and again.

"Well, here's ol' Rusty," one of the men announced as she approached a table that had been set up near the chutes. For the four-day rodeo, the only stock being kept in the waiting pens normally used by animals that were to be transported east were those participating in the various events. A young boy, looking about ten years old, sat next to the mayor.

Augusta's gaze automatically went to the pens housing the bulls. Bone Buster was the biggest, most dangerous looking of all.

"You ready to draw the names?" the mayor asked, offering his Stetson for her to do the honors and making her focus on the task at hand. "Young man," he addressed the boy, "we're glad you could join us on this prestigious occasion."

"I'm hoping that's something good, mayor."

"So do these cowboys, young man"—he grinned at his constituents—"so do they."

Augusta wondered who the boy was and why he'd been allowed to watch. Usually the drawing was left to participants and officials.

When Joey walked up, Augusta was surprised that he'd deliberately defied her orders to see if she would play fair. Maybe she didn't know the clown as well as she thought. Maybe she needed to be a bit more careful than usual. Augusta waved away the mayor's offer and pointed at another white hat in the crowd. "Let's use his."

Dally stepped up and placed his hat on the table, surprise darting across his eyes so briefly that she was sure only someone who knew him well would have noticed.

The young boy clapped his hands in approval of her choice. "Golly, Mr. Angelo. She's gonna use your hat. Maybe it'll bring you luck."

"Let's hope so, Jory." Dally grinned at the boy.

Don't count on it, Augusta thought as she held up strips of paper that had the bulls' names on them. She dropped them into Dally's hat and acted as if she were stirring them like a cook stirs his stew, then finally held up one paper high over her head.

"What's the first man's name on the list?"

"Buford Jenkins of the Lazy S."

Everyone looked at the cowboy straddled over the top of one of the chutes, then back at Augusta anxiously. She handed the paper to the mayor, who wrote the bull's name by the man who drew him. "Bad Company," she announced.

A rally went up. Bad Company was a good draw for any man. Jenkins would earn lots of bragging rights if he made the ten seconds. "Next?"

"Slim Doogan of the Double D."

Surprise registered across Dally's face as their longtime friend stepped up and waited for Augusta to choose the next name.

"Fulla Stomp!" Augusta read the name and noticed that Slim turned slightly pale.

"Serves you right for trying to ride with the big guns." Dally slapped his friend good-naturedly on the shoulder. "Want to back out while you still can?"

The other cowboys laughed, sharing in the fun. No man was counted coward for changing his mind about participating in the outlaw event. The competitions usually pertained to skills and talents used in their everyday working life on the ranch. Bull riding was meant for show, even to those who knew the event had started way back in '67 between two Colorado outfits, long before the Pecos, Canadian or even the Prescott competitions.

Slim shook his head. "Nope, I'll stick. But will you mind toting a tub of ice water to my tent later tonight, friend?" he asked Dally. "I got a funny feeling I'm gonna be sitting sore after that horn hooker gets done with me."

Everyone laughed but loudly congratulated him for his grit.

"Next name?" Augusta looked over at the mayor's list, needing to get on with the drawing. She and Joey had other responsibilities and the clown seemed bent on ignoring his until she got done here.

"Dally Angelo," the mayor announced.

A hush swept over the crowd. Anticipation etched Jory's face. Augusta's heart felt as if it leapt into her throat. She could feel her pulse beating at her temples, her cheeks, racing down her arms to her wrists. Thrum, thrum, thrum. Her hand shook as she reached in to draw a name from the hat.

Please don't let him see, she whispered silently. Dally was standing awfully close.

A band of iron reached out and clamped around her wrist, stopping her from grabbing the piece of paper from the hat.

"My hat. My draw," the sinfully sexy voice demanded, sending a brushfire of anxiety blazing through her.

Augusta couldn't protest without justifying her reasoning. She could do nothing but grant his request. God, what if he noticed what she'd done? What if everyone did? They'd never believe she only meant to affect the outcome for Dally and no one else.

His hand dipped in and out, his fingers unfolding the paper. Disappointment etched his brow as his jaw set hard and unforgiving. "Big Windy."

"Too bad, Angelo," someone said. "Maybe tomorrow."

"That bull can't hold lucky much longer," another offered. "Why, I'll bet—"

"Ahh, shucks," said Jory.

The wager was lost in a multitude of discussion about when Dally would draw Bone Buster.

Slim Doogan slapped his friend on the shoulder. "Bone Buster's looking a might relieved you didn't draw him tonight if you ask me."

The crowd laughed and took a collective glance at the object of their discussion. The bull snorted at all the attention, giving the back of his pen a good kick for measure.

"Yeah, real relieved," Dally muttered. "Looks plumb puny if you ask me."

Laugh it off, Augusta thought, knowing how disappointed Dally was at not drawing the brindle's name. She nudged the hat back from Dally and stirred the names again, this time making sure she grabbed the paper she had hooked on one side beneath the inner lining of the Stetson so that it would be difficult to dislodge. "Next name?"

"Gill Puckett of Jacks Bluff."

Augusta wished she had waited to dislodge the paper. Tempest wouldn't appreciate one of her ranch hands being mangled by the mankiller. She made a great show of looking surprised as she unfolded the paper. "Bone Buster."

"Lucky man," she heard Dally say beneath his breath before he offered a hand to Puckett, giving him a hearty, "Congratulations."

Six more men's names were chosen from the hat. Six more minutes of watching Dally study Bone Buster, the bull that always seemed to evade him. When the drawing was over and the others headed back to town, Augusta signaled Joey to the table.

"Hand Dally back his hat."

"No, I'm taking a break, boss." Joey shook his head and

started backing away. "You do it. Besides, he's busy telling that little boy good-bye."

Realizing the clown meant to leave her and Dally alone at the chutes, she protested, but it did no good. Joey grinned. "Time to pay for your past. I can't do that for you."

Augusta swung around and decided to show her coworker that she could deal with Dally without falling to pieces. But just as resolve rose to engulf her, it sank to the pit of her stomach. There Dally was, moving the way she remembered, with a purposeful stride and lean, muscular limbs.

His chaps, scuffed boots and a white chambray shirt were nothing different than what most of the other cowboys wore, but they looked a part of him—masculine and seductive in an earthy sort of way.

He'd lost none of his good looks over the years and she knew it was from spending time chasing the rodeo and riding wild stock. A man didn't sit a saddle long without staying fit. She had thought she would be long past any attraction she felt toward him but the surprise at seeing him again had sent her senses reeling like a fishing line cast in a fast current. She'd lost control of any solid reasoning not to kiss him. Touching him, kissing him, tasting him had been her downfall. She couldn't let it happen again if she was going to make it through these four days with any sanity left intact.

She walked toward him, eager to give him back his hat and get away from him. The longer she remained near him, the weaker her resolve to resist him became.

"So when did you start working the shows?" Dally brushed back his mussed hair as she approached. "I thought you were going to head east and go to school. Become a lady doc or some other such something."

She offered the hat and watched as he placed it on his head. "I said I wasn't going to settle for anything traditional. Tramping isn't exactly traditional employment for a woman."

"Then you didn't take it on just to follow me around?" He managed to look hurt, though she knew he was being arrogant.

"Of all the brazen, conceited—"

"C'mon, Stubborn Redhead," he teased, "I only meant that it's strange that your employment puts you in the same places I'm bound to show up. The shame of it is that you handle the hat and, still, you're too honest to rig the draw in my favor. It sure would have been sweet to put an end to all this controversy and let me have my reckoning with the brindle."

She caught her breath. Had he guessed or was this just lucky teasing? He'd never forgive her if he knew the truth that she'd deliberately held back Bone Buster's name for another man. "Drawing Big Windy was a good thing."

"How so?"

"No use taking on a ride with the brindle without getting a few practice rides under your belt. You'll warm up on Big Windy and then, if you're lucky, maybe have another ride or two before you draw Bone Buster."

A moment later Dally stood beside her, looking down at her with speculation dancing in his eyes. "What are you afraid of, Augusta? That I'll be hurt?"

She lifted her chin and stared back, willing herself to ignore how close he stood, how masculine he smelled, how loco she'd been to get into this discussion with him. Nothing would ever change and it served no purpose but to make her angry.

"God, I'd forgotten how beautiful you really are." Dally's heated whisper brushed against her cheek.

To her chagrin, his compliment sent a ripple of pleasure rushing to all the nerve endings in her body to beat steady drums at their pulse points. "Stop it, Dally. If you think I'm going to let you pick up where you left off, you're sadly mistaken. I refuse to—"

The next moment, his face paused only inches from hers. A band of velvet granite had wrapped itself around her waist as he captured her in his embrace. He smelled like the red earth that had been so much of their playground as youths and the Texas sky that had warmed their skin on days they'd spent learning to love each other in the sun-drenched Indian paintbrush and clover. Most of all, the secret scent of love wafted through her senses, the fragrance that arose when two hearts came together again with a renewed sense of belonging.

Her heart pounded as if she were competing in the horse race. Augusta gazed up at him and thought that she was lost forever. She'd forgotten how vibrant his eyes were, like the clear Texas sky Kasota Springs had been named after. She felt dizzy. Her knees trembled as if she were sinking in quicksand.

His breath mingled with hers as he leaned in to lay claim.

She wouldn't let him kiss her again. Her chin rose. She glared at him, daring him to defy her and take a kiss. She was no longer a teenager, so in love that she had no reason to her thoughts. He couldn't just ride in and think they could pick up where they left off.

He made no move to touch her. Instead, he asked very softly, "When do you think I'll get to?"

Augusta couldn't believe his arrogance, but she wouldn't admit to knowing exactly what he meant. She blinked, unable to hold his stare. "When do I think you'll get to do what?"

"Ride Bone Buster." His mouth lifted into a sinfully, sexy grin. "What do you think I meant?"

Oh, you just love it, don't you, seeing if you can test my willpower. Well, I'm older now. Wiser. I can handle your devilish good looks a lot better than I used to. "How should I know and why should I care?"

When Dally moved aside, she began to breathe again and found better footing. She hadn't meant to be so brutal about it, but he'd left her no choice. She hadn't felt so vulnerable in a long time.

"So, what do you think?" His voice held an edge of anger in it. "Do you think Puckett can ride the brindle?"

"Bone Buster is as rank as they come," she warned. "Gill Puckett will—"

"Get himself killed is what he's going to do." Dally didn't let her finish, glaring at her as if she were the Jacks Bluff ranch hand.

"And *you* wouldn't?" She couldn't believe what she heard. Envy stirred Dally's anger. She wasn't about to let him get away with making her feel more responsibility than she already felt at pairing the man up with the brindle. "You're afraid someone else is going to ride him the full ten seconds before you do, aren't you?"

Something dangerous flashed in Dally's eyes, intensifying the blue until it looked like the static display that ran across beef horns when lightning struck too close to the herd. She'd gone too far. Said too much.

"Hell, yes, I want to be the first. He killed *my* father, not anyone else's. Me and that bull's gonna come to terms with each other. It won't do if Puckett or anybody else rides him first."

She couldn't help herself. She reached up and touched Dally's cheek, unwilling to let him think she didn't understand what drove his anger. She'd always understood; she just didn't agree that this was the way to face the fact that his father was gone. Riding the bull wouldn't bring Flint Angelo back. Nothing would.

Her fingers lingered on Dally's cheek for a moment before she halfheartedly pulled them away. She remembered tracing the sharp angles of his face, the cleft in his chin one hot summer's eve, branding to memory every nuance of his cherished face. "I almost wish somebody else had ridden him after all these years, Dally. Maybe then we could have had a chance together."

Maybe she shouldn't have always made sure Bone Buster was matched with a cowboy who had no chance of riding him.

Maybe she shouldn't have always made sure Dally never had the luck of the draw.

Maybe she should quit rigging the draw and let fate decide Dally's destiny.

"Maybe when I make the ride"—Dally brushed her lips softly with his before she could react—"we'll finally talk about why you really walked out on me."

He walked away this time, leaving her standing and staring after him.

Chapter 5

Slim Doogan was an easy man to find. Wherever there was a skillet of sourdough biscuits and a bucket of bubbling, pepper-flavored beans, the man would be taking his fill. He might be thinner than a wheat stalk, but he had always been able to eat his weight in free grub. And he never failed to find something to complain about, no matter how good his fortune. Augusta approached the crowd lined up at the Flying G's chuckwagon and overheard him doing his best to stir up some sympathy.

"I . . . tell . . . you," Slim grumbled around a mouthful of beans, deliberately pausing between each chew, "drawing Fulla Stomp is about the worst stroke 'a luck what's ever befallen me. Why, I remember the day I rode ol' White Toe . . ."

A collective gasp of appreciation rippled through the crowd. Augusta did her best to hide her chuckle, almost glad for his stretching the truth. It got her mind off the reason she needed to talk to him.

"He was a ton of fury and three gallons of slobber and snot." Slim eyes widened as he tried to build suspense. "I weren't much bigger than I am now."

"Hell, you ain't never been bigger, Slim. Get back to the bull-honkey."

"Here, let me fetch another of them fine Flying G biscuits." He stepped in line and grabbed another biscuit from the skillet, instigating a quick rap of the ladle against his knuckles. "Dang it, Sam," Slim complained. "I can't help it if you got the best biscuits on the Llano."

"Get back in line, next time, Doogan, and let some other folks eat. And quit jawing about riding White Toe. Ain't nobody but Dally Angelo rode that white son-of-a-blizzard, so quit polishing your spurs 'bout it," Sam groused and went back to work feeding the hungry stream of people who were standing in line waiting their turn to receive some of the fine fare.

If Slim's yarn-spinning halted the speed of the serving line again, Augusta knew he'd learn soon enough that a bull was the least of his worries. Preventing a chuckwagon cook from doing his duties bordered on yanking the tail of a bobcat and expecting it to purr.

Realizing he'd been caught stretching the truth, Slim pulled his hat down to cover his eyes. "A man can't even fancy up a story round here without . . ." He let his words trail off as he crammed his mouth full of biscuit and walked over to one of the bales of hay that had been set out to provide a resting place for folks to sit.

Augusta glanced at the faces in the crowd and breathed a sigh of relief when she didn't see Dally's face among them. She walked past the others and asked if she could take a seat next to Slim. When he glanced up at her and realized who it was, Augusta noticed the embarrassment painting his cheeks rosy. She offered him a gentle smile. "It's okay, Slim. We all knew you were trying to pull our legs. Sam's just busy, is all. He doesn't have time to say it nice."

"Ah, heck, Gus"—Slim offered a wide-gapped grin—"I ain't upset at Sam. I know better'n to cut in line. Everybody knows that's a prime rule of camp—take your time when it comes up. Not before and not after." He sighed heavily, rolling his shoulders as if they ached. "I'm just sorry nobody thinks I got it in me to ride ol' Toe or any other bull worth his snot."

"You've got other talents, Slim. And you're a smarter man than most for not wasting your time on trying to ride those bulls. You aren't really gonna go through with riding Fulla Stomp tonight, are you?"

"Funny thing, you say that." Slim's lips curved into a conspiratorial whisper. "I've been trying to think of a logical way to get out of it ever since I drawed this afternoon. Trouble is, me and logic don't always sit on the same saddle of giddy-up, if you know what I mean."

"I tell you what—" An idea struck Augusta—one that just might work better than the one she'd planned when she first decided to approach Slim with her request. "You promise me that you'll talk Dally out of riding Bone Buster during this reunion and I'll see that my father pulls Fulla Stomp out of the competition before you're scheduled to ride."

His eyebrows drew together in a frown as he shook his head. "Can't do that, Gus. Dally's set on it. Maybe you just oughta wait and see if Bone Buster's luck holds true. Maybe Dally won't draw him this time, or maybe he'll have to wait till the next competition to get better luck. That's September or better, I'm thinking."

"There won't be a next time for Bone Buster," she said quietly. This was the first time she'd told anyone what she and her parent had decided. "That's why we brought the brindle back here. We're taking him out of competition after this one. He's only got another year or two at most before Father would put him out to pasture anyway. So, I've asked my parents to pull him for stud now."

Slim rose to his full six feet two inches in height. "You'll crush him, Augusta. You gotta let him have his ride. He won't be the same if he never gets it."

Frustration made her bolt to her feet, her hands gripping Slim's arms in an effort to keep him from walking away.

"Why, Slim? Why can't he leave it alone?" She tried to make him understand in a way she never could Dally. "Bone Buster won't bring his father back. Flint's dead."

Tears welled in Augusta's eyes, but she wouldn't let them fall. God knew she'd cried enough of them trying to understand, trying to find some sense in Dally's unrelenting bullheadness on the subject.

"You think it's about revenge, don'tcha?" Slim stared down at her hands until she let go of him and dropped them to her sides.

"Isn't it?" Right now she felt as sad as her tramp outfit appeared to others.

"No, Gus. It ain't." Slim pushed back his hat and stared into her eyes, looking suddenly full of gravity she'd never noticed in him before. "It's about having control. Dally ain't the sort what gives over easy to letting anyone or anything control him. That bull represents the time when life just up and slapped him in the face and took away the feeling that he would live forever. It was like life said, 'Look here, Dally Angelo, there's gonna be things no amount of true grit will see you through. Everybody who ever trod this big ol' patch of heaven we call Texas and the rest of that hell those other folks call home has to face it. Flint Angelo did. You do. You just gotta decide if you're gonna let it whoop ya or if you can be cowboy enough to accept it, learn from it and make yourself stronger because of it.'"

Slim had a talent far beyond one of riding bulls. He knew how to bring home a point. He had somehow shed a new light on Dally she'd never seen before.

Hadn't she faced the same sense of lack of control? Hadn't her life spun in a way she never anticipated? Hadn't she been trying to manipulate it so that the outcome would eventually be the way she wanted it?

Was she just as guilty as Dally for not letting go of what she thought was best, hiding behind the reasoning that she couldn't watch him kill himself?

Had she hung on to that justification so long that she hadn't been able to accept the curve life had thrown her, learned from it, and didn't trust herself to have the strength to see through whatever truce they might find together?

Trust was what she needed right now. Not trust in Dally, but trust in herself. Trust that she could do the right thing and tell him about Maddy. Tell him that they had a daughter together. Trust that if he hated her for keeping the secret from him and never spoke to her again, she could somehow live through the devastation of losing his love forever.

Augusta reached up and softly touched Slim's cheek. "Thank you, friend."

"For what?" He took her hand and slightly pushed it away. "It's the cowboy way, you know."

She stared at him, wondering which "way" exactly he was referring to. Cowboys did an awful lot their own way.

"Telling the truth when you're alone with a partner. Spinning yarns when there's a crowd to work up."

She laughed, grateful for the amusement twinkling his eyes and reminding her that he had dimples. "Now who's the clown? You're full of beans, Slim Doogan."

"Most the time if I can help it," he admitted.

"Walk with me over to the Springs Hotel?" she asked, linking her arm through his. She needed to see if her folks had made it to Kasota Springs. They were due in from St. Louis already and she hadn't seen them yet. Good thing she had paid for two rooms in advance or they'd have to stay in one of the tents in Clown Alley. There were no rooms to be had anywhere all over town. She'd heard someone say that the sheriff had let out a couple of the criminals on good behavior just so the county could rent out some of the jail cells to boarders.

The thought of sleeping in a cell next to Cherokee Bill Bartlett, the bank robber, would certainly have no appeal to her parents if she had to give up the hotel rooms. The LeDouxes might offer to put them up out at Jacks Bluff.

"I'll make a quick change and we'll go see about pulling Fulla Stomp out of the mix," she announced.

"Nah. I didn't make the trade, remember? I'll just see you to your hotel. I said I'd ride that bucker and I will." Slim reached up and playfully honked her nose. "Let's just hope he don't jar a bunch of them beans out my butt or the crowd's gonna wanta be borrowing that nose of yours, Rusty."

Her parents had not arrived by the time she completed her last routine and changed into the periwinkle teagown that matched her eyes perfectly. Her hair now hung in thick auburn waves down her back, brushed to a luster that could have rivaled sunset shining on the walls of the nearby Palo Duro canyon.

They should be here already, she worried, making her way through the hotel parlor and out into the crowded street. *They said they'd be here in time for the dance.* It wasn't like them to be late.

A throng of excitement swept over Kasota Springs as fiddlers, tamborine shakers and banjo pickers struck a lively tune together to entice everyone to join in the dance.

Women wore their best bonnets and graced the festivities in a kaleidoscope of calico, paisley and lace parasols. The men sported string ties, brocade vests and spit-polished boots.

"Dance with me, Little Lady?" a wrangler asked, taking his hat off as she approached the livery.

"It's my true regret I can't, Sir." She knew most of the women there would be expected to accept several dancing partners. Men outnumbered women twenty to one. Unmarried women were even more rare. "At least not until I find my folks. Maybe later."

"I'll hold you to that, darling." He returned his hat and moseyed on down toward where the musicians were drawing a bigger crowd.

"Where's Joey when I need him?" she wondered as she headed to Clown Alley. She doubted she'd find any of the tramps still there. All of them had put in a hard day's work and deserved a well-earned rest.

Sure enough, when she reached the tents and searched several, Augusta found them empty of anyone she might send out to see if her parents were having trouble along the trail. She hadn't seen any of the troupe among the dancers. After doing comic routines all day, dancing was usually one of the last things a clown wanted to do. They danced all day in one form or the other.

She concentrated for a moment and tried to recall what Joey might have mentioned earlier about participating in the evening's festivities. The bull riding. Dally had asked for some clowns to help distract the bulls if they got too dangerous for a safe retreat. Joey would be there most likely. If not him, then somebody else from the Flying G would have agreed to earn a little extra money.

It took her longer than she hoped, making her way through town and over to the chutes next to the railyard. Men kept stopping her and asking her for a dance. At some point this evening, she was going to have to grant all those she'd promised for later.

Just as she spotted Joey running around the arena waving his hands like he was swatting flies overhead, she realized what he was attempting to do—flag an angry bull away from a downed rider.

Her heart felt as if it dropped to her feet and took root in the soil beneath them. The bull raking his hoof deep into the red dirt, tossing its head and bellowing with rage was none other than Big Windy, the bull Dally had drawn. Dally lay sprawled across the ground, his back to the bull. Dally dug his boots in, digging for enough scramble to get away. His boot slipped. Someone yelled, "Look out!"

Before she could think about what she was wearing, before

she could feel the crash of lightning pulse at her temples, before she considered the stupidity of what she was about to do, Augusta threw herself against the chute and hurdled its top.

Material shredded, her feet tangled, she landed on her knees in the dirt. Her breath had gone somewhere. Where she didn't know. It didn't seem to be anywhere in her body.

"Ho, bull! This way, bull!"

She could hear Joey trying to distract the beast, could see him waving his hands, trying to get the bull to change its focus toward him. The demon's eyes rolled wild, its nostrils flaring, obviously taking in the smell of its new competitor. Augusta cursed herself for putting on that dab of perfume for the party, wishing now she still smelled like the animals she'd dealt with in the various routines. The perfume would infuriate the bull.

She found her breath. Made it to her knees.

The bull faced her, its eyes narrowed a second before it charged.

Augusta thought she saw Dally scrambling for cover. Joey yelled something about a barrel. Her gaze darted to a barrel a few feet away from her. A man standing on the other side of the chute near the barrel, punched it with his fists, sending it into a roll.

She and the bull reached the barrel at the same time. Self-preservation made her do the only thing she could think of at the moment. She jumped as high as she could, praying the leap would take her somewhere far out of reach of horns and thundering hooves.

Her toes touched the tip of the barrel giving her unexpected momentum. She leaped even higher, hurdling the bull's bowed head and one shoulder.

"To the gate, Augusta. Over here!"

Dally's voice came from a place of safety. Now, if only she could reach the same. Augusta called upon every skill she'd ever learned, prayed every prayer she'd ever been taught as the seconds ticked by and she ran faster than she thought possible.

"Here, Gus. Jump!"

Augusta did as she was told, jumping into the arms reaching out to pull her up and over the chute gate. One second. Two. Red dust swirled all-around her as the bull came to a shuddering halt behind her, the chute fence the only barricade between her and its fury. Big Windy lifted his mouth and bellowed discontent, throwing its tail over his back to fan the hot steam of sweat raising a musky bovine stink to the air.

All of a sudden, Dally was holding her, kissing her like no one but they were present and she hadn't just been running for her life. *His* life, damn it!

The crowd roared in approval, whether for the bull's defeat or Dally's amorous victory demand, she wasn't sure.

Augusta jerked away and slapped him hard across one cheek. "Grow up," she said, forgetting all the good sense Slim had made earlier in the evening and listening to the fear that still thundered in her heart. "Grow up before you kill the both of us."

She stalked away.

"Might've rode Big Windy the full ten, Angelo," someone yelled, "but that kiss didn't last long enough for bragging rights."

"Are you okay?" asked Joey, trying to keep pace with her.

"I'm fine." Augusta looked at what was left of her teagown, her mangled hair and her patience with any man who decided to come within ten feet of her at the moment. A wonderful sight to present to her parents. Just wonderful. "Don't I look fine?"

Joey threw his palms up. "Oh, okay, boss lady. Just wanted to make sure you didn't need me."

"I need you all right." She kept walking toward the hotel, punctuating her orders with every step. "Take one of the remuda and set out east of town. Go to Clarendon if you have to. Father and Mother haven't made it in yet and I'm worried about them. Make sure they didn't have trouble along the trail."

"I wish they'd come by rail." Worry filled his tone. "I thought they might being that Maddy's with them."

"They wanted to stop in and visit some friends over at the 6666 Ranch and then my grandmother in Clarendon. I couldn't talk them out of it."

"I'll change out of my costume and light out of here before you know it."

"Don't bother changing."

"You really think something's wrong?"

"I'm not thinking any such thing." She refused to consider anything might have happened to them. To Maddy. Oh God, Dally. What if she had to tell Dally that something had happened to—?

No. She wouldn't let it enter her thoughts.

But just as quickly as she tried to dismiss the possibility, Slim's words rushed to mind. Words that scared the hell out of her. *Sometimes life just ups and slaps you in the face.*

"Find them, Joey." She prayed that she would never be called upon to be that strong. No one should *ever* have to be that strong. And for the first time, in four years, she finally understood Dally's anger. Dally's fear. Dally's single-minded purpose.

"Please hurry," she pleaded.

Chapter 6

Most who visited Kasota Springs thought the town was named after a fingertip of the Canadian River that had been divided by a knuckle of mesa tableland from its mother river. Though dry much of the year, miraculously, the springs occasionally rose from an aqueous source deep beneath the loam to quench the prairie's thirst. Dally thought of it as the plains popped out in a sweat beneath a hot July sun.

Whatever fed it, he was grateful the springs still had enough water to cover the bullrushes. He strode past the Double D encampment, ignoring the circle of cowboys waving him in to join them at the cook fire.

"Too bad about Puckett," one of them hollered at Dally. "Heard that arm jerker threw him plumb out the back door!"

"Ol' Bone Buster's just chomping his cud waiting for a chance at you, Angelo," teased another. "Poor Gill was just a warm-up whooping, far as that brindle's concerned. Sure hope your luck opens up so that brute'll quit stomping so hard on the rest of us."

Dally didn't take the bait, knowing the men were teasing yet sincere about wanting the challenge between him and the mankiller to be finished—one way or the other. He'd stayed around long enough to watch Puckett's turn at the

brindle and, though he had wished the Jacks Bluff ranch hand
no harm, felt a sense of relief when Puckett didn't stay on the
full ten seconds. Still, he'd give him his due. Puckett had
lasted seven seconds, longer than anyone before him.

The man deserved the round of applause he'd received
when he'd gotten up and dusted himself off. Dally had gone
over and shook his hand, extending Puckett the greatest compliment he'd ever given another man when he said, "That was
some real try, partner."

Instead of everyone congratulating Puckett for the length
of time he had been able to stay on, they'd rushed in to get
Dally's comments on the near miss. There was always lots
of big talk about the cowboys' winnings and losses, but it
seemed as if Dally's intent to ride Bone Buster had cast a
shadow over the rodeo and the possibility that someone else
could break the bull's winning streak. A shadow that loomed
like a thunderhead and threatened to spill foul wind. A shadow that took away any sun that should have been shining on
others at the rodeo.

Dally wanted nothing but a good dunk in the springs, some
clean clothes and to settle into his bedroll for the night. He
had walked away earlier to let the crowd focus their attentions
rightfully on Puckett's tremendous effort and decided that he
should do the same here at the Double D camp.

He'd deliberately set his tent up farther down bank from the
others, seeking a bit of solitude from the day's speculation
about him and the brindle. Listening to all the controversy got
old, especially the part about the risk he was taking. It was his
life, his risk. To hell with what anyone thought about it.

Who are you fooling, man, he told himself as he ducked
inside the tent and immediately started peeling off his soiled
vest and shirt. *You care what she thinks.*

His thoughts returned to the real reason he'd watched Gill
Puckett make his ride. The real reason he'd actually found himself counting off those seconds the man had stayed atop the

bull. For the first time in his life, he'd found himself wanting another man to defeat the bull. To strip from him the goal he couldn't turn away from until Bone Buster had been broken. To release him from whatever this was that kept him from fixing what was wrong between him and Augusta.

The willingness to see someone else make the ride scared the hell out of Dally. Made him sway from the intense focus that had gripped him for so long. All of a sudden he wanted to know what would happen *after* he rode the bull. Riding Bone Buster didn't seem to be the ultimate goal anymore.

That's why you kissed her, Dally berated himself. *Not once, but twice today. You wanted to know that she missed you. That there was still something between you that might be worth fixing. That fixing it would bring a greater satisfaction than conquering the bull that killed Flint.*

The sting of the slap that August had given him might be long gone, but the hurt of believing she wanted no part of him ached like a mule kick in the gut.

Dally threw his clothes in a heap in one corner, muttering a low curse when he realized the vest was torn. His mother had made the vest for Flint the year before he died. Dally had worn it for luck every time he drew for the ride. Remembering his mother, he bent and retrieved the paper he'd left in the pocket of the soiled shirt. He started to put the note away somewhere safe, but his fingers trembled as he touched it. *Light a lantern,* he told himself, trying to shake off the sense of helplessness that engulfed him as he unfolded the paper in the dark—the sense of something fearful he couldn't put a name to.

But the sheer act of acknowledging the apprehension seemed too monumental an effort. Dally stepped outside the tent and allowed the moon to provide the light he needed, to ease the darkness of the unnatural fear that overtook him.

He strode to the bank where the moon glistened bright atop the water's surface, plopped down and rested his elbows on his knees. Dally folded and unfolded the paper, wondering if he could read it again, yet knowing the act was unnecessary because he had memorized every line, word by word.

Son, you were such a little guy when you rode your daddy's roping steer.

His mother's words came to him now, in the sigh of the wind, the whisper of the leaves in the cottonwood trees, in the snap and crackle of the campfire not too far upstream. Dally peered at the words his mother had written before she'd died from a broken heart that had lost its true love and no longer wanted to live.

Flint always laughed and yelled at you, "Son, do or die," and you always yelled back, "Ki yi, ki yi."

I know nothing I can say will stop you from trying to ride that bull. So when you do, Dally, remember this. I know your daddy. He'll be near. You just ride on luck and skill. Bow your head and ask the Good Lord to bless you, if He will. Remember that fear knows no pride. Fire up and ride, son. Ki yi, Ki yi!

The letter fluttered from his hands as Dally bowed his head on his knees and did what he'd never allowed himself to do until now. He offered up a prayer to the higher source he believed in, asking for more than a chance at drawing the bull's name tomorrow. Asking for something beyond his sake.

"Help me be done with this thing, Lord," Dally whispered. "You know I won't give up the ride, and if anyone knows how stubborn that redhead can be, it's You. She won't ever agree to marry me until this is done." He lifted his head and stared at the star-filled sky. "And the one thing You know best about me is that I love her with everything I am."

His hand swept through his hair as he attempted to put into words all he felt, all he longed for. But God had not been listening on that day four years ago when Dally had begged him not to let his father die, when he'd pleaded for him not to let Augusta walk out of his life, six months later when he'd buried his heartbroken mother. Why should He be listening now?

Dally studied the ever-darkening expanse of the Texas countryside for a long time until he suddenly noticed that, despite the shadows, the moon cast light so vivid that he could see far into the distance. The rooftops of town, the canopy of trees, a bank of clouds looming on the horizon all seemed sinister elements until touched by a light more luminous than their dark outlines. The unnamed fear that had overwhelmed him only moments ago now seemed to ooze out into the night as if it were a wound that needed bleeding.

Dally focused on the moon, wondering if maybe he was being told something he wasn't smart enough to understand. He craned his ear, trying to listen just as he wanted to be heard.

Then it struck him. Focusing on the light, he saw what scared him and he could see past the darkness. Was that the answer? To focus on what was beyond what he meant to do?

That was too simple. Too easy, to be right there in front of him if he just looked a different way. The *right* way, maybe?

"As much as I never thought I'd hear these words come out of my mouth"—he paused to garner a strength he'd never called upon himself to give—"will You help me do whatever it is that will put an end to this battle with the bull and bring me and Gus back together?"

The moment he prayed it, he knew he'd done the right thing. Maybe this time there would be a real chance to draw the ride that had eluded him for so long. Maybe for the first time in a long time he wanted to be done with it for some reason other than his own satisfaction. Maybe if he focused hard enough he could see life beyond the ride.

"You better ask for a lot more than that."

The voice startled Dally from his thoughts. The clown he'd seen with Augusta most of the day strode toward Dally, appearing eerily ominous in his face paint, wig and padded suit.

"Where I come from a man's careful about the trouble he throws a loop on." Dally didn't extend him any welcome and wasn't ready to take any advice from the stranger. Especially not where Gus was concerned. "I'll thank you kindly to be on about your business and leave me to mine."

"Sorry." Joey shrugged. "And I only meant to warn you that it's going to take more than praying to win my boss's heart again, Angelo. That's a good start, make no mistake, but you're gonna to pursue her just as hard as you've chased that bull."

"I don't remember asking you for your opinion on the subject." Dally stood and dusted off his pants leg. "And, besides, I thought you were off looking for the Garrisons." He tempered his growl with sincere concern. "I'm assuming they're all right since you're standing here eavesdropping."

"They broke an axle but lucked out when some other folks came along and offered them a ride here. Gus sent some of the hands out to fix the wagon and bring it in. She's getting the Garrisons settled in at the hotel."

Dally headed for his tent, making a mental list of what he needed to gather before he could help the Garrisons. A shirt, his saddlebags and horse. "I'll just get my riggings and see what Augusta wants me—"

The clown stepped in the way, forming a blockade. "No, Angelo. She asked me to tell you to wait until morning to pay your respects. And she said to tell you that she sent enough men to take care of things. You're to stay put."

Dally grabbed a fistful of bowtie and padded ruffles, jerking the clown's face close. Nose to nose, he made it clear that he wasn't a man so easily ordered around. "You sure she's the one asking or have you got something to say about it?"

Joey's palms reached for the sky, as if held at gunpoint. "Holster your pistols, Cowboy. They're all tired and Gus said since you're dirty from your ride she thinks it's best that you wait till tomorrow to visit. She said to tell you that we'll see you first thing in the morning before the Woolly Buckers contest, and I'll make sure Mr. and Mrs. Garrison know that you asked about them."

We'll see you. *I'll* let them know. Why did the Garrisons have time enough tonight to see this clown and not him? Not to mention that Joey had been standing around every corner next to Augusta today any time Dally had sought a moment alone with her. Seemed mighty convenient and not absolutely necessary despite the fact they worked a lot of routines together.

Helping six- and seven-year-olds learn how to ride the buck out of cantankerous bouncing balls of wool would take instructors with good hearts and lots of patience. The man must have some good qualities or he couldn't be of help with tomorrow's sheep riding contest. Dally wanted to dislike Joey. Had every need to. But all he could muster against him so far was that Joey did what his boss asked him to do, he called her by the affectionate name she allowed only a few people the honor, and her parents obviously granted him time and trust more than most. Just how close a relationship did he and Augusta have outside of their work hours?

"Okay, Joey, or whatever else the hell your name is, I'll bite." Dally knew that all clowns who traveled with the competitions were called joeys. Why didn't this one use his true name? Another reason to be irritated with him. Something didn't sit well in the saddle here. Something that was being left unsaid.

An overwhelming feeling that Augusta didn't want him to see her parents made Dally feel as if something was being hidden from him. Something that obviously was no secret to this Joey Cayuse. "Now tell me why it is, clown," Dally demanded, easing his hold only slightly, "that the Garrisons will still be awake for you to tell them anything but they're just too tired for me to pay my respects?"

Joey jerked away, ripping material from Dally's fist. "Maybe that's a question you should ask yourself, Angelo. I'll bet you'll find almost four years' worth of reason when you get the answer."

Almost? What the hell did he mean by that, Dally wondered, as the tramp disappeared into the night. Why hadn't he simply said four years?

Chapter 7

Parents and youngsters alike sat on bales of hay that had been placed along the wooden maze of corrals that held the sheep and other animals waiting their turns to outwit their riders. Augusta spotted her mother and father in the crowd and nearly tripped over the lamb that had just sent its six-year-old rider boots over bottom to the dirt. Was Maddy with them or had Joey managed to keep her daughter entertained at the hotel as instructed?

Dally was in the chutes working the animals. He didn't need to see Maddy until Augusta could conduct the meeting on her own terms.

"Let's hear it for little J.D. Williams, folks." The announcer led the crowd in a round of applause.

Augusta remembered to straddle the lamb, act like it threw her as well, then landed backward in the dirt. She jumped up, dusted off her backside and limped elaborately to the sideline. Anytime one of the children didn't make his ride, she or one of the clowns made sure he felt better by pretending an adult couldn't handle the job any easier. The clowns' main functions were to add encouragement to anyone's effort.

"Seems that nobody can sit that ornery ol' critter, J.D. Don't take it too hard, partner."

All of a sudden a little blond girl, no bigger than two bits, ran out in her hat and boots and laid a big kiss on little J.D.'s lips. The boy turned every shade of crimson, but his grin stretched for ear to ear.

"Hey, now. See there, cowboy"—the announcer chuckled—"there's always something fine comes from making a good try. Let's hear it for five-year-old Sandra Jean Goff for making that cowboy's ride worthwhile."

"Where's your shadow? I thought he was supposed to be helping with this."

Augusta swung around to find Dally waiting for his turn at the chute opening for the next ride. He'd spent most of the morning making sure the bellropes were secured tightly around the sheep's underbellies and each rider had a secure hold on the rope when the flag dropped to signal it was time to begin the ride.

"I let him sleep in," she informed, not wanting to think he could go searching for Joey and start any more trouble. She'd asked Joey not to participate in the children's event so he could watch over Maddy and give her parents an opportunity to visit with some of their friends. Knowing at some point she would have to admit the truth to Dally and let him meet their daughter, Augusta had tossed and turned all night trying to figure out the right way to tell him. To make him understand. "You shouldn't have been so unfriendly to him last night. He was just doing as I instructed."

"So he told you?" Dally stretched the rope around the lamb and made sure the boy was ready to ride. "He should mind his business where you and I are concerned."

Augusta was burning up in her clown suit, and Dally stirring her anger even more so didn't help matters. "You should remember your manners as well as the fact that we're not married."

"Not because I don't want to be," Dally reminded with a note of challenge as the flag waved and he swung the gate open wide. The sheep lunged out of the chute and made a mad dash for the other side of the field.

"Look at the wool fly," one of the chute roosters crowed, instigating a round of laughter from other critics who sat atop the chutes and passed judgment on the rides. "You'd think she was being chased by a coyote or something. Ain't got a bit of buck in her."

Dark, angry-looking clouds loomed over the western horizon, promising a possible summer thunderstorm. Though Augusta eagerly wished for some good old Texas wind to cool the day down, she hoped the storm waited to arrive until after the children's rides were finished.

"Storm's brewing," one of them noticed.

Both kinds, Augusta decided, praying for the contest to end for other reasons than the possibility of getting wet or muddy. Hell felt like it was fixing to break loose between her and Dally, and it was a bigger storm than the one that might be swelling on the horizon.

"I'm going to go talk to your folks as soon as this is over," Dally informed her when she made it back. Luckily the boy had ridden the lamb the full ten seconds and she didn't have to fake another spill on her backside.

"I'll wave them over now," she insisted, realizing that now was the better time for him to pay his respects. That way, she was sure Maddy was nowhere in sight. "I'll handle the chutes. You go take a break."

Dally stared at her a minute, then nodded. She waved at her parents to come this way and watched Dally make his way toward them, his lanky backside and stride still something that could set her heart fluttering no matter how angry she might be at him.

She had to concentrate hard on keeping her mind on the task at hand instead of on watching Dally with her parents. But as soon as she released the chute to let a rider go, she dared a glance at Dally. She liked the way he shook her father's hand and stood at ease with him. The way her mother smiled as she talked to him. Both of her parents thought a lot of Dally and had always considered him a good match for her. Both of them thought she'd been wrong for not contacting him and telling him about Maddy's birth. And even though she'd asked them not to talk to him about Maddy until she did, she'd also not asked them to lie if he found out the truth before she had a chance to tell him. She couldn't cause a rift between him and her parents when they had wanted her to tell him the truth from the beginning.

She'd known from the moment she made the decision to return to Texas that everyone would learn that Maddy was her daughter, not her sister, as most back east believed. She was tired of living a lie, and Maddy was getting old enough to start asking about the truth.

The promise of rain scented the air. Lightning flickered against the sky, its accompanying thunder silent at first, then becoming a low grumble. The crowd began to thin. Slim Doogan came hurrying up to whisper something in the announcer's ear.

"It seems, folks, that a decision had been made to swap out the team roping and wild cow milking events due to the inclement weather." The announcer held up his hands as if warding off an attack. "Now, folks, Mr. Doogan assures me that the committee thought long and hard about what was best for all concerned."

"Long and hard?" another man jeered. "The mayor probably got into a wager with Tempest LeDoux over it and lost. Everybody knows she's the one running the show."

"Hey, Doogan, speaking of running the show," one of the chute roosters yelled. "Anyone know who's looking strong for best all-around?"

Slim's gapped grin stretched wide. "Dang sure ain't me, that's for sure and shooting. I been bucked off everything that's crow-hopped my scrawny hide."

The crowd laughed.

Augusta had been keeping up with most of the events because she'd had to handle the clown routines between each of them. If she were guessing, it looked like it might be that cowboy who got in trouble a while back. Rowdy somebody. She never remembered his last name. She sure hoped he won. She'd never thought he got a fair shake about all that bad business that happened a few years back.

"Some feller who used to live around here," Slim confirmed her calculations. "A few folks' saddles are riding rough over it."

"Well, we're mighty thankful you gave us the news, Mr. Doogan." The announcer hurried Slim on his way. "We hope you draw a better ride tonight."

By the time evening came, raindrops patted tentatively, smearing Augusta's face paint and dampening her clothes. Two of the events had been delayed but not called off. She'd just finished the hat drawing and managed to waylay Dally's ride on Bone Buster one more time. He'd drawn Hell Fire and Slim, unfortunately, had drawn the brindle.

"That's a real shame, Dally." Slim held out the paper he'd drawn. "I'll trade'ja if you want."

Dally shook his head. "I'll take it legal or I don't take it at all."

Guilt consumed Augusta as he turned to her and stared, his eyes looking at her with a longing that broke her heart. Rain glistened on his Stetson, molding his shirt to define the muscular sinews of his shoulders and arms. He wanted the luck of the draw so much. He'd never forgive her if he ever learned the truth.

How could she tell him? How could she keep denying him the right? Watching him walk away and thinking that fate had dealt him a sorry hand was becoming too hard for her to bear. She'd made up her mind that she couldn't do it again. Tonight, after this ride, she'd tell him the truth. She'd let Fate decide whether he chose Bone Buster tomorrow.

Slim strode over and handed her the slip of paper he'd drawn. "I'm not gonna ride him, Gus. You can call me No-Grit if you want to, but I ain't gonna put my friend through the possibility of seeing me kilt or watching me make the ride he wants. I can't do that to him. It ain't in me."

"You're a true friend, Slim." She took the paper, wadded it up and let it fall on the ground. "No one will call you anything less."

"You're one too, so let him ride."

Augusta evaded his gaze. "I don't know what you mean?"

"Sure you do, Gus." Slim took off his hat and ran his thumb around the inner lining, silently informing her that he was smarter than he let others know. "Sometimes you gotta do the right thing so your man can find the courage to do the right thing for you."

He knew. Slim had somehow guessed or seen that she'd rigged Bone Buster's name to be chosen when Dally's name wasn't in contention. "I love him, Slim. I just couldn't watch him die."

"Love him enough to let him live then," Slim said softly. "Until he rides that bull, he's doing neither. Not living or dying. Just waiting. And, Gus, waiting's no kind of life for anybody." Slim tapped her bulbous nose. "Now, I'm going to take my own advice and find me a pretty little gal who's tired of waiting on some hunka bootstrap like me to come calling. I suggest you git over there and let that cowboy know you're tired of waiting too. I'm heading out to shuffle these boots on some sawdust."

Slim's advice set well with what she'd already decided. Augusta could only hope that the dance would be moved inside if the rain turned into a downpour. That way her parents and child would be busy somewhere other than near Dally. The threat of rain would never stop him or any other bull rider, so her secret could remain safe until after the outlaw event. That would give her time to see him through the ride and get him alone to talk.

Already wet and filthy from the day's routines, Augusta decided to ask some of the other clowns to stay and help with the event. As she and two others took up positions inside the wooden maze, the announcement was made that Slim Doogan had forfeited his ride.

A few jeers echoed over the crowd who'd braved the gusts of wind that now pelted them with stinging raindrops. Thunder bellowed a warning to all that the rides best begin or the clouds churning overhead might belch some black-biled wind and wreck havoc on their plans.

One rider, two, took their turns. The grounds melted into small muddy pools. Augusta and her crew added a sense of comic relief to the tension of the bulls blowing hot steam at their riders.

Dally was up next. He tightened the flat braided rope that he pulled around Hell Fire's girth, then tied himself to the back of the animal by putting his hand through the loop and pulling it tight. Wrapping the tail of the rope around his hand, Dally wove it through his fingers to make sure if he did get bucked off, he could easily let go of the bellrope.

The chute gate opened into a field of mud and muck. Dally turned out his toes and hung on as Hell Fire lunged out of the chute like a twister running amok. Hell Fire's shoulders hurdled one direction, his haunches kicking higher than his head. Dally read the spin just before the bull tossed his massive horns to the left, trying to throw his lanky rider.

"Ride 'im, Dally," Augusta yelled with all the others, too caught up in the excitement of the moment. She'd forgotten how thrilling it was to watch such a match of muscle and horn against a man's greater will. She also forgot that she was in the stomping line and left little room for escape. Hell Fire was coming strong and straight for her.

Realizing her mistake, Augusta darted to the left, taking a flying leap at the top of the chute but knowing she wasn't going to make it.

A gun went off. A clown appeared on either side of her. She heard her name yelled. Then something struck the back of her leg, sending her crashing over the wooden fence.

Augusta landed in the mud, face-first. It took her a moment to realize the wind had been knocked out of her. She gasped, sucking in damp air and spitting out bits of foul-tasting stuff she prayed was straw. Something hot and slimy oozed down the neck of her costume, but she was afraid to turn. Afraid that Hell Fire stood just behind her, blowing hot fury and ready to gouge her with horns.

A body hurdled next to her, grabbing her, lifting her. "Gus, are you okay? Did he hurt you? Talk to me, Redhead."

Dally's hands were all over her, checking, testing, making sure she could stand. The clowns rushed over to help her to her feet.

"I-I'm all right," she finally told them, spinning around to make sure they were all out of danger. If the fence had been any less sturdy, Hell Fire would have locked horns with a few of her ribs. She took a step away and started to raise her hands to wave at the crowd to assure them she was unhurt, but her right leg gave way. "Ouch."

Dally pushed the clowns aside and swept her up into his arms. "Where are your folks?" he asked, before she could utter a single word of protest.

She couldn't let him take her to her parents. Maddy might be there and she wanted time to tell him about her.

"No, it will just frighten them," she said. "It's just the back of my leg. I'll be okay. No need to worry them. Take me to Clown Alley."

"No." He headed for somewhere closer, a line of tents set up near the springs. "You almost got freight-trained by that bull. I need to see if he hooked you and anything's broken."

"Well, folks, it looks like Dally Angelo made his ride and won the girl for the dance," one of the onlookers said. "Some cowboys just get all the luck."

"Some luck." Augusta held tightly to Dally's shoulders, realizing how difficult it was for him to make much progress in the mud. "Sorry I'm such dead weight."

Dally halted in his tracks and stared down at her, for the first time allowing her to see the worry that etched his brow. "Choose better words when I'm carrying you, Gus, okay? Promise me you won't ever say such a thing again. That bull could've killed you."

And then it struck her and she couldn't resist saying it. No matter how much she loved him, no matter how much she'd made up her mind to let him have a true draw tomorrow. "It's not easy watching someone you love get hurt, is it?"

Chapter 8

She felt him stiffen. His boot slipped. Dally tried to correct the imbalance but the momentum forced her hands to unlock from around his neck. He couldn't regain his stride and catch her at the same time. They both went crashing to the mud, he to his knees, she on her backside.

"Just wonderful," she complained, once she caught her breath and tried to stand. Her leg hurt like sin, but she'd never admit it to the laughing hyena attempting to help her to her feet. At first she thought he had reacted to what she'd said about watching someone you love getting hurt and that it had made him lose his footing. Now it looked as if he had simply just tripped. "Quit laughing. It's going to take days to get this out of my costume, much less my hair."

Dally laughed harder, infuriating her when he started to walk away and leave her.

"I said, stop your—"

He turned and bent down to get something. All of a sudden, Dally spun around. A mudball sailed through the air and hit Augusta's right cheek. She opened her mouth to protest, then abruptly closed it, dodging the next wad of mud coming her way. Dally had already bent to grab a third handful when she decided to remind him that two could play the same game.

"So that's it, is it?" she countered and grabbed a handful. "You forget who you're slinging at, Angelo. I could always outwit, outrun, outthrow you any day of the week. So take your best shot."

The mud fight began in earnest. Chuckles and giggles riffled the space that divided them as each projection of wet, Texas dirt hurdled through the air to make contact. The rain persisted, only adding to their muddy mess. Augusta laughed hardest when Dally tried to close the space that divided them and his boots kept slipping and sending him crashing to the ground.

"Better be careful there, partner," she teased. "You won't sit old Bone Buster tomorrow if you keep slipping on your saddle. Want to give up now while you're ahead?"

"I haven't lost a mud fight with you yet, Redhead," he reminded, a grin splitting his face from ear to ear. "And the dirtier you get, the more I get to wash off. Remember?"

She did remember. All too well. Some of their best love-making happened after bathing the mud off each other. "No fair, Cowboy. Trying to distract your opponent with sweet talk. My hair's red, remember? I got a temper that doesn't cool down so easy."

"And I know just the way to cool that temper." Dally nearly stumbled again as he reached her.

"Better practice up on some of that swagger, Angelo," she laughed, helping him get to his feet despite her intention to resist his playfulness, "or you'll just be kicking up dirt."

"You're the one who puts the swagger there, Gus. If I've lost it, it's because I thought I'd lost you."

Time seemed to stand still between them, the rain washing away the past heartaches that made her want to ignore how close he stood, how utterly desperately she wanted just to lean into him and give herself to the swell of emotions that had been banked for far too long. The dark mass of his hair hung to his collar, his shoulders drenched from the drizzle of rain. But Dally had never looked as handsome to Augusta as he did now. He appeared as vulnerable as she felt. His eyes said he missed her as much as she had missed him. Desire ignited through Augusta, warding off the chill of all that had kept them apart.

"I missed you, Redhead."

The huskiness in his voice rippled along the surface of her skin in pebbled gooseflesh, its white-hot seduction surging through her bloodstream. She swallowed and licked her lips, her heart gripping at the sincerity in his tone.

Their gazes collided. "I'm sorry," their apologies echoed in unison.

"You first," Dally whispered, his lips pressing a kiss against her forehead, her eyes, against her neck.

A shiver of longing raced through Augusta and it was all she could do to remain standing. But she had to tell him. Had to find somewhere to begin to explain what she'd done and why she'd done it.

Augusta fidgeted, her body tensing as she realized that her confession might very well put an end to all this. And she wanted so deeply for this closeness to last. Just a moment longer. A lifetime if it could.

The prairie around them looked freshly washed, and she was filled with hope that the old had been cleansed away and somehow the moment was full of new promises. Her heart began to sing, her blood seemed to hum with some long dormant but well-remembered rhythm.

Dally smiled at the expression softening the contours of Augusta's face, aware of the exact moment she opened her heart to him again. "Let's go see about your leg, love, before I lose something more than a mud fight. You keep looking at me like that and I'm going to lose any sense I've got left. Otherwise, I'm going to throw you over my shoulders and carry you off to my tent and not come out for days."

She simply nodded and let him lead her by the hand, past the Double D camp to the privacy of his tent.

They spoke little while he pulled up her trouser leg and checked where she pointed that it hurt. Deciding that Hell Fire's head must have caught the backside of her leg but didn't break skin, Dally told her that it looked like it would be a nasty bruise but nothing more. She was lucky. No broken bones or gores.

"Would you like a drink?" Dally offered, retrieving a bottle of whiskey he had stashed away to use for medicinal purposes. He offered her the amber liquid. "It will take an edge of the pain away."

"I didn't think you drank before you rode." She was surprised to discover Dally kept a bottle of liquor among his things.

"I mostly use it to cauterize wounds or sterilize my knife." Dally opened the bottle, took a swig, then offered it to her. "But I'm not against enjoying it when it'll ease some pain."

She looked up, wondering what pain had instigated the swig he just took. She knew, but she didn't want to admit to being the cause of it. Augusta accepted the bottle and took a drink, tasting the essence of Dally on the bottle's rim. She closed her eyes, savoring the taste. "Hmm," a moan escaped her as she gave in to the memory.

"Good?"

"Delicious," she admitted. Let him think what he would. She knew what really drove her hunger.

"Hope I'm not disturbing anything," a familiar voice announced from outside the tent. "Augusta, could I talk to you a minute?"

Startled and embarrassed, she hadn't even heard anyone approach. She hoped he hadn't heard her moaning and misunderstood. "Of course," she finally answered and handed Dally back the bottle.

She tried to smooth down her hair but the wet muddy

strands did nothing but practically stand straight up as if they were railroad spikes. *Oh yeah, right. I look quite fetching, I'll bet.* "Why didn't you tell me I looked a sight?" she shot Dally a woeful glare.

"You look damned beautiful to me."

She swatted away Dally's hand as it reached out to pull her toward him just as Joey entered the tent. The clown stopped in his tracks and stared at both of them.

"What happened to you two? Did you get plowed through the mud?" When the flap swung back and left them in virtual darkness, he added, "You gonna light a lantern so you can see?"

"We weren't haven't any trouble seeing a thing." Dally's tone held a hint of unfriendliness toward the intruder.

The two men obviously didn't care much for the other, though she knew them both to be good people. Why was it men always felt they had to challenge one another? Why couldn't they believe a woman could love one man and simply be good friends with another? If she and Dally were ever going to be truly happy together, that was one thing she would have to get straight with him. She had men friends. Just no male lovers other than Dally. Served him right for being the jealous sort.

"We were just checking to see if Hell Fire did much damage to my leg," she told her friend. "It's only a bad bruise and won't be any more trouble than that time the donkey kicked me. In fact, come to think of it, it's the same leg. So, if you came to see if I'm okay, I am. No need to concern yourself any further. We have things well in hand."

Joey hesitated, not taking the hint to leave. "You sure you don't want me to walk you back to town?"

"If she needs walking, I'll walk her back."

"Then you're not going to join your *parents* for the dance?"

When Joey stressed the word parents, Augusta really knew he was asking about when she would return to Maddy.

"Tell them I'll check in later. To enjoy their evening and go ahead and go on to bed. Don't wait up for me. Like Dally said, he'll see me home."

"All right then," Joey relented. "If you think that's best, but could I talk to you a moment . . . alone?"

"I'll be at the spring, washing off." Dally moved past the clown and shoved open the tent flap. "Looks like the rain has let up."

"What's so important that you couldn't say it in front of him?" Augusta asked, not holding her tone to a whisper after Dally exited. She would keep nothing from him any longer. She'd promised herself that tonight would change things and now was as good a time as any.

"Are you sure this is what you want, Augusta?" Joey stood like a silent sentinel ready to guard her from all comers. "He's what you want?"

"He's always been who I want, Joey. That's never been any question about that." Augusta knew before the words came out of her mouth that she'd finally determined the reason she was willing now to meet Dally more than halfway. "I just finally realized that I've got to love him enough to let him have his ride. That all this time I've been chastising him for thinking it would bring Flint back, when all along I've been guilty of believing that *not* letting him ride would somehow save him and give me more time with him. All it's done was pull us apart. I'd rather have tonight in his arms, Joey, than years more of waiting for and wondering about what could have been."

"What if he doesn't understand about Maddy?"

"Then he's not the man I think he is."

"I only want what's best for you, Augusta."

"Dally Angelo is what's best for me, Joey. He always has been."

"As long as you love him, then I'll back off and not say another word."

It was then that Augusta realized that Joey had cared for her more than just as a friend. "I'm sorry, Joey, I didn't know."

He shrugged. "Don't be. I've always known the truth. I just figured that cowboy of yours would somehow mess it up. Guess he's got more luck than he gives himself credit for."

Joey disappeared into the night, leaving Augusta with a sense of sadness that she'd caused him pain. She left the tent and crossed the distance to the springs and stood directly behind Dally. He stiffened as she slipped her arms around his waist and pressed her cheek against his broad back. His shirt was damp and cold from the rain, the skin beneath it drawing her fingers to its warmth. She could feel his every breath, heard the exact moment the steady beat of his heart sped up to match the racing of her own.

"I love you, Dally."

"I've never believed any different. But what about this thing with Bone Buster?"

"I'll watch you ride him if that's what you want."

Dally braced his feet as if warding off an attack. An untruth. "I need to understand why this sudden change of heart, Gus."

She gently brushed his arms, urging him to face her, to slip them around her and pull her closer. She leaned back into the curve of his embrace, letting her gaze take in the blue of his eyes, the heaven waiting at his lips. "Because I discovered there's something we all fear beyond our control and that's death. Bone Buster represents that to you. There's nothing we can do to conquer it, Dally. Riding him any time will never make you any stronger a man than you already are."

She saw the hurt in his eyes, the wish that there was no truth in the words she spoke now. "It's only now that I realized that I'm chasing the same fear. I was losing you every day of the four years I'd spent trying not to watch you ride that brindle and, maybe, kill yourself in the trying. If I blame you for keeping us apart, then I have to do the same of myself. Don't you see, Dally. I'd rather have tonight with you than any other years without you."

Her eyes flooded with tears as she searched his face for a sign of understanding, of acceptance. "It's just that simple. I finally grew up. *Wised* up."

Dally's gaze seemed to study her, gauging her in some way. "I'd give the ride up forever if I thought you really mean this."

Their lips met instantly. Augusta's arms flew up to wrap themselves around his neck as he crushed her against him. His tongue traced the seam of her lips until she opened her mouth and met its delicious heat with her own. A heady feeling engulfed her, overwhelming Augusta with a need so torrid, she thought she would melt in his arms.

She moaned against Dally's lips, shoving her hands into his hair and pulling him closer. As she tasted him deeper, he swept her into his arms, carrying her toward the tent.

"Make love to me here on the bank," she whispered, "like we did when we were so happy."

"There aren't any wildflowers or clover."

"I don't care," she muttered, unbuttoning his shirt as he lowered her to the ground. "We can use this."

He stripped off his shirt and spread it like a blanket, worshipping her with his eyes. Augusta sucked in her breath in anticipation of his touch, her fingers fumbling with the buttons of her padded costume to unfasten them.

It was then she noticed the string of rawhide around his neck, the ring that dangled there. Tears rushed to well in her eyes. "You still have it."

His smile alone could hold her captive. "I've worn it since the day you threw it at me."

Dally lifted it from his head and took her left hand. With the gentlest of movements, he slid the ring over her finger and pressed a kiss that fanned his breath over her knuckles. "This is where it belongs. Forever."

Augusta laughed with the pure joy of the moment, then kissed him fiercely, wanting to seal the pledge their hearts were making. Suddenly, a fierce impulse to press him closer overwhelmed her. She began to tug the buttons loose from his waistband.

Without breaking the kiss, Dally started working the clown costume off her shoulders and down her arms. When she realized what he was about, her fingers raced to help him.

He gently halted her hands. "No, there's no hurry, love. Let's take all the time we want. All the time we need."

Ever so slowly, Dally peeled away the garments that hindered their closeness, letting them fall one by one to form a blanket against the moist earth.

"I've missed you so much," Augusta whispered in a heated rush. "I've waited . . . wanted you to touch me again for so long."

He heard the words from somewhere far away. She was welcoming him back into her heart, into her life, and the forgiveness in her heart gladdened him, brought a sting of tears to his eyes. He pressed his length against her and kissed her ever so gently, the miracle of her love tasting like heaven on his lips.

Augusta's hands traced a trail across the expanse of his shoulders, down the flat plain of his abdomen to explore the wanting it took everything he had within him to control. In a move rougher than he intended, Dally covered her mouth with his, his tongue driving between her lips to taste and savor. Augusta moaned, her arms wrapping themselves around his neck. He wanted to inhale her, to consume her, to absorb her until there was nothing left of either of them but one all-enveloping flame.

Dally held her fast, unable to let her go now that she was in his arms. She belonged to him. She had bound herself to him since the first day he met her and he had gladly born those reins of friendship and, ultimately, love.

Augusta tore his lips from his long enough to demand the one thing she wanted more than anything in this word. "Make love to me again, Dally. I want to know where I belong. To know I'm yours."

He nuzzled her neck, scattering kisses along her jaw, tracing his tongue around the lobe of her ear, branding her with a desire all his own.

She moaned, urging Dally to capture her lips again and kiss her long and hard. His hands explored the silky length of her, along her sides, caressing one nipple until it strained against his thumb. She clung to him, wordlessly begging for more. Dally bent to suckle one hardened peak, then the other, causing her to cry out with need. He slid down the length of her, kissing his way to the hollow of her abdomen, nipping until she whispered his name over and over again.

As his hot tongue moved over her, Augusta's flesh felt as if it were set afire. She gripped his shoulders, clinging to him in an effort to ground herself, but her senses swirled unrestrained. She wrapped her legs around his hips to draw him even closer, writhing against him in desire.

Dally moaned, his hands cupping her hips and lifting her to him, probing the intimate welcome she offered him. Like a moth drawn to the flame, Augusta thrust her hips toward him, gasping when he filled her so completely. Suddenly he held still, and Augusta sensed that he was remembering. Remembering how eager they had been as teens to learn the ways of love. Remembering how well their bodies strove to please and teach each what the other liked. Remembering the wonder of their joining.

She could endure the wait no longer. Softly, she implored, "Please, darling, I've waited so long for you."

Before the exquisite torture drove her over the edge, he silenced her with a savage growl of a kiss as he claimed her completely. She swelled around his length and together they began to move in a rhythm never once forgotten but kept sacredly stored away until just this moment, for just them.

He whispered endearments in her ear, forever imprinting themselves in Augusta's heart. The tension mounted as she met his driving thrusts. Higher and higher they climbed toward some unfathomable release. "Please," she entreated against his lips, knowing that he knew exactly what she was asking of him.

Just as she thought she might scream from the pure pleasure of being in his arms, Dally buried himself deep within her. She began to shudder. The world seemed to shatter as she clung to him, crying out his name.

Several minutes passed before their ragged breathing subsided. Dally kissed her slowly, reverently, drawing himself up on his elbows to look deeply into her eyes. Alive with light and shadow from the moonlight, his body glimmered. Augusta licked her lips in anticipation of tasting the sated essence of Dally.

His lips curled into a smile that set her heart to pounding so loudly, she was certain it could be heard by everyone at the Double D encampment. But she didn't care. Staring back at her from the blue depths of Dally's eyes was a love so bold, she would never, ever let anything, anyone keep her from his arms again.

Tears stung her eyes as powerful as the emotion giving voice to the ecstasy she shared with him. "I won't let anything ever keep us apart, Dally," she pledged. "I promise."

Dally's fingers traced the tip of her nose, down her jaw, to spread across her abdomen. His gaze followed the trail his hands had made, stopping at each place to lay equal claim. He gently smoothed the old scar where she'd been horned by a billy goat. He drew a figure eight around her navel. His fingertips traced the marks where her belly had been stretched to make room for Maddy.

Augusta tensed. Dally's hand jerked away. The one thing, the only thing that might make a liar out of her just had.

The truth about Maddy just might be the one thing that could break them apart . . . this time forever.

Chapter 9

Reality sank in, turning the passion that had seared his blood only seconds before to ice harder than hailstones. Those were not the injuries from a rodeo wreck but the marks of a woman who had borne a child.

The thought of her keeping such a secret from him stabbed a wound so deep within Dally that he couldn't seem to breathe. He had to move, to get away from her. He needed time to think. Dally rolled over, rose silently and put on his pants, unable to find words to express the betrayal he felt.

Why hadn't she told him? Why had she hid the fact from him? Her child was probably traveling with the Garrisons. He knew Gus well enough to know that she would never be far from her flesh and blood. That would certainly explain why she hadn't wanted him to pay his respects at the hotel. She must have known he would spot a little one that looked like her.

Dally's stomach knotted as if someone had punched a fist there. God knew he and Augusta had talked about having kids and what they would name them—Maddy, for her mother, if the first one had been a girl, Flint for his father, if they'd been lucky enough to have a boy. They'd planned to have a herd of them, the more the merrier.

The thought that some other man had been given that

privilege, had spoiled his dream, hurt like nothing else Dally had ever felt. He glanced back at Augusta and noticed she was getting dressed, not saying anything, not looking at him. His attention riveted to her hands. She wore no wedding ring but his.

The small pleasure that filled him didn't last long because he didn't want to know what her lack of another ring really meant. Had she married someone and repeated her pattern by leaving him? Or had she carried the child without the benefit of a ring? Did she still have any feelings for the man? The image of Joey loomed large in Dally's mind as he recalled how much Augusta had shared her confidence with him.

"Is that why you refused to give me an answer to my question all these years?" The betrayal finally took voice and he hated that he sounded so pathetically vulnerable.

Her eyes lifted and focused on Dally, the moonlit blue of their depths awash with a sheen of tears. "I couldn't agree to marry you when there were things to make right between us. You were bent on riding the bull, and I"—she paused as if she were mustering strength—"I had hidden something from you that might break us apart forever when you learn the truth."

Dally wasn't sure he could listen to anymore. Listening seemed harder than strapping a bellrope around a rank bull with a reputation. She'd been right about what she'd said concerning having to wait. Waiting to hear what she might say now was nothing but pure hell.

Grab horn, he told himself. *If she can find the grit to tell you, then you can find the courage to saddle up and listen.*

"I caused F-Flint's death," she sobbed.

Of all the things he'd expected her to say that wasn't it. He felt like he was crow-hopping, one buck worse than the next. She had a baby without him. She caused his father's death?

"I knew he wanted to ride Bone Buster that day," she began slowly, tears streaming down her cheeks. "My father and several of our hands had gathered up a purse and bet no one could ride the brindle. Flint was almost the first one to take up the challenge and he bragged to everybody that he would give the purse to you and me so we could marry and have a better start on our own place than your folks did."

Dally cursed. "I told him I wouldn't accept the money unless I could match it dollar for dollar."

"I knew that, Dally. I even agreed with you, but your father wouldn't hear any different. He was as stubborn about making the draw as you've been about riding the bull." She reached out to Dally, but he didn't take her hand, his arms folding across his chest stubbornly.

"I knew he'd never be satisfied till he made the ride," her voice squeaked with a tension that caused her to start pacing. "He told me that nothing I could say would make him change his mind. So I did the one thing within my power. I asked my father if I could handle the hat and draw for the rides."

She sighed, letting out a long, slow stream of breath. "I tucked the scrap of paper with Bone Buster's name on it inside the inner lining so that I could draw the bull's name whenever I chose." She faced him, her eyes full of anguish. "I couldn't stand not to give him what he wanted since he was being so single-minded about it. Don't you see, Dally. I deliberately chose Bone Buster for Flint. I caused him to die."

Dally's stone-carved face triggered Augusta's worst fear. She'd lost him. He'd never forgive her interference. Never forgive her for trying to control the outcome of their future by being so stupid.

"Didn't you think we loved each other enough to find another way? To give me time to find a way to make our life together?"

"Is that it? You're not going to blame me for helping him die, but you're infuriated because I didn't give you enough time? You're angry because I didn't trust you?" Yet his accusation rang true. She hadn't trusted him. Hadn't believed in him. Thought him too young at seventeen to deal with the fact that there was a reason their marriage should happen more quickly than they'd planned.

If he was this hurt by knowing she'd rigged the drawing, how much more so would he be when she told him about Maddy? This was too much. Her emotions were too raw. They both needed time away from each other. Maybe morning would bring better sense to all this. Maybe then she could decide to tell him the rest.

"Please forgive me about the drawing, Dally. I never meant to hurt you or your family."

His legs were now apart, his hands deep in his pockets, his shoulders rigid as if he were bracing for a showdown. "Then I'm guessing that you've rigged the drawings where I'm concerned too."

She nodded. "Every time you showed up at a competition where we took Bone Buster."

"You were at every one?"

"If I wasn't, I made sure you didn't make the draw."

"You going to keep your hands out of it tomorrow? Let somebody else draw?"

"I tried to tell you I would earlier when I said maybe tomorrow would be a luckier day for you. I had already planned to let fate decide."

"And I'm supposed to believe that now just because you say it."

"Only you can decide what you choose to believe." Everything she'd ever hoped for was no more. They had no future together if he wasn't willing to trust her again. Augusta took one last, long look at him, feeling a crushing sense of sadness as she realized that lack of trust was its own death.

Dally couldn't sleep. He'd tried to shut away his thoughts but failed miserably. As the first light of dawn shone beyond the walls of his tent, he decided to go ahead and get up for the day. Maybe a walk would do him good. It sure couldn't hurt.

He glanced at his saddlebags and thought about packing up his gear and getting the hell out of Kasota Springs. But he was a man who faced his troubles and refused to let lies run him off. Best thing for him to do was stay and find out what else Augusta Garrison had kept from him.

Restless and angry, he exited the tent and strode past the still sleeping Double D encampment. Only Sam was stirring about. The cook had probably been up for hours preparing the morning meal that would come sooner than some of the sleepers preferred. He'd heard dancers returning to camp long past midnight and some of them had clearly imbibed in libations.

Dally glanced toward the half tent that rose over Slim Doogan's bedroll and wished that his friend was already awake. He needed someone to talk to. Someone he could trust. But the stringbean was snoring loudly. The man had taken a lot or ribbing about not riding Bone Buster. His friend deserved a decent rest from all the jeering.

Dally peered past the encampment to search for the rooftop of the Springs Hotel. Maybe he ought to have himself a long talk with his old friends, the Garrisons. He'd bet they'd have a thing or two to say on the subject of their grandchild. Why hadn't they mentioned the fact to Dally? He knew Augusta well enough that had the subject come up, she would have never asked them to lie to him. But he couldn't put them in that awkward situation. They'd never been anything but kind to him and his parents.

Hell, he didn't even know if Gus had given birth to a girl or a boy.

A child. Augusta's child. Envy, unlike any he'd ever known, filled Dally. No matter how hard he tried, he couldn't get Joey's image or the possibility of his being Augusta's lover out of his mind. He would have chuckled at the image of a miniature clown with face paint running around Gus's dress skirts, but this was no laughing matter.

What did the kid look like? Did he have Augusta's red hair? Was he smart as a whip like Augusta or have her ability to do acrobatics? What if the child was a girl? Did she make that same funny snort Gus did when she was tickled? Did she have her mother's fetching blue eyes?

Dally wanted to know the child, wanted to become part of his or her life. It didn't matter that *he* wasn't the father. He wanted to be, *needed* to be the man who had the privilege of helping Augusta raise her child. Would she ever consider the possibility?

The thought of Gus sharing her life with some other man hurt like nothing else Dally had ever felt before. He'd always thought of her as his. She'd said she was, didn't she? Less than seven hours ago. Was that a lie too?

Weary of questions that had no answers, he headed toward the maze of wooden chutes that held the rodeo stock. He needed somewhere to vent the crushing weight of unhappiness that enveloped him, and there was only one thing that sprang to mind that might satisfy such a need for now. To confront Bone Buster. Right now. Without the benefit of an audience. Without the approval of the woman he loved. Maybe he could ride this hell out of his system.

But as he neared the chutes, he saw Augusta standing at the brindle's pen, her outline a beauty unlike he'd ever known. Her hair cascaded like an auburn waterfall past her shoulders. She was dressed in a riding skirt and blouse the color of her eyes.

He didn't speak but simply strode past her, hitching his boot on the low rung of the chute and throwing his weight up to hurdle the top.

"What are you doing?" she demanded, grabbing his shirt and yanking him backward.

He didn't let her have her way, holding tightly to the chute.

Finally, Dally leaned back and stared at her. "I'm going to ride the bull. Here and now."

"I'm not going to stop you," she said slowly, "but we need to talk first."

"The time for talking is over."

"I didn't tell you everything, Dally. There's more you have to know." She pointed toward the tents of Clown Alley. "Could we go inside. I'm cold."

Her cheeks were pale, her eyes bright with something other than tears. They'd made love last night in the rain and mud. He didn't like that his first concern was worry and concern about her welfare. "You should've worn a shawl."

"I'm finding out lately that I should have done a lot of things differently." She made a move toward the tents. "Couldn't your ride wait till we've had a cup of coffee?"

He didn't agree; he just started walking toward the tents. The large one where she kept her props and costumes offered little warmth and was no more inviting than when they'd been out-side. "You already got a fire going or do I need to start one?"

She grabbed a blanket from out of one of the trunks and wrapped it around her. "There's a pot on the tripod still warm from Cookie's fire. I try not to build one inside the tent unless I know I'm going to be here awhile to make sure the fire goes out when I'm finished."

Dally waited until she poured two mugs of coffee and of-fered him one, sipping the brew with more gratitude than he felt at the moment. He took a seat on top of one of the trunks, waiting for her to tell him what he was doing here.

Damned if she didn't look as pretty as he'd ever seen her. "You feeling okay? You look a little pie-eyed."

"I didn't sleep well."

"That makes two of us."

"I'm sorry."

"I'll get over it." He didn't mean to sound so curt, but he was tired of all this polite conversation

"You have a right to be angry with me," she said, twisting one end of the blanket between her fingers. "And I want you to know this was the hardest thing I ever kept from you." Augusta took a deep breath and met his gaze. "You have a daughter. Her name is Maddy."

A daughter. Named after Mrs. Garrison. The baby was his. Hearing Augusta's confession didn't make it any easier to accept.

He thought he'd feel pleased that he would have the honor of being in her child's life. He thought he'd be jumping in his boots with gladness that there hadn't been another man involved. Instead he only felt an overwhelming sense of being cheated.

"How old is she?"

"Three and a half. I had just found out that I was with child the day your father died."

Almost four. Joey's words came back to haunt Dally. The man was trying to tell him. He'd been trying to be a friend while still not betraying Augusta's confidence. Dally owed the man a huge apology.

"I couldn't tell you that day, Dally. I just couldn't. Then when you said you were going to ride Bone Buster or die trying, I . . . well, I knew I had to protect her from losing you. Just like you lost Flint."

"Protect her from losing me?" He bolted to his feet, slamming the mug of coffee down on the trunk. The liquid would have burned him if it had been any hotter. He'd have had hell riding the bull. "Dammit, Augusta, you cheated me out of three and a half years of her life."

"I had to think of Maddy." Her eyes glared at him as sharp as an eagle's protecting her nest. "Think about it, Dally. Can you imagine how it would be if you had ridden Bone Buster and died? She would have just known you long enough to care. This way, well . . . she never knew you. Never loved you enough to have to feel the hurt you experienced after Flint's death."

"It should have been my choice," he argued, slamming one fist into the other. "You don't know how things could have been."

"I know that you wouldn't have let anything, not even Maddy, make you give up the ride."

"The sad thing is that I would have, Gus." His heart spoke for him. "If I'd been given a chance. She was life. And I would always choose to protect what was best for our baby. I love you, dammit. I wouldn't have loved her any less. I want to know her, Augusta. To be part of her life."

Augusta's eyes glistened, tears turning them a deeper shade of blue. "I know you do."

"So where do we go from here?"

She patted the seat beside her. "Could we sit and talk together? Without yelling?"

He took a seat beside her. "So talk."

Her eyes searched his. "Do you forgive me about Flint?"

All night he'd thought about what she'd done and couldn't fault her for trying to give the man his opportunity. "I'd have done the same if given the chance. Nothing would have stopped him from making the ride, we both know that."

"I was scared, Dally. Seventeen, scared and stupid. Can you forgive me for not trusting you and walking away?"

Maybe if he hadn't been so intent upon doing things his way, been too proud to accept the money. Maybe if he hadn't been so afraid that everything was out of his control, he would have been more aware of how she needed him. The fact that he'd failed her miserably was something he had to live with the rest of his life. "I was scared too," Dally admitted, wrapping his arm around her trembling body. "Afraid that I couldn't handle everything life threw at me, no matter how hard it came."

Dally confessed that his pursuit of the bull led nowhere but to a future without Augusta. "Don't you see? If riding Bone

Buster means losing you and Maddy for good, then I lose and my father rode for nothing. Bone Buster would win twice."

To his surprise, she grabbed his hand, stood and pulled. "Come on, I've got something I want you to do."

He allowed her to lead him back to the Spring's Hotel. When they reached the lobby, she told him to wait there and she'd be right back. Minutes later, she came rushing back with a little girl cradled at her hip. The child was dressed in a Stetson the same color as Dally's, with big expressive blue eyes the shade of a clear Texas sky peeping up at him. Lustrous curls of red curled from beneath the Stetson.

"T-This is Maddy," Augusta's said tentatively, though her face beamed with pride as she introduced father to daughter. "And, Maddy, this is Dally Angelo."

"He's got a name just like me."

So Augusta had given Maddy his last name. Pride unlike any he'd ever known compelled Dally to pull Augusta into his arms and look at his daughter in wonder. "Will you please tell your mama to answer me, yes or no?"

Staring at the woman whose face would always be the most beautiful to him, no matter if she wore painted freckles and a big, fat nose or she looked as lovely as she did now, he asked, "Which is it, Gus. Will you marry me or not? Yes or no?"

"Let's leave it to the luck of the draw, shall we? Maddy take off your hat and turn it over." Augusta's laugh ended in a snort, instigating an echo from her daughter.

At the sound, Dally grinned from ear to ear. Maddy was her mother's daughter. He couldn't wait to see how much of her was like him.

Maddy held the hat out to him upside down as instructed. He looked inside and there in a dozen pieces of paper or more was all the answer he'd been hoping to hear. On every single piece of paper one word had been written . . . *yes.*

"Mommy said to draw one."

Epilogue

Augusta watched as Slim Doogan and Gill Puckett loaded Bone Buster into the chute. Each man was pulling for Dally and all attention was riveted on the rank bull. The beast bellowed discontent against the confined space, kicking its hooves and trying to lock horns with the wooden prison to free itself.

Anticipation hung in the air as all eyes watched Dally throw his leg over the brindle and tighten his suicide wrap around his hand.

Augusta's eyes met Dally's, and she gave him a thumb's up. She and two other tramps, Joey among them, were positioned on each side of the corral to play bullfighter if Dally got into trouble.

Dally patted the pocket of his vest where he'd placed his mama's note and gave Augusta a brief nod of thanks for patching up his father's vest so that he could wear it for the ride.

"Let 'im go, boys, let 'im go!" Dally yelled, giving the signal that he was ready.

The flag went down. The gate swung open. Augusta's gaze latched on Dally's face. She forgot to breathe, forgot to blink, forgot that she stood seconds away from danger herself.

A ton of muscle and fury left the chute fast, sunfishing into the air so high that she could see the brindle's underbelly. Then just as quickly as he'd reared left, Bone Buster sucked back and changed directions, kicking his hind legs so high she was sure he would flip forward. Dally had his hands full just to stay seated but, to Augusta's surprise and great relief, he settled into a spurring lick, matching the action of the animal, buck for buck.

Unable to unseat his rider, the bull hurled himself toward Joey. He was a headhunter that one, looking for someone to vent his fury upon. The bull just didn't want to throw Dally, he meant to hurt someone in the process. Joey dodged, Augusta darted, the other clown started hollering like a squealing piglet as he ran out of the raging bull's path.

Some help they were. If the clowns continued to help the bull riders, they were going to have to be braver souls than the three of them.

Dally held on, bending so far backward that Gus thought he would surely lose his hat. Bone Buster's shoulders rolled one way, his haunches the other.

"Seven," the crowd began to chant. "Eight . . ."

"Nine," Augusta counted with them, tears erupting in her eyes as she dashed out of harm's way. The gun went off, the flag dropped. "Ten seconds!" she yelled. "Dally, you did it. You rode him."

A cheer went up over the countryside when Dally removed his hat and fanned the beast's head, the worst insult a cowboy could give an animal he rode. Finally, Dally threw his Stetson high into the air in exaltation. He bailed off the bull, ran straight for Augusta and gave her a resounding kiss for all the world to see.

"Way to go, Angelo," yelled Slim from the gates. "Kiss the gal and break that old brindle."

Together Dally and Augusta hurdled the fence and found themselves laughing and holding each other in pure delight.

Something stronger than fear had defeated the mankiller today and both of them knew what had conquered the beast— their love.

"Hey, Dally, look at me," Maddy hollered, trying to catch his attention. "Think I can ride 'im?"

Augusta looked over to where her daughter played with several other small children. Each rode atop a lamb no bigger than its mother's knobby knees, doing their best imitation of Dally's ride.

"You'll ride that woolly, sweetheart. You come from a lucky family." Dally laughed again, wrapping his arm around Augusta and staring proudly at their child. "And that's *Daddy*, darlin'. Not Dally."

Author's Note

My readers often ask me how I get ideas. I wanted to share with you how I got this one. After we experienced the tragic passing of my youngest brother, my older brother had to find a way to deal with his grief. The way he did that was through a cowboy song he wrote. I was so touched by this that I asked him if I could write a novel about Dally. Such a hero deserved to have a special heroine to love him. With my brother's permission, I share his song with you.

Thanks, Jim, for allowing me to give Dally the love and resolution he deserves.

"Ki Yi, Ki Yi"

All he had from his momma
he had folded in his shirt.
A saved piece of paper held the words his momma wrote.
"Son, you were such a little guy
on Daddy's roping steer you'd ride.
Daddy laughed and yelled, 'Son, do or die.'
You'd holler back, 'Ki yi, ki yi.'"

Dally gathered up his rigging.
It was time to rodeo.
Strapped it on that killing Brahman
that took his daddy's soul.
Bull bucked the chute in anger.
Cowboy's face was full of fear.
He remembered Momma's promise,
"I know your Daddy. He'll be near.
There's no guarantee.
You just ride on luck and skill.
You got to bow your head and ask the Good Lord
to bless you, if He will."

He was born to ride; it was Daddy's life.
Swing that gate and let him go.
Lord, that cowboy's gold was the bull he rode.
Hey, long live rodeo.
Cowboy cry, "Ki yi, ki yi."
Keep the Good Lord's spirit deep inside.
God is your strength: Fear knows no pride.
Fire up and ride!
"Ki yi, ki yi."

By permission of Jimmy Williams, November 2008

TEXAS
TEMPEST
Linda Broday

Chapter 1

The smell of dust mingled with brimstone as McKenna Smith rode past the cemetery that perched on a rise above Kasota Springs, Texas. Under the midday sun, he paused to wipe the sweat from his eyes.

A lone woman caught his attention as she stooped to lay fresh flowers on the last of five neatly lined graves that were separated from the rest of the dearly departed by an ornate iron fence. It wasn't that the smartly dressed woman bore the weight of grief, or that she wore a scarlet dress instead of the usual black mourning apparel, which caused the spit to dry in his mouth.

What brought discomfort was the way she lovingly brushed Panhandle dust from each tombstone. Those who rested beneath the soil evidently meant something special to her.

The lady spent time to keep the graves tidy.

McKenna's blood chilled. No one would give a damn when he passed on. No one would shed a tear. And no one would bring him as much as a smelly weed.

His would be a cold, untended grave on some rocky hillside. When the time came and he found himself in a corpse 'n cartridge condition, they just might leave him to the vultures where he fell without bothering to dig a hole. He'd used

up all his chances for a long peaceful life. He faced the harsh
reality that befalls the fate of someone like him, particularly
one who'd become a legend of sorts from outrunning the results of hard living and dodging bullets.

Not that he'd dodged them all. The pain in his shoulder was
quick to remind him.

The leather creaked when McKenna slid sideways in the
saddle. From beneath the low brim of his hat, his narrowed
gaze assessed the row of granite tombstones. It appeared the
climate in Kasota Springs was a tad on the unhealthy side,
either by disease or misfortune.

For a moment he pondered whether the bad luck was catching and considered bypassing the Panhandle town. He could
ride past and keep going. After all, he had a far piece to travel.
But he guessed one place was as fitting as another when it
came time to turn up his toes. The good Lord wouldn't care.

It didn't ease his mind any to know that every undertaker
from Cimarron to Austin kept his measurements in a handy
place, just itching to be the one to use them.

Suddenly, the petite mourner in the cemetery rose. She removed the sheer black veil that shrouded her features and
folded it carefully. Completing the ritual she'd likely repeated
umpteen times, she tucked it and her fancy handkerchief
inside the beaded bag on her arm and snapped it briskly shut
as if the handbag locked up the souls of her deceased kindred
and she was afraid they'd get out.

She met his curious stare, lazily peeling some flimsy, spi-
dery sort of gloves from each of her fingers.

A flush rose that she'd caught him watching. But, in truth,
he couldn't turn away. The slow, sexy way she skinned the bits
of lace away held him in a spell. She stripped out of one
person into another right before his eyes like an actress who
played many parts, with each involving costume changes.

McKenna's chest tightened from the quick intake of air.
The lady's fingers were long and well formed. They could

probably unkink all the knots in a lonely man's soul and take him straight into glory.

Damn, the woman invited too many thoughts of the purely sinful variety!

He was an authority on hands and long fingers. Take his for instance. He had calluses on the outside of his thumb where the gun handle molded into his palm much too often. But his fingers were nimble enough to undo the tiny row of buttons down a willing lover's dress so he could caress her skin.

Still holding his gaze, the striking grave-tender cocked her left eyebrow. Jamming the bits of black lace into her pocket, she flipped out a pair of rawhide work gloves and had them on in a flash. A jolt skittered up his spine the way a skittish horse danced around when a rider put his foot in the stirrup.

Before he could blink twice, she hitched up her skirts. Pulling the hem between her legs, she tucked the tail into her waistband to form the feminine equivalent of britches.

Her long stare never wavered from his face as if daring him to comment. Without waiting for one, she untied a spirited, bloodred bay from the fence.

Dumbfounded by the swift transformation from a sedate picture of womanhood into a scandalous wanton, he could do nothing but touch the brim of his hat and give her a nod with a quirk of his head. Had he gotten his tongue unglued from the roof of his mouth he might've spoken a word of greeting.

Except he couldn't.

Thrusting one dainty foot in the stirrup, she threw her leg over the saddle while the horse made a tight circle.

Someone oughta tell her that was too much horse for such a slight woman, although he wasn't fool enough to apply for the job. He had enough trouble without adding headstrong fillies to the list. It turned out he shouldn't have worried over her lack of ability. Expecting to have a ringside view to her unseating, he was once again surprised.

McKenna took a slow turn up and down the arresting

figure and her exposed length of leg as she applied a firm hand and calm voice to the bay.

Favoring McKenna with a glimpse of white teeth framed by a lush mouth, the colorful woman whirled, thundered down the hill and into the middle of the small town.

A swirl of grit, aided by the sweltering July wind and the tramping of cattle below in the stockyards, momentarily blocked his vision. It took a second for the air to clear.

With the cemetery sitting up high, it provided a good view of Kasota Springs. He grinned at the mystery woman's breakneck speed that nearly knocked a man from his ladder. He teetered precariously, clutching the end of a banner that he was doing his damnedest to hang across the street.

Despite its drooping, McKenna read the lettering that proclaimed a July Fourth Cowboy Competition. He shifted his attention back to the horsewoman who'd reined up hard in front of a gathering of onlookers in front of the saloon and leaped off. From their black expressions they weren't too happy.

Now that he was alone with the dead, McKenna could satisfy his curiosity. He rode up to the row of graves and squinted.

Each of the five stones bore a name and below that was a simple line that read: *The Beloved Husband of Tempest.*

He reckoned he'd just met the Lady Tempest, even though they'd yet to speak. Five beloved husbands? And they were all dead. She must be rough as a cob. Didn't look it though at first glance. Only her brash display afterward told the tale. Her no-nonsense attitude told him she could wear out a whole regiment of battle-hardened soldiers.

Judging from the testament on the markers, she'd evidently done her best with one shy of a half dozen good souls.

Nudging his horse into a jog, McKenna proceeded into town, taking in all the hammering, sawing and the like. The town buzzed with more commotion than a hangman preparing for a big send off. But the charged atmosphere took on the makings of a riot when the man who'd been on the ladder climbed down in a stew and appeared ready to string up the pretty widow.

Pulling alongside the blood bay, McKenna eased from the saddle and tossed the reins over the hitching rail.

"I swear, Angus Murdoch, if you don't take down that sign I'll yank it down myself," bellowed the Lady Tempest, whose skirt sprang from the waistband and into a more proper position during the commotion. "You know what I told you to put on it and that's not close."

Mindful that he was in front of the saloon and a beer with an inch of foam on top had been in his dreams, he decided it would wait. The spirited woman was a sizzling lightning bolt that a man couldn't drag his attention from.

"Loosen your rigging a little, Miz LeDoux, before you have a runaway conniption. You ain't the only one with an opinion." The irate sign-hanger flushed. "No one ever called these celebrations a rodeo before. It's always been a cowboy competition or a cowboy reunion. The mayor said we gotta stick with one or the other. And his word is official."

"Yeah, Tempest. When you fill the mayor's shoes you can call it whatever you like," informed another exasperated onlooker who likely had to stand twice to make a shadow. The skinny fellow wore a carpenter's apron around his waist and clenched a handful of nails.

McKenna hooked his thumbs on his gunbelt, wondering how long it'd be before she made the carpenter mad enough to eat those nails. From the looks of it she was damn close.

If their looks could kill, she'd be maimed for life.

"Rodeo has a manlier ring to it. Cowboy Competition is just flat wimpy. The Spanish brought the word 'rodeo' with them when they came to Texas and if it was good enough for them, it's good enough for us." Tempest LeDoux jabbed a finger into Angus Murdoch's chest. "Now get it changed."

"Don't you order me around."

"I beg your pardon; the lady does have a point." McKenna rested his weight against the heavy rail constructed of railroad ties that were probably left over from when they brought Kasota Springs into the transportation age. Despite knowing she needed no help in saving herself from a bloodletting, he added his voice to hers. "Pecos changed theirs to the Pecos Rodeo and it gave the town's yearly occasion quite a boost."

Sure a damn sight better than cowboy reunion.

"Who the hell asked you?" The swelled up sign-hanger spun around, clearly intending to tear into McKenna. Instead, his Adam's apple worked hard to swallow when recognition came. His face drained. "Uh, never mind. You're probably right."

Flustered, Angus punched the carpenter who'd been venting his spleen and loudly whispered, "It's him."

"Him who?"

"The gunfighter, McKenna Smith. You know, the man that fitted that outlaw, Slim Pickford, with a coffin suit last year."

"Why do you reckon he's here?" the carpenter whispered back.

The lovely widow LeDoux turned and favored McKenna with a wink before she walloped the two. "It's rude to talk about someone, especially when he's within earshot. Number one, I might've invited him here. And number two, tend to your own rat killing and get busy changing this banner. I want it up before dark. Visitors start arriving tomorrow."

Angus Murdoch ground his teeth, jerking up the long piece of thick burlap. "Damn woman. Wouldn't be surprised if she hadn't tried to knock me off the ladder on purpose."

McKenna was hard-pressed to hide a grin. He wouldn't doubt it in the least.

The Little Lady with Texas-size character had livened up his day. He'd sure try not to tangle with her. While she hadn't specifically said she *had* brought him to Kasota Springs, she'd certainly implied it. She likely did that to pretend she was privy to information they didn't have.

Sounded about right. He couldn't be a hundred percent sure though.

But McKenna couldn't exactly recall the last time he got invited anywhere, least of all anyplace close to Cimarron, New Mexico, and the slew of enemies he made during the Colfax County War.

And by a woman? Well, the last time he got an invite she wasn't a lady. And he sure wasn't in some fancy parlor at the governor's mansion.

This time was different. Tempest LeDoux was clearly more woman than any man could tame.

Wouldn't pay to let her catch him saying that though.

Chapter 2

McKenna tumbled right into bottomless eyes the color of newly plowed earth and skidded to a stop.

The amused scrutiny Tempest LeDoux turned on McKenna almost made him swallow his spit sideways. And, yet, her smile appeared rusty as if she didn't get a chance to use it every day. One thing was crystal clear though, the sun seemed barely the flicker of a candle beside her sultry heat.

"Here for the rodeo, cowboy?" Her voice was like aged wine, mellow and smooth.

Dimples in her cheeks created little pockets and told him the lady could charm the pants off him and nary break a sweat. Speaking of sweat, he was mindful of his need for liberal use of soap and water. He added a bathhouse to his short list along with a shave before he rode on.

"Just passing through; don't expect to stay long enough to ride any wild horses, bulls or rocking chairs."

Tempest LeDoux definitely wasn't a shrinking violet. But then the graves lined in a row told him that. She was probably used to working fast.

He'd better make it clear real quick that he wasn't looking to be notch number six on her belt.

Even though he yearned to have someone care enough to

tend his grave, he'd have to draw the line when it came to marriage. His jaw hardened. Love maimed, it hurt and it destroyed.

But whiling away a few hours in pleasant company was another matter.

With the hitching post supporting his weight, he crossed his ankles, fished a match stem from his pocket and stuck it in the corner of his mouth. His gaze took a leisurely stroll down the petite figure. Pausing at her bosom, his throat went as dry as a sun-parched raisin. Her overendowment, confined by the snug fit of some sort of clingy material, molded each bosom as though they weren't covered at all.

Lord have mercy on a poor man!

Once he could go on, his measure of the flare of her hips suggested she could give him a run for his money and then some.

His glance returned to the curve of Tempest's rosy lips that were slightly parted in anticipation. Of a kiss maybe? Her pink tongue made an agonizing slow turn around them.

McKenna struggled to silence the need.

Then her mouth turned up unexpectedly in a smile as bright as gold flecks in a miner's pan. In that moment, he forgot everything except how much he hated the thought of an empty bed and an itch that hadn't been scratched in so long he couldn't recall.

"Most men say hello before they begin doing that."

"Doing what, ma'am?"

"Relieving me of my clothes."

A quirk lifted the corner of McKenna's mouth. He removed the match stem before he replied. "One thing you'll find out about me—I'm not most men. And you're in a category by itself from other women, if you don't mind me saying."

"I'd be real disappointed if you didn't."

"You don't fool me; you like being admired." He straightened, pushing away from the rail.

The top of her dark head almost reached his shoulders. Almost, but not quite. He spared a fleeting smile, preferring to keep things simple until he got acquainted.

This lady was a stick of dynamite sure as hell.

"Does it show that much?" Her voice was a breathy purr.

"Only to someone versed in the subject." Arching an eyebrow, he nudged his hat back with a forefinger. "Why did you let everyone believe that we have a business arrangement?"

"Those meddling old goats are worse than a patch of prickly pear, always looking for a chance to jab me. Wanted to rile 'em up a bit is all." Tempest slipped her arm through his. "Buy a lady a drink and tell me where you've been all my life."

The request, coupled by light pressure on his arm, was like slow, cool water trickling over baked rocks that thirsted for a bit of relief. Waves of pleasure tumbled through him, creating a roar in his ears that drowned out every lick of sense he had.

For a moment, he almost forgot the dry dust in his throat that a cool glass of beer could make a distant memory.

His longing glance at the local watering hole ended in a black scowl. The Slats and Fats Saloon looked far too rough and rowdy for a lady. Even though he didn't doubt Tempest could hold her own, he wasn't about to take her into that den of iniquity unless she left him no choice.

But if she insisted, he'd fight a pack of rabid coyotes to protect the widow who tended lonely graves.

McKenna swung her around, pointing her toward the hotel café across the street from Cattleman's Bank. "I prefer a good cup of Arbuckle. What I make can't be mentioned in the same breath as fresh ground coffee."

The lie slipped through his mouth like it'd been coated in axle grease.

Tempest knitted her brow and dug in her heels. "Don't you need something stronger to wash the grit from your teeth?

Most men prefer a stiff slug of whiskey coming off the hot trail."

He wondered if she tried to latch on to every stranger who rode into town and drag him into the saloon. The notion sat about as well as a load of green watermelon in his gut.

"Like I said, I'm not most men."

"Indeed not." Her mouth twitched in humor. "And you appear a very healthy one as well if I dare say."

What an odd thing to observe. McKenna was still trying to figure it out when he felt a tug on his sleeve. He looked down at a youngster whose reddish hair turned a shade of burnished orange in the sunlight.

"Mr. Smith, would ya like me to take your horse to the livery for you?" The boy grinned. "Won't be no bother."

The free use of McKenna's name took him aback. Word sure traveled fast. Kinda unnerved him, but at the same time it flattered that the boy knew who he was.

"Sure, kid." McKenna tossed the lad a nickel for his trouble. Hard Tack deserved a rest. Deciding to lay up for the night, McKenna fished another coin from his pocket. The silver glinted in the bright sunlight as he flipped it into the air. "Here's a quarter for some oats too."

"Thanks, Mr. Smith. I'll take real good care of the dun."

"Much obliged, son." He grabbed his saddlebags, tossed them over a shoulder and politely offered the widow his elbow.

Tempest's gloved fingers nestled around his arm. "Appears you're staying after all."

"Don't get your hopes up for the rodeo, Mrs. LeDoux. It's only for one night. Reckon me and Hard Tack can get an early start come daybreak." McKenna firmly let her know she couldn't manipulate him like she apparently did everyone else.

If he had a nickel for every woman who'd tried it before, he'd have a fair to middling stack, although he knew Tempest was by far the most expert at it. And the loveliest, he added.

His spurs jangled as she fell smartly into step with him
on the wooden sidewalk, her pretty scarlet dress swishing
against his britches leg to beat the band. Odd contentment
filled the cupboard that'd been bare too long.

"Thank you for taking pity on a dusty saddle stiff."

"Anything I can do to make your stay more pleasurable."

McKenna felt a bit like Moses parting the Red Sea the way
the crowded sidewalk opened up to let them pass. He doubted
it was due to any religious zeal, but more because of his skill
with a Colt.

He scanned the street for trouble. Only took one fool who
wanted to make a name for himself to try to force a showdown.

One middle-aged man gave them a rude stare as he moved
aside. In a low voice, he remarked to his female companion,
"Don't know what that crazy Cajun woman has up her sleeve.
Suspect she's the reason Smith is here though."

"I'd shore like to know what the hired gun can help her
with," sniffed the woman. "Lord knows bullets can't help her
keep a husband."

Bright spots rose in Tempest's cheeks and he felt her spine
stiffen. Never making a peep or acknowledging the speculation with a flicker of an eyelash, she raised her chin and
stared toward some distant speck. McKenna had the utmost
respect for her ability to ignore the spitefulness.

Took a lot of doing to keep walking. Times had been when
he hadn't. And given this lady's hair-trigger temper, he was
even more astonished that she could maintain her dignity.

That told him she'd had more practice than she should've.

Some kind of war waged between the beautiful widow and
the rest of the town. This wasn't his fight, but he'd always
rooted for the runt of the litter. Aside from Tempest LeDoux's
bold, scandalous behavior, she was nothing but a runt who
tried to pretend she was the biggest hound on the porch.

From beneath the shaded brim of his hat, he studied her

proud features that seemed too lonely and sad. Everyone needed a willing ear, something she didn't appear to get much of in Kasota Springs.

Even if she used him for her own purposes, he didn't mind. In fact, he was happy to help her feed these people some crow.

Laying a protective hand on the small of her back, he held the door of the hotel and ushered her inside. She waited while he quickly removed his hat, then she took a deep breath and reached again for the crook of his arm. Amid a steady hum of whispers, he escorted her into the dining room.

Little tendrils of her hair tickled his nose when he leaned next to her ear. "Seems your plan to rile folks up good and plenty is working. They don't appear able to find much else to get google-eyed over or yap about."

She nodded. "The famous Guardian of Justice on the Jacks Bluff payroll, now there's a tasty morsel to chew over."

"But I'm not. You having any particular trouble?"

"No more than usual, but nothing I can't handle." Tempest slid into the seat he held for her, removing her rawhide gloves.

Putting his hat on the table, McKenna sat opposite her and propped the saddlebags against the side of his chair. "I'm probably butting in where I don't belong, but if you're having problems you oughta talk to the sheriff. I've seen my share of tinderbox situations. Not a good idea to keep glowing embers around dry grass."

She propped her arms on the table and stared straight into his soul. "Enough about my piddly problems. Satisfy a woman's burning desire to know what brings you to our little corner of the world."

"Just passing through on my way up to Horse Creek in Colorado. Seems the town got in my way."

Tempest smoothed back a strand of hair that escaped from the red ribbon tying it back. "On business or pleasure?"

The lady said that like it was a choice between sugar and pickles. For McKenna everything was pickles. He couldn't recall ever having sugar on purpose. Something told him he'd missed out on a lot by focusing on his job of protecting the weak, righting wrongs and upholding justice.

Damn the need for someone to do it!

No one ever wired him to come unless they wanted someone dead or gone. There was a major difference between him and other guns-for-hire. He had scruples. He never drew his Colt unless he knew he fought on the side of right. But his work was unending and it had piss-poor benefits.

Not a day went by he didn't wish he'd had a little more sugar to offset the sour taste that lingered in his mouth. The stench of death ruined the ability to savor each victory.

"I'm sorry, ma'am, what did you ask?"

"Are you going to Colorado because you want to or because you have to?"

A dull ache sat in McKenna's midsection. "It's business. A promise made to a friend."

"Sounds like you take those favors real personal."

"Do for a fact." Especially when it came to fulfilling a dying wish. He eyed the smooth leather of the saddlebags.

"We're a lot alike, Mr. Smith. When I give my word to someone you can take it to the bank, no matter what it costs me. A person who can't keep their promises isn't worth a plug nickel."

Just then the waiter rushed over, bumping into the table and dropping his pad and pencil. He seemed to have a case of the nerves like everyone else in town except Tempest. McKenna's gaze traveled the room. Each person who had been staring suddenly discovered a speck of dirt on their clothes, a missing button or swatted at a fly that had landed on their table.

"What'll you have, ma'am?" The waiter looked at Tempest.

"Do you still have some sarsaparilla left, Oscar? I need something more exhilarating than coffee."

"Yes, ma'am. And you, sir?" The man kept his focus anchored on the furniture when he addressed McKenna.

"I'll have a bowl of stew and a piece of pie to go with coffee. I seem to have a hollow spot."

"Very good choice, sir. Right away." The Nervous Nelly retrieved his writing utensils and scurried away.

"I tell you one thing, Mr. Smith. You certainly put the fear of God into the people of this town and I don't think it's all due to your reputation either." Tempest twisted a gold band on her finger. "I do declare, you're one of the tallest men I think I've ever seen. And most forceful."

"I haven't done anything, yet, that'd scare folks."

"It's what you haven't done that has them in a tizzy."

"Then I'll try to hurry up my stay so things can return to normal." McKenna met Tempest LeDoux's gaze. She appeared so fragile, yet had the strength of fifteen men. "You've had more than your share of hard times. I saw the graves on the hill."

"Jacks Bluff and my daughter, Alaine, are all I have in this world and I'll scratch and claw to keep them. Nothing is going to take them from me. Nothing."

"You have some mighty fierce determination." His voice softened more than he'd planned. "But sometimes that's not enough to protect the ones you love." He cleared his throat. "I take it Jacks Bluff is the name of your ranch?"

"I came by it right after husband number two passed on. Phillip LeDoux was a hell of a man. There wasn't a horse he couldn't ride or a woman he couldn't tame. My heart broke right in two when he died after Alaine was born. If it hadn't been for my daughter, I'd have climbed into that pine box with him." Tempest dabbed at the corner of her eyes with the handkerchief McKenna handed her.

"I'm sorry. I didn't mean to pry."

"And I didn't mean to drip all over the place."

Sadness leaked from the angles of her face like a cistern that had sat empty too long and was suddenly deluged with rain. She'd apparently borne enough sorrow and despair that would've killed a lesser woman. "It's the first time I've talked about him in a good long while."

McKenna reckoned he wasn't the only one who'd had way too many pickles. It appeared Mrs. LeDoux hadn't seen a primrose path either.

Chapter 3

Tempest admired the rugged Texan across from her. His unshaven jaw sported what appeared a week of growth. Some men had a dark shadow even when they were clean shaven. She had no proof of it yet, but she fit McKenna in that department.

Warmth stole into her face under his steady regard. She studied the menu on the chalkboard, all the while casting fleeting glances at him.

The man whose energy and power charged into a room like a herd of wild mustangs on locoweed stirred old longings.

This day that began so ordinary had taken quite a turn.

She tried to put her finger on what exactly about McKenna Smith drew everyone's eye. Sure he had the widest shoulders she'd ever seen, wider than husband number five who had been a large man. And McKenna's easy, but deliberate, stride put her in mind of flowing water that knew where it was going but was in no hurry to get there. That was an attention-getter.

With this Texan it seemed more than that though.

Maybe part of the fascination was due to the black leather britches that tapered along muscular legs and disappeared inside tall boots hugging his calves. Or it could be the leather vest studded with silver conchas and a denim shirt the color of sin that gave the famous paladin the aura of a man to reckon with.

Sweet mercy! Her breath snagged on the flutters in her throat. Perspiration marched down her spine like a bunch of army ants storing food for the winter.

He was by far the most electrifying man she'd ever crossed.

"Mr. Smith, it's quite an honor to have your presence in Kasota Springs. Sure gave these twitter-patted fools a whole new set of speculations to flap their gums over."

"It wasn't intentional I assure you." His mouth quirked in an almost smile.

That was another thing she'd noticed. He doled out smiles with the care of a watchdog guarding a henhouse. Spending so much time among bad people likely didn't give him much to be happy about.

"All the same, I'm glad to finally meet you. I've heard so many thrilling stories of your exploits."

For years, rumor ran rampant of his quick dispersal of outlaws, his dogged persistence in the pursuit of justice and about the line he wouldn't cross. Wild talk was generally what made legends so she'd always chalked down the reputation of the black-clothed figure to nothing but scuttlebutt. Until now.

"Don't believe everything you hear, Mrs. LeDoux."

"That sounds so . . . old." She wrinkled her nose. "Call me Tempest."

"Yes, ma'am."

Quiet conviction loomed about this man. She found it in the vibration of his deep voice, felt it in the strength of his touch. McKenna Smith wasn't someone looking for vainglory.

Her gaze dropped to a rawhide pouch dangling around his neck. The Indian medicine bag seemed out of place with the black leather apparel of a gunslinger.

Shifting to his hat lying on the table, she took in the beaded hatband rimming his Stetson.

Hats spoke a language of their own about the wearer. The shape and style told where a man came from and where he might be going.

McKenna's whispered more than a few secrets. A bullet hole had put an extra dent in the crown. The sweat around the band told of hard work and long hours in the sun. The felt headgear had provided shade, protection from the elements and a drinking cup to scoop up river water.

And the white owl feather sticking from the beaded band mentioned a reverence for the earliest Americans.

Curiosity nibbled. But they were things a person didn't ask a stranger right off.

"I didn't know your services were required as far away as Colorado." Tempest toyed with the sugar bowl. "Is it customary to travel that far to help someone out?"

"Not generally. I made an exception in this case."

She had to bite her tongue to keep more questions from spilling out. Quizzing him would be ticklish at best with the potential to land her in a hot skillet. She frowned when he didn't volunteer more.

"All the same, I wish you'd stick around for the rodeo. Lots of roping, riding and dancing. Maybe you'll reconsider?"

"Don't hold your breath, ma'am." He rubbed his eyes as though to rid them of seeing the things they must.

The waiter hurried back with their order, catching the bowl of stew before it slid off the round tray. Again, he retreated very quickly as if he feared staying too long in McKenna's sights would buy him a six-foot hole on the hill.

Hiding behind the glass of sarsaparilla, Tempest imagined how the famed cowboy's sun-streaked hair the color of sorrel would look all tousled and mussed from lovemaking.

Wicked tingles shimmied the length of her as her mind leaped to the picture of him shirtless. Better yet, lying in bed with a sheet draped over the important parts and a bare leg curling from one side of the cover.

And kissing. She didn't have to close her eyes to envision his mouth, his tongue tracing the curve of her lips.

Oh, saints in heaven!

She sighed, reining in that stampeding horse, reminding herself she'd sworn off men. Besides, a black cloud hung over her head. She'd buried more companions than God allowed. She couldn't bear for anything to happen to McKenna and that it'd be her fault.

Men met with a hurried end when they got too close to her.

And old proverb spoke about when two pecan branches touch one of them dies. It was definitely true; she'd witnessed it.

Tempest trembled.

A long gulp of her refreshing drink cooled desire pumping through her blood like hot liquid metal.

Well, almost. At least it tamped it down to a sizzle.

Lowering the thick mug, she found herself caught in the golden depths of his dusky gaze. And she had no strength to resist the attraction, no matter what she'd sworn.

Damn her Louisiana Cajun roots and the curse put on her!

"Jacks Bluff the name of your ranch did you say, Mrs. LeDoux? Sense a story in that. Takes a lot of stamina to carve out a successful cattle operation here in the Panhandle." His words came out all rough and husky as if his throat had closed up and sound got all bruised struggling to get through. "Few women know how to run a herd or have the gritty spirit to sustain a ranching enterprise. My hat's off to you."

"When my back's against a wall, I have only one way to go and that's forward. I'm a survivor, Mr. Smith. And I was fortunate to hire good help. My foreman, Teg Tegeler, is one of the finest cowmen this side of the Brazos."

"All I can say is that you're mighty tough to have weathered the loss of so many husbands. Takes some godawful fortitude."

"Are you prone to disease or accidents, Mr. Smith?"

Sudden gunfire fractured the dining room conversation and the quiet clink of silverware but few people blinked.

"What in the hell?" Hardness stole across McKenna's eyes, turning the golden hues into colorful shards of glass. He started to his feet.

"Don't pay that any mind." Tempest attempted to contain embarrassment that rose to her face. Truth be known she was mortified. She tried to cover with a short laugh. "I'm sure it's only my fool daughter. Alaine's probably practicing."

He settled back into his chair. "Doing what? Shooting up the town? Or giving people a heart attack?"

"Nothing that child does surprises me. Over my strenuous objections, Alaine works herself to a frazzle these days trying to get ready for the rodeo shooting competition. She dreams of joining a Wild West show. If not Buffalo Bill's, then another. Her behavior is certainly unladylike. I've impressed upon her my severe displeasure."

"Kinda dangerous for a girl. Could get her in trouble."

Tempest sighed, feeling the weight of single parenthood. "I've done everything a mother can. If I forbid it, she just sneaks around my back. Figured it's best to be able to see her so I can go for the doctor. Don't know who she takes this rebellious streak after."

McKenna murmured, "Begging your pardon, ma'am, but a wild goose never raised a tame gosling."

"What are you saying, Mr. Smith?" she asked sharply.

Before he could reply, a frantic man burst through the door. "Bank robbery! Someone is robbing Cattleman's Bank."

Some diners crawled under their tables and others sat speechless, their forks frozen halfway to their mouths.

McKenna leaped to his feet, grabbing his hat. Tempest was right behind him, thankful that Alaine hadn't caused the commotion after all.

They almost reached the door to the street when a bullet shattered a window, zipping past her head.

"Get down!" McKenna pulled her behind a bronze planter. Impatiently pushing the tangle of fern from her eyes, she noticed he'd drawn the heavy Colt. The steel in his hand looked as natural as the fluid way he walked.

"Stay here," he ordered. "You'll be safe."

He edged to the door and slowly opened it. Tempest peered around his broad form and froze. Across the street from the hotel in front of the bank, a masked robber was struggling with a kicking, clawing, red-blooded female in an attempt to get her on a horse.

She'd recognize that flying black cloud of hair anywhere.

"No!" Fear settled in Tempest's bones like a frigid winter ice storm. The picture of cradling Alaine, holding her baby girl's lifeless body out on the dusty street, swam circles in her mind. "Stop him. He's trying to steal my daughter. Please, don't let him hurt her."

Chapter 4

Not that the outlaw had overpowered Alaine yet by any means. Nor did the possibility appear particularly rosy either, judging by the way the girl clawed, bit and screeched like a cat that had her tail caught in a meat grinder.

Pride briefly calmed Tempest's heart that pounded worse than a wild yearling herded into the branding chute. Some of her spunk had rubbed off on her daughter after all.

McKenna grabbed Tempest's shoulders and shook her. "Get the sheriff. I'll stop him."

Clutching the hotel door frame for support, Tempest's knees sagged. "Sheriff Barnett's visiting his sick mother in Mobeetie." Her dry mouth worked to keep panic from rising in her throat. "Won't be back until tomorrow. Dear God, Alaine!"

Her cry evidently spurred McKenna to action. He charged for the ruthless outlaw who had one arm clamped around Alaine LeDoux's waist, attempting to throw her on the horse with no regard for the pain he inflicted.

Polished sunlight glinted off McKenna's silver spurs, their measured clink delivering their own dire warning as the tall figure cut through a billowing cloud of dust. Even the birds appeared to stop fluttering about, lining up on the banner stretched across the street to watch the spectacle.

Without a second thought, Tempest lifted her skirts and dashed behind the man who righted wrongs and restored justice.

Saving her daughter might require both of them.

Cold fear strangled her. She'd had everyone she loved ripped from her life. Alaine had to survive. She wouldn't bury her daughter too. The fates couldn't ask that much of her.

And then, just when Tempest thought the odds were about to turn, the mangy robber spied McKenna striding straight for him.

The rotten scoundrel swung. Using Alaine's wriggling body as a shield, the man fired his pistol, heedless that innocent people might be struck.

Tempest ducked behind McKenna.

"Get on this horse, little missy, or you'll wish you had," the outlaw snarled, raising his pistol as if to strike Alaine.

"I wouldn't do that." McKenna's warning sliced the air with steely calm. The warrior in buckskin and black leather planted his feet in the middle of the street with his Colt leveled. "I promise you, you don't wanna harm her. You just think you have problems with the girl."

Tempest covered her mouth with her hand. This was insane. Why *this* town and why Alaine?

"Who are you?" The man squinted, likely to better see who spoke with such bold conviction. "Don't look like the sheriff."

"Let's just say I'm someone who's gonna stop you."

"That so?" The man licked his lips and cast a furtive glance. "Ain't no two-bit cowpoke gonna do that."

Two-bit cowpoke? Just wait until the dumb fool found out who McKenna was.

"Turn the girl loose and we'll discuss things." McKenna edged toward the outlaw. Tempest followed suit.

"I ain't no fool. Discussing won't lead me anywhere except to the end of a hangman's noose."

Tempest would surely arrange that had she but a length of rope. How dare the piece of scum ride into their town, steal their security, their money and their children!

"Takes a mighty brave man to hide behind a girl's skirts. Let her go." A muscle bunched in the hard line of McKenna's jaw.

The thieving desperado seemed in an awful big hurry to get to hell. If anyone could send him there, McKenna Smith could.

Alaine's thrashing abruptly stopped and she went limp. The sudden dead weight caught her captor off guard. A blood-curdling scream escaped Tempest's mouth. Her heart hammered in her chest. No, this couldn't happen! The outlaw couldn't have killed her precious baby girl.

For a split second, the famed Guardian of Justice had a clear shot.

McKenna squeezed the trigger.

But at that very instant, an impeccably dressed stranger in a dark suit and derby hat dashed into the fracas, coming from behind the bandit to help Alaine. Tempest watched in horror, expecting another poor soul to succumb to violence.

Thankfully, McKenna's bullet grazed the Good Samaritan and struck the intended target.

Cursing, the masked desperado stared at the blood staining his shirtsleeve.

With the man's attention on his wound, the dapper stranger grabbed Alaine who had sprung to life, tugging her free of the assailant.

"Alaine!" Tempest sprinted from behind McKenna's dark shadow. The monster had better not have injured her girl. She didn't care that she might have to go through, around, or over the top of the desperate criminal to get to Alaine.

"Damn you!" With a flying leap, she flung herself onto the outlaw's back and clung to his neck.

"Get the hell off me." The man shook until he finally dislodged her and jerked loose from McKenna's grasp, then seizing the last chance for escape he jumped on his horse and galloped from town.

A hail of gunfire followed as McKenna took aim through the thick acrid smoke that filled the street.

Out of breath from fear and worry, Tempest reached her daughter's side. "Alaine, honey, are you all right?"

McKenna turned. "Need to borrow your horse, ma'am. Mine's at the—"

"Take him."

"Guard my saddlebags with your life. I'll be back."

"Just be careful." She reached out to him, but he was halfway to the hitching rail. "Don't get . . ." Her caution trailed, the word hurt or injured or dead left unspoken in the air as the tall gunslinger with his holster slung low on his hip bolted toward death, destruction and duty.

The man who'd awakened sensual longings and things better suited for dark privacy vaulted into the saddle of her beloved bay, Ace High.

He barely shook the reins and the powerful animal sprang forward as though shot from a cannon. She watched until they vanished from sight before turning her full attention to Alaine. She ran her hand down each of her daughter's arms, checking for broken bones.

"Are you hurt, honey? Let's get you over to Doc Mitchell."

Her daughter pulled her gaze from the handsome stranger and blushed, pushing Tempest away. "Mama, please. I'm fine."

"But maybe the doctor should determine that."

"I don't have time for this right now. I have to get ready for the rodeo." Alaine's eyes narrowed as she crooked a dark eyebrow at her savior. "Besides, I need to repay this gentleman for his . . . daring gallantry."

Tempest watched her daughter sashay away from her just like she had done when she fell from a tree and skinned her knee sixteen years ago. Alaine had gotten up, brushed herself off and skipped off to play with the foreman's son. Looked like she'd found someone her size to play with once again. Only what was this dandy-pandy's idea of fun?

The dandified Easterner seemed a tad too concerned with his appearance for her liking. He was a little too soft, too neat, too perfect, and he smelled of lilac water for God's sake.

Tempest scowled after the pair. For all she knew he might use Alaine for some nefarious means. Regardless of his intentions, she didn't want her daughter getting involved with him. Not that she'd ever managed to have a voice in Alaine's affairs. The girl was quick to tell her what she could do with her advice. But a grudging thought came. She had to thank the dandy for helping Alaine escape the clutches of that animal.

She sighed in defeat and turned toward the Springs Hotel.

No, Alaine danced to the beat of her own music.

Too much like her mother most would say.

Full of gloom, Tempest sank back into her chair in the dining room a few minutes later. She frowned at the mysterious saddlebags with which McKenna had entrusted her.

No one listened to her. That was a sad fact.

McKenna Smith was accustomed to danger. Nothing would happen she told herself. Her bad luck didn't usually work this fast. But what if?

Propped beside his empty chair, the saddlebags taunted her.

With a tentative feel, she stroked the worn leather that must have a million tales to tell if only they could. Must hold something all-fired important, for McKenna hadn't let them out of his sight for a moment. God forbid that he meet with misfortune.

She undid the buckle of one and slowly eased up the flap with the tip of her fingernail. Just one little teensy glance. What would it hurt?

After all, she reasoned, if she knew what was in them, she'd know what to do in the event it became necessary.

But Jabberjaws Edwinna Dewey watched with her beady, little eagle eyes from the next table. The woman actually leaned forward in order to get a good eyeful.

Heaven help her. Tempest couldn't do a blasted thing without half the people in town taking her to task.

She jerked back her hand, fastening her sweaty palms around her half-empty mug of sarsaparilla. Under Jabberbox Edwinna's piercing gaze, she tried to forget that McKenna Smith made her feel she was all woman with certain needs.

Tried to forget the ache that lodged in her chest right behind the wall of steel she'd erected from haunted memories.

But she didn't have enough voodoo magic to make that happen. She might as well face the reality that she'd lasso a herd of buffalo to have the one thing she'd longed for ever since she caught her mother and father wrapped in each other's arms when she was eight years old. They hadn't needed the rest of the world when they were together.

Was having that too damn much to ask?

Once, just once in her life, she'd like to love a man and have him love her back without worrying about how long he'd keep breathing. She dreamed of the kind of permanence other women spoke of, the security of having someone else to help solve her problems and to feel the early dawn on her face with the love of her life lying beside her. She'd be warm and thoroughly satisfied, both mentally and physically.

And in her dream they'd be old and gray and happy as larks.

Chapter 5

McKenna clenched his teeth, letting the spirited animal that seemed to share a lot in common with its owner have full rein. At the speed with which they skimmed the ground, it wouldn't take long until he had the robber in his sights.

Then it'd be hell to pay.

He didn't cotton to thieves who stole hardworking folks' money or tried to steal a pretty widow's sole reason for living. He didn't rightly have a plan, but he wouldn't go back to Kasota Springs without the loot. That much he knew.

How he got it would be up to the outlaw. If blood was spilled, then that would be the way of things he reckoned. The choice would be up to the lowbred skunk.

McKenna wished it hadn't befallen his lot to pursue the bastard who'd stolen other people's life savings. But with the sheriff away, no one else had stepped up. They'd all looked to him to do the job. He'd discovered it almost always happened that way.

That was the price of a reputation.

Most days he wished for an ordinary life, one that didn't require the use of a Colt or knowledge of the ways of bad men.

He thundered down a little arroyo and skirted a rock wall. A cloud of dust up ahead gave him hope. He made out one horse and rider through the haze. No one besides a mangy thiever had reason to torture his horse this way.

When he caught up to the man, he was liable to kill him just for mistreating the animal.

Tracks led toward Palo Duro Canyon, a logical place for someone who didn't want to be found. Given the miles of canyon littered with caves, dugouts and heavy undergrowth, McKenna would have a devil of a time tracking the bandit.

At least McKenna had wounded him. Wasn't sure how bad though. Evidently, not nearly bad enough.

He let out a ragged breath and checked the position of the sun.

Dark would fall in a few hours.

On his side . . . there was only one easily accessible way in and out of the canyon.

A wry smile formed.

It'd take time and patience to wait at the entrance though since water was abundant and plenty of rabbits and small game would keep the outlaw fed.

Regretfully, McKenna had never been a patient man. Especially since he had a deathbed promise to fulfill.

Pushing the bay, McKenna reached the old Indian trail that led into the deeply creviced prairie a short while later. He eased down the steep grade, sweeping the rock ledges.

Hair on his neck prickled like he was caught in a lightning storm.

He pressed his knees to the horse's side to stop.

Gentle rustling of the short grass, the skittering of a mule deer through the brush and the feeling in his gut whispered a warning.

Suddenly the wind stilled and a flock of blackbirds in a large cottonwood took flight.

Every nerve ending raised, McKenna searched the branches of the cottonwood that obscured the trail. A mass of shimmering leaves and shadows made it impossible to spy anyone lurking in their midst. Saddle leather creaked as McKenna reached for his sidearm. Sliding the Colt from the holster, he nudged the horse slowly forward.

The lush green canopy brought welcome relief from the sun's heat. McKenna kept his feet rigid to prevent the rowels of his spurs from jingling. A hitch knot in his stomach cinched tighter.

Good sense told him to turn around and ride back out.

He started to do that when the sneaky bastard dropped from the branches onto him, knocking him from the saddle.

His Colt flew from his hand in the scuffle, skittering to the rocky ground.

With a sinking heart, he watched Tempest's horse rear and gallop down the slope, farther into the canyon.

And sitting on his chest with a pistol pressed to his forehead was the outlaw.

Darkness descended over Kasota Springs and Tempest LeDoux continued to wait for McKenna in the Springs Hotel lobby with the saddlebags at her feet. She chewed her lip, keeping her attention riveted on the door.

Her foreman, Teg Tegeler, eased his lanky figure onto the sofa beside her. "Reckon Mr. Smith ran into a passel of trouble."

"Appears that way." She stared at the yammering group of men gathered in a knot in the hotel saloon. "Can't believe those fools would lay odds on whether he'll come back or keep riding. Makes me mad enough to swallow a horned toad backward. McKenna Smith is an honorable man."

Teg raised a craggy eyebrow. "Shoot, don't take it personal. You know Murdoch'll bet on which direction a bird will fly from a tree. So will a few of the others."

"Doesn't excuse them."

A grin spread over the weather-beaten face. "Never thought I'd see you turn down a chance to gamble."

"See no sport in this. Something terrible's happened."

Tempest said a silent prayer for the valiant keeper of justice. She grew cold as visions of him lying in a pool of blood on a lonely stretch of prairie drifted across her mind.

Flying bullets were deadly. Ask husband number four.

She swallowed hard and reached for the saddlebags, pulling them into her lap. The leather pouches might be all she had left to remember the tall Texan by. What would she do with them if he never returned? Again, she thought of looking inside when a shadow fell across the worn leather.

"Mrs. LeDoux, I have it on good authority that you're in possession of Mr. Smith's belongings."

She raised her gaze to Phinneas Jenkins, the surly malcontent and owner of the survey and land office. "I do, not that it's anything to you."

Phinneas puffed out his barrel chest, his mouth drawing in a tight line around a fat cigar. "I'm taking charge of those saddlebags in the sheriff's stead."

Tempest clutched them tighter. "When the devil sprouts wings and beats the flames from his scrawny rear end!"

Teg's feet had already hit the floor. "Touch 'em and I'll rip off your fingers. Smith left them in Tempest's keeping and that's where they'll remain, by God."

"I happen to believe they may contain loot from other robberies," Phinneas blustered. "No doubt he was in cahoots with the bank robber and they hightailed it out together."

A spewing sound leapt from Tempest's mouth. "And you truly think he'd leave it behind! You're a halfwit."

"Peddle your notions somewhere else." Teg poked the man's chest. "Or better yet, keep 'em to yourself."

"I ain't the only one of that opinion." Phinneas Jenkins swaggered off to join the betting frenzy in the hotel saloon.

"Ma'am, why don't you have the clerk lock the bags in the

hotel safe for now?" Teg motioned toward Phinneas who'd captured the group's attention. "Could get ugly. Not that I don't think you can handle those blowhards. You've chopped off their heads before and served 'em to 'em on a silver platter. Just might save on bloodshed."

"Probably wise. These are awfully important to McKenna."

While Tempest stowed the saddlebags in the safe, the noisy crowd moved their bet-taking into the lobby, congesting it with sweaty bodies, schemes and stupidity. She scowled at the unholy mess.

"If you don't need me, I'm riding back to the ranch, ma'am," Teg announced over the din.

"Don't see what else there is to do tonight. I'm going to take a room here. Want to be close." When the tall lanky foreman turned to go, she grabbed his arm. "Teg, keep an eye on Alaine. So many strangers riding in for the rodeo."

"Always do, ma'am. Today ain't no different from the rest."

Tempest made arrangements for a room and headed for the stairs. But her attempt to escape the crush ended in frustration. They swallowed her up in the madness.

Angus Murdoch caught sight of her and waved a piece of paper. The sign-hanger would relish locking horns with her again. "Placed your wager, Mrs. LeDoux? A sure bet we won't see hide nor hair of Mr. Smith or our life savings again."

Tempest favored him with a withering glare. The man never missed a chance to stir a boiling pot or poke her with a sharp stick.

"Wasn't going to, but I've changed my mind." She opened her handbag and held up a coin. Raising her voice above the clamor, she announced, "This shiny ten dollar gold piece says McKenna Smith will bring back the outlaw *and* the loot."

Hoots of laughter followed Tempest's bold prediction. Wasn't the first time they'd jeered her.

Angus pocketed the coin. "I'll take your bet."

"Gives us a chance to get back some of what you took from us in your poker games," growled Phinneas Jenkins.

Turning on her heel, Tempest whirled to push through the rabble-rousers but found her way blocked by a quiet neighbor she'd not shared more than a half dozen words with in his six years in the Panhandle.

"Thank you, ma'am." Tears glistened in the hardscrabble rancher's blue eyes. "I know Mr. Smith's gonna make these fools eat their words. I'd put my money on him, but I lost everything I had in the robbery. Nothing much between my family and starvation. I trust McKenna Smith. He'll do us right."

Tempest patted his shoulder. "I believe that."

A man in overalls, a farmer by the looks, overheard and raised his voice. "The mangy outlaw stole mine too, but I have two hogs I'll wager that we get it all back."

"I got two dollars to my name in a fruit jar at home that says Mrs. LeDoux is right," yelled another.

Amazed at the unaccustomed support, Tempest beamed. She had friends she didn't know she had. Her chest swelled.

A young man about Alaine's age that she knew only as Pony Boy stepped forward, gripping his hat in his hand. "I watched my maw wash other people's clothes on a rub board until her fingers bled. We ain't never had more'n two cents to rub together." His voice hitched with unshed tears. "But my maw, God rest her soul, saved up three dollars and thirty-two cents before she died. She opened up an account at the bank for me. That no account weasel took it. Mr. Smith is my only hope."

"Pony Boy, I'm truly sorry about your mother. If I recall, you lost your father too when a horse fell on him. If I can help in any way, will you let me?"

The boy's face tightened. "Ain't asking for a handout, ma'am."

It was all Tempest could do to keep from wrapping her

arms around him. But that'd make him draw further into his shell.

Instead, she added a business tone to her gentle reply. "And I don't give charity. I offer work for those who need it. You'll get your money back. And if you want the job, come see me or my foreman. We're always looking for willing hands."

"Appreciate it, ma'am."

"Where are you staying?"

"Here and there." Pony Boy swallowed hard. "House burned down a few months ago. Mostly I bed down under the porch of the church. Ain't complaining. It's okay and no one bothers me."

She choked back a lump in her throat. She'd been that poor once. She'd never forgotten the despair. Even when she crawled between the fancy sheets on her big four-poster bed, she remembered nights when she had nothing but a ragged blanket to ward off the chill and a rock for a pillow. Before tears spilled, she shoved through the gaggle of buffoons and stumbled into the street. Couldn't go anywhere else since they'd blocked the hotel stairs.

Damn! Why did life have to be so cruel sometimes? And why did McKenna Smith ride into the middle of her heart if he was just going to get himself killed?

At daybreak, Tempest could stand the sound of her frantic heartbeat no longer. She smoothed her wrinkled clothes and hurried down to the hotel desk. The clerk was Joe, the same fellow who'd locked McKenna's saddlebags in the safe.

"Please tell me Mr. Smith rode in."

Through bleary eyes, Joe peered over the rim of his spectacles. "No, ma'am."

"Might you be mistaken? Maybe someone relieved you for a while? Or maybe you dozed?"

Joe straightened and adjusted the red garters that held his

shirtsleeves at the proper length. "I assure you, madam, I take my job very seriously. He didn't enter this hotel."

Tempest sighed. "I didn't mean to get your nose out of whack. I'll be in the dining room having breakfast—"

"Yes, I'll come get you if he comes in."

She leaned to kiss his cheek. "You're a good man, Joe."

Wasting an hour and a half dawdling over eggs and coffee, she still saw no sign of McKenna.

If only Sheriff Barnett would get back. Maybe she should send Teg out to try to find McKenna.

She finally took up residence on a velvet sofa, had lunch at noon in the dining room, and then wandered onto the sidewalk for a good breath of air. It seemed wise to get out of the hotel for a bit since everyone had grown tired of placing bets on when she'd give up on the gunslinger.

Besides, she'd decided at last to send someone to the ranch for Teg. Pony Boy would, but he probably didn't own a horse.

That's when she remembered McKenna's dun over at the livery. She didn't have to send for Teg; she could go herself. Her skirts whipped around her ankles as she made tracks for the gelding. Just before she reached the livery, the sheriff galloped into town in a swirl of dust.

Breathing thanks, she sprinted toward the jail.

"Sheriff, we have major problems," she began.

The hefty man dismounted and raised his hand to stop her. "Already heard about the bank robbery, Mrs. LeDoux."

"But I'm concerned for McKenna Smith. He lit out after the varmint yesterday afternoon and hasn't returned."

"Yep, I know that too." He opened the door to the jail and stepped inside.

Tempest nipped at his heels. "If you're not going to look for him, I'll go myself. He could be hurt or in the clutches of that man." She swallowed hard. "Or dead."

"Settle down, ma'am. Don't need you to do my job for me."

"Meaning?"

Sheriff Barnett sighed deeply. "As soon as I get my rifle and a fresh horse, I'll head out. Good enough?"

She jutted her chin. "It is. Thank you, Sheriff."

"Fine. Then I reckon I have things to do."

With that accomplished, Tempest wandered back to her post at the hotel, dodging horses and sidestepping all the newcomers who'd come for the rodeo. Wagons by the drove turned onto Main Street. And in the distance she could see tents already dotting the countryside. If this bore any indication, the Independence Day celebration would be a resounding success.

Tempest beamed with pride at the banner stretched above the street with the word RODEO in bold letters.

It was her finest hour, but she couldn't relish it.

Then she swung around to see if Sheriff Barnett had saddled up yet and that's when she saw Ace High jogging up the street as if the horse marched in a parade.

She shielded her eyes from the sun's glare to get a clear look.

A sharp intake of air hurt her lungs.

The tall figure perched in the saddle bore no resemblance to the dashing figure of McKenna Smith.

Chapter 6

But the rider was him.

Tempest could only tell McKenna by the throng he'd attracted since he turned on to the main thoroughfare.

Her heart pounded, slamming into her ribs.

She raised her skirts and raced to meet the Texas legend, afraid to blink or swallow, afraid he was a mirage.

A crowd of adults and children alike ran alongside the horse, whooping and hollering, trying to touch whatever part of McKenna they could, be it his britches leg, his boot or the horse. She watched in amazement as dogs scampered into the mix, yipping with excitement.

Sheriff Barnett burst from the jail with rifle in hand.

As Tempest drew closer to McKenna she was appalled. One sleeve had been ripped almost off and barely hung by a thread. Lord only knew what'd happened to his vest with the fancy silver conchas.

Layers of dirt and filth covered his dark clothes so that she was hard-pressed to recall the shade they'd been.

And then she spied the blood staining his shoulder.

A quick breath hissed through her teeth. Dear God! What on earth had he suffered on their behalf?

Tempest grabbed a young boy by the arm. "Get the doc."

"Yes, ma'am." The child bolted for the doctor's office.

Satisfied she had help on the way, Tempest turned her attention back to the heartbreaking sight.

That's when she noticed the outlaw stumbling behind the horse, tethered by a rope tied to the saddle horn. The robber appeared to have gone through the far backside of hell. But she spared no sympathy for anyone who'd try to steal her daughter. She'd hang him herself if she could lay hands on a good rope.

Reaching them, Tempest stroked her bay's powerful neck and stared into McKenna's weary, golden gaze. She took special note of the haggard lines etching his face.

"Mrs. LeDoux." McKenna tipped the brim of his hat.

"Mr. Smith."

He'd performed a miracle for them exactly like she'd known he would. His name was synonymous with justice and right, a noble shepherd who defended and protected the innocent.

Even dirty, bloody and bruised, he was more man than any she'd known.

She followed McKenna to the jail where he swung with fluid ease from the saddle, looping the reins over the post. Untying a burlap sack, he tossed it to the sheriff.

Sheriff Barnett accepted the bank loot with a nod. "Reckon you're the missing Mr. Smith. I was just fixin' to head out searching for you." The burly lawman's gaze flicked to Tempest. "Mrs. LeDoux threatened me with bodily harm if I didn't. She was convinced you were dead or hurt."

From under the shadow of the tall-as-sin cowboy's hat, he gave her a bone-tired flicker of what she almost took for a smile. "Appreciate your concern, ma'am."

"Wasn't near enough for saving Alaine."

"Just doing my job." McKenna swiveled back to the sheriff. "Hope you've got room in your jail for Cherokee Bill Bartlett. Last report has him wanted for a whole string of robberies from Galveston to the Oklahoma Territory."

"Happy to take him off your hands. Sorry I was gone when all the hullabaloo took place."

McKenna pulled Bartlett forward and handed him over. "He admitted to watching the bank for a few days. Seized the opportunity when you left town."

"Guess he didn't figure on you being here."

McKenna's face darkened. "A mistake on his part. But then he also miscalculated on his hostage's fierce will. Alaine LeDoux alerted us and bought some time. Without that, Cherokee Bill might've gotten away."

"That girl's always been wild as a March hare, just like her mama." The lawman wagged his head and vanished into the jail with his prisoner.

"Thank goodness you're alive." Tempest's voice cracked with pent-up emotion. "I was afraid . . ."

"Makes two of us. My saddlebags?"

"They're in the hotel safe. Didn't want anything to happen to them."

"Knew I could trust you."

A warm flush swept from the soles of her feet. "I'll take care of my horse. Don't worry about Ace High. Will I—?"

"McKenna Smith," Tazwell Redgrave interrupted her. "I'm Kasota Springs' mayor. Let me shake the hand of a true hero."

"Nice of you to say, Mayor, but I didn't do much."

"There are no words to express our gratitude."

Just then Doc Mitchell pushed through the crowd that pressed around McKenna. "Tazwell, all this hoopla can wait. This man needs medical attention." Doc waved his arm. "Now everyone go about your business and let me tend to him. Mrs. LeDoux, that means you too. Now skedaddle."

An hour later, McKenna finally escaped the doc and his fanatical need to bandage each little nick and scrape. He waited until just outside the door before he ripped off the gauze that wrapped him from stem to stern and wadded it up. It left big brown splotches of some concoction the doc had mixed up.

There was an epidemic in Kasota Springs all right . . . an infestation of bedbugs in the brain.

Cherokee Bill's bullet only did minor damage. No need for panic or telegraph for McKenna's coffin measurements yet.

For God's sake, all he needed was a bath and forty winks.

Intent on that, he weaved his way through the crowd still gathered outside the doctor's office and strode toward the public bathhouse. After he scrubbed the last traces of Panhandle dirt from him, he'd collect his saddlebags, get a bed to fall into, then head for Horse Creek bright and early.

He'd lost a day's ride. Didn't want to waste more.

Mayor Redgrave approached, cutting McKenna off. "Mr. Smith, may I have a moment of your time?"

"I'm dirty and tired and my stomach's gnawing on my backbone."

"Won't take long. Say ten minutes?"

"Make it fast then."

"Step this way, sir."

The mayor threw open the double doors of the Opera House that sat next to the Springs Hotel.

McKenna stared at the packed place that couldn't hold another person. "Mayor, I don't have time for some type of theatrical performance. Thought I made that clear."

"This isn't what you think."

Before McKenna could wrest himself from the mayor, burly arms hefted him into the air. Men carried him to a podium and set him down. Tempest LeDoux stood beside the mayor.

"Mr. Smith," Mayor Redgrave said, "to show our gratitude and deep appreciation for saving the town's money, we'd like to offer you the keys to our fair city. Not only that, the dance kicking off the rodeo tomorrow night will be in your honor."

Redgrave held out a large key that had a blue ribbon tied around it.

"I can't accept. Really. I have to be moving on."

But the mayor had already pressed the key into McKenna's hand. To refuse it would cause a lot of hurt feelings.

Tempest stepped up. "That's not all, Mr. Smith." At her signal two men joined them.

"I'm throwing in free board at the hotel long as you want it." The proprietor pumped McKenna's hand as if trying to get water from a spout. He'd evidently thrown on his best Sunday suit in a hurry because the buttons were in all the wrong holes.

The second man cleared his throat. "And no need to worry about your vittles during your stay in Kasota Springs. You'll have all you want free of charge at the Red Rooster Café."

"You don't have to do this." McKenna stared out at the sea of thankful, grinning faces. Each pair of eyes let him know the dire straits their lives would've been in had they'd lost what little they'd accumulated in the bank.

He needed to head out. He had things to do. Hell! But it meant a lot to these people to show their gratitude. And Tempest LeDoux . . . he couldn't exactly turn his back on her.

Clearing his voice, he quipped, "I usually work a lot cheaper."

A smattering of laughter ran through the crowd.

Tempest beamed. "We haven't forgotten your horse, Mr. Smith. I'm providing feed for the animal until you leave us."

McKenna lifted his dusty hat and waved it. "Thank you. Thank you all very much. It'll be my pleasure to accept your kind hospitality."

His head swam with the town's benevolence as he hurried toward a bath, a hot meal and a bed. Muscles that weren't stretched or bruised throbbed, and the ones that were told him he was too old to wrestle bears and wily outlaws. Capturing Cherokee Bill had taken all the cunning McKenna had.

"Yoo hoo, Mr. Smith!" a female voice called.

Without looking, he knew it belonged to Tempest LeDoux. He kept going. He was in no mood for socializing at the moment. Quickly gaining entrance to the bathhouse, he was greeted by the smell of soap and cleanliness.

A hot bath and shave would go a long way toward improving his mood. Then he'd tackle the widow. He owed her proper thanks, no two ways about it. She'd been the driving force behind the town's collective generosity.

The persistent woman seemed to have a finger in every pie. Not that they wanted her to; she just plunged in both fists and dared 'em to object.

And she'd watched over his saddlebags. That alone was worth a lot. He owed her and he'd see to that. Later.

But if he thought to escape her, he was sadly ill informed.

Tempest marched into the men's establishment behind him like Custer intent on making a last stand. "Mr. Smith, I must have a word."

Men in varied states of undress grabbed for their clothes.

McKenna groaned aloud and faced her. "I see you're not going to let go of the bone between your teeth. I give up."

A ruddy-faced man stormed from a back room with his apron flapping. His muttonchop sideburns twitched with indignation. "Ma'am, you cain't . . . women ain't allowed in here. Ain't decent."

The widow's dark eyebrows arched. She cast a wide smile at the patrons who tried to shield themselves with their shirts or britches. "You don't have anything I haven't already seen before, boys. Wouldn't win any prizes that's for sure."

Saving her from a second lynching since arriving in town, McKenna grabbed her arm and hustled her toward the door.

"If I hear you out, do you promise to give me some peace?"

"Certainly. I'm a perfectly reasonable woman." Her voice dripped with sugar. "I only wanted to invite you to the weekly poker game at the ranch since you'll be staying and all. It's tonight at six sharp."

McKenna seethed. There would be no way he'd get a long, quiet soak unless he agreed. "I'll be there, now go."

"Don't be late. Ask anyone for directions. They know." With her head held high, she sashayed from the building.

"Uh-oh. She's got it bad for you, Mr. Smith," said Mr. Muttonchops. "You ain't got a prayer; you gotta go. She don't take no for an answer. Truth is no one's ever had the nerve to turn her down and live to tell it."

"He's right," confirmed a patron. "Ask anyone."

"Do tell." If McKenna hadn't been so desperate to get shed of her, he'd never have agreed. He was far more interested in checking the back of his eyelids for leaks.

But surely the men exaggerated.

Tempest LeDoux was just a small thing he could toss over his shoulder like a sack of potatoes.

A little package of dynamite that understanding could diffuse.

No reason for a grown man to fear her.

A game of poker wouldn't take long. He could leave early.

Chapter 7

In the kitchen at Jacks Bluff, Tempest dug out her mother's old recipe books that'd been passed down for generations and blew off the dust. She wasn't sure she had all the ingredients that might help assure her plan's success.

She'd not only charm McKenna but keep him healthy as well.

From jars of herbs, roots and berries she measured exact amounts into a pot. While it simmered, she carefully took down pieces of cut crystal from the carved china cabinet.

A bit fancy, but sure to impress the rugged Texan.

McKenna Smith would see that she wasn't some uncouth, blackwater Cajun. She might've been once, but the swamps of Bayou Goula were a long way from the Texas Panhandle.

Spreading a cloth of old lace on the poker table, she stepped back to view it. Much too formal. She gently folded it up and wrapped it back in the tissue paper. Didn't want to have him laughing at her.

Flowers might add a nice touch though. A dozen vases of her Seven Sisters roses would give the room a pleasing fragrance and cheer. With snippers in hand she hurried to the garden.

A few hours later she had everything ready.

Alaine always disappeared on poker night and this would

be no exception. The girl usually stayed in town or hung out with Teg Tegeler and the boys at the bunkhouse.

But maybe Alaine was busy with that Eastern popinjay— Morgan or whatever the hell his name was. Tempest chewed her lip. For once, she prayed Alaine would go shoot at targets or practice knife throwing or something.

Tempest glanced through the window in time to see riders pass under the high crossbar and enter the Jacks Bluff compound. She adjusted the mass of dark ringlets that cascaded down the right side of her head and onto her shoulder. The gentlemen were here. Four to be exact. Three she summoned at the last minute just to make her interest in McKenna a tad less obvious.

She groaned, recalling the scandalous way she'd barged into the bathhouse after him. All these years and she still had the social graces of a lop-eared mule.

Hurriedly lighting the kerosene lamps, she pulled aside the finest lace curtains money could buy and scanned the horsemen. Though too far away yet to distinguish their faces, she knew without a doubt the broad-shouldered one who sat more erect, more proud was McKenna. He rode natural and easy, the flow of a river following the curvature of the earth.

He also appeared healthy as a new calf too.

Her heart beat faster when she whispered his name.

McKenna dismounted in front of a ranch house that seemed more suited to a lush southern plantation than the high plains of Texas. Every outbuilding, animal and blade of grass was well maintained. He admired the lonely widow's handiwork.

"Well, we might as well get this show over with," drawled the tallest of McKenna's three companions, a man named Curtis.

"Yep, shore wisht I would've had the gumption to turn her

down." Doc Mitchell scratched his bald head. "More fun to watch the moon rise and bet on how many stars'll pop out."

"Least that way we wouldn't have to worry which one of us would draw the short straw," said the short squatty owner of the land office, Phinneas something.

McKenna was still trying to decipher the meaning of the short straw remark when Tempest threw open the door. Every thought flew from his head as he stared, stunned by her transformation into a southern belle. The wide skirts of her dress must've required miles of fabric.

But he was more focused on her ripe breasts, the way the clingy federal blue bodice molded them, and the delicate pink rose peeking from the plunging vee.

Tempest LeDoux wore more costumes than a troupe of actors. And wore them very well, he decided.

"Come on in, boys, make yourselves at home."

"Mrs. LeDoux." McKenna touched his lips to the back of her hand.

"I see I was right." Dimples in her cheeks winked.

"About what, ma'am?"

"It's Tempest, remember?" Humor crinkled the corners of her eyes. "I made a bet with myself that you'd still have a dark shadow no matter how often you shaved."

Kasota Springs was sure a town fond of wagering. Seemed the whole kit and caboodle of them placed any number of bets on an endless variety of subjects. He'd learned about the pot the men got up after he lit out after Cherokee Bill and how Tempest won it. Again he wondered how the name of the Jacks Bluff Ranch came about. It certainly had something to do with betting.

"You have a beautiful ranch here. You'll have to tell me what prompted the name."

"Perhaps I will. If you share the details of what happened between you and the outlaw." The barest brush of her hand on his arm was more enticing than a full embrace by most of the women he'd known.

Through the fog in his brain, he recalled a certain spider that lured a fly into her web with the promise it wasn't sticky.

Her heady fragrance swirled up his nose, battering against his defenses. She smelled of dark woods full of moss and fern and musky secrets.

Tempest LeDoux was a whole lot of woman for any one man. But then she'd had at least five he reminded himself.

"Ah, me and Cherokee Bill . . . not much to say other than he was convinced he wasn't coming back to face justice and I convinced him he was. Now he's in the hoosegow. And I'm in the home of the most beautiful woman in Texas."

"You're a silver-tongued devil."

"Just speaking the truth."

"Hey, do you mind if we get this card-playing done so I can turn to better pursuits." Curtis gave them a black scowl.

"You're in a mighty big hurry to lose your money, Curtis. You'll be glad to know I've chosen One-Eyed Jacks for tonight."

Doc and the others groaned, burying their heads.

"One-Eyed Jacks?" McKenna crooked an eyebrow. "Never heard tell of it and I thought I knew every form of the game."

"Tempest made it up, that's why," explained Doc.

"I did not," Tempest protested. "My granddaddy taught me how to play. It's easy; you'll get the hang of it real fast."

Seated at a card table minutes later, surrounded by so many damn roses it would put a funeral parlor to shame, McKenna had second thoughts. And it had nothing to do with the indoor garden.

He recognized a professional at work in the way she shuffled the deck, expertly bridging and then fanning them out. If he were a betting man, he'd say she'd spent some time in a large gambling house—maybe in New Orleans from the mellow accent wrapping certain words.

The thronelike chair she perched on made her look downright queenly.

"I do declare, I forgot to offer you fine gentlemen some refreshment." She laid down the cards. "Bourbon anyone?"

"Might dull the ache when I go home broke," said Doc.

McKenna rose. "I'll help you."

"No, thank you. Absolutely not. You're my guest."

Sipping smooth bourbon whiskey from cut crystal wasn't anything he'd planned. Neither was losing every round of cards to the lovely widow.

Maybe it was the heady fragrance circling his head.

Or the flashing dimples and the amber glints sparkling in her gaze when she favored him with a brilliant smile.

And maybe it was the way her curls cascaded onto her bare shoulder from the high upswept hairdo that made him think of more pleasurable activities that could scratch that itch.

Tempest LeDoux had taken a damn quick course in charm school. The results astounded him.

A desire to get close . . . intimately, indecently close to her silenced the old warnings that had always kept him from wading onto a patch of quicksand.

The complicated game was hard to follow and it soon became apparent that no one was going to win except her.

The minute he latched onto a good grasp of the game she changed the rules, insisting that was what she said to begin with. The urge to strangle her pretty throat grew stronger with every passing second.

Suddenly, his vision blurred and a dizzy whirl made it hard to keep from falling out of the chair.

Whatever the cause he knew it was something more than her wishy-washy rules and fine bourbon.

He was probably beat from twenty-four hours without sleep.

A few minutes passed and McKenna seemed unable to gather his wits. He couldn't be drunk. He'd only had what amounted to two jiggers of bourbon. Funny thing though.

She'd always taken *his* glass to the sideboard to fill, where with the others, she brought the bottle to the table.

Four hands later, Doc Mitchell and his two friends laid down their cards and jumped up, clearly relieved. "You've wiped us clean again. Reckon we'll mosey back to town."

"Better luck next time, boys." Tempest seemed pretty jovial. "Watch out for the coyotes."

McKenna tried to stand and leave with them, but his legs wobbled, buckling beneath him. He sank back into the smooth, imported leather. He'd rest awhile and try it again.

"Another bourbon, McKenna?"

He quickly covered the top of the glass. "I've had enough. Any more and I'll be laid out on your floor."

"Now that would be a pity." Her grin belied the words.

"The shame would be in not using my free room at the Springs Hotel after everyone went to so much trouble. It'd slight their feelings." Damn this dizziness—there were two of everything he looked at.

"I daresay they'd live over it. They have before."

"You're full of devilish contention, my dear lady."

"Perhaps." Tempest shuffled the cards. "Anyway, looks like it's just us."

McKenna shook his head. "Count me out. You helped yourself to all my money. Don't have a cent left, so reckon I'm done too. I'd better head back to town. My bed'll look mighty welcome."

He tried to force some stiffness into legs that insisted on folding. They were a little better but not well enough to make it to the door and mount a horse.

"Are you feeling puny? You look a little white around the gills."

"I'm fine. Maybe I'll just sit another minute though."

"Then while you're resting, how about some Slippery Sam?"

Anything was better than One-Eyed Jacks. At least he'd played Slippery Sam. Considered himself an expert at it.

"There's still the matter of nothing to ante up with."

"Want to make it interesting?"

"Isn't it already?"

"Let's say that whoever loses a hand has to remove one article of clothing." Her fingers drifted down her slender throat, stopping just before they reached the rose winking from her low neckline. "Either my bodice or your britches."

McKenna was already imagining her breasts, lush and bare. "That's quite a proposition."

She dealt them each three cards and laid the remainder in the center of the table. He had to draw a card from the top of the undealt stack that would be higher or the same suit as one of the cards he held in his hand.

Since he had a two of hearts, four of diamonds and the queen of clubs he already counted it a win. He glanced at the wisp of fabric between him and pure heaven.

A spiraling shaft of heat curled through his body.

He pulled himself from her dark gaze and drew. "The ace of spades; I win, Tempest."

"Hold on there. The ace is low in this game."

"Not where I came from, lady. Stop changing the rules."

"You lost. Quit stalling and shed those britches, McKenna."

Damn those dimples and the sugary smile!

"My dear Lady Tempest, you cheat at cards. But a deal is a deal." Many people spent half their lives in hesitation and the other half in regret. At the moment, McKenna was doing both and wondering how she always wound up with the upper hand. He slowly unbuckled his gunbelt and hung it on the back of the chair. With considerable effort, he tugged off his boots. Then he slid from the leather britches, thankful for the faded red drawers that hid his modesty somewhat.

"I can't believe you'd accuse me of cheating."

"You oughta be ashamed of yourself, taking advantage of

an unarmed man who hasn't slept in two days," he growled, testing his legs while he was up. They held his weight this time and his head was clearing.

But he had his pride to avenge first. He wouldn't sit back down though and he damn sure wouldn't have another thing to drink.

"Go ahead and draw your card," he said. "If you win again, I'll know you're up to no good."

Tempest drew a three of hearts and lost as well.

Odd that she didn't seem all that heartbroken.

"My, my, I hate to see you hafta strip off that pretty bodice." The corner of his mouth lifted.

"Anyone tell you that you're an eager man, Mr. Smith?"

"A few."

She pushed herself from the throne-chair, removed the rose and laid it aside. Those long fingers enticed him as they dallied with each button and untied lace fastenings. Finally, when he thought his lungs would burst from the wanting, the scrap of satin slipped from her arms.

The spit in his mouth dried.

All he had to do was reach out and pull her against him.

Her chemise was thin and lacy and left nothing to his imagination. Exactly something he would've guessed she wore. Nothing but the most expensive for the runty woman who still tried to prove she was the biggest of the litter.

One good tug on the flimsy chemise and she'd be exposed.

Both of them now stood.

Yearning crackled the air in the inches separating them. She was so close he could hear her heart racing to match the rapid pulse in the hollow of her throat.

"My daughter won't be home for another hour."

"Darlin', what I want to do with you requires nothing short of an entire night. Not going to start something I can't properly finish."

Chapter 8

"It must be lonely up there on that mountain all by yourself."
Tempest's forefinger etched a silken trail down the dark
shadow of McKenna's jaw.

Maybe she could get him upstairs if she put her mind to it.

This was a man who whispered a dream in her ear and gave
her hope. He made her think she could have a life of promise
and fulfillment. She wanted to believe it. She really did.

"I've grown accustomed to the inconvenience."

A wry smile flitted across his face before it vanished. Had
she blinked, she would've missed it.

"Surely you've wanted more. Ever think of putting down
roots, owning a home and a piece of land, and having someone
to share the good times and the bad?"

"I'm not in the habit of wanting things I can't have."

"But you can have them. Nothing's stopping you."

"When you get my age it's too late for castles in the sky."

"What happened to drain all the happiness from you?" It
was more than simple curiosity, she truly wanted to know.

McKenna ran a hand across his eyes and sighed. Light
from the kerosene lamps created an interesting mural on the
pressed tin ceiling and deepened the lines around his mouth.

She sensed he was about to reveal something sadly profound.

"I'm a man with regret as a bedfellow. The things that nag at me the most are the ones where I had a choice, the ones when I knew I could've stopped myself. And the ones when I stare in the mirror, look deep inside, and know I shouldn't do something and do it anyway. I've had a thousand such moments where I chose the wrong path and paid the consequences. I've used up all my chances for anything normal."

"Maybe. But you're not dead yet." She tilted back her head to look up at him. "McKenna Smith, would you grant one request?"

"Depends."

She stared into the golden twin windows, into the tortured soul beyond their depts. Her breath hitched.

"Would you please kiss me? Nothing else, just a kiss."

Without replying, he tenderly cupped her face between his large hands and stared for a few seconds shy of an eternity. Then his head lowered. Tempest closed her eyes to savor the moment.

As gentle as the first spring rain, he touched his full lips to hers.

She'd expected the scorching heat because she couldn't imagine anything less between them. When the kiss deepened into a wickedly thorough one, she wouldn't have felt it if someone had poured kerosene under her and lit her with a match.

Sweet mercy!

McKenna pulled her to him with a fierce need, a wild storm soaking arid Panhandle land with life-giving moisture. A groan rose from somewhere deep inside him. She clutched his shirt, never wanting to let go, and silently begged him to fill the nagging emptiness that hollowed out her insides.

She'd give anything for someone to give a damn.

Someone who could lift her bad luck curse.

And someone to desire her as a woman.

Through the thin chemise, her swollen breasts met the hardness of his chest. Friction against the rough texture of his shirt created a bonfire inside her. Maybe **someone** *had* lit a puddle of kerosene under her.

"Oh, McKenna, I do love a man who knows his way around a woman's heart. Ever think of marrying up with someone?"

Abruptly, McKenna set her aside as though she had something contagious. It was over, all the magic, all the sexual longing that created a sheen of moisture on her bare skin.

"I need to get going." He snatched up his britches.

Panic and fear pulled tight inside her. "What did I do? Tell me and I'll fix it." She couldn't keep the tremble from her voice.

"I can't give you what you want." He stuck his long legs into the pants and buttoned the waist. "I'm sorry."

"But—"

McKenna plunged first one foot and then the other into his tall boots and tugged them on.

"If we could just talk, I'm sure we can—"

With the britches back inside his boots, he stood. His raw anger whipped the air. "People always kill the ones they profess to love. Love destroys."

"Are you saying . . ."

McKenna had strapped on his gunbelt and was tying the leather strip around his thigh. He froze as cold as a rocky mountaintop. "No, I'm not saying that."

"Help me understand what happened. Who kill the ones they vow to love?"

"A ghost. You wouldn't understand." He jammed his hat on. "This is one of those times I spoke about where I have to make a choice. I'm trying to do the right thing for once. Let it be."

She jerked up her bodice and swept toward the wide staircase.

"I've been kissed by a lot of men in my time. I can tell a dutiful kiss that men don't really mean when they're trying to coddle you. But that one came from someplace deep inside and it was real. You can deny it until Gabriel blows his horn, but all your naysaying doesn't hold water."

She wouldn't look at him or she'd wilt just like a weed that thought she was getting a drink of water only to find it'd been a figment of her imagination.

In the Slats and Fats Saloon the next day, McKenna replayed the events of the poker game over a cool mug of beer.

The reason for the dizzy, weak spell last evening puzzled him. Nothing made sense. Tempest almost certainly put something in his bourbon. She had to. There seemed no other explanation. But if she had why? To mess with his mind? To lure him into her bed? To get him to kiss her?

Put the saddle on the right horse, he told himself.

He kissed her because he'd wanted to in the worst way and not because of anything Tempest LeDoux had said.

Ah, those perfect breasts and lips that tasted of sweet passion as old as time itself. He'd almost taken her up those stairs and quieted the longing that wound him tighter than an eight-day clock.

Until old memories left bitter gall in his mouth . . .

Lacy Lorena had tossed him away like a meaningless scrap of paper and merrily traipsed off. His dear mother.

He turned to hard bedrock. People did kill the ones they professed to love. He was proof. No package deal for him.

If a woman wanted a romp in the hay, he'd rush to oblige.

But love and marriage? She'd best go paddle that canoe up a high waterfall.

A young cowpoke squeezed up to the long bar, jostling McKenna's arm. Seemed the population had tripled overnight with folks arriving for the start of the rodeo. The carnival-like atmosphere outside had burst into the saloon and Angus Murdoch was furiously taking bets.

"I got two bits for Dally Angelo," yelled one fellow.

"That cowboy ain't gonna stand a chance," said another. "My money's going on Bone Buster. That mankiller ain't ever been rode and he ain't ever fixin' to be."

"Just because Bone Buster killed Dally's pa don't mean Dally cain't tame that bull. Angelo's tough," came the reply.

"Well, he's got guts, that's for sure. Too bad he's gonna get those guts stomped to a pulp."

Angus caught McKenna's eye. "Mr. Smith, you gonna wager?"

"Nope."

"Gonna be interesting. Follow the crowd this evening to the pasture near the chutes at the railhead." Angus whirled. "Hey, Carlos, I know you're a gambler. Where's your *dinero?*"

McKenna took his beer to a table apart from the frenzy.

Watching, he reaffirmed his conclusion—the town was hell-bent on betting and did so with zeal unequaled anywhere.

The batwing doors of the Slats and Fats Saloon suddenly swung almost off their hinges. "Crazy Mrs. LeDoux's coming and she's wearing her wedding hat. Run!"

Tempest LeDoux in a wedding hat? Seemed an odd thing to rile people over, but it seemed to spell some sort of doom.

An amazement to behold, the bug-eyed man's cry busted up the gambling venture. Men tripped over their feet in a mad dash for the back door. Those who remained had ridden in for the rodeo, but despite staying seated, they seemed awfully jittery.

"What's going on?" McKenna asked the bartender named Slats.

He thought of checking his pistol to see if it was loaded.

"Miz LeDoux seems to be shopping for a new husband again and they know what's good for 'em." The tall, thin man, nicknamed because he resembled a bed slat McKenna was told, showed all his teeth and continued to polish the glasses. "I'll distract her if you like while you escape, Mr. Smith."

"How do they know she's looking for a husband?"

"She always wears the same . . . trappings . . . when she's out beating the bushes—a fancy white wedding hat she's worn to all five of the occasions and the frilly parasol she carries, I assume to beat the poor bastard into submission." Slats shrugged his bony shoulders.

"Why aren't you and the rest of these men hiding?"

"We're hitched. You might better hightail it outta here before she walks through those doors or you're a goner."

"She wouldn't come in here, would she?" But he knew she would. The woman had busted into the men's bathhouse hadn't she? There seemed no end to her daring. She lived life as if it was a .45 with a full cylinder and she had to shoot all the bullets out in rapid succession.

Sure enough, she calmly strolled in as though she owned the joint and they catered specifically to female clientele.

McKenna's tongue got caught in the roof of his mouth when Tempest waltzed over and plopped down beside him.

"I declare, Mr. Smith, fancy seeing you here." Her dimples flashed as she fanned herself. "It's so hot outside I feel just like a June bug dancing on a tin roof."

"Mrs. LeDoux." He nodded his head.

He couldn't unglue his eyes from the hat covered in big white flowers. Thin netting fell from the brim to the tip of her pert nose.

Yep, she put him in mind of a bride all right.

And if he could believe expert opinion, she was looking for husband number six.

His last swallow of beer floundered in his gut. He'd have to tell her real quick to cast her net somewhere else because this fish wasn't biting.

Slats huffed over. "Ma'am, you got no business in here. This is a drinking man's establishment. We got rules."

"Oh, pooh! Every rule is made to be broken," she answered.

"Mine ain't. Men ain't gonna go for you coming in here, ruining the one place where they can hide from their wives."

"Your partner, Fats, doesn't run off paying customers." Quite unconcerned, she leaned the parasol against her chair and tugged the lacy white gloves from each digit. "Quit griping and be a dear man. Bring me the coldest sarsaparilla you have."

Slats glared. "Just one. And then you gotta leave."

McKenna lifted his mug. "What brings you to town?"

"Today's the opening ceremonies to kick off the rodeo. As presiding officer of the rodeo committee I have duties."

He relaxed. Maybe he'd jumped to the wrong conclusions and she wasn't interested in him after all. "Slats, bring me another beer while you're at it."

The slender bartender set down both mugs and collected twenty cents from McKenna.

"You're a gentleman, but I pay my own way." Tempest handed Slats a silver dollar and grinned at McKenna. "You said I cleaned you out. Shame on you for holding out on me."

"Only a fool takes everything he has to a poker game."

"You're a smart man. Did you have a good time?"

"You did yourself proud, ma'am. You're a worthy opponent."

"It's Tempest, remember."

He remembered all right. Had hell getting her name and the taste of her out of his brain long enough to catch some sleep.

Sheriff Barnett strode in and marched straight for their table. "Have a word with you, Smith?"

McKenna followed the sheriff outside. "What is it?"

The sheriff pushed back his hat and stared down the street. "You seem a nice sort and don't know the workings of some of the people in this town so I thought I should warn you."

"Right kindly, Sheriff. What people in particular are you warning me about?"

"Mrs. LeDoux. She's got her mind set on adding you."

"To what?" McKenna wished the man would speak clearly.

"Dammit, Smith, she's got you marked for husband six."

"I've given her no reason to think I'm interested in applying. Appreciate the concern, but I can pretty much take care of myself. Been doing it for a while now."

"You don't know her." The sheriff left shaking his head.

McKenna went back inside in time to see Tempest stuffing a small bottle into her purse. Probably smelling salts. Most women carried them for the vapors.

Although Tempest didn't seem the sort to swoon.

In her no-nonsense way, she'd slap a fainting spell silly if it tried to jump on her.

The sheriff was out of line in McKenna's book. Tempest LeDoux was a lonely, harmless widow just looking for a little companionship. But it might not hurt to tell her again in no uncertain terms that he wasn't interested.

Chapter 9

From where McKenna sat, he could see the whites of several pairs of frightened eyes peering through a crack in the door that led to the alley behind the saloon. A brave lot.

He tipped up the mug and took a long swallow, letting the cool liquid slide down his throat.

"Mr. Smith, will you dance with me tonight?" Tempest's silken request slid over him like warm sap oozing down a tree.

McKenna frowned. "I don't dance."

"But the affair is in your honor. You have to be there. Even if they don't know how, most men at least try."

"I don't know how much plainer I can get that I'm not most men. I don't dance." Funny how thoughts were swirling inside his head looking for a place to light. He seemed sorta dizzy again. "And I want to make something crystal clear . . . I'm not looking for a wife. Don't chase what you can't catch."

Tempest's eyes widened innocently over the rim of the mug of sarsaparilla. "I never said you were looking for a wife."

"Folks around here appear to have the impression that you've set your sights on me." He leaned forward. "Get that notion out of your head right now. I admire you. I think you're a heck of a woman. And I find your company pleasurable."

"No one's told me that in quite a while. Thank you."

"That's as far as I'm willing to go."

The dimples flashed when she grinned. "Shoot, McKenna, I'm not asking you for a date with the preacher, I'm only asking for one little teensy weensy dance. That's all."

"You can lead a horse to a river, but you can't make him swim it. I'll be there, but you can forget me dancing."

He hadn't kicked up his heels since the time he got drunk in Cimarron and danced like a fool on the bar. He swore then to lay off all dancing.

Several hours later, he leaned back in a chair on the sidewalk in front of the hotel with his hat pulled low over his eyes. The cow town had gotten livelier once the speechifying by politicians blowing hot air was done. Around noon, a noisy parade with no shortage of pretty fillies marched up the street.

Tempest outshone them all by far in yet another fanciful costume. She dazzled in a white gypsy bodice that fell off her shoulders. A shimmering skirt hugged her shapely hips, secured at the waist by a wide belt with gold bangles.

He pushed his hat back with a forefinger.

She looked the part of a gypsy fortune-teller who could rook you out of the fillings in your teeth before you could get your butt parked good in the chair.

Damn if it wasn't a carnival after all.

Try to deny it or not, the lower regions of his anatomy responded to the woman who could steam hot water on a cold stove. Half the time he wanted to strangle her with both hands and the other half he wanted to throw her over his shoulder and take her to a private island and explore her curves.

It was all he could do to keep from yanking her out of that wagon, petticoats and all, and hauling her right up to his room.

Tempest caught sight of him, smiled big and blew an airy kiss. It was then he knew he was in danger, the mortal kind, the kind a man couldn't easily get out of.

McKenna propped his feet on the railing in front of him. He should saddle up Hard Tack and light out for Horse Creek with his parcel. The town's generosity be damned. He'd caught Cherokee Bill and gotten their money back because it was the right thing to do, not because they owed him for it.

At the sound of a pistol, he was on his feet with his Colt in his hand before he realized it was the signal for the horse race to start.

Paints, buckskins, roans and all thundered down the street and into the countryside. He'd just eased back into the chair when he noticed a commotion near the livery. It wasn't any surprise to see Tempest fly at a big stout fellow with her fists raised. A young man lay on the ground at their feet.

McKenna's spurs clinked as he strode into the fray.

"Get her off me," yelled the man.

McKenna grabbed Tempest around the waist. "Stop!" One of her feet landed a kick to McKenna's shin as he pulled her loose.

Tempest's chest heaved. She had fire in her eye and fury in her voice. "Turn me loose. This brute deserves to be horse-whipped and I intend to do it."

"She's crazy," the man hollered.

"Just settle down, Tempest." McKenna had his hands full with the hellion. "If I let you go, will you behave yourself?"

Casting her adversary a bitter stare, she nodded curtly.

McKenna gave the young boy a hand and pulled him to his feet. Blood trickled down one side of his dirty face.

"She was only trying to protect me," murmured the boy.

"I would've thrashed this clod within an inch of his miserable life if you hadn't stopped me." Tempest lifted the hem of her skirt, tore a strip off her petticoat, and carefully cleaned the boy's face. "The louse has nothing better to do than beat an unfortunate boy who has no one to take up for him."

The big-boned fellow spat a curse. "The dummard should've

done what I told him. Next thing I know this crazy hellcat jumped right in the middle of me and my business."

Cold rage filled McKenna. In that moment, he stood in the boy's shoes. "Is this young man under your employ, Tempest?"

Her eyes glittered with rage. "As of this moment, Pony Boy works for me. I'll not see my ranch hands abused by anyone."

Deadly calm reverberated inside McKenna when he turned to the ill-mannered devil. "I see you lay a hand on this boy or Mrs. LeDoux again you're a dead man, mister."

His warning delivered a strong, dangerous message that he was more than willing to back up with force.

The man's Adam's apple bobbed a little, an indication McKenna had put the fear of God in him.

Tempest flashed McKenna a crooked smile. "Thank you. I'm going to find my foreman, Teg Tegeler, and have him take Pony Boy to Jacks Bluff. He needs a home and I have a big place that needs more young people."

Pony Boy wiped the blood from his eye. "Thank you, ma'am."

"Seems a good solution," McKenna agreed.

Tempest glanced at the clock hanging from the corner of the bank. "Good heavens, Alaine's shooting competition begins in fifteen minutes! I need to get moving. I'll see you later. Don't be late for the dance tonight."

He parted with a flicker of a smile. "Wouldn't dream of it."

Taking his time, McKenna sauntered down the crowded street where the shooting competition was about to commence.

He hadn't meant to go, but curiosity won out.

McKenna wanted to judge Alaine LeDoux's skill for himself.

And nothing wrong with wanting to see the girl's mother. Her eager smile and sultry voice was addictive.

She drew him like a hard beetle to a lantern on a hot night and he didn't even care if his butt was getting singed.

His body instantly responded to images that flitted through

his head, the ones that kept him awake and drove heat into his belly.

He wanted her.

Oh God, he wanted her.

Tempest stood near with her feet braced and hands clenched over her heart when Alaine strode confidently to the shooting mark. McKenna knew Tempest was praying and knew what she prayed for. First and foremost she wanted her daughter safe. But he'd recognized the torn look in her eyes. She wanted her daughter to win, to show these people that LeDouxes were as good as anyone.

The girl raised the 16-gauge Parker and drew a bead on the target.

Alaine appeared to know what she was doing.

As blue smoke burst from the business end of the rifle, it was Tempest, instead of her daughter, who recoiled as if it were she holding the weapon.

Alaine's bullet went wide. The miss took all the stuffing out of the bewitching, prideful woman.

With death stealing five hapless husbands, not to mention a mother and father, it stood to reason that Tempest would be on edge with her daughter, afraid that any second she'd lose her too. The idea of Alaine toting guns must terrify her.

And yet, the mother let her daughter chase her dream. In spite of all Tempest's objections, even though she denied her own dream, she truly championed Alaine.

The widow had a good head on her shoulders . . . and a soft spot for wayward daughters and homeless boys.

McKenna eyed Alaine stalking toward the nearest alley with her chin held high. He tasted her disappointment. But the youngest LeDoux wouldn't give up, that much he knew. She was like her mother; clamp her teeth in something and it'd take forty mules and a jenny to pull her off. That girl would practice until her trigger finger wore down to a nubbin and even then use the stub.

Mother and daughter had a lot more in common than they realized. The girl would come back better than ever tomorrow.

He whistled as he strode toward the bathhouse. He'd arrived at two decisions.

He'd ride on out come morning, complete his task and cut a trail back through Kasota Springs on his way home to Austin.

And he'd go to the dance and give the pretty widow a little sugar to offset all those sour pickles she'd had to eat.

Chapter 10

Purple twilight had drifted over Kasota Springs by the time Tempest galloped into town after a hurried ride to the ranch to change clothes. It'd taken more time than she wanted in choosing the right outfit, but she wanted it to be perfect.

She drew up hard on the reins and dismounted in front of the town square. Fiddle music already played, drowning out the shuffle of the dancers' feet.

Tempest swept the crowd. No sign of the handsome cowboy whose mere glance made her heart quiver.

McKenna Smith wasn't going to come despite his promise.

An ache rose more powerful than when she'd buried her husbands.

It still worried her that she would somehow cause his death, that the bad luck curse put on her long ago under a Cajun moon would continue to steal those she loved. The potion she made had thus far worked. But the secret herbs and roots had limited power. If only she could cure McKenna of the need to live by the gun. That would be a crucial step.

Don't chase what you can't catch. McKenna's warning.

How true were his words that no woman would ever rope him.

She couldn't imagine not trying though.

Not to change the curse. No, the sad fact remained that she'd fallen hopelessly in love with this gunfighter in black.

McKenna Smith had fire and passion and strength.

She weaved her way around the edge of the dancers and took an inconspicuous place with the other partner-less women. She smoothed her soft calico skirt and returned their smiles.

No one would ask her to dance. No one ever did.

Men cut a wide path around her out of fear that they too would meet with the fate each of her husbands had and to touch her would invite a handshake with the undertaker.

She looked for Alaine, but didn't see her. She'd have given anything for a chance to console her daughter after missing the target at the shooting competition, but Alaine had stalked off alone to lick her wounds.

A seamstress could've cut Alaine and her from the same bolt of cloth in that the girl wanted to nurse her wounds in private.

Seemed they both might have raw hurt to soothe tonight.

Against Tempest's will, her booted foot tapped in time with the music and she began to sway. With eyes closed, she pretended strong arms wrapped around her. She was gliding across the wooden planks with the one she loved.

Just one song and she'd ride back to her lonely life at the ranch and seek solace in the lavish furnishings she'd collected.

"The prettiest woman here and you don't have men lining up to dance?" The deep husky voice from behind sent hot waves sweeping into her belly. "Thought I'd have to beat 'em off with a stick just to get to the front of the line."

Tempest's eyes flew open. She whirled and plunged into McKenna's glistening golden stare.

"I didn't think you'd come."

"Always keep my word, you can count on that. Had to say good-bye and thank you for making a saddle tramp welcome."

Her breath caught on the ball of spiky thistles in her throat.
"You're leaving?"

"I have a matter of utmost importance to take care of."

Whatever was in the saddlebags she suspected.

"But you agreed to stay awhile."

Lanterns hanging around the town square twinkled with
the brightness of a thousand dreams but each held illusion.

"Plans change." The shadow deepened beneath the rim of
McKenna's hat and along his jaw. "Dance with me, Tempest
LeDoux."

The tall paladin with long legs that took him anyplace he
wanted to go gave her a real, very blinding smile.

"I thought you'd never ask."

The circle of his arms enfolded her, transporting her
straight to heaven. Millions of tiny trembles burst inside her.
She pressed her face against his broad chest, inhaling the
scent of shaving soap, sage and free spirit.

He was a maverick who roamed the wild country.

Tipping her head back in order to look up at him she murmured, "You said you didn't dance. Yet here we are."

"Yep, here we are. Didn't think it proper to head out at first
light without saying good-bye."

Unshed tears blurred Tempest's view of McKenna's high
cheekbones and strong jaw. She'd lost him before they even
had a chance.

She lowered her eyes and felt his chin rest on the top of her
head. He was a man of steel and principle. Together with him
she could've banished the ghosts from her past. His heartbeat
was soft and sure. She clutched a handful of shirtsleeve and
wished for strength to let him go.

McKenna's grip around her waist tightened as though he
read her mind. "That was a fine thing you did today, fighting for that boy and taking him under your wing."

"Pony Boy reminds me of myself. Did you know he's

been sleeping under the porch at the church? Doesn't have a soul."

"This land is hard and takes what it wants." McKenna's voice carried a brittle edge.

"Sometimes far too much for a grown person, let alone a frightened young man." Tempest knew just how fast the land gobbled up men and dreams.

"Something tells me you've not always lived a life of luxury. You've done without many times I gather."

More tears filled her eyes, although she was much too prideful to let the weakness show. She blinked hard. "My mother and father died of the black fever in the swamps of Louisiana. I've been on my own since I was ten."

"I've found life doesn't stand hitched. You've gotta ride it like you find it. It bucks and paws and snorts. Sure isn't for a sissy, that's a fact. You've had a hard row to hoe."

"It threw me more than once, but I did it and the trying made me strong enough to weather the storms."

"It certainly did. At least I was right about something."

"What's that?"

"Took you to be from the south. Sometimes you wrap your words in dogwood and magnolia blossoms. Knew I recognized that mellow accent."

Tempest sighed and wrinkled her nose. "I can't tell you how long I've worked to get rid of it. People here would never accept a girl who came from the swamps. Bad enough they know I'm from Louisiana. They just don't know how deep."

"You try too hard to fit into this town. Can't force respect."

"I've never gotten a blasted thing I didn't have to bulldog my way into, wrestle it to the ground and take."

McKenna's eyebrow lifted. "My point exactly. And you never got to keep any of it other than material things that don't mean a damn, did you?" His sigh ruffled her hair. "I'm sorry. That was uncalled for. Life kicked you in the teeth and I'm no one to criticize the way you turned out."

Tempest didn't trust her voice to speak. Truth be told, he was right. She always ruined everything by trying too hard.

He twirled her under his arm. The man was no stranger to dancing so she wondered why he'd been adamant, refusing to do it. A wisp of jealousy rose.

How many women had he held like they meant something?

The music ended. McKenna steered her away from the dancers. "Let's sit a spell."

His big hand on the small of her back made her tremble as he led her to one of the bales of hay that had been scattered around the perimeter of the dance floor. She noticed the one he directed her to was half hidden from view of the dancers. She watched him bend his lean, lithe form and seat himself beside her.

"None of us here are the people we planned to be, McKenna."

"I reckon I own that. Know better than most."

She twisted her hands in her lap and chewed her lip. "I've never had real peace inside. Seems I was born worrying about one thing or another. But you have this way about you. You make people . . . me . . . believe the impossible. I didn't mean to settle down in the Texas Panhandle. I intended to go to Montana, but I gave up on it."

McKenna leaned and tucked a strand of loose hair behind her ear and caressed her cheek. "What's stopping you?"

"Alaine. The ranch. I have obligations . . ." Her voice trailed when he moved closer and tilted her chin toward him. She grew weak with longing.

His kiss seared the air around them and every denial lodging in the far corners of Tempest's soul.

"Let's say good-bye like we said hello," McKenna murmured against her ear.

"With clothes or without this time?"

"Darlin', I want to crawl inside you and love you like you're the last doggie out of the chute and the world's gonna end tomorrow."

Chapter 11

McKenna rose as the first blush of dawn crept through the window of his hotel room. He quietly dressed. Kissing Tempest's bare shoulder, he gave her lush form a long stare, threw his saddlebags over his arm and closed the door.

Damn, he hated leaving her.

If she hadn't still slept, he'd never have been able to.

Wanting for her was a heat that threatened to consume. The desperate need wound itself around his heart and pulled tight.

If only they lived in a perfect world, where a man could reach for those desires and be confident he deserved them. In a perfect world, he could count on people and know they wouldn't disappoint. And in a perfect world, love would last a lifetime.

The livery was a short walk. Although McKenna had to admit he had fond memories of Kasota Springs, he itched to keep his promise to a friend.

If not for that, he might hang around just to watch the fireworks that popped when the fetching widow was around.

But he had to put distance between him and Tempest LeDoux.

For now at least so he could do some thinking.

She'd left her brand on him and it'd take 'til doomsday to

scar over. He didn't even have a rustler's running-iron to brand over it and try to erase her mark. He might not want to.

The woman with a sensitive heart full of caring tempted him in a million different ways to forget who he was, why he could never take a wife.

Damn Lacy Lorena! And damn the Colt sheathed in his holster. A muscle twitched in his jaw as he stepped into the livery.

Hard Tack's stall seemed unusually quiet. When he reached it, his curse rent the early morning stillness. The dun gelding lay listless on the dirt floor. McKenna didn't have to be told the horse likely had colic. He had to work fast.

Hell and damnation! He knelt, tugging on Hard Tack's neck.

"Get up now, boy. You have to stand up."

Hard Tack lifted his head. Pain filled the gentle brown eyes. Then the horse let his head fall back to the stall floor.

McKenna grabbed the tack and carefully slipped it over the gelding's head. He dug in his heels and pulled. At last he got the animal on his feet and out into the corral. Around and around they walked. Then giving Hard Tack a little rest, he walked him some more.

The sunrise came as an orange ball of heat by the time the beefy liveryman stumbled from his bed, wild-eyed and suffering the effects of too much rotgut the night before.

"The gelding colicky, Mr. Smith?" the stout farrier asked.

"Yep." McKenna whirled. "What have you been feeding him?"

Scratching his head, the liveryman frowned. "The alfalfa Miz LeDoux's been sending from her ranch and a few oats."

"Are you sure that's all?"

"Well, Timmy's been coming around right regular. He's the boy you paid to bring him here." The liveryman's eyes grew wide. "I recollect Timmy always has this burlap bag with him."

McKenna left Hard Tack's exercise to the farrier and made tracks for Timmy. Scaring the boy out of a year's growth wasn't his intention, getting to the root of the problem was all McKenna was after. A few minutes later, he had his answer. The cause of the colic was sweet feed and green apples. Timmy didn't know Hard Tack had problems digesting those when given too much. The poor boy had thought he did McKenna a favor.

At least it hadn't been worms as McKenna feared. A day or two and the horse would be good as new.

Traveling was out for now. He didn't even consider leaving without Hard Tack. The gelding was family. They'd both stay.

After breakfast at the Red Rooster, McKenna returned to the stables and spent the rest of the morning with Hard Tack, thankful for signs of improvement. For all his slackard appearance, the beefy farrier showed diligence in his care. McKenna would add extra to the bill when they settled up.

Deciding to take a stroll, he made for the Slats and Fats Saloon. A beer might be just the thing.

He might even have one or two of those hardboiled eggs they kept on the bar in a big jar full of vinegar.

On this particular day, the barkeep was the one everybody called Fats. Half the height of his partner, Fats was so short he'd have to climb a ladder to kick a gnat on the ankle.

Seeing McKenna, Fats hustled behind the bar and stepped up on something in order to peer over the polished wood. A second later, he slid a cool beer in front of McKenna. "Mr. Smith, you gonna ride in the wild bronc competition?"

"Nope. For the last time, I'm not here for the rodeo."

Angus Murdoch crowded around. "Bet you could tame the wildest, meanest bronc in the chute."

"I've done my share of competition riding," McKenna replied. "Don't see much sport in getting busted up just for the pure hell of it."

"Ain't meaning no disrespect, but you're riding a mighty mean back-breaker already," Angus cackled.

Everything went quiet inside McKenna. His narrowed gaze raked the sign-hanger. "How you figure that?"

"Well, you're still breathing and unhitched after the Widow LeDoux's most determined assault."

"It's early yet," laughed Fats. "She's not done."

McKenna fixed the pair with a piercing stare. "Only fools know to keep running their mouths. I'd keep quiet about Mrs. LeDoux unless you'd like me to show you what happens to men who forget how to treat a lady. When you mention her, I suggest you use a heap of respect or you'll answer directly to me."

Angus flushed, hastily paid for his beer and left. Fats found pressing business in washing dirty glasses.

McKenna returned to the livery to check Hard Tack's progress. The gelding wasn't as lethargic. The tight bands about McKenna's chest loosened a bit. The horse would be okay.

Currying a handsome buckskin, the farrier paused with his brush in midair. "You fixin' to head over to the churchyard for the box lunch before the bronc riding starts, Mr. Smith?"

"Didn't plan on it."

"I'd go if I had a lady to cotton to. Guess it's just as well. Cain't get interested in anyone since the missus died."

"How long has it been?" McKenna asked quietly.

"Almost a year. You might as well take part. Who knows, you might get lucky." The man grinned, leaving McKenna to wonder if the town had started taking bets on Tempest and him. He wouldn't doubt it. But the thought aroused anger. He wasn't going to marry her. Wasn't gonna happen.

Against his better judgment, he walked to the church, his silver spurs clinking with each step.

He looked forward to glimpsing Tempest, who'd be busier than a weathervane in a stiff wind. She was determined to fulfill every last one of her rodeo committee duties. Including some that weren't covered under that responsibility.

They'd said their good-byes. Facing her again would make leaving that much harder . . . on them both.

Some things were too much to resist he found.

And Tempest strained his will to the breaking point.

McKenna stood at the back of the enthused crowd where he could watch in secret. He drank in the widow's beauty, remembering the feel of her skin that was soft as the full bolls of Delta cotton.

People of all shapes and sizes, from near and far packed the churchyard. A mess of children chased each other around a big cottonwood tree, the only shade around in the whole blamed town. McKenna stood in the shadows as men shyly bought up the ladies' pretty boxes that were tied with fancy bows and the like.

All except one. The box that remained was the best looking of the bunch.

He wondered why it was left but soon got his answer. A pinched-faced woman he'd heard everyone refer to as Jabberjaws Dewey leaned and whispered to another. "Ain't nobody gonna buy Tempest LeDoux's. Ain't a man alive who'll touch it. Lord only knows what she put in it."

Anger swept him like a raging river, swollen from heavy rain. A searching gaze located Tempest at the front near the lonely box. Waiting.

Even from the shadows, he could see that her shoulders were fiercely straight and her eyes stared straight ahead. If he'd been close enough to tell, those eyes the color of freshly plowed earth would likely glisten with unshed tears.

"Well, reckon no one's gonna step up and buy this last box," announced Mayor Redgrave. "Sorry, Mrs. LeDoux."

How dare they treat Tempest with such open scorn.

"I will." McKenna raised his hand, pushed through the

tangle of bodies and darting children. "I'll buy the lady's box. I'm sure it's the tastiest of the whole lot."

A wave of snickers drifted aimlessly among the onlookers.

Of course, they kept it low, mindful of McKenna. But he'd heard and it didn't exactly make him all that charitable.

Claiming the fancy lunch, he shot the cacklers a withering scowl. Heads ducked and feet scurried.

"You don't have to do this to save my stupid pride," Tempest murmured, trying to hide the red flush in her cheeks.

Capturing her sweaty palm, he tugged her toward the bank of a small creek behind the church.

"What if it so happens I want to?" The corner of his mouth quirked. "And I'm not saving your pride or anything other than my growling gut. I happen to be starved. Besides, this smells like fried chicken, my favorite."

Finding a smidgen of privacy amid the nearby trickling stream, McKenna let her choose the first piece of chicken.

Tempest selected a drumstick. Framed by long dark lashes, her brown gaze met his, creating a wave of smoldering heat where they touched. "I thought you left town."

"Found Hard Tack listless in his stall with a bad case of colic."

"How serious?"

"Should keep me here a couple more days. What do you have to say about that, Lady Tempest?"

Her eyes twinkled and dimples flashed. "I certainly know how we can fill the time."

Chapter 12

The day was heavenly despite a dark cloudbank building in the west that promised rain. Tempest grinned and nibbled on the drumstick. Yes, she could fill his days and every single night, even Thanksgiving and Christmas, if he'd stay.

She'd looked for a man like McKenna Smith her whole life.

He was number six. He just didn't know it yet.

The potion seemed to be protecting him from taking dangerous risks and keeping him healthy. Could've been what kept him from leaving, not that she wished ill on the gelding.

She still had the little vial in her pocket.

If something distracted him long enough, she'd pour the last of it into his cider. A small amount had worked very well. A lot should get even more amazing results.

Her mind drifted to the previous night they'd spent making love. His hotel room had smoldered with a heat they couldn't put out. Lord help her need to be in his arms, entangled in the sheets, hopelessly, impossibly in love. He hadn't ridden out of her life just yet. She had a second chance. Maybe.

She chewed her lip. After McKenna witnessed the matter with her box lunch, would he think her too damaged? Few men would want to hitch themselves to a ridiculed woman like her.

She couldn't offer him very many advantages beyond a ranch.

"I'm sorry about that incident back there."

"You mean at the church?"

She nodded. "If you didn't see the majority of the town's dislike before, you saw it blazed across the entire Panhandle."

McKenna gently kissed her cheek and winked. "One thing you'll learn about me—I form my own opinion about things. Never been one to follow the herd."

"I admire a fearless man. More cider?" she asked.

"Don't mind if I do. It's mighty good."

With one hand holding a wishbone, he picked up a small pebble with his left and threw it into the creek. He looked around the ground for another. Seeing her chance, she added the rest of the potion to the contents and handed it back.

"May I ask something personal, McKenna?"

The shadow of his dark hat hid the glisten of his eyes, but she sensed a darkening. He cleaned the meat off a wishbone and held it up. "Get the long piece and I'll tell you anything."

Game for the fabled lucky charm, Tempest grasped her end and tugged. She grinned, waving the longer piece of bone.

"Looks like you lose again, McKenna."

"Nothing new in my dealings with you." He dropped the short piece of bone into the box and licked his fingers. "What is it your pretty, inquiring mind wants to know?"

"What's so important that you left me guarding your saddlebags? And what's in Horse Creek?"

"When I was born, my mother, and I use the word loosely, left me behind in a dirty hotel room. Lacy Lorena was an actress in a traveling show. A newborn son didn't quite fit her lifestyle."

"Did they put you in an orphanage?" Her throat tightened.

Damn. She struggled to swallow a hard lump, her chest aching for the unwanted baby boy.

"An acquaintance of Lacy's took me to raise. Martha Wren was also an actress, but she had a heart big as the sky and a stable life. I grew up around the stage. When she died early of a lung disease, I came west. Got mixed up in the Colfax County and Lincoln County wars and learned how to stay alive."

He jerked off his hat and ran a hand through his hair before he jammed it back on. "If there was a fight, I found it. Couldn't abide rotten land-grabbers taking from honest folks."

"I can see how you became the Guardian of Justice."

"Someone had to do it. Reckon I appointed myself. Started hiring out my services." McKenna parted with a wry smile. "This is a long way to get to the bunkhouse, but I'm getting there. In my hell-raisin' days I met up with John Two Feathers. He became the father I never had. Part of me died when he recently passed on. I gave him my word I'd take his amulet and medicine bag to Horse Creek, bury them on the sacred land of his ancestors."

"Oh, McKenna, no wonder you guarded the saddlebags with your life." Her heart swelled with love.

"Yep. I'd severely hurt anyone who messed with them. Or you," he added quietly with a measure of gritty calm.

Not knowing how to answer or trusting her voice if words had come, Tempest's heart swelled as she wrapped up the left-over chicken and put lids on the jars of butter pickles and beets.

McKenna was stuffing the contents into the fancy hatbox that generally held her wedding hat when Doc, Angus Murdoch and Phinneas Jenkins approached. The three could be sold as a matched set. Where one went the other two were close behind. Tempest rose and eyed them warily, in no mood to tolerate them.

"Mr. Smith," began Doc. "Can we have a word?"

"You're wasting your time, gentlemen." McKenna rose to his full height, towering over them all. "Not in the mood."

"Hear us out," begged Angus. "The wild bronc competition is fixin' to start. We'd like you to enter."

Tempest put her hands on her hips. "He said he's not interested. It's too dangerous for someone like McKenna. He could get hurt." Or worse. She shuddered.

"You gonna let some woman speak for you?" asked Angus.

Doc's quick hand kept Tempest from stomping Angus into the middle of next Friday. "A fellow from down Laredo way said you won the competition two years ago. Said you're a hell of a bronc rider. The fellow had never seen anything like it."

"I'm done with bronc riding. Don't have anything to prove."

A red stain crept up Phinneas's neck. "Don't be so hasty. You can make some easy money here, Smith."

"You mean make *you* some easy money, don't you? Put the saddle on the right horse. And if it's so blessed easy, how come one of you don't ride the damn thing?"

"Well . . . well . . . we ain't suited for it," blustered Doc.

"If you'll excuse us, gentlemen, I have to get this lunch put away so I can attend to my rodeo chairman duties. Don't see why we'd have a reason to give you the time of day anyhow."

"Best get on your way before I lose my temper and do something I'll sorely regret." McKenna's glacial squint scattered them like a flock of nervous geese.

Tempest folded up the tablecloth, thanking the Good Lord that McKenna wasn't a foolhardy man or one given to big ideas.

It was just fine and dandy with her if he never looked at a wild mustang. She enjoyed the warmth flooding her.

Chapter 13

Tempest and McKenna parted company at the livery. He went to check on Hard Tack while she stashed the lunch remains in her room at the hotel and continued on to the livestock pens and chutes next to the railhead.

She had to keep an eye on Alaine and try to curb the girl's enthusiasm. She would keep her daughter safe if it killed her.

In the face of Tempest's severe displeasure, Alaine had insisted on taking part in the roping. But who knew what other events the girl would try to tackle. She wouldn't put it past her wild-and-woolly daughter to sign up for the bronc riding or the wild cow milking contest.

Good heavens, that child would be the death of her yet.

Tempest normally loved a rodeo when it was strangers putting themselves in mortal danger. And being head of the committee certainly brought satisfaction. But this time she had other things she'd rather do—like snuggle in McKenna's bed at the hotel or in her huge, four-poster one out at Jacks Bluff.

Strip down to the bare skin and make slow passionate love until neither had energy left for anything except sleep.

Her Texas Guardian had saved her from total humiliation. Tempest had wanted to sink into a deep hole and pull it in after her. But then McKenna had stepped up bold as could be and bought her box despite everything.

McKenna had honor and knew how to care for a woman's feelings.

Only someone who'd experienced the same embarrassment and fear would've stood up and dared anyone to cross him.

But that was typical of the man who'd made love to her. She was the last doggie out of the chute. She just prayed the world wouldn't end tomorrow. Oh God, how she prayed.

She thought about their lives. Both had come up the hard way, except Tempest had known the love of a mother and father. McKenna lived knowing the very person who should've loved him most had thrown him away. Like Pony Boy, McKenna had needed someone to fight for him, someone to slay the dragons in the dark of night.

Tucking those thoughts away, Tempest made sure the wild bronc competition got started and settled down to watch the raw power of the animals and the gritty men who tried to tame them.

Her attention was riveted on a wild mustang just loaded into the chute. The animal was rearing and snorting, trying his best to bust free of his wooden prison. She pitied the cowboy who tried to ride the beast. He'd better be tough.

The mustang was a killer.

It'd be just like Alaine to try to ride it.

Tempest gripped the wooden plank that served for seating. But it wasn't Alaine striding toward the chute.

Her heart lurched painfully.

It couldn't be. But it was. McKenna was surrounded by a dozen or so men and it seemed he meant to climb onto the back of the crazed animal.

Thick foreboding blocked the air from Tempest's lungs.

At the creek he'd said he wouldn't ride. What'd changed?

He'd gotten a pair of leather chaps from somewhere. The

sound of them flapping against his long legs was like whips tearing into her flesh.

Hazers held the mustang tight while McKenna threw his leg over the saddle and got a firm grip on the reins.

She squeezed her eyes shut. She couldn't watch, couldn't breathe, couldn't bear to bury another good man.

But when she heard male voices shout, "Waltz with the lady!" her eyes flew open.

A thousand pounds of muscle, rawhide and rage left the chute fast, bucking and twisting its body first to the left and then to the right. It was the kind of horse some would say warped its backbone and hallelujahed all over the place.

For all his seasoning, McKenna had his hands full just to stay seated. An icy chill swept through her as she raced to the thick posts that formed the arena.

She got there just as the bronc intentionally hurled itself backward, the trick of a killer. It wasn't content merely to unseat McKenna, the mustang meant to kill him.

Despite the gut-twister's plans, McKenna held on and rode straight for hell. The horse crashed into the fence, the chutes, everything in its path not caring what it went through.

Tempest gasped. The horse had turned into a blind-bucker.

Then with blood in the crazed killer's eye it turned and came straight for Tempest.

A blood-curdling scream left her throat.

She'd never get out of the way before it busted through the corral fence and trampled her.

But, just as she felt the horse's breath on her neck, McKenna leaped and with a mighty heave pushed her to safety.

The horse's hooves caught McKenna, dragging him under. By the time the rodeo clown distracted the animal and outriders roped it, McKenna lay in a silent heap on the ground little more than a bunch of limp, bloody clothes.

"McKenna! Someone get the doctor." She knelt and lifted him into her lap. "Don't you die! Don't you dare die on me."

Chapter 14

"Doc's gone out to deliver the Whipple's baby," yelled a man's voice.

"Then get a buckboard." Tempest's fingers trembled as she loosened McKenna's shirt. "I'm taking him to Jacks Bluff."

She would not, by God, lose another man!

Carefully, a half dozen men lifted the still, pale form into the back of the buckboard and they made the arduous journey to the ranch. Once there, ranch hands carried McKenna into the big house.

Tempest barked orders right and left. Soon the men had rigged a bed in the downstairs study and she began the work of getting him undressed and comfortable.

All the while she kept up a running prayer.

This was her fault. She'd given him too much potion and it'd made him crazy. She should've known this would happen.

Tears sprang to her eyes. He'd saved her life. His last thoughts had been for her safety, not his. By all rights it should be her lying there with blood oozing from her head.

Calming herself, she washed out the gash, cleaning away the blood, dirt and wood fragments from the busted corral. Stitching the wound closed the best she could, she bound his head, giving thanks that her fingertips hadn't detected a depression or break in his skull. That was a blessing.

She quickly moved to his other injuries. A few needed attention but weren't serious. And he had some broken ribs.

Tempest placed her hand on the broad chest of the man who'd given her much more than one night to remember. She was thankful he'd been unconscious while she stitched his wounds.

She wouldn't be the cause of any more pain.

Leaning, she planted a kiss on his dark whisker-shadowed jaw. Sudden reality created ice in her veins. In trying to assure he was safe and healthy she almost killed him.

"Dear Lord, if I can't have him without the help of potions and sheer stubbornness, I'll give him up." Her prayer seemed to ricochet off the walls, bouncing back in her face. "It'll be his decision or none at all."

Tempest sat beside his bed through the long night, watching him go in and out of consciousness. The times he'd been awake he'd been disoriented, not uncommon after having a thousand pounds of rawhide stomping a man's head into a soft melon. She took heart though in his recognition of her. Seemed a good sign, but she kept listening for the doc's horse anyway. She'd feel better having a medical opinion, even from Doc Mitchell.

Cook was stirring in the kitchen by the time McKenna opened his eyes and slowly looked around the room.

Tempest grasped his hand. "McKenna, you're at my ranch. Do you have any memory of what happened?"

"Last I recall I was on top of a rip-snortin' mustang bound for hell." A shadow crossed his golden amber gaze. He touched his bandaged head. "Then he turned straight for you. Reckon I ended up under the angry beast?"

"You saved my life." Her voice was ragged from the tears clogging her throat. "I wish . . . oh damn, I wish . . ."

"The main thing is you're all right. Real glad of that."

"Are you hungry? Cook can make whatever you want."

"Just some coffee for now. Smells good."

"I'll be right back." She stepped smartly out the door.

McKenna wondered how he came to be in her study. He looked around the room filled with expensive paintings, leather-bound books, a piano and more vases of roses. Too much for a room this small. He sighed. His Lady Tempest. She seemed to think having more and better of everything would fill the emptiness inside and make people accept her.

Only it hadn't.

When Tempest returned, she carried a tray of food that could've fed an army and all its horses.

"I just wanted a cup of coffee," he growled.

"You might change your mind." She handed him his coffee. "Besides, some of this is for me. Now that you're better I'm hungry." She broke off a piece of toast, plopping it into her mouth. "Doc Mitchell should be by shortly to check on you and see if my stitching measures up to the old goat's standards."

"You stitched me up?"

"Did the best I could. Doc was out delivering a baby at the Whipple's when the accident happened."

"You're something, Miz Tempest LeDoux."

Tempest shrugged her shoulders. "Sewing up nasty wounds comes with the territory on a ranch. I do what it calls for."

"Yep." He changed the subject. "Must've taken you years to amass all these trappings of wealth. Makes me wonder why a little girl who came from the swamps would need this to prove who she is."

Her chin jutted. "Are you criticizing me?"

"Just trying to understand. You're a fascinating woman."

She relaxed. "Seems people look up to others when they most envy them."

"Tempest, you have more heart and soul than most of the people in this town combined." His voice grew soft. "Things like saving Pony Boy, caring about the less fortunate and taking such excellent care of your daughter make me admire you, not what you own." He wanted to add grave-tender to the list, but he didn't.

"Those things come as natural as breathing."

"Natural is good." He waved his arm. "The rest of this is fake. You're too worried about appearances."

She jumped to her feet and snatched up the tray of food. "I'll wait in the parlor for the doc if you don't mind."

The whip of her skirts spoke a language he had no trouble deciphering. He'd gone and said the wrong thing. He tried to call her back, but he was met with the loud ticking of a clock.

McKenna rubbed his eyes. He'd give her a little time to un-bunch her tail feathers. Then he'd try to make her see *she* wasn't fake, just the things she surrounded herself with.

He'd barely finished his coffee when Doc Mitchell arrived. Tempest showed the man to the study door, then vanished.

Reckon he'd raised her hackles good and plenty.

"Well, Tempest sewed you up fine," the doc said after examining him. "A mighty lucky man. Word in town said you were fit for the boneyard after that mustang got finished. Take it easy for a day or two. Headaches will likely come and go. Best if you stay here at the ranch."

McKenna didn't know if that was best or not considering how mad he'd made Tempest. Somehow he'd have to try to unkink the mess he'd made. He wouldn't leave with her angry.

But hours passed and she didn't step foot into the room. He finally dozed.

He awoke to find Tempest tiptoeing through the door. The sheets rustled when he moved. "There you are. I thought you'd ridden back to town for your rodeo duties or something."

"Angus is taking care of the rodeo affairs. Did you want something? Are you hungry?" Her manner was distant.

"I could use a bite to eat and some more coffee."

Without a reply, she raised her pert little nose and left, presumably for the kitchen. He wasn't sure if she'd bring the food to him or throw it at him. A short while passed before he heard approaching footsteps. He sat up, propping himself against the brass headboard that must've taken every hand on the ranch to move it from God knows where.

Tempest quietly entered and placed a tray across his lap. The smell of the juicy steak made him realize how empty he was. He was disappointed when Tempest didn't keep him company.

How could a man say he was sorry if she wouldn't let him?

When she came for the tray, he threw back the bedding and grabbed his britches determined to set things right.

She scowled. "What on earth are you doing? Doc said—"

"He didn't say to laze around in bed, letting a woman coddle me. I'm getting up and don't try to stop me." If she could be stubborn, so could he. "I need air. Lots of it."

She clamped her pretty mouth shut and carried the tray to the kitchen.

He almost reconsidered when his head started spinning. Determined, he buttoned his pants, pulled on his boots and strapped on his gunbelt. Reaching for his hat, he marched from the room to find Tempest. He had some things to say.

McKenna found her on the wide front porch. Sweating from exertion, he dropped into the chair beside her. She kept her gaze focused on the distant horizon.

"Tempest, are you going to let me apologize?"

"Whatever for, Mr. Smith? I'm sure you know far more about me than I do myself."

He took her hand and smoothed the back. "I never said *you* were fake. That's not what I meant at all. I wish you could see what a special lady you are and how any man would be thrilled to have you as a wife and friend."

"You don't owe me anything; it's the other way around."

"All the same, I wasn't criticizing you." He cupped her face and turned her toward him. "But that's not the whole of it is it? What's really going on?"

Eyes the color of rich melted chocolate stared into his. He hadn't expected to see her lip quiver. She bit it to still the tremble and swallowed hard. "McKenna, I'm to blame for you being on that crazed mustang."

"How do you figure that?"

She closed her lids for moment. When she opened them, he saw a flash of tears. "I put some potion in your cider at the box lunch affair when you weren't looking."

"Potion? What in the world are you babbling about?"

"After we first met, I made a secret potion out of herbs and roots from a Cajun recipe handed down from my grandmother. It was supposed to keep you healthy and ensure your safety." She chewed her lip again and a sob broke free. "I gave you too much. I poured the entire vial into the cider."

"That's why I was dizzy the night of the poker game?"

She nodded.

"And why I felt the same way in the saloon that day?"

She nodded. "I'm not proud of it. As you said I try too hard. And I almost killed you. You should've let the beast trample me, no more than I deserve. But I'm done. I have no plans to marry you. I'm letting you go."

He thought a proper reply would swim to the surface, but it seemed to be bogged down in quicksand. He rose to stand at the railing and stared out across the green pasture, trying to sort through the contents of his scrambled brain. He owed her the truth and she'd know if she got shortchanged in the tally.

After what seemed forever, he finally remembered the reason why he'd gotten on that bronc.

"Tempest, you're not at fault for me riding that animal."

"I'm not?"

"Nope. I got on it to keep Pony Boy from riding. He was bound and determined. I saw the boy in the livery and he told me he was going to win the prize so he wouldn't be beholden to anyone. I knew he didn't have what it took for a bronc like that so I rode it in his place. Any money I got from the bets belongs to him. So you see, it wasn't anything you did."

"Oh, McKenna." She came to stand beside him at the porch railing and put an arm around his waist. "I didn't know."

"Hope I made the boy a mess-load of money. He can use it."

"I was so afraid I caused the accident."

He took off his Stetson and placed it on her head. She tilted back to look up at him. A grin formed. "Nope, you didn't. You still letting me *go* as you put it?"

"Yes. I'm through trying to hold you, bend you to my terms. Some things are born wild and untamable."

"That's a pure shame and quite admirable, Miz LeDoux, since I refuse to let you go after I waited so long to find you."

"You want me in spite of everything?" Her dimples winked.

"In spite of, regardless of, and because of all that you are and all you can give a man like me. Isn't gonna be easy trying to teach an old dog like me to take to the leash."

McKenna bent his head and kissed her long and hard. She tasted like fine wine, fermented, aged to perfection and very heady. He could spend a lifetime with her. Tempest was nothing like his mother. She'd taught him a thing or two about the need to forgive the past, take what he could from life and make the best of it.

"You asking me to marry you, McKenna Smith?"

"I am for a fact . . . unless you object."

"How soon? I have to think of Alaine and the ranch and—"

"Rein up on them horses, lady. Don't go stampeding on me."

"No harm in making plans."

He laughed and kissed her again. There'd be no changing her. "You still have a bee in your bonnet about seeing Montana?"

"Yes, I do."

"How about going along with me to Horse Creek, then we can ride on to Montana? Who knows where we'll decide to

settle down. Figure we'll marry here first of course. Alaine
should be at her mother's wedding. Only fitting."

"You sure you want me? I have this cloud of bad luck
hanging over my head."

"A person makes their own luck and, yes, I'll always want
you."

Three days later they stood in front of the preacher. Tempest wore a brand new hat at McKenna's insistence. Alaine,
Morgan and Teg sat in the front row. Pony Boy, whose bank
account had grown from three dollars and thirty-two cents
to over one hundred and eleven dollars, grinned like a silly
fool who'd inherited the kingdom of God.

Tempest glanced up at husband number six. There was a
quickening in her heart as his lips lowered to hers, sealing
their vows with a kiss.

She was a lucky woman. This marriage would endure everything life could throw at them. She felt it in her bones.

Leaving the church, they walked toward the fancy buggy
McKenna had rented for the occasion. Old shoes, empty cans
and cowbells were tied to the back. They'd leave the buggy at
the ranch and collect Hard Tack and Ace High.

The matched set, Angus, Doc and Phinneas Jenkins stood
blocking their path.

"Well, I see you lassoed yourself another husband, Tempest," said Angus. "How long you figure this one'll last?"

McKenna stiffened; his jaw becoming hard as steel. He
stepped forward. "Already taking bets, gentlemen? If you are,
you're gonna lose. Not any of your business, but I plan on
lasting forever. And I have a very long memory. One day I
may ride this way again and settle up on my wife's behalf."

The trio ducked their heads and headed for the saloon.

Tempest grinned as McKenna lifted her into the buggy. "You
shouldn't scare them like that. They might just believe you."

He draped an arm around her shoulders and pulled her close. "They better believe it. Be unhealthy if they don't. I'll show 'em what happens when they poke a bear with a sharp stick."

"I hope you don't regret taking up with me."

"Darlin', when I rode into this town and saw you in the cemetery, I was thinking about dying and leaving nothing worth a damn behind and not a single soul in the world to care. I was a legend without a legacy. Now I know my legacy is tied to a slow waltz under a starry sky and my own Texas Tempest in my arms."

ROPING
THE WIND

Phyliss Miranda

To my Aunt Martha,
who taught me to be a lady, and
Lola, my mother-in-law,
who taught me how to be a woman.

Special thanks to Bobby Thompson,
a real-life rodeo star who is
not responsible for any of my rodeo faux pas!

Chapter 1

Kasota Springs, Texas
Fourth of July Rodeo, 1890

"What in the . . ." Morgan Payne wasn't sure whether to cuss or fight. "Son of a . . ." He stared across the alley at a young woman holding a bow. He damn sure knew where her arrow had ended up.

"Lady . . ." He flinched in pain. He'd been shot at, and even hit more times than he could remember, but never by an arrow launched by a slip of a gal barely out of her teens.

"May I please have my arrow? They are quite expensive."

"Do I look like I'm in a mood to give you anything but a hard time?" He pulled the sharp point from the crotch of his pants. "My suit is damaged and all you care about is this dern stick?"

"I think someone woke up grouchy." There was a faint glimmer of humor in her eyes.

"Little Lady . . ."

Her brows knitted together and her eyes, the shade of sun-struck amethyst, lost their humor and now flashed in anger.

Whoa! He'd apparently hit a nerve, but he continued, "I haven't been in town long enough to even eat my first meal, and I can already see that this place is nothing but trouble."

He stepped forward, while she seemed to ponder his comment.

"Nice trousers," she finally said.

Damn, she didn't seem to think she owed him so much as an apology. Morgan Payne hadn't done anything to deserve having an Indian weapon planted way too close to his privates for his liking. A man who loved the chase and was happiest running down desperadoes, rounding up rustlers and busting bank robbers, he hadn't ever been this poorly treated by an outlaw.

It was bad enough that his assignment as a Pinkerton agent required him to go around looking like a damn Eastern dandy—a little too soft for his liking. The worst part, he couldn't wear his gun belt in sight, making him feel naked. Not that it would have helped in the situation he seemed to have gotten himself into. Shooting a female was pretty much against his religion even if she'd almost neutered him.

But so far his initial exposure to Kasota Springs, Texas, deep in the heart of the Panhandle, had flabbergasted him.

First the Springs Hotel had no beds to rent because of the Fourth of July festivities. He'd been thankful to find a room no bigger than a jail cell above a saloon. Where no doubt he'd share the floor with soiled doves and rowdy cowpokes looking for a good time, but he'd call it home until his mission was accomplished.

Morgan Payne was an expert horseman and could shoot the sweat off a rattlesnake at twenty paces. He enjoyed his reputation—a man who lived by the Old West's motto of fair play and quick justice.

Right now he was only interested in locating a hemp committee to help him tame the gal who seemed to now direct her anger toward his trousers. If he hadn't been a tad bowlegged, he'd have the dern piece of jagged flint in his cojones instead of only a nick in his thigh.

He studied her. Tall and slim and about as suntanned as

he'd ever seen a woman, the gal stood there staring at him like an angel—with horns obviously hidden beneath a brimmed hat that sagged because of age. Buckskin thongs hung from the brim. Strips of rattlesnake skin were threaded through slits near the edge. He suspected she might have skinned the rattler with her sharp tongue.

A mane of midnight black curly hair flowed over her shoulders from beneath the buff felt hat, and a wicked look shone in her eyes.

Her fitted jacket with buckskin fringe and leather pants surely made all the old maids shudder. But the scarlet sash around her tiny waist—he was certain his hands could fit around it nicely—caught his attention. He'd seen Wild Bill Hickok wear a similar sash, but it had a purpose: to hold pistols hidden beneath his jacket.

Now Morgan was the one to shudder, wondering if it'd be worth the effort to haul her pretty little butt over to the sheriff's office and let him handle her irresponsible actions. On second thought, it seemed the whole dern community couldn't decide on anything. So why would the sheriff be any different?

When Morgan first arrived in town the banner hanging across Main Street read "Cowboy Competition." Then by the time he rented his room it had been changed to "Rodeo." Hellfire and brimstone, if they couldn't decide what to name their cowboy reunion, how would they handle this gal?

All he wanted to do was get the job done, put the bad men out of business and get back to being a lawman.

"You should be apologizing, not discussing my trousers. You came close to ee-masculatin' me."

"Hm. You're lucky I was using a bow instead of my rifle."

Then he noticed her strong voice. Boardinghouse English tinged with a lazy Texas accent.

"You shoot a gun in town?" he asked.

"Only when I'm practicing."

"What are you practicing for?" Morgan knew he probably didn't want to know but seemed to want to humor the girl.

"To be as good as Annie Oakley."

"It's obvious that isn't bound to happen. Didn't anybody tell you she uses guns, not a bow and arrow?"

"The townsfolk don't much like it when I practice with a gun." She held up the bow. "Shooting this contraption cross-alley gives me the perfect distance and better accuracy. It doesn't make any noise, so nobody cares—just as long as I don't use my gun. But sometimes I use *this*." She whipped a knife from a sheath hung on her belt sash.

Steel flashed in the sunlight. There went his bright idea of taking her to the sheriff. The whole town was in cahoots and ignoring her unruly behavior.

Morgan twirled the arrow he held. His thigh stung like hell, and he felt a draft but was uncomfortable examining himself. A tad difficult with her staring intently at his crotch. He wasn't sure whether to return the thing or break it in half, but resisted the urge to do the latter, remembering that he had to remain detached and try not to draw too much attention to himself.

He was supposed to be a visiting flannel-mouthed Philadelphia lawyer who wanted to buy a small spread of his own. The ruse would at least get his foot in the door, where he could hold talks with locals about their operations.

Capitalizing on the famous Texas hospitality, he knew the folks of Kasota Springs couldn't resist helping a damp-behind-the-ears dumb Eastern dandy.

"I doubt you're as skilled at shooting or throwing steel as you think you are." He decided to go for broke and see how she'd react. "Most women aren't."

"I'll have you know, I'm very good. The best around—"

"If you're the best, then everybody better stand back or they'll get their toenails pared with a butcher knife," Morgan retorted, eyeing the knife in one hand and the bow in the other.

"If I hadn't intentionally missed your family jewels, you'd be riding sidesaddle for the rest of your life." Her chin set in stubbornness. "You were just in the wrong spot at the wrong time. And if you know so much about tossing steel, then teach me." She offered him the knife with a smile.

Something in his mind screamed caution. "How stupid do you think I am?"

"I don't know, I just met you."

"Give me the knife!" He took two long, purposeful strides toward her before she handed it over, handle first.

Accepting the dang thing, Morgan squared his shoulders and shifted his weight to the ball of his right foot. Taking aim at the bale of hay across the alley, he effortlessly nailed the target and offered some sage advice. "Keep your wrist stiff. Stretch your arm out completely, but be careful not to stretch it to its fullest or your muscles will get sore."

"Thanks. You don't look like someone who would know about tossing knives or firearms."

"Just a piece of advice I picked up somewhere in my thirty years of living." He realized what he had done. Letting her know he was crafty with a knife was a mistake that could blow his cover and get him killed.

He corrected his blunder. "Any man worth his salt knows how to hunt." Cautiously keeping his eye on the arrow, he added, "If I return your weapon and go on my way, will you promise not to shoot me in the back?" He tried to keep his sarcastic tone controlled, but knew he failed miserably.

"If you promise not to tell who shot you." She gave him a mischievous look. "And, by the way, nice-looking rear end."

Surprised at her brazen comment, Morgan decided to quit while he was ahead. He needed a drink in the worst way. He flashed a reserved smile, the best he could scrounge up, and handed over the weapon.

"Good day, Little Lady." He tipped his derby hat to the young thing with way too much woman in her to deny. "That's a good nickname for you. Think it fits?"

"I'm nineteen and no lady."

"You got no argument from me." Morgan Payne headed down the alley toward Slats and Fats Saloon, praying that she didn't shoot him in the butt to punctuate her displeasure.

Chapter 2

Morgan Payne hotfooted it toward Slats and Fats saloon and was greeted by a bartender with shoulders barely coming up to the edge of the bar. He made up for his lack of height with girth. Morgan wasn't sure where Slats was, but he could pretty much account for the Fats's side of the partnership.

Nodding politely to the man, Morgan ordered a mug of coffee with a side of whiskey, paid him two bits and ambled toward a table in the corner. Far enough away from the center of the hubbub yet close enough to get the lay of the land without drawing a lot of attention. Even a greenhorn agent would never sit with their back to a door. Not one that planned to survive long. Damn, he wanted a beer, but he was a stickler for the rules—no alcohol for a Pinkerton. His mouth watered a tad. Maybe this was the time to bend the rules, but he wouldn't give in to temptation.

Morgan quenched his thirst by downing the lukewarm coffee, leaving little more than grounds before he added the whiskey, and set the cup aside, hoping nobody noticed he hadn't consumed the fiery liquid. He sure didn't need his cover blown this fast.

He removed a couple of coins from his vest pocket and fiddled with them, as if they would draw his thoughts away from the gal in the alley whose image he hadn't been able to shuck.

Settling back in the chair, his elbow touched the Colt .45, the peacemaker, hidden in his shoulder holster beneath his waistcoat. He smiled to himself, comparing his situation to the girl with the red sash who concealed a knife under her own jacket. The woman he couldn't get out of his mind.

He listened to first one, then another local discuss the annual ranch competition that was on tap for the weekend.

A middle-aged man, a black leather apron hanging over his paunch, darted into the bar and announced, "McKenna Smith just rode into town." He vanished just as quickly as he had appeared.

All ears perked up. "The gunslinger?"

Not looking up, the bartender dried a shot glass.

"Yep, the Guardian of Justice they call him. Bet he's on the bankroll of one of them English money outfits," someone Morgan couldn't see alleged.

Mumbling and nodding in agreement, the men were stirred up. Whether they agreed from fear or excitement, Morgan didn't know, but he knew one thing for certain, he planned to steer clear of the notorious gunman. Morgan knew McKenna too well to get within spittin' distance.

A young buck, wearing a dirty Stetson that had seen better days, tossed back a slug of whiskey. From the looks of his shaky hand, it wasn't his first drink of the afternoon. "I've got money that says Buckaroo LeDoux could best him. The kid's a shoo-in for the sharpshooting competition. Nobody can—"

"Clayton Snyder, you better quit calling that kid Buckaroo. At least not while any of those Jacks Bluff riders are within earshot," said the bartender.

"Who's gonna make me?"

Eyebrows raised at the challenge, and even the silence seemed to await an answer.

Clayton must've got the message. He turned all of his attention to his empty shot glass.

As though only taking a momentary break in the action, the hullabaloo in the saloon resumed.

"Sure-fire alive, no doubt the Slippery Elm cowboys will win the competition," bellowed a cowpuncher.

"*Rodeo*," another butted in. "Now they're calling it a dad-gum rodeo, not a *com-po-tition* or a challenge."

"It'll never last. Need to go back to the ranch roundup. I bet in a hundred years nobody will even know what a rodeo is," spouted another cowpoke.

"I guess Tempest LeDoux has been up to her usual shenanigans."

"Yep. Should of known when they put her in charge of the shindig she'd demand the stripe off a skunk and make him happy to oblige."

Obviously unable to hold his tongue any longer, Clayton mumbled loud enough for everyone to hear, "And her kid, Buckaroo, is bound to win if that bunch of mother hen cowpokes from the Jacks Bluff have anything to say about it."

"I'll put two bits on the Jacks Bluff boys," spouted a patron with a handlebar mustache that would put a full grown longhorn to shame. He tossed coins on the bar.

"Four bits on the Slippery Elm." A newcomer dug in his pockets to add to the pile.

"That's sour grapes, Angus Murdoch. You're madder than a hornet 'cause you locked horns with that unpredictable Cajun LeDoux woman. You know the Slippery Elm doesn't have a chance against the Jacks Bluff," the bartender added.

"Ain't so. Here's another four bits to prove it." Cowboy Mustache butted in and plopped down his donation. "That widow woman who thinks she knows about ranching is flat crazy . . ." He trailed off, taking heed that trouble was brewing.

Morgan looked up in time to see the batwing doors open

into a full swing, allowing a tall, lanky man to enter. The weatherbeaten codger filled the room with his presence. Voices hushed, as though the men expected to be blessed out by the newcomer.

"Go ahead and say what's on your mind, you bunch of ho-nyocks. You stick together like flies around a bull's butt anyways. But jest don't forget I ride for that brand."

"Hey, Teg, they don't mean nothin'," the bartender said, as he shoved a beer in the ranch foreman's hand.

The territorial hierarchy had just been established, leaving no doubt in Morgan's mind that the Jacks Bluff Ranch ran the railhead. Now he had the first piece to the puzzle.

Teg didn't agree or disagree with the bartender, just picked up his mug. He suddenly became interested in Morgan. The tough-as-strop-leather cowpuncher moseyed his way, as if Morgan was a long-lost cousin who just showed up for a visit. "Here for the festivities?"

"Nope," Morgan answered nonchalantly.

"Need a fresh cup?"

"Got one, thanks."

"Kinda cold, ain't it?"

"Nope. Just like I like it."

"Teg Tegeler, foreman of the Jacks Bluff." He offered his hand.

Morgan stood and the two men shook hands.

"Morgan Payne, Esquire." Damn, he would have preferred to introduce himself as Morgan Payne, lawman, and it twisted his trousers that he couldn't, but he had no choice.

"Take the weight off for a spell." Sitting down, Morgan motioned toward the empty seat.

"Been in these parts long?" The foreman eased his sinewy frame into the chair.

"Nope, just got here. Come out West thinkin' about buying a little spread and settling down."

"Don't look much like you'd know anything about ranching." Tegeler took a gulp of beer.

"Haven't been a lawyer all of my life."

Teg seemed to have sized up the stranger and figured him for a good ol' soul. Probably dumber than hammered horse dung for thinking he could waltz into town and buy a ranch without knowing a cockroach from a cow chip.

"Other than a couple of shoestring operations and a nester or two, most of the land in these parts belongs to the Slippery Elm and Jacks Bluff." Teg set his mug down. "The Lazy S brand is owned by a bunch of Yankee bankers who only care about what they own, not what their riders know or who they are. They're too scared of Texas to show their faces, but not so scared they won't take the money from their operation." The old timer's jaw set. "The other outfit is the one I ride for, Jacks Bluff. I reckon you ain't gonna find nobody wantin' to sell in these parts."

"Much obliged. Just what I needed to know." Morgan fiddled with the coins. "Guess with only two big operations around and barbed wire to keep the cattle corralled, nobody is being bothered with rustling now'days."

"Other than an occasional varmint who wants to show us he can snatch a beef from right under our nose, or an Indian who jumps the reservation and heads back here in need of food for survival, there ain't much thievery going on." Teg leaned back in his chair and stuck his thumbs in his vest pockets. "There'll be twenty or so outfits here for the rodeo, some as far away as Nebraska, so if I get wind of anybody wanting to sell, I'll keep you in mind."

"Appreciate it." Morgan tossed the coins on the table and stood. "But think I'll see for myself if there's anybody around interested in selling."

"Good lookin' boots," Teg said and leaned forward, more interested in his beer than the man walking away.

Blasted, the whole town seemed interested in the way he dressed!

Morgan left the saloon and headed toward the bank. He wanted to take another trip down the alley but couldn't take the chance that Miss Fancy Pants was still terrorizing the town.

Dang it, the best place to get information was the alley. It was notorious for drunks, misfits and saloon girls out for a smoke, who were light on ambition and long on desires and who would always get loose lips when they thought the coins in his hand were intended for their pockets.

Sometimes another bottle of booze would make information flow and the inquirer's name be forgotten.

Morgan made his way along the dusty boardwalk toward a café he spied earlier, trying to ignore his front sides gnawing on his backsides. A good meal with a pot of decent coffee would improve his disposition.

Even in the short time he had spent in the saloon, the town had nearly doubled in size. The streets filled up with people, horses and carriages like a buffalo wallow during a rainstorm. Horses snorted and pranced as though coming to town was a special event for them. Women all dolled up in finery and men in their Sunday best milled around the streets. He dodged frilly parasols and petticoats as he made his way along Main Street.

A shot pierced the air.

That dern gal isn't practicing again, is she? Morgan wasn't sure he wanted to know. Besides, he thought she had more gurgle than guts.

Suddenly, pandemonium broke out and folks scattered like cattle dodging thunder.

Confusion spread in epidemic proportions. An uproar singed with volatility hovered in the air. Something more than simple excitement—more like fear and it was accelerating by the second.

Women grabbed their children and darted inside the first

doorway they found. A crowd of the town's bravest quickly formed in close proximity to the Cattleman's Bank.

The natural peace officer in Morgan Payne sent him into action, long before his brain reminded him that at the moment he was a lawyer—not a lawman. He shouldered his way to the front, while he slipped his right hand under his jacket and touched the butt of his Colt. By that time, his brain reminded his hand to keep the weapon out of sight.

He heard the next shot only a fraction of a second before the bullet shattered the window of the Springs Hotel.

With his weapon drawn, a tall man edged from the hotel and darted toward the fracas with a screaming frenzy of scarlet satin following closely on his heels. The woman cried, "He's trying to steal my daughter!"

Morgan immediately recognized the man as McKenna Smith, and began zigzagging his way through the crowd toward the bank.

He halted as though he was a bogged steer. A masked robber tried to overpower a kicking, clawing and biting woman. Her hat hung by its thong around her neck and her black hair flew as she continued her assault on her captor. He might kidnap her, but not without skinned shins and bruises galore. The bandit gripped her with one arm while he aimed his pistol in the direction of Smith. He seemed not to know which required the most attention, the squirming furious woman fighting for her life or the approaching gunfighter.

A flash of red fabric caught Morgan's eye. Recognition clutched at his heart. The hostage was the woman in the alley—the woman who had assaulted him. Although he had threatened to tar and feather her, she didn't deserve death at the hands of an outlaw.

Quickly, Morgan circled the crowd with the intent to come up behind the bank robber and if he could get a clear shot, he'd give it all he had to save the woman.

Using the hostage as a shield, the gunman raised his pistol to her head and demanded that she get on the horse.

McKenna Smith leveled his Colt and shouted something Morgan couldn't hear.

Unexpectedly, the girl went limp.

Dead silence.

In the distance, her mother screamed.

The girl's dead weight caught the bandit off guard, and he lost his balance but only for a second.

Suddenly the bowels of hell gobbled up Main Street.

The petite woman in red came from behind McKenna and shrieked, "Alaine!"

Not paying any regard for her own safety, she raced toward her daughter and the bank robber.

As though in slow motion, to a mind's eye, a bluish haze circled from Smith's revolver and whizzed by Morgan's ear, grazing his head. Thank God for the derby hat that was the unwelcome recipient of the Guardian of Justice's bullet.

"Sonofabitch . . ." Morgan didn't rightfully give a rusty rat's ass if anyone heard his profanity. "Mother of Joseph . . ." He touched his temple—just another wound to add to his day, this one a testament to his efforts to help Alaine.

Taking the last five feet in one leap, the girl's mother flung herself onto the outlaw's back and clung to his neck, riding him like she had a hold of the tail of a bucking bull. The outlaw fought the scratching, clawing woman off his back. Jumping on his horse, he raced out of town like he had a bee-hive up his butt, with McKenna Smith on his trail.

One of Morgan's concerns about his cover getting blown had just ridden off on the heels of the robber.

The Little Lady, who had make it clear earlier that she was no lady, allowed Morgan to help her to her feet.

"Thank you." She smiled sweetly, as though she'd simply lost her footing. "You are a true gentleman."

Before he could respond, her mother swooped down bombarding the girl with questions.

Morgan eased away, watching the young woman he could now put a name to—a pretty sounding one, Alaine.

Alaine assured everyone she was fine and not in the least shaken by the experience. She had simply used a ploy that she knew would distract the bank robber.

Dismissing her mother's concern and insistence that she see a doctor, the fearless gal brushed herself off and sashayed Morgan's way. Taking his arm, she leaned into him and in a voice meant only for him, she pled, "Please don't embarrass me."

He clenched his jaw. Morgan touched her fingers, clinging to his arm like he was a life jacket, knowing his vow not to get involved had just been shattered.

She turned to her mama and raised her voice, "Mother, I don't have time for this right now. I need to repay this gentleman for his daring gallantry."

Morgan Payne didn't know whether to spit or get drunk.

Dozens of pairs of eyes, heck the whole cow town, watched as he escorted her away from the crowd as though they were going to a church social. Never veering from their noble stroll with quiet emphasis, Morgan said, "Miss Alaine, let's get one thing clear. I have a rip in my trousers, a bullet hole in my hat, and I'm not in a mood to be your gallant anything."

She set a smile on her face and looked him straight in the eye, whispering softly, "Oh, but you are."

No doubt trying to tame this Little Lady would be nothing short of ropin' the wind.

Chapter 3

Catawampus from the town square and hidden in the shadows of the hallowed storefront of the newspaper office, Alaine LeDoux sat on a bench and watched a haze of gold and purple-veiled blue sky turn into an opalescent sunset.

She had a good view of the bandstand but just didn't feel like joining in on the festivities. It had been two days since she had been held hostage at the bank robbery, and her mother was still furious at her. That last thing was nothing new.

The tournament race had been grueling. Even her palomino's rich golden body was still gleaming with sweat when she left him at the livery. His dark eyes pled to be left alone. Much like she felt at the moment.

He had made her proud, giving her his all, blazing down a straightaway and slowing just at the right time, so she could grab rings off a bar extended from clips on poles up and down Main Street. Winning that event was girl's play, but missing her shot in the first round of the shooting competition was true defeat.

She rested the back of her head against the windowpane, thankful the opening ceremonies were over. Her mother was pleased with the turnout. Every politician, ranch owner and cowboy in five states had shown up to settle the question of superiority—whose ranch would win the competition. Oops, she meant rodeo. Her mother had pounded the new word into her head. A new era for Kasota Springs, Texas.

But to Alaine, it was nothing but four days of men versus livestock, vying for bragging rights. The outlaw event, bareback bull riding, was all about guts against glory.

Hopeful, would-be champions from various different outfits came to demonstrate their everyday working skills: riding bucking horses, roping steers, cows and calves, competing for the honor and prestige of the ranches they worked for and their bosses who owned those ranches. Even a contest for the top wild cow milker had been included.

Added to the carnival atmosphere were chuckwagons set up at the end of the street, competing for the honor of being the outfit who made the best biscuits.

Crowds would jostle, cheer, laugh and sing until the last day of the celebration when weary families would climb aboard creaking buckboards, dusty buggies and faithful horses and return home to the daily tasks that made up the foundation for the new frontier.

The band kicked off its first tune. Fiddle, guitar and harmonica music filled the air. Dancers took to the wooden dance floor put up just for the occasion to cut a rug beneath the Texas sky.

Alaine smiled, drawn between wanting to join the merrymakers and knowing if she did, she wouldn't be asked to dance. It seemed most fellows around were either intimidated by her mother or afraid they might be tagged as her next husband. Alaine suspected some feared she might have inherited her mother's bad luck where men were concerned. Nobody would question why a healthy, feisty woman like her mama had caused more than one man to get happy feet when they discovered that she was a five-time widow.

Edwinna Dewey flittered by, not wasting so much as a polite hello on Alaine. Maybe the town gossip feared that her crinoline and lace might be contaminated by Alaine's buckskin and cotton. She wanted to stick out her foot and trip the busybody, but that took more energy than Alaine wanted to exert.

Perhaps Alaine should have taken more time with her dress, but she saw nothing wrong with her leather-fringed riding skirt in a nice mahogany color. She tugged at the matching bolero, trying to pull it together over ample breasts. Dang, she should have gone with a loose-fitting blouse, like she generally wore. But her mama had talked her into the linen V-necked contraption. Even a tiny glimpse of skin at her neckline was too much for Alaine's liking, but it'd been a hot day and comfort won out over prudishness. If nothing else, she had hung her hat on a nail in her horse's stall, replacing it with a piece of rawhide tied around a ponytail. Now locks of hair sprung to life around her face. The curse of having curly hair.

Twitching her nose, Alaine drilled a stare in Edwinna's backsides, before mentally counting the Jacks Bluff cowboys she scoped out. Blasted, who was watching the ranch? It seemed every one of her mother's hands were at tonight's dance for the rodeo. She smiled to herself. At least she had become comfortable calling it a rodeo.

Teg Tegeler, all spiffied up, headed her way. Spurs jingled as he neared. His starched white shirt contrasted with his weatherbeaten features. She wasn't in a mood for a lecture from the only man she considered a father figure.

He slowed down just long enough to say, "Good evening, Miss Alaine." He tipped his hat. "Cheer up, Little Buckaroo. You're gonna win. I can promise you that." The foreman lumbered away, headed toward the square and no doubt the group of women frothing at the mouth to dance with the legendary codger.

Hoping to catch a glimpse of the man from the alley, Alaine studied the expanding crowd of dancers. She sighed, not particularly being proud of her actions at their first meeting. She couldn't believe that she had shot the dandy, and then he turned around and saved her from public humiliation by getting her away from her mother. Yet, after depositing her at the Springs Hotel, he walked away with little more than a tip of his hat and a gruff, "Good day, ma'am."

Mr. Grouchy Trousers had done all of this for her. And she hadn't even asked his name. She had fretted away the best part of the night thinking about what a good-looking butt the man had. Shame on her! How rude! For not asking his name or thinking about his backsides? She wasn't sure.

Her attention was drawn back to the dance as her mystery man came into sight. She lowered her head, not wanting to be obvious in her admiration of the devilishly handsome rascal. Guilt washed over her. Although she hadn't taken time to ask his name, she certainly didn't fail to recognize his physical attributes that could make any woman happy to wake up next to.

Glancing back to the dance area, she caught eye of the dandy again. He wore a trim, neat-styled suit with pants that didn't have a hole in them. She couldn't help but chuckle. Maybe she should offer to buy him a new pair? No doubt in her mind that the mercantile wouldn't have a thing in stock even close to the quality of the ones he possessed. It'd take weeks before a catalog order would reach Kasota Springs. But then the clothes he wore didn't look like anything she'd seen in a catalog. Obviously, tailor-made and probably imported from France.

From his vest, her mystery man removed a pocket watch with what looked like a braided watch fob attached and checked the time. She would have expected a fancy gold watch fob for a man of such perfection.

She watched as he moved among the crowd and sought out men to engage in conversation but never stayed long. It wasn't as though he did it to be sociable but methodical, reminding her of a politician trying to kiss as many babies as possible a day before the election.

He neared a gathering of women waiting for ladies-choice to be called.

Sadness crept into her heart as she caught eye of her mother standing alone. Not far from her a group of ladies fanned themselves as though a particularly disagreeable scent invaded their space, while a threesome conversed behind fan-masked faces, most likely discussing one of the LeDoux women's new escapades.

Alaine had heard others talk about poor, pitiful wallflowers, but her mother was far from poor or pitiful. She was bold, outspoken and didn't take crap off anybody. If that labeled her a wallflower, she'd be at the top of the list.

McKenna Smith approached her mother, and said a few words. She nodded and smiled up at him, and he guided her to the dance floor. The endearing act raised Alaine's opinion of the gunfighter two notches. He obviously was more like her mother than Alaine first surmised—he didn't seem to give a damn what people thought.

Suddenly, the man Alaine had wronged disappeared in the crowd. Probably to dance with some pretty woman, who would swoon over his charm. She knew he had some, but seemed to make a point of her seeing little of it.

Movement a few yards behind Alaine unnerved her and drew her attention away from the dance floor. She listened as the voices of Clayton Snyder and a Slippery Elm hand, only known as Gimpy, became distinct. She became intensely still, not wishing to be detected. They stopped near the corner of the building, but not close enough to see her. The sulfurous scent of lighted matches and cigarette smoke assaulted her nostrils.

Clayton spoke first. "Didja hear that that LeDoux woman hired on that kid they call Pony Boy?"

"He's as weird as that crazy Cajun, so he'll fit right in with those misfits who ride for her." Gimpy chuckled. "He don't even know which end to put his spurs on."

"I wanna see him on a horse." Clayton snorted. "Maybe we oughta tie him to one of them renegade bulls everybody's bettin' on. Maybe Bone Buster. I heard he killed a feller."

Furor raged within Alaine. Over her dead body would they touch Pony Boy. He couldn't help the way God made him. Her jaw set. If she had listened to her gut instead of her mama, she'd be armed and would take them on for even thinking about hurting the kid. As scrappy as Alaine had been raised, if she came after them, they'd have to work hard to keep her from hanging their clawed-out eyeballs on a hitching post for the buzzards. She gritted her teeth and clenched her fist.

Just one more word, Snyder, and you'll have the toe of my boot somewhere between pleasure and pain. She didn't trust him or his cohort Gimpy one iota, never had, never would.

"Naw. The boy ain't worth it. I'd rather get that crazy Cajun alone," Gimpy snickered.

"Don't even try," Snyder said. "If she ain't any better than her kid is a shot, she wouldn't be worth the effort."

"Didja see how far off Buckaroo was with her target? Goes to show that somebody should've told her that she's outgrown her cute age and since she cain't hit a lazy bull's butt, she needs to realize her abilities stink."

"Ain't your beeswax, Gimpy. Besides, we need to stay clear of trouble. Got work to do. Gotta move some of them Lazy S heifers."

"Yep, with all them cowboys more interested in breakin' their bones to show who's the best or dancin' them foolself to death, nobody will be watchin' the henhouse, so to speak."

They each snuffed out their smokes, laughed and retreated back into the stink hole they came from.

Alaine's heart broke at the words. Not about the cruel

things Clayton and his cohort said about her abilities but the asinine comments they made about her mama.

Lifting her head, Alaine searched the crowd for her mother. Nothing, but she didn't see McKenna Smith either. "Not unusual for Mama," she whispered to herself.

Tempest had probably scared Smith off and then headed for the Springs Hotel where she had a room, so she'd be up early to start the next day's activities.

Was Alaine just like her mother?

Why do I have to live under the shadow of such a powerful, proud woman? Only an apple comes from an apple orchard, she told herself.

Lowering her head, Alaine tried not to think about the ridicule she had forced herself to become immune to. Couldn't anybody see that her mama was nervy and strong? Why couldn't she simply tell them to go to hell? Alaine's mama had buried five husbands, one being Alaine's father, so why didn't they leave her alone? She wasn't crazy, just liked to have fun, and because she thought for herself, they labeled her mad.

Alaine thought back to the first round of the sharpshooting event. Dern! She wouldn't have missed her target if she'd stayed focused instead of letting the man who exuded masculinity in every breath overshadow her confidence. Mr. Grouchy Trousers sure did carry himself with a commanding air of self-confidence. And his well-groomed appearance didn't match his suntanned skin. His blue eyes seemed to hold secrets—secrets she wouldn't mind exploring. When she had seen him watching her perform, it unnerved her.

If it hadn't been for the sight of him affecting her confidence, she could've won the first round.

"Hey, Little Lady," a voice as strong as steel, yet as soft as down, broke into her silence.

That voice—she'd know anywhere.

"Hey, back-atcha." She replied to the man who stood over her like a giant oak. His expression a mask of stone.

"Mind if I sit awhile?" Not waiting for an answer, he eased his strapping frame beside her.

"Suit yourself." She didn't feel like company, but at the same time, she longed for this man's notice.

"Nice night." He removed his derby and laid it beside him on the bench.

"I've seen better."

"You're Alaine, right?" he asked, and this time his voice was more friendly.

She nodded. "LeDoux. Alaine LeDoux."

"Pretty name."

His thigh touched hers, and as much as she knew to move away, she couldn't. As though he were a magnet, he drew her to him.

"Excuse me, ma'am, but couldn't help but overhear those bastards talk about your mama. They don't have enough sense to hobble their lips or spit downwind."

"So now you're coming to my rescue again?"

"Nope. Just figured you needed a friend." He turned slightly toward her and broke into a pleasant smile. "I know I don't know you all that well. Hell, barely know your name, but those coffee boilers don't even have a vocabulary big enough to string three words together to make an intelligent sentence." His shoulder touched hers, as he twisted in his seat slightly. "Hypocrites, they are. Dumb ones to boot. Why do you let ignorance rule your heart?"

"You don't know anything about my heart."

"I know about hearts. Got one myself, you know." He gazed down at her, a half smile on his lips. The late-evening shadow of a beard gave his classically handsome face a manly aura.

She tried not to return his smile, but failed miserably. "That's good or I guess you wouldn't be walking around, huh?" The merciful shadows hid her awkwardness. She felt the need to explain. "Mister, my mama isn't crazy and those who say so are fools."

Eyes as blue as the Texas sky held her gaze, brimming with tenderness and passion.

Trying to explain to her that he understood was like fencing off sticks and stones with a feather duster. Morgan knew more than he wanted about protecting a loved one from ridicule. He'd lived it but that was years ago. His mother hadn't been condemned to a life of mockery; she'd been damned to a life of mental illness. After his father died, Morgan was destined to a lifetime of shielding her and his three siblings from cruel remarks by the ignorant and the just plain mean folks. He swallowed hard, remembering his vow that he could not—would not—allow himself to dwell on his growing-up years, but he couldn't stand seeing the same hurt crush the gal sitting next to him.

She was no gal—she was a full-fledged woman. Smelled like one, too—sweetbriar roses. And her thigh resting comfortably against his reminded him that she was a hot-blooded woman.

Morgan's heart broke with the knowledge that Alaine carried such a heavy burden. Her mama was her mama, after all. Yet his vulnerability where she was concerned made him uneasy. She could present serious problems if he continued to let feelings for her get in his way.

He laid his hand on hers. "Why don't you do what you've probably always done? Go over to the dance, hold your head high, be yourself, and not give a flying frog what others think." Impulsively he added slight pressure to his touch. "I sense you've been doing that for a long time."

Her brow furrowed. "Because I'm scared," she managed to reply through stiff lips.

He figured she didn't admit that very often. The gal didn't appear to be intimidated by anything or anybody.

"You know if I lose the sharpshooting event, I'll embarrass Mama and the ranch. Maybe I should drop out." It was no question but a simple statement.

"I didn't peg you as a quitter. One question, though. Why is it so important to be another Annie Oakley, anyway?"

"Crowds, cheers and cowgirls. She's independent and gets paid a thousand dollars a week, plus she doesn't have to answer to anybody."

He wanted to ask if Alaine ever considered that Oakley had to do what her boss Cody or her husband said, but didn't, deciding to change the subject instead.

"Heard the ranches donated the prize money for the all-around drover. How's that work?"

"Each ranch participating ponied up a dozen head of cattle, rounding out a purse of between two and three hundred head. Not a bad start for a ranch."

A soft Texas waltz floated in the air as they both absorbed themselves in thought.

Morgan broke the silence. "Want some advice?"

"Seems if I don't say yes, I'll get it anyway." A rosy tint kissed high yet delicate cheekbones.

"This morning was calm, and I'm betting you are accustomed to practicing with pretty good gusts of wind. Using a 16-gauge hammer-type?"

Nodding, she replied, "A Parker."

"I suggest going to a 20-gauge. It'll eliminate some of the recoil. Because of the lighter weight, you'll have to make up the difference with skill."

"Makes sense." She mulled over his suggestion. "It just might work."

Leaning into him, she touched the small graze on his temple. When she lifted her face, their lips touched briefly. She whispered, "Thanks—"

He cut off her words with his mouth. Her lips were warm

and sweet against his. Soft, yet firm breasts brushed his arm
as she quickly pulled away, leaving his flesh burning with fire.

Morgan hadn't intended to kiss her. It was wrong in so
many ways, but it just seemed the right thing to do.

"Would you partner with me for the rodeo, uh, the . . ." She
wavered, as though considering taking back the invitation.
"Wild cow milking?"

Damn, she completely ignored the kiss! Good. It meant as
little to her as it did to him. But one thing for sure, this cowpoke wouldn't be milking any wild cows.

"Why me? There's lots of seasoned cowboys chompin' at
the bit to partner with you. Why a greenhorn?" Dang, it hurt
him to say the word "greenhorn."

"Nobody will team with me because they're scared of
her—"

"Her?"

"Mother. They think because she's always husband-hunting,
I am too. But it sure isn't true."

"No beau?" Way too personal, he figured but the words
had already escaped.

"No," she said as though she wasn't sure, but quickly
added, "Wanna go pretend this day never happened and release some of that bottled-up energy?"

"Excuse me, but I don't have any bottled-up energy," he
replied.

"But you're always grouchy."

He glared at her. "What was it you wanted to do?"

"Shoot!"

Chapter 4

Bottled-up energy. The words rumbled around in Morgan's head like stones in a wagon bed. He didn't know what possessed him to accept Alaine's challenge, but somewhat later he had snatched up his hat and stalked after the leather-clad woman toward the livery stable.

He knew he'd just purchased a ticket for a stampede, but he had a feeling he needed to see how it played out.

At least he could check on her horse and get her back to the hotel before retiring for the night, thankful she'd be out of his hair for another day. He had a feeling she wouldn't be that easy to get rid of.

He definitely recalled the conversation where he had unequivocally stated his position—he would *not* be hornswoggled into any of her games. "Not here, not tonight, not anytime," he steadfastly retorted.

"But you haven't asked what I want to shoot."

He didn't even want to know her weapon of choice. "Not with a knife, bow and arrow or a gun. Nil, nada, nothing," he had said.

Alaine suddenly stopped and he almost plowed into her as she turned to face him. "Dice." A tad of a smile touched her lips. "Surely you know how to shoot craps."

"I'm not in the wagering mood."

"Are you ever in a good mood?" she asked.

"I'm not grouchy, if that's what you mean, so quit asking me that." Morgan fumed, wondering if she thought he was so dense that he didn't know she'd already made her point. "Besides my disposition is none of your damn business."

Blasted, he had offered her friendship, but drew the line when it came to being her playmate. After all, he was on assignment and had a small window of opportunity to get the job done. The Pinks didn't earn the motto "We never sleep" by going off on tangents with pretty women. They even had their slogan painted beneath an open eye on their office doors. Morgan hated to be called a private eye, the nickname it had garnered.

Even the thoughts of shooting as a sport bothered him. Only one reason to shoot existed—self-preservation.

He could help her improve her skill in sharpshooting, but partnering with her for the title of wild cow milking champion was *not* going to happen. No doubt they'd win hands down. With Alaine's long, agile fingers and his quickness, they'd make a good pair, but he didn't have the time or patience to mess with her. The other side of the coin: she stirred feelings that he was desperately trying to ignore. The kiss was nothing less than dynamite, and no doubt would stick with him for a while—a distraction he couldn't afford.

Morgan exhaled and realized he was fast losing sight of the job he had to do. He had only scratched the surface of his investigation. Although he knew before he left Philly that the big syndicate ranches were despised, he hadn't realized the magnitude of the problem until he spoke with Tegeler and some of the other ranch owners. Armed with the facts, he still had to make sure that nobody knew the Slippery Elm owners had engaged the Pinkertons to investigate their own operation. And that was secondary to the major trouble. He couldn't allow anybody to know that he worked indirectly for the British belted earls or the door to his investigation would be slammed shut so fast it'd slap a flea in the face.

The Slippery Elm seemed to be the only ranch reporting abnormal incidents of cattle rustling. Not only in the frequency but the numbers stolen.

Why the Lazy S and no one else? Even Tegeler confirmed Jacks Bluff had no problems, and the foreman for the shoestring company called the Rocking J, which was catawampus between the two biggest operations, professed to having no awareness of problems in the area.

Cattle and rustling went hand in hand, so why were Kasota Springs pastures off-limits? Nothing added up.

He thought he'd made headway toward gaining the trust of one rancher. Now he wasn't even sure about that. But the best way to reinforce their relationship was to patronize the wild child of Kasota Springs and her whim-whams, one of which he was currently up to his ears in.

The Pink and the Little Lady entered the livery stable. The stalls had been mucked out recently, leaving a sweet, musky smell of hay, which wouldn't last long.

Morgan watched Alaine spread an Indian-woven horse blanket on the dirt floor. Opening her fist she showed him the dice. Smiling up at him, she said, "Best four out of seven and I promise not to call you grouchy."

An angelic look made her features glow, reminding him of a schoolgirl making a promise she had no intention of keeping. Oh yeah, she was an angel through and through. With a devilish smile. But then she sure did have a great pair of . . . lips. Full, red and ripe. Her strength and stamina seemed at odds with her exquisite beauty.

"And what's the reward?" He generally had fair luck playing and reasoned that good fortune would shine on him today.

"You name it."

"Okay." Damn, it was getting hotter by the minute and he couldn't remove his jacket since he had his shoulder holster on. "The question of partnering for the rodeo." He squatted down across from her.

Her bosom bulged at the neckline, disturbing his thoughts.

She leaned forward, exposing tanned flesh. "Okay, when I win, you agree to be my partner."

"No, when *you* lose, I don't have to be your partner!" He tried to say it with conviction, but her allure made him dithery. "Women first." He couldn't keep his eyes off her neckline, which seemed to swell with every move she made.

Alaine leisurely rolled the dice between her palms.

"Said I'm not in the wagering mood, but to oblige I'll play until one of us shoots a seven or eleven, then game's over." He tried to peel his gaze away from her. "Quick and painless. No quarrels over rules. Understand?"

"Understood." Amusement flickered in her eyes. She tossed the come-out roll.

The dice cartwheeled before stopping on a five and a one.

"Oh dear me." She looked up at Morgan and leaned forward, handing him the cubes. "I believe I lost, so that makes you the shooter. Right?"

He nodded and followed suit, throwing snake eyes.

They continued alternating tosses, until Morgan bested her with three winning rolls to her two.

Morgan slid the dice to her.

Alaine followed her same practice of rolling the cubes between her palms, cupping them and blowing before she shot. "Three and six! Goodness gracious, but I'm still in the game, I believe." She clutched the lapel of her blouse, leaned forward, exposing a great deal of cleavage, and laughed. She reveled in her glee longer than Morgan thought necessary before sitting upright and dropping the dice on the blanket.

"I don't want to take advantage of a woman. Roll again," he directed.

He knew from the first toss that she was up to something. The gal apparently couldn't play it straight if she had thirteen

diamonds in her hand. He'd been around. Won and lost his
share of scammed crap games, and recognized her trick from
the get-go. He had played along with her so far, but that was
coming to a halt—if she didn't cheat him out of his drawers
in the meantime.

"Oh gracious, kind sir." She picked up the dice, flung her
hands to her chest and giggled. "I knew you were a gentleman." She hesitated and gave him a coy look, almost as
though he perplexed her. Unhurriedly, she made her play and
lost.

She bent over to give him the dice, exposing more of her
velvety bronzed skin. It was as though bit by bit she was slipping out of her corset. Something she probably planned all
along.

Hell's bells, here he went again, getting all preoccupied.

"Show 'um to me," he said, keeping an eye on her nicely
constructed chest. He watched as she lifted her hands to her
neckline, and as though she got caught, she gradually lowered
them allowing the dice to drop to the blanket.

He continued, "I meant, I know you're cheating. Those
aren't the dice I'm wanting. Give me the loaded ones or I'll
physically take them off you."

She peered up at him, bewildered as a chicken on a chain,
flabbergasted he'd actually called her a cheater. "And, I
thought you were a gentleman."

"Most of the time I am, but Little Lady, when you put
yourself into a cheater's position, all bets are off."

"I do believe you're calling me a scallywag!" Her violet
eyes flashed with anger. "Just how do you think I could hide
them? Everything is out in the open."

"I'm warning you, lady. I don't kowtow to scammers, so
give 'um up."

"Come get 'um," she challenged him, showing off a sensu-
ous smile, "if it's that important to you—"

And he did.

In one quick motion he sprang across the blanket and nailed her beneath him. "Give 'um up."

"I don't have them." She squirreled and wiggled, bringing her knee up close to the most sensitive part of his body. He countered her attack with his own knee and flattened her, pressing his full body against her.

His grip tightened, his position very clear.

Morgan enjoyed her nearness, the feel of her skin against his. The rawhide strip holding her raven hair in a ponytail had come off, and long ringlets lay on near naked, ripe breasts, making his senses spin. Alaine's riding skirt slipped up, exposing nice long legs. His imagination took care of what lay between her thigh and shoulders.

His body was heavy and warm, and his heart thudded against hers. Alaine refused to give into her squirming and resisted his touch, while she marveled at his strength—the feel of his hands. He made light contact with her cleavage. His fingers were tough and callused, used to hard work, not fine and supple like he spent his time behind a desk.

Northern businessmen were supposed to be soft, not accustomed to the physical labor needed in the new frontier, but Morgan was tough both physically and mentally. There was nothing soft about him, except his lips which were only inches away from hers. So close that she could feel his breath against her cheeks. Blue eyes closed in on hers, electrifying the very air around her.

He seemed to lessen the intensity of his hold, and she seized the opportunity, taunting him with her womanly persuasions. She shifted her weight, pressing her breasts into his rock-hard chest. Letting her hips wiggle just in the right places. She hoped to distract him—to make her play.

Mr. Grouchy Trousers, who was anything but cantankerous at the moment, pulled up slightly, allowing her to wrap the calf of her leg around the back of his knee, where she shoved with all her might, figuring she could flip him, but it didn't work. She twisted and arched her body, seeking to get free. He came down hard on her, his mouth catching hers and claiming a kiss. A slow naked kiss. Above her head, Morgan's huge hand held both her wrists together, while his free one explored the rise and fall of her breasts.

She heaved forward, dislodging the dice. They tumbled over her chest and landed onto the blanket face-up. A six and a five.

Alaine made a daring try to reach for the dice but a booming voice shattered the air.

"Touch her again, you sorry flannel mouth, and I'll rip off your fingers."

Morgan rolled off the woman, got to his feet and pulled her up behind him.

Alaine brushed her skirt off and pulled straw from her hair. "Teg, the uh . . ."—she seemed to weigh her words carefully—"the gentleman wasn't attacking me. We were—"

"Shooting dice," Morgan spoke up.

"I guess they got lost." Teg eyed the cubes on the blanket, and then turned to the young woman. "I'm warning you for the last time—no gambling." He picked up the dice, tossing them to Morgan. "Keep 'um for a souvenir."

"We weren't *exactly* gambling, Teg." She looked like she was about to cry. "And he wasn't bothering me. He's agreed to be my partner in the rodeo." She smiled persuasively at Morgan. "We were playing to determine which event we'll enter."

"And?" Teg switched a curious, yet uncompromising glare between them. "It'll be?"

"Wild cow milking," Alaine said simultaneously with Morgan's, "Steer roping."

"Hum," the old codger guffawed. "I still think I'll take you out behind the barn, son, and teach you some manners." Teg put his thumbs in his vest pockets and never moved his eyes from the younger man.

"You ol' goat," Alaine spoke to the foreman and stepped up beside Morgan. A playful frown crossed her face. "You can't beat up my partner." She patted him on the arm. "I need him."

Morgan didn't need the woman to plead his case, and certainly didn't need a woman to need him, but neither Alaine nor the ranch foreman gave him an opportunity to defend himself.

"Better get in your entry fees for both events. And, what's your partner's name, anyway?" Teg said, disapproving.

"It's, uh . . ." Alaine turned to Morgan, and in wide-eyed innocence said, "I don't believe I caught your name."

"Because you never asked, but it's—"

"Morgan Payne, Esquire," Teg interrupted, looking at him as if he were Morgan Payne the impersonator, someone who didn't have enough wits about him to know his own name. "And, I ain't gonna have you lookin' like a broomtail in a cornfield, shaming the Jacks Bluff or her mama, so you're gonna spend every minute from now 'til the rodeo events begin learnin' about ropin' and ridin'." He raised craggy brows. "Starting tonight. Gotta be ready at first light 'cause this ain't gonna be an easy job." Tegeler looked his student up and down, as though appraising his value. "Don't look like much of a cowboy to me, but think I can teach you enough to keep you from killin' your dern self and our Little Buckaroo here."

Don't let the ol' guy call your bluff, Morgan repeated in his mind. He clenched his fist at first then relaxed it. Mentally, he patted himself on the back for a job well done. Even the veteran ranch hand figured Morgan for an Eastern dandy who thought he could beat the devil around a stump.

"Can you ride?" Teg surveyed him again, answering his own question. "Probably not, but you got hands that look like you could rope."

Silence was golden, Morgan had always heard, and at the

moment he was up to his ears in bullion. He set his jaw. Whatever it took to get the job done, he was prepared to give.

"Get yourself a horse, Payne, while Miss Alaine goes over to the dance and tells her mama that she's not staying in town tonight."

Morgan wanted to hit the man for being such a hard case. He had him by the cojones and Morgan knew it. So did Tegeler.

"Skedaddle, Little Buckaroo," Teg called after Alaine, as she shot a confident smile at Morgan and a frown to the foreman. Morgan half expected her to stick out her tongue to emphasize her discontent at being bossed around.

Quietly, Morgan watched until the woman was out of earshot, while keeping a steady eye on Tegeler. Once he was sure she was gone, Morgan said in a tone that left no doubt to its meaning, "You're a sorry sonofabitch, Tegeler."

"You better make it your best shot, son." Hostility sharpened Teg's voice.

Morgan's fist connected with the other man's chin, sending the ol' coot sprawling to the ground.

Tegeler pulled himself to his feet, rubbed his jaw and picked up his Stetson. Dusting the dirt from the hat, he said, "I'm warning you. You may have gotten in the first lick, but I'll get the last."

Chapter 5

The male bravado in the shadowy stables was so dense that Alaine feared she might grow whiskers by simply smelling the air.

Tegeler nearly plowed her down as he exited, barking over his shoulder, "Payne, be saddled before I change my mind or you can walk to the ranch. Makes me no never mind."

Clearly he was still in a tiff over Morgan's manhandling Alaine.

"Adios, Teg." She raised a questioning eyebrow at Morgan. "I see he's still out of sorts. But then you and Teg are kinda alike—either in a testy mood or no mood at all."

Morgan's jaw clenched and his eyes slightly narrowed. "If you say so."

"As long as I can remember, Teg's been with Mama and seems to have made it his duty to look out after me. Him and every cowhand, prairie dog and cottontail on the ranch." She walked to her horse's stall and snatched up her hat. "He's forgotten that I've grown up, but then, sometimes I forget it too." She smiled and tried to ignore the hammering in her heart.

Placing the hat on her head, she adjusted the rawhide straps. She deliberately baited Morgan. No doubt he recognized she wasn't a child any longer, or at least his body said as much when he wrestled her to the ground and searched her bodice for the dice.

"Every woman needs protecting." Morgan rubbed the palomino's nose. "Did you find your mama?"

"She'd already retired for the night, so I left a note at the hotel desk. She won't be surprised that I'm going back out to the ranch. I spend as little time as necessary in town. About ready?"

"Not quite. Wasn't planning on needing a horse right away, so I didn't make any arrangements for one," said Morgan.

"No need. It's taken care of. I ran into Pony Boy. He's helping out in the livery during the rodeo." She led the gelding out of the stall, picked up a currycomb and ran it through his flaxen mane. "Mama hired him on, but he refuses to come out to the ranch until he completes his duties here. He's taking care of finding you something to ride."

"Hey, Diablo," Alaine spoke to her horse, "meet Morgan." She patted the animal's neck. "Diablo's good between the ears, Teg says."

"Only kind to have." Morgan reached out and took the comb, letting his fingers linger on hers longer than she thought proper, yet not long enough. He commenced to groom the palomino, brushing the saddle area twice.

"A horse has to be trusted." His blue eyes narrowed speculatively. "If you can't trust 'um, they're apt to get you killed."

Getting the point, Alaine felt her face flush. He might as well have added "like a woman."

Alaine watched as Morgan worked with Diablo, eventually placing the blanket several inches forward, leaving room for the saddle to settle in its proper place, while smoothing the coat, making sure the gelding's hair wasn't rubbed the wrong way.

She eyed the rugged fine-looking man who didn't act like he was a stranger to a horse. A greenhorn would have plopped on a saddle, not caring whether the cinch and stirrups injured the animal or he got spooked.

For a Philadelphia lawyer who professed to know little about the new frontier, Morgan had done his homework . . . lessons not learned from books. Knowledge not taught but experienced.

She needed to find out more about this man. His words were too guarded not to be hiding something. And she questioned herself as to why he wore his gun hidden beneath his coat. Not to mention boots broken in like he'd worn them forever. With a business suit, no less. Maybe it was an Eastern custom.

For the life of her, she trusted him . . . but didn't know why.

Walking to the horse's opposite side, Morgan lowered the cinches and stirrups so they hung neatly. As though reading her mind, he said, "You don't know me, Alaine, so why do you trust me enough to be your rodeo partner?"

She grabbled for answers. The simple truth—she felt something in her heart that told her to do so, but letting him know that might lead to the wrong idea. She hem-hawed. "Well, for one thing, you don't look like a man who would take advantage of a woman. I mean, you don't have wandering hands."

Oh damn! Did the man ever have strong, great-feeling hands that seemed to be experienced in wandering about anywhere they wanted to—especially on a woman's body.

A stone cold look came from his eyes, and he said nothing, probably thinking . . . *and my hands weren't wandering when I wrestled you to the ground?*

"Plus, Mama figures you for a dandified Easterner who seems a tad too concerned with your appearance for her liking." She tilted her head to one side and stole a slanted look at him, just to see his expression, as she continued, "Says you're too soft, neat and perfect. To quote her, 'For God's sake, he smells of lilac water.'"

"Lilac!" He quirked a questioning eyebrow and tightened the cinch. "And, I paid two bits for a shave and haircut. The barber threw in the shave lotion for good measure."

"You got your money's worth, but you do make me think of Mama's lilac bushes." She couldn't help but grin. "I kinda like it."

In reality, he smelled nothing like a flower. More like leather on a fall morning, a tad musky and totally manly.

"What else did your mama have to say about me?" He laced the latigo through the cinch ring while he spoke. "Something tells me that I don't wanna know."

"She thanks you for saving me from the bank robber."

"I didn't save you, you saved yourself." He tightened the leather strap, snugging up the saddle. "You never did give me an honest answer about why you trust me."

"Not until you tell me why you're in Kasota Springs."

"To find me a little spread to buy. Settle down. Learn to be a rancher." Patting the horse, he added, "Your turn. Why do you trust me?"

"Because Teg does." She studied Morgan's lean, dark face, watching for a reaction. "Not to mention that he would hogtie and castrate any man laying a hand on me. Nobody is that foolish."

But she remembered Morgan Payne had been just that fool.

Morgan didn't show any outward reaction to her comment, only adjusted the bridle and bit before he said, "Since we're being honest with each other, we still have an issue. Are you going to admit that you cheat?"

"I'm not admitting anything. You have the only pair of dice we used—"

"Then you're going to force me to prove it?" He dropped the reins over the saddle horn.

"If you're big enough." She dern well knew he was big enough, but also fairly certain that the dice he had in his pocket were legit. The fact that the total of the two dice landing on the blanket had come up to eleven was nothing but a stroke of luck.

Alaine was pretty sure she had the loaded dice in her blouse when she left the livery. Because she didn't have a lot of time to find her mama, she hid the blasted things in some tall grass not far beyond the door. She probably should have found a better place, but it was too dark to traipse off into the night just to get rid of the evidence.

Diablo swished his tail so wide it slapped Alaine on the side of the face. She laughed and patted him on the rump. His ears twitched. The gelding pranced and pawed the dirt, letting everyone know his patience had run out. He was ready to go home.

In the near distance a donkey brayed like someone was pulling him by the ears down Main Street.

Teg barged into the stables, tugging the sorriest excuse for a pack animal Morgan had ever laid eyes on. He'd seen his share of plugs, but the hip-shot donkey Teg towed as far as the door was flat-ass bigger than any Morgan had ever seen and was crow-bait at its finest.

And he was wearing a sombrero with gaudy sunflowers, nonetheless!

Alaine explained, "He was in today's parade and won't let anybody take off the trappin's."

At the mention of the straw hat, the dern animal stopped dead still and refused to move.

"You ornery, fly-bitten sunfisher. Just sit there all you want, but you're gonna get saddled anyways." Teg dropped the lead rope. "I should've left you out there and let the wolves gnaw off your ears one at a time."

Morgan had to agree with Alaine. Nothing had sweetened the ol' coot's disposition.

Once the foreman turned his back, the dang donkey dropped down on his butt, and set into hee-hawing like he had a belly-ache from eatin' green corn.

Teg wiped his sweaty brow and stuffed the neckerchief back in his pocket. "He's all yours, Payne. Get him saddled and ready to go." He shot Morgan a frown that said don't-argue-with-me before heading toward a stall where a hand-some buckskin nosed him a welcome.

The donkey stopped bawling and raised to all fours.

Morgan surveyed the sorry animal. Stepping in front of

him, Morgan stared him right in his eyes. The nincompoop
went to bawling again and then plopped down.

"Do you expect me to ride that thing?" Morgan called out.

"You can ride him or carry the sorry sonofabitch, makes
me never mind." Teg lifted the latch on the horse's stall. "Ain't
nothing personal, Payne. With that blasted rodeo in town, I
couldn't beg, borrow or steal something suitable to ride."

Nothing personal!

And this blockhead was considered suitable? Morgan wasn't
sure which part of the lie to believe—nothing personal or nothing available. Did he really look that stupid? He couldn't help
but wonder whether he was the *stu* or *pid* part of stupid.

Turnabout was fair play. After all, a guy couldn't slug a
man like Tegeler and expect it not to get personal.

Alaine smiled mischievously as though they shared a
secret. "Teg, Mr. Payne and I can ride double on Diablo."

Teg barked, "Not no, but hell no," leaving no room for argument.

Alaine shrugged her shoulders and nodded toward a nearby
saddle. "There's some of the ranch's extra tack. Use what you
need." Her smile twitched with amusement. "Jughead's been
around a long time. Be tender with him."

Clamping his jaw tight, Morgan mumbled, "I'm always
tender with a fool-ass."

He turned his back to the animal and waited. As sure as
shootin', Jughead shut up, stood and then let out a melodious
hee-haw as if he missed Morgan more than his own mama.

Morgan picked up the lead rope without looking at the
creature. Jughead followed his new best friend to an area
where he could be saddled.

"Don't look a donkey directly in the eye or they'll balk. Rebellious in nature," he mumbled just loud enough for Alaine
to hear.

Not much different than the Little Lady standing beside
him watching his every move.

"You know I could probably borrow one of the Jacks Bluff mounts," Alaine said, more as a statement than a question. "Anyone who is still in town probably doesn't plan to go back to the ranch tonight. Besides, we could have him back by morning."

"And have your mama lynch me for horse stealing?" He had the dang animal half saddled before he spoke again. "Right, ol' boy." Morgan pulled the cinch tighter, realizing Jughead had resorted to ol' fashioned horseplay. His belly had swollen up to twice its size.

Morgan had seen mules do it many times before, and suspected Alaine had too—Teg definitely had. Might be the first time for a donkey. The rider knew that as soon as the confounded animal felt weight on his back, he'd pull in his belly, loosening the saddle and sending the cowboy sliding underneath him.

Morgan would play their game if only to sidetrack Alaine from questioning his horsemanship.

Alaine effortlessly mounted her palomino, and he followed suit.

Jughead pulled in his belly and the saddle tilted.

Expecting the trick, Morgan deliberately fell hands first on the ground, eating hay and dirt. The only problem, he hadn't calculated for fresh horse apples.

He dusted off his tailor-made suit, now sporting unsavory patches of horse dung, and blessed out the stupid animal, obviously to the amusement of Tegeler. Morgan tightened the rigging and mounted for what was guaranteed to be a very long ride across the prairie.

Talk about a motley team! A surly, quintessential cowboy wearing a Stetson riding high in the saddle on his stallion; the beauty with her hat hanging down her back on strings, ebony ringlets flying in the breeze; and a Philadelphia lawyer, derby hat and all, lumbering along on a stubborn donkey refusing to give up his sombrero.

Little was said on the ride, mainly because Jughead seemed to want to stop and rest every hundred yards. Morgan lagged behind by a good quarter of a mile, which was probably good because he could hardly stand his own stench.

Jeeze, it'd be first light before he would reach the Jacks Bluff. He wanted to tell the other riders to go ahead, he'd walk and lead the blasted fool to the ranch, but didn't want to give them the satisfaction of knowing their joke was irritating the hell out of him.

Well, ain't this fun? Morgan reared back in the saddle, trying to make the best of a bad situation. He was enjoying the clear skies and a zillion stars blinking, not to mention watching Alaine ride light in the saddle, letting her hair blow in the wind. She truly matched the horse's strength, ability and agility. The view was almost enough to take his mind off his predicament.

Damn Teg Tegeler!

Leaning farther back, Morgan rested his hand on Jughead's flank. He felt the donkey's back arch and its legs get rigid only a fraction of a second before the animal tucked his head between his legs, bowed up and pitched straightaway as though he was leaping to the beat of an Indian war drum. He smoothed out long enough to lull Morgan into thinking Jughead had tired himself out, then suddenly he twisted and turned trying to unseat his rider. But he didn't.

Almost as quick as Jughead got rattled, he settled down . . . all the way down on his backsides, bellowing like he was mad enough to suck the skin off a snake.

Morgan rolled away from the balking, bellowing donkey.

Teg circled back toward Morgan, reined in and hollered, "Forgot to warn you. Jughead's kinda sensitive to being touched on his flank." He looked down at Morgan sprawled on the ground. "Ain't hurt, are ya?"

"Not even a scratch."

Teg gave his horse his head, "Didn't figure you for a bronc buster. Seems there's a lot about you we don't know."

Chapter 6

Alaine twisted in her saddle to see what the ruckus was behind her. She watched the dern donkey pitch, trying to send Morgan head over teakettle. Her heart plunged with every jump.

Feeling as if her chest was about to burst open, she fought to keep raw emotion in check, as she watched Morgan hit the ground and roll away from the animal. Terrified the greenhorn was seriously injured, she turned the palomino and galloped his way, dust billowing behind.

Diablo slowed and she slipped out of the saddle. She rushed to Morgan's side and gathered him into her arms, then shot Teg a frown that left no doubt how peeved she was at the ol' toad.

"Are you hurt?" She realized she was more frightened than Morgan.

"Nope." He picked up his hat that looked like hell, and pulled to his feet. Putting on the filthy, crumpled-up derby, he added, "Just my pride."

"I can't believe you stayed in the saddle as long as you did with that spoiled fool." She gave him an encouraging smile, while she shot another go-to-blue-blazes look Teg's way. Not that it would faze the tough foreman.

She ran her fingers along Morgan's jaw line and caressed a bloody scrape smaller than her little finger that ran parallel with the one he'd gotten from McKenna's gun.

He caught her hand with his. "Thanks for your concern, but I'll be fine."

His touch sent a ripple of excitement through her.

"Good. I don't need a lame rodeo partner."

At least her team member hadn't gotten killed before they had a chance to share a real kiss. Not a light substitute for a sensual, searing one not so easy to forget.

Morgan straightened to his full height, towering over her like a giant cottonwood. He was tougher than she had imagined. He had shown what he was made of—certainly not whipped cream and feathers. The delectable man was strong, stalwart and all male. More cowboy than lawyer.

"I insist that you ride the rest of the way with me." She watched for any sign of disapproval on Teg's part, while she picked up the donkey's reins and handed them to him.

The foreman seemed to know any objections from him would be shrugged off, so he snatched up Jughead's reins and spurred his stallion, giving the donkey little choice but to pick up speed or be dragged all the way to headquarters.

"Appreciate it." Morgan swung into the saddle, gave Alaine a hand, and shifted his weight to allow her to settle in front of him. Very snug fit. There was an air of efficiency about the man that fascinated her.

Without warning, Alaine become extremely conscious of Morgan's virile appeal. A reasonable woman would sit stiff in the saddle, and after her companion got settled, knee the gelding forward, but Alaine enjoyed the feel of his strong arms around her waist and leaned back into him, taking pleasure in his hard, well-sculptured chest.

The day had been a real scorcher—a cherry-red branding iron of a day—but night brought relief, as if the hot iron had been doused with cold water. But now, clouds wove cobwebs across the moon, giving the prairie a romantic air.

She closed her eyes, wishing the evening would never end.

The rangeland was so quiet she swore she could hear the twinkle of the stars. Except for an occasional coyote howl and the crunch of prairie grass beneath Diablo's hooves, the universe seemed to stop and listen as two hearts beat as one.

Morgan's unbridled energy nestling against her could start a flame not easily put out. She inhaled, trying to ignore the heavy, warm thighs pressed against hers every time he moved.

Any other man's hands on her waist would've had her clutching her bolero tighter across her breasts. Morgan was different. He made her feel safe. Her muscles relaxed, sending the tension from her body. She loosened her grip and let the vest gap open.

Maybe she had stopped being afraid of her own reactions to him. Alaine let her head drop, half expecting the big man to kiss the nape of her neck. Her body didn't object when he shifted his position, tucking her nicely in the circle of his arms.

Maybe it was time that Alaine stopped calling him Mr. Grouchy Trousers, because Mr. Daring Drawers seemed more fitting . . . at least at the moment.

The couple rode along absorbed in their own thoughts, until the trail turned north toward a valley, something Morgan hadn't expected.

Descending off the wide-open plains, Diablo increased his gait, clearly knowing home was close at hand. They cut down through an arroyo. Shortly after crossing a stream, the main house came in view. The home reminded Morgan of ones he'd seen in Galveston. Stately, but not ostentatious, a cross between the traditional rambling ranch houses of the Texas Panhandle and the grandeur of a southern plantation.

Morgan broke the silence. "So this is Jacks Bluff?"

"Welcome to our humble abode." She twisted around and flashed a sweet, endearing smile that made him feel truly welcome.

As they neared, Tegeler's outline became more clear. He sat on the veranda that wrapped completely around the house, rocking in a chair, obviously making certain his Little Buckaroo met curfew.

Diablo halted near the barn. Morgan helped Alaine to the ground and slid out of the saddle, making sure he made as little contact as possible with the pretty lady.

Alaine adjusted her bolero and kept an eye glued to the foreman, who stepped from the porch and sauntered their way.

"Thank you." She raised her voice to make sure Tegeler heard her. "I insist you stay in the main house while you are here." Morgan's eyes met hers and he saw amusement flickering there. She shot him a mischievous smile. "Mama would skin all of our hides if we didn't show proper Texas hospitality to the gentleman who saved my life."

"Like hell will he sleep under the same roof!" Teg gave Alaine a warning scowl and snatched up her palomino's reins. "Animals to tend." He turned around, and continued. "And, find you a place to bed down. Guess you can have Ol' Nevada's bunk. He won't be needin' it."

"I can take care of Diablo," Morgan snapped.

"No need. You need to get settled in the *bunkhouse*." Reaching the barn door, he spit tobacco juice in the dirt. "Besides, you smell like the south end of a northbound bull."

Alaine raised an eyebrow and laughed softly. "Sometimes it's impossible to reason with Teg. Without Mama being here to back me, disagreeing with him would be like arguing with a knothole."

"Thanks for your hospitality but the bunkhouse will be fine." He tipped his hat. "Evening, Miss LeDoux."

Morgan watched the old man disappear but was fairly

certain he wasn't far enough inside that he couldn't hear and see the couple's every move.

"At least you can join me for a cup of hot tea before you retire." She offered him a sultry smile, as though she might consider offering more than a drink.

Surely meaning to antagonize Tegeler, she raised her voice, "It'll help you sleep better."

Alaine looked so enticing that she made it hard for Morgan to resist, in more ways than one.

"While I find that tempting, I certainly don't smell like lilacs anymore." Damn, he needed to get cleaned up and get some rest. He had a feeling tomorrow would be one helluva day, and with the ol' geezer's temperament, a long one to boot.

"I'll have the tea ready in ten minutes."

Before Morgan knew what had happened, Alaine darted off toward the main house, tossing over her shoulder, "Don't dally."

"Coffee," Morgan called into the night.

What is wrong with that woman? He knew he was articulate enough to pronounce "no" and Alaine was certainly educated and knew what the word meant, but for some reason his "no" always ended up "yes" where she was concerned.

Not wanting to rile the ol' codger any more than he'd already done, Morgan headed off to the bunkhouse to see if he could get rid of as much of the horse crap as possible.

As he passed the barn, he heard a loud hee-haw from Jughead. He couldn't help but stop and check in on him. Besides, he owed the donkey a thank-you for not killing him. It wasn't Jughead's fault that the true ass was Tegeler.

Finding a bucket of carrots in the corner, Morgan fed the ornery varmint a treat.

His next project: find water and see what he could do about cleaning off trail dust and dried horse dung. At least the smell had subsided. Although falling headlong into the first bunk he came to sounded better than tea, Morgan was amenable to sharing some refreshment with the Little Lady at the main house. If to do nothing else but rile Tegeler. Or prove she cheated at dice.

On the way to the ranch, Morgan had plenty of time to examine the ones Teg had tossed him. Not only could he feel a marked heaviness in one corner, but could feel the spots on one side being deeper than the others.

The lawman in him, who was trained to find the man, find out what happened and find the hoosegow, wanted to prove she had finagled him into being her rodeo partner, yet the gentleman in him wasn't about to let it happen.

Almost before Morgan got the bunkhouse screen closed, Tegeler and a trio of ranch hands lumbered inside.

"Tuffy, Bobby, Jimmy—this here's Alaine's rodeo partner." Teg held a smug look on his face and a twinkle came to his eye. "Don't mind the muleskinner smell."

The men shook hands and welcomed the younger man like leery coyotes eyeing a piece of burro meat. He introduced himself, "Payne. Morgan Payne."

"What brings you to these parts?" Tuffy looked the newcomer up and down, no doubt recognizing he wasn't a grubline rider.

"He's from back East, trying to find some land to buy," Tegeler offered.

Jimmy surveyed Morgan from head to toe, as if to say—not that the derby hat didn't give him away—"You're not with one of those syndicate operations, are ya?" Before waiting on an answer, he continued. "Ain't no land for sale around these parts. At least not to any of them cocklebur British outfits."

"Just looking for a small spread for myself."

"Pert near all of the pasture belongs to the Slippery Elm and Jacks Bluff, and they ain't for sale." Tuffy hitched up his britches, then drawled on, "Going out to the corrals to check on the livestock, then play some dominoes. Anybody comin' along?"

The foreman nodded. "Be there directly."

Blasted, Morgan wanted Tegeler to stick around because he had a few issues to discuss with him, beginning with why in the hell Teg set him up with that damn donkey, but there were too many eyes and ears registering every move he made.

Tegeler motioned toward a cot in the corner. "Might as well use that one. Ol' Nevada passed on and nobody's been brave enough to take over his bunk." Shoving an apple crate from the foot of the cot, he opened it. He surveyed Morgan and then said, "About the right size. Poor fella had nobody to claim his belongings, so these don't need to go to waste."

No doubt Teg was well respected and his word was law where the Jacks Bluff hands were concerned.

Bobby and Jimmy followed Teg and Tuffy out the door and moseyed toward the corrals.

With the bunkhouse empty, Morgan wondered what in the hell he'd gotten himself into.

Thoughts of ending the day in the company of the beautiful rancher's daughter fueled Morgan's desire to get cleaned up with no lollygagging. After changing clothes, he took time to wrap his gun and holster in his filthy coat and hid it deep inside the crate, taking mental note that he needed to replace the shoulder holster with a hip type when he went to town.

He plopped on a battered dove-gray Stetson sporting a pheasant feather stuck in an Indian-woven headband. Feeling more at home in rough pants and a boiled shirt, even without a gun belt, than he had in weeks, he glanced in a tin mirror. Not bad. He even looked the part of a cowboy . . . a profession he felt more comfortable with than being a damn Pink.

As an afterthought, he slipped the dice in his pocket.

Moments later, he stood in the ranch's fancy parlor, more fitting for a southern plantation than a West Texas town.

Everything in the room was in excess. Exquisite paintings worth a mint overlooked a piano that sat cockeyed to shelves of leatherbound books.

Bright lamplight illuminated the parlor as though to show off the bluish-lavender floral wallpaper. Alaine's mother had a lot of cojones to complain about him smelling like lilacs when she had the blasted things plastered all over the room.

He hung the Stetson on the hat rack, just as Alaine returned from the kitchen carrying a silver tray with a fine porcelain tea set.

"Are you sure I can't get you something stronger than coffee?" She set down the tray. "It seems more fitting after such an exciting day."

Morgan eyed the teapot and cups, again decorated with some type of gawd-awful blue flowers. Thanking the heavens he didn't have to drink out of one of the dainty thimbles that he might crush just by holding it, he accepted a heavy coffee mug and practically emptied it with two swallows.

She poured some tea, before situating herself on one end of the settee. "Please join me."

He eased next to her, aware of how fetching she looked in the parlor light. Alaine had changed into a simple muslin dress in a soft shade of violet that emphasized her amethyst eyes and skin as delicate as the cup she sipped from. She had secured her onyx hair at the nape of her neck with ribbons.

Visions of Morgan's three stair-stepsisters shot through his mind. One helluva sorry time to start reminiscing about family!

"Thank you for the coffee." Morgan didn't feel as awkward as his voice probably sounded. Seems that thanking her was about the only words he'd uttered since he saddled her horse back in town. Although it'd only been a few hours ago, it seemed like an eternity. He had enjoyed the last leg of the trip, sitting behind Alaine and holding her tight, making sure she didn't slip from his grip when she dozed off.

"I uh . . ." She seemed to stammer for words herself. "Is yours okay? I tend to make it too strong."

"Thank you, but it's fine." Damn, what was he supposed to say? *The coffee's good, but I really want to make love to you until Jughead decides not to be so stubborn*—or Teg, for that matter.

Morgan tried not to look at her bust, although it was covered completely with an ivory chemisette, a word he'd learned from raising three sisters. Her breasts seemed to bulge at the fabric. His mouth went dry just thinking about all the softness lying underneath. He had to draw his attention away from his ungentlemanly thoughts about the pretty woman sitting next to him.

Besides, he had no idea where Teg might be lurking, just waiting for him to make another mistake with Alaine. Not easily intimidated by any man, Teg griped the hell out of Morgan.

He had to think of something to talk about fast or his whole conversation would exist of "thank you" and "fine."

"Did I understand you correct? Are there twenty outfits entered in the rodeo?"

"Yes. Mama is rather pleased. With that many, the winning purse is quite respectable."

"Presume the Slippery Elm donated the same as everyone else?"

"Oh, yes. Ten head." Alaine covered a yawn with her hands, and smiled sheepishly at him. "Pardon me."

"So that's what Clayton Snyder and his cohort were talking about when they said they had to move some heifers?"

"I found that comment strange, Morgan. They had brought in their donated stock to the pens days ago, so I didn't exactly know what Clayton meant."

"He's their manager, so he outta know."

"No. Their manager is Gimpy. The one with the lame leg."

Her eyes blinked, surely not trying to flirt but from the need to sleep.

"That answers some questions." Morgan set his cup on the table. "As much as I'd enjoy visiting longer, I need some sleep."

After helping her to her feet, he walked to the door and put on his hat. He reached in his pocket and fingered the dice.

"Here." He placed them in her hand. "I forgot to return these."

"Thank you." Her face blushed a hot pink. She seemed hesitant to continue. "Are you still going to be my partner?"

"Of course. I'm a man of my word, but Alaine, if you want me to teach you to be the best marksman you can be and put my life on the line to partner with you at the rodeo, you have to be honest with me." A single thread of understanding formed between them. "And, if you can't, at least be honest with yourself. Otherwise, you better find yourself another calf to rope."

"I understand." She bit a quivering lip. "I know I wasn't exactly honest with you. And, I don't want to find another calf to rope."

"Just remember lack of confidence in the rodeo arena can get you killed."

She smiled but didn't answer. Her amethyst eyes drew him. Her sweet, irresistible charm made it impossible for him to be near without touching her.

Common sense abandoned Morgan, and he pulled the pretty lady into his arms. Crushing her to him, he claimed her lips, sending spirals of ecstasy through her. His passion was more persuasive than she cared to admit, and his moist, firm mouth demanded a response.

Alaine returned the kiss, savoring every moment, realizing it was as challenging as it was rewarding.

He suddenly released her.

"Good night, Alaine," he said, as if such physical affection was a customary farewell.

"Sleep tight, Morgan." She hesitantly closed the door.

Morgan shut the screen, thinking how the hunger of her lips had shattered every ounce of calm within him. Why had he touched her in the first place? Especially with every cowboy on the ranch taking turns as chaperone.

Deep in the shadows he saw Tegeler's towering silhouette.

Meandering closer, Teg stepped forward and shoved a gun belt into Morgan's hands. "Figured you might need this." The ol' coot let loose with a string of tobacco juice, almost hitting Morgan's boots. "Be ready to ride at first light. Gotta keep you away from that gal—one way or another."

Chapter 7

Morgan didn't get much rest and woke long before sunup. He'd pretty much had his fill of the odor of musky old newspapers insulating the bunkhouse walls and the assortment of foul smells that would insult a skunk—sweaty men, licorice-smelling tobacco chaws and dirty feet. Then add snores that could wake the Devil, and a rooster who didn't seem to know night from day—Morgan had tossed and turned before giving up on sleep.

Mulling over the day before, he sat on a wooden barrel outside and watched as the sun barely cracked the horizon.

The lawman in him had a character flaw he detested. Everything had to come to a satisfactory conclusion before he could proceed further. So what if he had weakened? Hopefully he had driven his point home to Alaine—she must have confidence in herself if she wanted to be a winner.

Up in the main house, lamplight flickered in the corner bedroom upstairs and Morgan watched as a shadow crossed only a second before the room darkened. He never saw another light come on in the house except in the kitchen where the smell of bacon frying wafted through the air.

He leaned back and enjoyed daybreak. One thing about the Panhandle he had quickly learned to like: although it might've been hot enough to sizzle the legs off a grasshopper during the day, by evening the constant West Texas wind cooled things down.

Coffee sure did sound good. Pulling to his feet, he stood and stretched, trying to ignore the soft scent of roses. Only a woman rancher like Mrs. LeDoux would plant flowers around a bunkhouse. Morgan fingered a petal—a Seven Sisters rose, one of his mama's favorites.

The old ache in his heart twitched. He suddenly had a desire to go home and check on his sisters. To hell with solving some crappy rustling case for British moneymen who were so greedy that they had offered him a nice bonus if he could find more land to add to their portfolio.

Morgan was beginning to like the folks in Kasota Springs, some more than others—particularly one pretty lady—and figured the syndicate owners had enough land. Besides, he didn't see anything just right except for the little spread between Jacks Bluff and the Slippery Elm.

On his next trip to town, he had to finagle a meeting with the Slippery Elm's foreman and manager. Snyder was bossy and Gimpy seemed easily influenced. The information the owners back East gave the Pinks didn't jibe. But after overhearing the Lazy S duo talk about Alaine's mama in such a disrespectful fashion, the last thing he needed was to get into a confrontation with the stupid asses.

Blasted, Morgan had a job to do, get the information he had acquired back to Philly so the owners could take the necessary steps to protect their investment. His personal opinion on how they operated didn't count.

He was losing his objectiveness, damn it! His orders were to investigate cattle rustling on the Slippery Elm. He had a cardinal rule: never get personally involved. But the one element nobody figured on was a beautiful, dark-haired, sassy-butt daughter of a rancher.

The sound of gunfire ripped into the tranquility, but it

didn't seem to stop the ungodly snoring coming from the bunkhouse. Morgan glanced over his shoulder. Teg's cot was empty.

Deciding to look into the commotion, Morgan headed in the direction of the gunfire, just as another shot rang out. Passing the barn, he followed a path beyond the corrals toward a pasture where the dangest thing he'd ever witnessed came into view. He couldn't resist stopping and taking in the breathless sight.

There stood Alaine in her nightclothes, complete with a red sash around her waist, taking potshots at a bullet-riveted target nailed to a post—more a piece of shredded timber than a bull's-eye.

He cleared his throat and called out a customary warning before approaching from behind. "Morning."

"Back-atcha, Morgan." She reloaded and took another shot, pulverizing a sliver of wood barely hanging on. "Heard you coming."

Alaine lowered her gun and offered a friendly, good morning smile. "You were right. Since you suggested that I change to a 20-gauge, I'm much more accurate." She smiled with an air of pleasure. "Thanks."

"No thanks needed. Just practice and keep the confidence."

"I saw Teg slewfooting it toward the main house about an hour ago. Probably trying to get in good with the cook, so if you want any breakfast, better shake a leg," she bantered. "Don't want him to catch you with me in my unmentionables, do you?"

"No, ma'am." He headed for the house, hungrier than he'd been in ages. And it wasn't just the thoughts of biscuits and gravy that whet his appetite.

Today was bound to be tough but not as difficult as if he got caught ogling the wild child of Kasota Springs with a shotgun in her hand, wearing nightclothes—red sash and all.

Breakfast was tasty and ample, no doubt one of the reasons the Jacks Bluff ranch hands were so loyal.

Teg stuffed the last bite of biscuit in his mouth and washed it down with coffee. He stood and barked, "We've got work to do." He wiped his mouth and grabbed his Stetson. "Tuffy, make sure Alaine gets to town safely. She'll fight you tooth and toenail, but you know what I want."

"Yes, sir."

"Tell her we'll be comin' in town tonight like I said." Teg finished off his coffee. "I'm taking Payne with me. Don't expect to be back before supper." He motioned toward Morgan, indicating he was ready to leave. "I sure as hell ain't gonna get in a predicament where I have to eat one of those box suppers that Miz Tempest is wantin' us to buy."

Bobby spoke up, "Last night, I ended up with Edwinna Dewey and you wouldn't believe the horsemeat she tried to pawn off as good vittles." He shuddered. "Won't do it again, not even for Miz LeDoux."

"And, Payne, I'll warn you, don't go playing poker with her either. She cheats," Jimmy piped up.

"Don't forget whose brand you ride for, boys." Teg shot over his shoulder as the back screen slammed shut. "If they can't be loyal to their brand, they need to call for their time and ride outta here."

"Just old-time cowboy joshing," Morgan remarked and then laughed. "So the apple doesn't fall far from the tree."

"Where gamblin's concerned, like mother, like daughter."

Nothing more was said until Morgan and Tegeler entered the privacy of the barn. There Teg mumbled, "Payne, gotta admit, you're one helluva muleskinner. If you ever need a job, I know a freight company who could use you."

The old man punched him on the shoulder, and a flash of humor crossed his face.

"You ol' egg-suckin' dog, I could knock you on your butt

again if I had a mind to," Morgan retorted. "I knew when you headed directly for me in the bar that my gig was up."

"You're too good of a lawman to let that happen. Besides I trained you, so figured whatever brought you here was none of my concern." Teg took a plug of tobacco out of his vest pocket and chewed off a piece. "Jest glad to see you, son."

"You were one of the best Texas Rangers around. Never knew what happened." Morgan glanced sideways.

"The Rangers weren't the same after they reorganized. After I served my time training honyocks like you to be the best trackers around and experts at catching rustlers for the Pinks, I hired on with Jack LeDoux down in New Orleans and followed him up here. Spent many a year trying not to look back on the days of cold coffee, rations not fit for a prairie dog, and women who cried every time they saw the backsides of her man ride off not knowing when he'd be back or if he'd be back."

"You still do the Texas Rangers proud, Teg."

Obviously finished talking about history, the foreman opened a stall gate and walked out a big bay who neighed and shook his black mane in welcome. "Sniff's nice and gentle. A good thinker. He needs somebody like you to challenge him."

Teg opened the next gate and brought out his stallion.

The men said little while they saddled the horses, and once finished, rode north past the area where Alaine had been practicing her sharpshooting.

A tinge of regret settled in Morgan's gut. The right and proper thing to do would have been for him to have spent more time with Alaine, although he still figured her confidence level, not her skill, was her enemy.

"One thing, Payne. Our little Buckaroo has to win the shooting competition for her mama's sake. Think that's possible?" He spit tobacco to the offside of his horse.

"Just because a chicken has wings doesn't mean it can fly."

Morgan chuckled and spurred the bay, who seemed to know exactly where they were headed. "But, she's improving."

"Good. Didn't do very good in the first round, but she has a second chance," Teg said. "Just make sure she wins."

They rode across the gentle rolling plains sprinkled with Russian thistle and mesquite brushes. Scrunch grass crumpled under the weight of their horses' hooves.

In the distance Morgan watched as the banks of the Canadian came into sight. Fringed with wild berry bushes and plum thickets, both sides sloped into the river. Huge cottonwoods towered over a coppice of smaller trees and shrubs scattered along both of its banks.

Morgan had seen most of Texas, but he couldn't think of a place closer to heaven than the Canadian River.

With their backs to the sun, they rode the fence line, checking for broken posts and cut or downed barbed wire.

"Didn't want to bring this up back yonder, and it's none of my business what brought you to these parts, but we could use your help, if you wanna stick around," said Teg.

For a big man Tegeler rode easy in the saddle.

Morgan knew Teg would show him common courtesy and not press him for details, but maybe he could repay the hospitality of the LeDouxes by helping out, if he could. "What kind?"

"Rustling."

"But you said you weren't having any problems."

"That we know of. But the whole kit-and-caboodle don't add up. There's something going on and we need it stopped before it boils over into a full-fledged range war."

Morgan figured this was a good opportunity to needle the ol' rascal. "If you wanted my help, at least you could've found me a decent horse, not a pack donkey."

"You're undercover, so thought it was fittin'." Teg laughed. "Plus you smelled worse than that dang donkey."

Teg reined up beside Morgan. "See that." He pointed to a

bull tangled in barbed wire and downed fence post. "Now that's a heap of trouble, son."

"You're not running cattle in this pasture. Why's he out this far?"

"I can bet a double eagle he ain't ours."

They dismounted and Tegeler opened his saddlebag, producing wire cutters, and the two men went to work.

The blasted bovine wasn't in much of a humor to be saved and sent both cowboys grabbing air more than once. "Notice anything odd about his brand?" Teg asked, trying to catch his breath while attempting to cut away more barbed wire in order to release the varmint.

"Definitely a Lazy S bull, but he's hair branded. And I don't think it's as old as it looks." A barb tore into Morgan's arm. "Sonofabitch."

"Yep, cold brand, slow brand, all the same." Teg struggled with the barbed wire and cutters. "Should've worn heavier gloves."

"If you can keep this bastard from killing us before he kills himself, we'll have him free in a minute or two."

Just another day covered with manure and blood, Morgan figured, as he tore away the last of the fencing, giving the bull his freedom. "Damn sure glad he wasn't any older than a yearling." Morgan had to stop and take a deep breath before continuing. "Only one reason to hair brand, Tegeler."

"Yep." He wiped sweat from his brow. "Only one reason."

Morgan wrangled his way through the twisted barbed wire and stepped over the downed fence, carefully trailing the animal for several hundred yards before calling back to Tegeler, "Bring our mounts, you ol' geezer. We've got work to do."

Tegeler led the horses toward Morgan, lagging behind him knowing exactly what needed to be done. Besides Teg, Morgan was one of the best trackers around, and if there were any telltale signs to be had, between the two of them, they'd find them.

"See what I see?" Morgan pointed at a mound of ashes. "Certainly not Indians." He leaned down and picked up some coals and rubbed them between his fingers. "Probably went out late yesterday afternoon."

"No campfire for sure." Teg's brow furrowed. "A branding fire. Cattle's been though here not long ago either."

Morgan nodded toward a trail of mashed-down pasture. "Grass has been bruised and is still crunched down. Had lots of weight on it."

Tegeler poked at the ground with the toe of his boot. The dust stirred easily. "Four horses here. None carrying more than a man's weight."

Inch by inch, Morgan examined the brush around the branding fire, not discounting any possibilities, while Teg took the opposite side for signs.

"Might be what we're looking for." Teg pulled away from a mesquite bush and squatted. Separating a limb, he picked up a piece of burlap. "Yep, jest as I suspicioned."

Morgan neared and took the cloth. "Ol' rustler trick, using damp burlap between the cow's hide and the hot iron to make the brand look older than it is." He smelled the fibers. "Smokers, too."

Teg knelt down and took a whiff. "Yep, for sure. Reckon it to be tobacco."

"Whatcha learn from the tracks?"

"Four riders. One with a limp." Teg moved a little to the right and pointed to boot prints. "Twisting on the sole and drove his lame leg's foot deeper into the ground than the other one. Bad left side, I'd say."

"Know anybody around these parts who fits that bill?"

"A gimpy leg is the sign of a working cowboy. Let's go. Wanna follow this trail and see where these cattle end up."

Both men swung into their saddles and followed the

trotted-down grass until they came to a clearing where a herd of cattle leisurely grazed.

"Hope to hell if we get caught out on Slippery Elm land, they don't shoot first and ask questions later, Teg."

"Ain't Slippery Elm pastures. We came off it back at the fork. This here's that shoestring operation they call Rocking J." Teg stood in the stirrups, took off his hat, and wiped the sweat with his sleeve. "Whatcha see, Payne?"

"A herd of lazy, fat cattle ready for market."

"Nope." Teg plopped his Stetson back on his head, and sat back down. "What you see is a shirttail herd too fat to be grazing off this little tad of ranch land. Pasture ain't even overgrazed. They've been feedin' somewhere else and I'm bettin' if you get close enough to 'um you'll find the Lazy S has been changed to a Rocking J."

"Easy brand to alter. Just add a J below the Lazy S. Who's runnin' this outfit?"

"Don't know for sure. Homesteaded to a fella named Bandy Jameson, I've been told. Has a couple of hands and a few head. Nothing more."

"The hell you say." It was Morgan's turn to sit back in the saddle and enjoy the rolling plains dusted with white and yellow prairie flowers he didn't recognize. "Ever met Jameson?"

"Nope. Another of those absentee owners. Don't really even know any of their hands. They stay to themselves."

"I'm bettin' he's the same man you know as Gimpy."

"From the Slippery Elm?"

"That's how I figure it." Morgan almost cackled out loud, but it would have given Tegeler too much pleasure to know he might've just solved Morgan's case for him and he didn't even know it.

A flash of light shot through the sky.

"Whatcha think, Teg?"

"Got a visitor. One too dumb to know that the sun reflects

off anything shiny. He's over to the right, probably a thousand yards."

"Yep. Think I'll mosey back outta here. How about you?"

"Plan on staying in the saddle and staying out of trouble."

Gingerly the duo turned their horses and trotted off, as though they apologized for happening into the wrong pasture.

"Payne, you might have reason to be on their land, but I sure as hell don't." Teg spurred his stallion. "Not with wire cutters in my pocket."

Chapter 8

Alaine sat on a bale of hay and watched the sky. To the west of the rodeo grounds dark angry clouds groaned and cursed vengeance, promising a summer thunderstorm.

Adjacent to the railroad tracks, holding pens and chutes created a wooden maze around corrals. Steers, cows, calves and horses impatiently stirred waiting for their turn to outrun, outbuck and outwit cowboys just as intent on beatin' them.

Alaine had traded her leather skirt for a pair of britches, red calico blouse and black vest, along with broken-in work boots. Her mane of curly black hair was snugly held in place by her ever present felt hat.

Suddenly she seemed more interested in one tough Philadelphia lawyer who looked larruping good in tight fittin' pants that showed off a nice butt. His front side wasn't all that bad either. Didn't know where he got 'um but they fit him as if they'd been tailor-made just for the man.

The banter between two chute roosters, rodeo-wise youngsters who perched on the top of the rails and knew how everything should be done and didn't mind giving out advice, put a smile on her face.

"Storm's a brewin', sure as shootin'. Gonna cause havoc if this dirt turns to mud," one said.

The second railbird concurred. "Good thing about these here parts, one minute it'll be sunny and the next stormy. Nobody knows what to expect except the good Lord and he ain't talking."

An ache in her heart quickly replaced her smile. Morgan hadn't gotten there yet, and she knew all hell was about to break loose.

She had been surprised to learn that the wild-cow milking and team roping had been switched because of the inclement weather. She guessed the committee, headed by her own mama, figured the roping deserved better conditions than the lowly milking competition.

Morgan surely would think she had rickydoodled him again. And he'd made it abundantly clear he would *not* participate in that event come hell or high water.

From the looks of the clouds boiling in the west, Armageddon was headed their way and was sure to bring high water.

To please her mama, Alaine had to win an event—any one of them. Tempest had been disappointed when her daughter missed her shot in the first round of the sharpshooting contest, and it wounded Alaine's heart to think about letting her down.

Not to mention the hunk of manhood Alaine couldn't get off her mind, who had instilled much needed confidence in her and at the same time made her think twice.

After all, Alaine had barely made the cut to the finals, and she suspected that being the lone female entered had cinched the spot. She wouldn't put it past her mama or Teg to make sure she qualified. This was her one chance. Although she'd been shooting really good of late, she couldn't be guaranteed a win.

But she'd make damn sure she didn't embarrass her mama and the Jacks Bluff. Even if it meant only winning one regular event—the wild cow milking, which could be as dangerous as bronc busting.

She glanced into the crowd to see how many of her mama's hands were around. Plenty. Apparently Teg had done his usual and made sure she had plenty of chaperones.

Once, just once, she'd like to be able to go somewhere and do something without being followed. But as long as she lived under the shadow of Tempest LeDoux, and ultimately the foreman, that wasn't about to happen.

Folks were gathering for the evening's festivities, but men were noticeably missing. She knew where they were and what event they were waiting to watch. And it dern sure wasn't cow milking.

No doubt in her mind, they were exactly where she'd like to be; the outlaw event—bucking bulls. Where brutally strong, rough, tough, and maybe some of the most foolish cowboys around competed for bragging rights. Most of the ranch owners didn't like their hands getting involved with it—the sport could maim or kill. Injuries were a given and the possibility of death loomed overhead, but she also knew many of those same owners had bets on the winner.

Soundless lightning flickered against the threatened sky and served to increase Alaine's concern that something ghastly had happened to Morgan.

Between Teg's stubbornness and Morgan's impatience, they might be laid out on the range dead from butting their heads together. Morgan had to learn in one day what most cowboys took years to accomplish.

Now she had the unpleasant task of informing him that all of his efforts meant nil, because they had missed the roping event. And she wasn't confident that Teg and her mama hadn't gotten into cahoots just to keep Morgan and her apart.

While having lunch at the Springs Hotel, she had overheard gossip about McKenna Smith, the infamous gunslinger her mama had taken a shine to, getting injured in one of the events. The tight group of gossipmongers led by Edwinna Dewey hushed the second they saw Alaine at a nearby table, so she figured he was over at Doc Mitchell's being put back together.

The days since the bank robbery had been filled with talk about McKenna Smith this, McKenna Smith that. Everywhere she went they yammered about how the Guardian of Justice saved the day. The mayor gave him the key to the town in gratitude for chasing down Cherokee Bill Bartlett, the bank robber who held her captive, and returning the town's money. Since he'd been injured, they'd probably rename Main Street for him.

But nobody seemed to acknowledge that the real hero was Morgan Payne—the man who took a bullet for her. Well, it wasn't a mortal injury, but still, it was a bullet. And he hadn't even complained. Nary a mention of his bravery had been made.

For the umpteenth time, Alaine moved from the bale of hay to the fence. Hugging a post, she prayed for his safe return. A good and proper thank-you was in order.

Alaine watched the second round of the team roping, and although she spent most of her time lost in thought she couldn't help but laugh at her clown friend Augusta, as Rusty the Tramp, went about entertaining the crowd with her funny antics. With her bulbous fake nose, bright red hair, exaggerated freckles and white-painted mouth turned down into an exaggerated frown, Alaine knew that Augusta smiled on the inside.

Not caring about other's opinions, she was one of the few females who bothered to speak to the LeDoux women.

When the steer roping ended, the corral emptied and her clown friend disappeared. Alaine kept her faith that Morgan wouldn't let her down.

The early evening wore on and raindrops patted tentatively on her hat, and she continued to fret over Morgan's absence.

Just one more event and the dance would begin. No doubt

Teg had kept his pledge to keep them apart, even if it meant that his student wouldn't show for the rodeo.

The crowd began to thin. Ladies trailed off to prepare for the evening dance. The one Alaine had hoped to attend, thinking all day about what it'd feel like to be held in Morgan's arms through a whole waltz. She had been in the circle of his embrace but each time it seemed much too short.

The announcer gave the thirty-minute warning before the wild cow milking contest would commence. She needed Morgan more than ever. They had already missed the team roping, and she was sure he wasn't going to be happy one iota.

Augusta reappeared wearing an ice blue tea gown with layers of ruffles, looking a bit frazzled. Well, she didn't blame her. Scrubbing off that face paint and making such quick changes of clothes during her routines would frazzle anyone.

Sometimes Alaine swore that she had more Indian in her than Cajun. This was one of those times. She smelled and felt Morgan before she heard him.

"Lookin' for a partner, Little Lady," he said from behind.

"Nope." Relief made her smile. "Got one."

She turned and looked at the handsome man all decked out in pants and a shirt that would do justice to any cowboy. His suntanned face reflected the whiteness of his shirt. He looked nothing like the dandy who arrived in town less than a week before. Where had the Eastern lawyer gone?

The shadows lifted from her heart. "I thought—"

"That I'd bailed on you?" Drops of rain shimmered on his Stetson.

"Did cross my mind, but knew you'd be true to your word. We have less than ten minutes."

"I helped Pony Boy bring around Diablo and I rode Sniff in," Morgan said with cool authority. "Who's header and who's heeler?"

Knowing that the thunder rumbling was nothing compared

to the roar she'd get from Morgan when he found out they weren't in team roping, she took a deep breath.

Oh, he'd rope okay—a wild nursing cow.

"Guess I'll repeat myself." His smile was brighter than his shirt. "Who's header and who's heeler?"

She scrounged up courage and stammered, "You mean who'll mug and who'll milk."

The look on his face hid none of his displeasure. He clenched his jaw and frowned. "No, ma'am. I didn't stutter."

Regardless of her explanation, none would satisfy the big man.

"No," she lowered her voice as if it'd soften the blow. "Mugger and milker."

He stared ahead like an Indian lookin' at the moon, as sprinkles turned into raindrops. "We missed the event, didn't we?" He pursed his mouth, obviously trying to corral his frustration. "Damn Tegeler's hide."

"It's not his fault, Morgan." She wasn't sure, but thought this might be the first time she'd ever defended the foreman, but for once he was innocent, although she was certain he would have made it happen if he'd thought of it.

She continued, "They had to switch the team roping semifinals with wild cow milking."

"Why?"

"To be honest with you, they claim it was because of the storm coming in, but I suspect it had more to do with the men wanting to watch bull riding to see if Dally Angelo rides Bone Buster without getting killed. A lot of bets are floating around on both."

"Hell of a reason." He pulled gloves from his pocket. "I'll be the roper and mugger."

Thunder boomed, then faded as though waiting for an encore.

Damnation and tarnation, he'd been hornswoggled again by

the Little Lady. One thing for sure, this would be the last game he'd play with her.

By morning, he'd have confirmation from his home office that his job was finished and he'd be on his way back to Philadelphia leaving behind Miss Prissy Pants and her tomfoolery before the closing ceremonies commenced.

But then there was the issue of helping Tegeler protect the LeDouxes from rustlers. A man of integrity, Morgan took his reputation seriously. He shook his head. There wasn't anything else to do except keep his promise.

"I take mugger," he said. "Besides, have you seen the size of those cows? I've seen bulls who would give them a run for their money." Morgan tried to disguise his annoyance, but was sure she saw right through him. "Plus, can't let all of Teg's hard work go to waste. I'll rope and mug, you'll do the milkin'." He pulled a coin from his pocket. "Or we could flip for jobs."

"And, have Teg on our butts? No way!"

They both enjoyed a good-hearted laugh, and headed for the chutes.

Soft rain peppered in earnest and was quickly absorbed by the thirsty soil.

"So you're not mad at me?" Alaine asked.

"Mad? Can't say I'd call it mad."

The smaller of the chute roosters hollered, "Better hurry, looks like a gully washer's on its way."

A second one ordered, "Chute's loaded. Got two minutes."

Clouds churned overhead and a heavy caisson of thunder bellowed a warning.

Only a handful of folks remained. Mostly those intrigued with the couple and who wanted to be the first to spread the latest gossip about another of the LeDoux women's fiascos.

Swinging into the saddle, Morgan brought Sniff up to the start line in the northwest corner of the corral. "Sure as hell hope we got a good, wet cow," he mumbled to himself. The gelding pranced sideways, eager to be pressed into action.

Pony Boy climbed up beside the other chute roosters and hollered, "Use small loops, Mister."

Lightning arced from cloud to cloud, followed by claps of thunder that made a calm and obedient horse like Sniff fret.

Morgan centered his butt in the saddle and watched the southeast corner chute, where a nervous nellie jumped and kicked, banging the sides. She swished her tail, and searched for a target.

He knew her kind. A free-roaming, fresh off the range cow with painfully swollen utters who had never had any human contact. Frantic because she was lookin' for her lost calf, she reminded him of Alaine's mother when she thought her daughter was being kidnapped. He saw the same wild panic in the mama cow's eyes. Hell, it kinda reminded him of Alaine.

Intermittent gusts of wind turned to unrelenting fury and threw bucketfuls of rain hammering down.

The flag dropped and a gunshot rang out.

Time started.

Morgan spurred Sniff.

Ready for a fight, the wild cow lunged out of the chute like a rattler had hold of her tail . . . and that was just the beginning.

The ol' gal ducked right and hung Morgan out to dry.

Cussing for dropping one, Morgan tried his damnedest to keep her running in a straight line, but she crow hopped around in no particular pattern.

By that time, maybe some of her sour disposition had sweetened or she was distracted by Sniff running after her and decided he wasn't about to catch her. She zigzagged across the corral, faking Morgan out. She jumped forward and turned right, twisting her short horns, taunting the roper.

Maybe the kid was right. Morgan adjusted the lariat and this time he made a good catch. Her head passed through the loop and he tightened the rope.

Being slowed down didn't set well with the cow, and in one leap that would make any bull proud, she belly-rolled, jerking Morgan out of the saddle. Uprooted, he held onto the rope for dear life, letting the damn fool pull him through the mud.

The rain slacked up, only to regroup and assault even harder, turning the grounds into a small playa lake.

Morgan spit water but swore the battle ax wouldn't best him. He used every cuss word he knew and some he made up along the way.

He wasn't sure if the old mama got tired of hauling him around or she decided she was just flat-assed tired, but she stopped dead in her tracks. In the slick mud, he hammered against the cow's hide, taking an uppercut to the chin.

Getting a good hold on her horns, he thanked his lucky star that she was a muley cow without the usual dangerous, long and twisted ones.

After catching a second wind, the cow took off again, which he managed to bring to a halt, hoping she'd stay on her feet long enough to be milked. How in the hell they ended up even in the vicinity of where Alaine was he had no idea, but they did.

From roper to mugger, Morgan held the bovine, while his partner milked her . . . very slowly.

The cow never got what Morgan would call still, but Alaine managed to get in a squirt or two. He wanted to yell at her to hurry up, but didn't want to scare the damn critter again and prayed they'd get their dern milk to the judge before another clap of thunder scared the ol' gal dry.

Alaine was covered with mud as much, if not more than Morgan. Bits of wet earth hung from her hair and the rain made her blouse cling to her like a mold.

"Let me milk awhile," Morgan said. "Before she remembers she's mad at us."

"She isn't mad, she's just grouchy," Alaine retorted.

From the looks of the white river flowing downhill, he was sure a jug of milk had hit the ground. Only a trickle in the bottle, but he wasn't about to complain.

"You got enough," he yelled.

Lightning lit up the sky and the damnedest roar of thunder he believed he'd ever heard reverberated the air.

That was about all the ol' cow planned to take. She lunged forward, almost knocking the bottle out of Alaine's hands and ran off at breakneck speed.

He watched Alaine and the cow race across the rain-soaked grounds—one for the chute and one for the judge.

Alaine lost her footing and slipped in the slosh, coming up unharmed with the bottle but drenched with mud and slop.

Morgan took off toward her. He glanced around, not that he expected applause for being humiliated, but there was not a sole present. Even the chute roosters had left their perch.

Swinging back in his direction, she looked about as down to earth as any woman he'd ever seen in his life . . . covered with mud, straw and other unpleasant things he'd just as soon not think about, and yelled, "Morgan, there's no judge! Where do I put it?"

"On the table, and they can measure later."

She looked up and his pulse skittered alarmingly. He joined her at the judge's stand, and swept her into the circle of his arms. Her nearness kindled feelings of fire. A blaze not easy to ignore. Enjoying the feel of her wet body, he kissed her long and hard.

Raising his mouth from hers, he gazed into her eyes, just as she recaptured his lips.

The heavens opened with another gush of rain, but he didn't care. He'd had more fun in the last ten minutes than he'd had in years.

He drew her face to his in a renewed embrace, first kissing the tip of her nose, then her eyes and, finally, he took satisfaction in kissing her soft mouth, leaving him burning with fire.

Alaine whispered softly, "How does it feel to try to rope the wind?"

Chapter 9

Morgan and Alaine raced back to the Springs Hotel in the howling thunderstorm that seemed to pass over about as quickly as it gathered. He had made sure she was safely on her way to her mama's room, where she planned to spend the night, so she could be up early to prepare for the following day's activities.

Nodding a good evening to the goggle-eyed desk clerk, Morgan stopped by the dining room and ordered a supper special, along with a pot of tea, to be taken to Alaine's room. He had to keep her strength up. The sharpshooting finals were only twenty-four hours away, and he had promised to do everything he could to see that she won.

He hightailed it for his room. It had been so long since he had been there that it came to his mind the shifty buzzard owning the shabby saloon below it might've rented it out by the hour in his absence. He'd heard talk that they let the prisoners, except for the bank robber, out of jail for the weekend and rented out their beds.

To Morgan's surprise, the room was just as he'd left it—stinky with a washbasin and a pitcher of insect-infested water. At least the mice had someplace to get a drink. He scooped out the flies and washed away most of the grime. It was too late to use the public bathhouse, but that was on the top of

Morgan's agenda for the following day. A hot bath and shave, not just washing up as far as he could, then down as far as he could, then washing "could"! He scraped the stubble off his face with a blade that was about as dull as a rusty ax head, but it'd have to do until morning.

Nevada's hat was beyond saving, so Morgan switched it for his own black Stetson he'd hauled around the country—from Galveston to Philadelphia and parts in between. He still favored the hat, much as he did his boots and watch fob. Oh yeah, the Pinkertons had given him hell about the boots, but in the long run, he'd prevailed. Next to a man's horse, his hat and boots were his most prized possessions.

But for Morgan it was his watch fob. The last gift his daddy had given him before being trapped in a mine shaft. At the age of twelve, Morgan had to provide for his three stair-stepsisters and a mentally ill mother, who became too frightened to step out of the house for fear of being kidnapped.

Morgan vividly recalled every tortuous hour working in the box factory on Second Street in Colinderville, Pennsylvania, where he made crude wooden boxes to hold squibs that were used in the mines.

Every evening was spent studying, when not shielding his siblings from the townsfolk's ridicule. They got called poor little ragamuffins and worse. He worked to feed his family until the girls were able to take care of themselves. His mother went into an institution only weeks before the good Lord relieved her of her worldly pain and took her into his arms. Putting her away, as folks called it, became a burden Morgan carried with him ever since. To escape, he had joined the Pinkerton Agency.

Morgan neared the Springs Hotel and in the distance heard the music and racket of the merrymakers attending the dance. He wished he and Alaine were there. One thing that had kept him going all day was thinking about holding Alaine in his arms and waltzing across Texas, but it wasn't bound to happen. He planned to look in on her first, then find Tegeler to see what, if anything, he had found out about the rustlers.

Pony Boy came up behind Morgan so fast that if he'd had a gun he'd probably have drawn it on the kid.

"Mister," he hailed. "Hey, Mister Payne, gotta wire for you." He almost skidded into Morgan. "Mister Dewey's wife over at the telegram place says that I gotta make shore I give it to you and nobodies else."

"Thanks." Morgan tossed him two bits, and the kid darted away holding the coin up to the light, as though checking for its authenticity.

Morgan walked into the lobby of the hotel and found a quiet, well-lit spot to read the message, after which he tore it into tiny pieces and stuffed it in his pocket.

"Didja find out anything?" a voice called from the shadows.

"Sonofabitch, Teg," Morgan bellowed. "You could walk through a den of rattlers and never disturb a one."

"Too many years of scouting." The old man motioned with his head to follow him.

Once they were in the empty dining room, Teg led him to a secluded corner where they could have some privacy.

"Need to talk, son," he quickly began. "Trouble isn't on its way—it's here." He smashed a cockroach that scampered across the floor. "Found two dead steers near the fence line. Gutted, mangled. Sending us a message."

"Not surprised. Just got a wire from Philly confirming that Gimpy is the same Bandy Jameson who owns the Rocking J." Morgan frowned. "Pretty sure he was the one who saw us on his land."

"Damn it!" Teg clamped his lips together in anger. "Gotta keep Alaine in town and safe. Don't care how in the hell you do it, but make sure she doesn't come back out to the ranch until this blows over. I've got my hands full out there and can't protect her right now."

Morgan didn't have to listen to the rest of Teg's reasoning. He knew full well that she'd be safer in town under his watchful eye than traipsing between Kasota Springs and the Jacks Bluff.

Teg continued. "I'm leaving some of the guys I trust to give you an extra pair of eyes or three."

Jeeze, it'd take them and a dozen more to boot to make sure the most stubborn person Morgan believed he'd ever dealt with didn't misbehave.

"One thing more, Payne. McKenna Smith got hurt and Alaine's mama took him to the ranch to doctor him up, so better stay away. Don't need him blowing your cover this late in the game."

"Smith's honest and levelheaded. Never killed a man who didn't draw on him first, but we don't need another gun involved in this mess." Morgan defended the gunslinger and eyed the foreman. More trouble was coming, Morgan was certain from the look in Teg's eyes. "Something else?"

"Gimpy and Snyder have disappeared. Just upped and walked off, stealing everybody's money for both operations. Got some mad hombres out there ready to string 'um up. We need to find the bastards before they do."

"Wish to hell somebody would have thought about asking Gimpy for his given name before the rustling began."

"You know better than that. It ain't polite to question a man's name. What his mama tagged him with ain't none of our business. Besides, some of their names are downright embarrassing."

A young couple entered the dining room.

Not giving Morgan an opportunity to tell him more about the telegram, Tegeler sauntered off.

"Don't let our Little Buckaroo get out of your sight without making sure one of the guys are there or you got me to deal with, Payne," he said over his shoulder before stopping and turning around. "Hogtie her if necessary." The ol' buzzard stared Morgan straight in the eyes. "And you sure as hell better not break her heart."

Chapter 10

Damn, Morgan wasn't sure when he signed on to be Alaine's bodyguard, but it kinda happened, just like him saying "no" and her hearing "yes." Seems everybody at the Jacks Bluff had a ciphering problem.

Glad the hotel clerk was nowhere in sight, Morgan climbed the stairs to Alaine's mother's hotel room. He gave a deep sigh of relief, knowing if he was seen going into her room the rumor mill would grind overtime. He knocked lightly.

"Alaine, it's Morgan."

"Come on in." Her voice sounded soft and inviting.

This might not be such a bad chore after all, he thought, before Teg's words reminded him otherwise.

The room was dimly lit, with only a lamp in the far corner of the room. The sweet, heady fragrance of lilac filled the stuffy room, which needed fresh air in the worst way.

Water swished gently like a mountain stream trickling over stones after a rainstorm.

At first he thought Alaine was hiding, but after taking a second look he saw her only too well.

Sweet mother of Joseph! The lamplight behind a thin dressing screen as she bathed served to highlight the silhouette of the most exquisitely created woman Morgan had ever seen. Only God could have made anything that perfect.

"Mama left a note at the desk that she's going to the ranch for the night," she called from behind the screen. "And, thanks for the supper. I was starving."

His mouth was spitless, but he finally muttered a couple of words. "You're welcome."

Teg had burst Morgan's plan apart like a balloon pricked by a bowie knife. He had figured he'd check on Alaine and when her mama got there, he'd set up watch outside the door.

His eyes returned to the vision behind the screen. Morgan couldn't tear his gaze away. A gentleman would have excused himself and left the room while she finished bathing, but he certainly wasn't in the mood to be that gentleman.

"Mama left a boxed supper, but I found the meal you sent much more inviting," she said in a silky voice. "Help yourself."

Water sloshed, and he could see the silhouette of her body wedged between the screen and the lamp as clearly as if there were no veiling between him and the lady.

She raised one leg and leaned forward to wash her ankle. The outline of full, well-developed breasts anchored the images in his mind, sending a reminder way down south that he was a hot-blooded male in need of immediate attention.

"Need anything, Morgan?" Her voice was a velvety purr.

"No, ma'am." He tried to remember his pledge . . . to protect her, and he couldn't do it sitting outside of her door, not with a window facing Main Street directly across from the mercantile's upstairs.

Although the window was covered with dainty lace curtains, she'd be right in the line of fire if someone decided hurting her might serve as a second reminder that they knew Payne and Tegeler were on to their scheme.

He swallowed again and needed a distraction. He looked

around. The room, void of pictures, reminded him of a Civil War battlefield hospital.

Evidently, Alaine's mama had planned for the worst, as there were enough bandages, bottles of tonic, even a jug of whiskey, to doctor about anything that could happen at the rodeo. They were prepared even if a range war broke out.

He could study the wallpaper only so long. He finally said, "Believe I'll take you up on supper."

Snatching up the decorated box, he tore it open like it was the newest Sears Roebuck catalogue.

Morgan grabbed the first piece of chicken he came to—a luscious, tender and succulent breast. Well, that wouldn't keep his mind off the naked woman. It was about as tricky as trying to stab fleas with a butcher knife when a fully grown bull was roaming through the room.

"Try a breast if one's there. You look like a breast man to me," she said in a honeyed tone.

Holy cow! Tossing the piece back in, he fingered his next choice. A meaty, mouthwatering thigh, which reminded him of the fine-looking part of her body that got exposed while they wrestled for the dice.

"Maybe you're a leg or thigh man. They're always my favorite," she commented.

Back to the box.

"Guess I'll hush so you can enjoy your supper." Her voice rose a little, making her statement a polite half question, half comment.

Words escaped him.

A neck. Kissing her got between him and the skimpy part of the chicken that his mama told him was the sweetest meat of the fryer.

He waited for Alaine's next soliloquy, and when none came he settled on the bony chicken back with the tail suggestively hanging on for dear life.

Hell's bells, he couldn't even eat supper for letting thoughts about the woman who made him crazy get in the way.

A jar caught his eye. He opened it and helped himself to a pretty good-size whole pickle. He munched on it. Surely there was nothing about a plump, mouth-puckering pickle that could remind him of how much he'd like to make love to the woman soaking in the tub.

Sitting the jar aside, he replaced the lid on the box, nearly crushing it with the force.

Morgan began to pace the room. Maybe that would take his mind off Alaine's soap-slickened body.

"Morgan!" She spaced the next two words evenly. "Come here."

He whirled just in time to see her stand up, giving him full view of every inch of her body. Long, luscious legs, tempting thighs, pert breasts—he corralled his thoughts about the rest of her.

"There's a roach in the tub. Get him out."

"Alaine, I can't come behind that curtain. You're not appropriately dressed."

Well, wasn't that about the dumbest observation he'd ever made . . . but he didn't know how else to describe her short of . . . sweet jumpin' Jehoshaphat, he'd like to see her without a damn divider between them.

"Don't be such a fuddy-duddy." She leaned around the panel, her dark hair hanging in wet ringlets over her shoulder, smiled and extended her hand. "Here he is."

Morgan accepted the squiggly insect that theoretically should have drowned. Not sure what to do with him short of stomping its guts out, he opened the jar of pickles and dropped the pest in, not really caring if anybody mistook the cockroach for seasoning or not.

Water sloshed again as Alaine eased back into the water. "Morgan, it's so nice in here that I think I could go to sleep," she said wistfully.

Teg's reminder not to touch Alaine, keep her safe and not break her heart hit Morgan like a one-ton bull in a nasty mood. He set his jaw and almost laughed out loud. The ol' man's words surfaced. Yep, paybacks were hell.

He strolled to the table, picked up a pen and jotted on the back of an envelope—*Deliver to Teg Tegeler, Jacks Bluff Ranch.*

Opening the door, he set the pickle jar on top of the note right outside, knowing one of Teg's spies would be within spittin' distance and would make sure the gift was delivered to his ol' buddy.

Every inch of Morgan was drenched with sweat. He couldn't recall being so hot in all of his life. The rain had served to turn a scorcher of a day into a muggy, humid night. The outdoors was more of a sweat lodge than anything. Now the hotel room was stifling, a sultry mistress waiting on a lover—steamed up from bath water, humidity and—Morgan was pretty sure he was adding several degrees of body heat to the mix.

Alaine chatted away, recounting the events of the day, talking about people Morgan didn't know and probably wouldn't ever meet, yet the sound of her voice lulled him into a relaxed mood. The underlying sensuality of each word captivated him and made him think of a silken rose petal. But underneath he knew there were thorns essential to protect its beauty.

"What?" He jerked upright.

"I said why don't you take your shirt off and hang it over the chair to dry? Rest awhile. I know you're exhausted, and I truly believe I can sleep a week in this tub."

"No argument from me. Might cool down by then." He unbuttoned his shirt and pulled it off. This might be the best idea she'd come up with yet.

He settled back in the only other chair in the room, a wooden hotel-issue piece, and rested his head against the wall.

Thoughts of what he had to do to complete his assignment filled his mind for the moment.

The telegram had given him instructions on how the corporation that owned Slippery Elm wanted him to handle the rustling case. With a directive from his home office, those developments would detain him another day or two. Then he'd head back to Philadelphia where he figured it was about time for him to do something that'd been on his mind for a long time. For starters, resign from the agency and return to being a lawman who enjoyed capturing untrustworthy, natural-born killers like Black Jack Ketchum or the Dalton Gang.

But before he could do that, he had to make sure that the wild child of Kasota Springs was kept safe . . . without getting himself killed.

Chapter 11

Alaine jerked awake. Shivers ran up her spine. She was about as cold as she'd ever been in her life, not to mention her skin looked like a prune that had been dried too long. Her bath water was not even tepid, close to freezing compared to the heat in the room.

She had literally fallen asleep in the water while chatting with Morgan, although he really hadn't said much.

Light flickered from the lamp. Everything in the room was quiet, except for the soft snoring coming from Morgan. Not a disturbing sound, not that she'd ever heard a man snore, but one that a woman could feel comfortable with, knowing she was being protected by a man she loved.

Yikes! What was she thinking? What she felt was more of an attraction. Wanting to get your hands on a male kind of magnetism but certainly not anywhere close to love. It was lust, a need, longing, a million other words besides love!

Ashamed that she let her thoughts run wild, Alaine dried off and slipped into a white muslin gown trimmed with tiny blue rosettes and pulled on the matching robe.

Rounding the corner of the screen, her breath caught in her throat and her heart pounded in an erratic rhythm. The sight of Morgan asleep in the chair sent a delightful thrill of desire through her like kindling catching fire.

What a magnificent specimen of a man! His naked chest was gorgeous, more than she had imagined, and she'd given the matter a lot of thought. Powerful, broad and muscular, and so tempting to touch. His strapping arms were bare too, with a silky covering of dark hair finer than what was on his chest, which was layered with a mass of coarse, touchable hair trailing down into a vee that disappeared into the top of his pants.

She took another step toward him, compelled by her own need to be near the man. Her eyes moved over his body, back up to a rugged, handsome face that needed a good, close shave. Drops of moisture clung to his damp forehead.

Alaine had never noticed that his chocolate brown hair had sandy streaks. Probably lightened by the sun.

He smelled of soap and leather.

There was no other way to describe the man except as powerfully built and devastatingly handsome. Raised on a ranch with brawny men who washed up sometimes in the horse trough, she'd seen her share of shirtless cowboys. He put them to shame.

With legs stretched out in front of him, Morgan rested his head against the wall. She considered straddling the man, in a not-so-ladylike fashion, and exploring every inch of his perfect body.

Society dictated that a lady wouldn't entertain such wicked thoughts . . . but at their first meeting she had made it clear that she was no lady.

She took another step toward him and noticed, in contrast with his perfection, his assorted cuts, scrapes, scratches and bruises, some scabbing and some rather new. It was all she could do not to reach out and touch them, caress away the pain.

She knew where the two parallel scrapes on his temple had come from. One from McKenna Smith's bullet when Morgan saved her from the bank robber. And the other, served up by that dern donkey. Morgan had taken a pretty good bang on the chin where the cow had given him an uppercut and she was fairly certain that the gashes on his arm were from barbed wire.

Her heart sank. Teg must have really put him through hell if he got tangled up in barbed wire. She smiled, thinking back to the wild cow milking. No way had he learned to rope so proficiently in one day. She added that to the list of things she planned to find out about the big man. He was no more a practicing lawyer than she was a saint.

Quickly, she gathered a wad of gauze, a bottle of witch hazel and a tin of salve. The least she could do was clean and doctor his wounds . . . most of them caused by the messes she had gotten him into.

Alaine squatted down, poured witch hazel on a piece of gauze and reached out to tend to his chin.

In a flash, Morgan captured her by the waist and pulled her into his arms. She was certain her heart had jumped from its usual place into her throat. His instinctive response was so powerful that it created a purely sensual thrill in her.

"I wouldn't do that, Little Lady." Tantalizing blue eyes stared into hers.

Pretending not to be affected by his presence, she said, "Do you always wake up grouchy?"

Morgan released her and smiled but didn't answer.

Alaine straightened up. "I'm sorry that I scared you. I thought—"

"You'd take advantage of me in my weakened state?" A glint came to his eye, and he broke into a wide, teasing smile. He moved his hands to her shoulders, sending an involuntary chill through her.

"Absolutely not!"

He quirked a questioning eyebrow at her. "Give me that gauze. They're nothing but scratches, and I can tend to them myself." He took it from her hand and stepped to the highboy where he began to pat the medicine on his scrapes and bumps. "But, I appreciate the concern."

Sweet Moses and his mama too! Morgan thought he'd died and gone to heaven when he'd opened his eyes and saw Alaine standing before him like an angel, complete with a flowing white robe. A vision of beauty like nothing he had ever experienced.

He finished tending to his injuries, and put the lid back on the tin of salve. He thanked her again, but she didn't respond.

Morgan turned away from the dresser to find her sitting in his chair with her head leaning against the same wall that had held his up for an hour or more.

"Alaine." He spoke softly, although he knew that a steam engine whistle couldn't have awakened her.

Sweeping the woman up in his arms, Morgan carried her to bed. He wasn't sure how he would manage it, but eventually he got her robe off and tucked her in.

The gentleman in him fought the rogue, and he gave her a tender good night kiss.

Morgan turned down the lamp and returned to the chair, where he tried not to think about the one wound he hadn't been able to tend to. The soreness between his legs. The graze in his thigh from her arrow had already healed.

Damn Tegeler anyway!

Morgan shifted his weight and drifted off to sleep, dreaming about the things he might've done with the Little Lady if the sandman hadn't carted her away.

Chapter 12

The following morning Alaine sipped her coffee, enjoying the peace and tranquility that a good restful sleep brought her. During the night, she woke twice and both times she stayed awake for a few minutes watching the man who slept in the chair nearby. His presence gave her comfort, sending her right back into her dreams.

A strange feeling warmed her when she thought about how Morgan didn't seem to want to leave her side, even standing outside her door while she dressed. Then he'd rushed her downstairs to the hotel's dining room where she now sat breakfasting alone.

Morgan had downed a cup of coffee with her before he had excused himself to take care of business.

Just as he left, he turned back to her and made it abundantly clear that she was to wait for him and under no circumstances leave the dining room before he returned.

The waiter filled her coffee cup and she idly stirred in a tad of sugar.

But the strangest part of the morning was Morgan's last question before he kissed her on the forehead. Rather ballsy of him to do that in public. "Do you trust me?" he had asked.

After she told him she did, he only said "Good" before heading out the door.

Something was wrong; she felt it in her bones. Other than McKenna getting hurt and her mama taking him out to the ranch, there was trouble brewing, as evidenced by a passel of their cowboys having breakfast in the dining room. Completely out of character for them.

But she trusted Morgan, and if she was in danger, he would have never left.

Alaine heard Pony Boy calling her name before she saw him.

"Miss Alaine." The young man clutched a jar in his arms, and stopped in front of her. "'Cuse me, Miss Alaine."

He scuffed the toe of his boot on the floor as though he really didn't want to look at her.

"Miss Alaine . . ."

"What is it, Pony Boy?" Immediate concern for her mama came to mind, but it was quelled with the knowledge that she'd never send bad news by anyone except Tegeler.

"My mama always told me to do the right thing no matter how much you don't wanna. Only I sometimes don't 'xactly know what's right. I figure I gots to be loyal to Miz LeDoux on account of I ride for the Jacks Bluff now. But, I like Mister Morgan. He's real nice, next to you and your mama, that is." Embarrassed, Pony Boy ducked his head.

"Just tell me what it is that's bothering you." She wanted to ask him to sit down but knew he wouldn't.

"It's Mister Morgan . . . I heard he's workin' for the Slippery Elm and I didn't want that you should get hurt."

Shock shot through her. "Are you sure?"

"Yes, ma'am. Real sure. Mister Morgan got this wire an' it was from them foreigners. You know, the ones that speak all stiff like they got a corncob up their . . . 'Cuse me, ma'am."

"That's okay, Pony Boy. Tell me the rest."

He stammered, shifted the jar to his other arm, but refused to look up.

"Who told you all of this?"

"Them Slippery Elm men. They were fixin' to ride outta town to takes care of some of that ranchin' stuff, I reckon. The gimped-up one mostly did the tellin'."

"Gimpy?"

"Yes, ma'am. They said I oughta tell you on account of it's the right thing to do."

"Have you heard anything else?"

"Yes, ma'am, but I was told to keep my lip buttoned up."

"Remember you're riding our brand now, so you're duty bound to let us know if there's something we need to know." She detested putting him on the spot but had no choice. "So you have to tell me everything."

"Yes, ma'am." He stammered. "Mister Payne got a bucket load of money deposited over to the bank this mornin'. More than the Dewey's . . ." He hesitated, trying to cover his slipup. "I mean, more than anybody's ever laid eyes on."

She prodded him along, knowing he was uncomfortable telling what he knew. Yet he seemed to take pride in taking on his duty to be faithful to his new employer.

"Go ahead, Pony Boy. You gotta trust me."

"Miz Dewey—oops. I mean *somebody* told around that Mister Smith and Mister Payne are in cahoots and wanna take over Jacks Bluff by gettin' you two ladies all swooned up over them. But that's just talk. Not fact. They wouldn't do that, would they?" Pony Boy shifted uncomfortably. "Mister Payne bought hisself a ticket back east on the next train goin' thata way."

Her heart plummeted, torn by the emotions that raged within her. She felt as though her breath was cut off, half from apprehension and half in dread of the truth.

Holding back tears of disappointment and aching with an inner misery that was eating her alive, she took a deep breath.

In her mama's absence, she had to play the part of the mistress of Jacks Bluff to reassure Pony Boy that he'd done the right thing. Squaring her shoulders, she lifted her head and tried to ignore the pain in her soul. She asked the young man if she could buy him breakfast. He eagerly agreed.

Off to the side, she saw Tuffy motion Pony Boy his way.

"Ma'am, if'n you don't mind, I'll go sit with Mister Thompson."

"Certainly, but I think he'd want you to call him Tuffy."

"Thank you, ma'am." He ducked his head.

"Your mama would be proud of you. You did the right thing, so we can protect the ranch." She bit her lip, hoping he didn't see she was about to cry, but curiosity got the best of her and she asked, "What are you going to do with that jar of pickles?"

"These here are for Mister Tegeler, ma'am. Gotta take good care of 'um." He shuffled off.

How could she eat? She pushed her plate away. Her world was falling around her. Morgan had asked her to trust him and she had, now it'd all been a lie. She looked around, not sure who she should trust. Who had the charismatic dandy drawn into his conspiracy to take over the Jacks Bluff?

Alaine's mind was filled with sour thoughts. Terrifying realization washed over her. The harder she tried to ignore the truth the more it persisted. She couldn't close her eyes to the facts any longer. The boots. The hidden gun. His ability to rope, ride and wear pants and a shirt like no cowboy she'd ever imagined. If he worked for the Slippery Elm all along, he had deliberately played her for a fool.

The greedy British belted earls weren't satisfied to have one of the biggest operations in Kasota Springs . . . they wanted control of the whole damn Panhandle!

But, for some reason that she couldn't put her finger on, something was missing. Facts, rumor or speculation, Morgan

Payne could not be involved with such a scheme. She knew it in her heart and her soul.

Daintily, she folded her napkin, placed it on the table and picked up her hat. Loud enough for everyone to hear, she said, "Pony Boy, if Mr. Payne returns, please inform him that I'm in my mama's room. Resting."

One of Teg's men followed her as far as possible without trying to be noticed, but he was about as invisible as the eyes of a coyote on a pitch-black night—you knew it was there but not exactly where.

Reaching the room, she tossed her hat on the bed and went to the wardrobe where her mother's dresses hung in an orderly fashion. The shelf above held matching trappings for each outfit.

For once in her life she was pleased that she and her mama wore the same size.

She considered the scarlet and black dress, but it brought back memories of the bank robbery and how frantic her mama was to keep her safe.

Cocking her head, she looked over the Federal blue day dress. It was nice. Although she was about to start a second War Between the States, no self-respecting southern born-and-bred lady would be caught dead in Federal blue.

Alaine selected a promenade gown that her mother had planned to wear to last night's dance, off-the-shoulder, trimmed with puffing and bows and accented with pink ribbons in scalloped lace. She stripped off her leather skirt and jacket and changed clothes.

Swooping up her hair in ringlets that hung down her back, she added a bonnet with yards of tulle and pink roses. Slipping on lace gloves, she gathered the beaded bag and parasol, pulled the veil over her face and walked out of the room.

Stopping at the top of the stairs, she raised the parasol and prayed that bad luck wouldn't come her way for opening the blasted thing indoors. She held her head high and proceeded down the stairs.

"Good day, Miss Tempest." The desk clerk greeted her without looking up. She smiled to herself and strolled through the lobby.

By damn, she'd get the truth from Morgan Payne if it was the last thing she'd do, and nobody would dare follow her!

Chapter 13

Heads turned and lips flapped as Alaine lifted her veil and tromped down Main Street, but she held her head high. For once, she honestly didn't care what people thought. In the past she acted like she didn't, but deep inside she did and it hurt. But no more.

She recalled Morgan saying that he planned to get a shave as soon as the barber shop opened, so she headed that way.

It seemed every man in town had decided to go to the barber by the number of men sitting on benches outside, along with others standing around making bets on who would be the all-around cowboy.

Alaine excused herself as she walked between two groups of men crowding the sidewalk. They tipped their hats, no doubt wondering what in the hell had happened to little Buckaroo LeDoux, the ornery gal of Kasota Springs.

The barber hopped around like he had fire ants biting his ankles when he spied her in the mirror. "Miss LeDoux, you cain't come in here," he said, although her arrival didn't stop him from sharpening his razor on a leather strap. "This here's man's territory. No ladies—"

"Excuse me," she interrupted, catching sight of Morgan, who lay back in the barber chair, draped in a white cape, with frothy, white shaving cream on his face. "I see the gentleman I wish to visit with."

Morgan must've heard the commotion long before she spoke, because by the time she crossed the room, he had sat straight up and came to his feet.

"What in the hell!" He grabbed a towel and wiped froth from his face, leaving a full beard reminding her of Santa Claus, except for the white on his forehead. A smudge of lather hung from one ear.

He threw the towel down and in long strides advanced toward her. Not backing down she marched on . . . two warriors prepared for battle.

"Little Lady—"

"Don't call me that." Triumph rolled through her when he winced at her words.

"Okay, Alaine! What's happened? Is something wrong? Are you okay? Hurt?" He bombarded her with questions. She'd expect that from her mama but not from Morgan.

His words were uncompromising yet gentle, while his expression stilled and grew serious.

She saw concern on his face, panic in his eyes, as if she had frightened him. She stepped back and looked him directly in the face. The man wasn't angry, maybe a little surprised, but definitely alarmed.

Suddenly much of her anger evaporated, leaving only confusion. Strange and disquieting thoughts raged a war in her mind. Something was terribly wrong.

"What's the matter, Morgan?" To her, her voice sounded far away.

"Tell me!" He demanded before stepping forward, taking her by the arm and leading her toward the door where he stopped long enough to tear off the cap, snatch up his Stetson and plop it on his head.

"No! You tell *me!* You, you, Yankee scoundrel." She didn't like him pulling her out the door in the least.

"I might be Yankee, ma'am, but I'm sure as hell not a scoundrel."

"You don't deserve someone like me to love." She stopped dead still, not sure where the words came from, but decided that wouldn't deter her confrontation. "You told me to trust you and I did . . . and, and—"

A crowd quickly congregated. She jerked out of his grip and whirled toward the pack. In the best boarding house English she could manage, Alaine looked directly at Edwinna Dewey, who seemed to be hanging on every word, and said, "So you all can go about your business without missing a word, I'll have this printed in the newspaper!"

The crowd dispersed. He partially dragged and almost pulled her into the alley . . . the alley where they originally met. How coincidental, she thought.

"Since you won't confess—"

"Alaine, I don't know what I'm confessing to."

"That you're not who you—not a lawyer, not anything." Tears wet her eyes. She was damned if she'd cry. She choked them back, and considered bopping Morgan on the head with her parasol for making her bawl.

"Sit down." He pointed to a wooden crate. "I can explain."

"About time." She took a seat, but didn't move her gaze from him.

"On the outside, Alaine, I'm not who you thought I was, but I am on the inside. Deep down, I'm the same man who fell madly in love with you." He jerked his hat off, ran his fingers through his hair and set it back on, obviously buying some time. "And I do love you."

"Morgan, I can't give my love to someone who has lied to me and done the things they say you've done. You and that McKenna Smith."

"Leave him out of it. He knows nothing about why I'm in Kasota Springs." His brows furrowed together in a frown.

"I'm not a lawyer, and I'm not looking for ranchland to buy for me or anybody."

"So far the rumor mill is one and you're zero."

"Don't get ahead of yourself. I'm a Pinkerton Agent on assignment. Alaine, I couldn't put you in jeopardy by telling you what I was working on. You had to trust me."

"A Pinkerton in Texas." She almost laughed at the idea. "That's about like a Texas Ranger in New York."

"I'm a special agent trained in a new area of law enforcement they call corporate fraud."

"Answer me one thing." She looked into his eyes and thought of a million reasons not to trust him. However, she did. "A yes or no, Morgan. Are you here to make sure that our ranch gets in the hands of one of the syndicate operators?"

"Absolutely not. If I were, why would I have warned Teg about the rustling?"

"You brought Teg into it!"

Alaine listened as Morgan explained the rustling scheme. How Clayton Snyder and Gimpy hair branded Slippery Elm cattle before moving them over to the shoestring operation that Gimpy owned. Then they'd alter the brand, making them Rocking J cattle, and sell them, depositing the money in Gimpy's account.

She tried to take in everything he said but was having a hard time of it.

"Gimpy and Snyder disappeared, taking the payroll and operating money for both operations. Got a wire about twenty minutes ago that they didn't get far. A Texas Ranger captured them over around Mobeetie and they're in jail up there."

"And the money you deposited in the bank?"

"Operating funds." He crossed his arms. "Hell, they had to get their hands paid some way. The owners asked my bosses if I could stick around a day or two to watch out after the Slippery Elm, so they could send new management down here."

"That's a logical explanation."

"I have little choice. My bosses directed me to stay."

"That was the wire you got last night?" Alaine asked.

"Damn, the gossipmongers in this town are really good."

"So the Slippery Elm owners needed someone they could trust—"

"Yes, ma'am. I'm not sure how much solving of the case I did and how much Teg did, but we got it done."

"So you're going back to Philadelphia?"

"Not right now. Might be a spell even. Got some of their bookkeeping to work out. Snyder charged out the owners with fifty heifers for the rodeo, instead of ten or twelve. Stuff like that."

"Morgan, I remember you telling me if I wanted a partner I had to trust you. You said you weren't going to put your life on the line for someone who didn't have confidence in themselves."

"I remember that."

"And you'll probably believe I'm lying, but I honestly trusted you. Even when the facts looked differently, I knew deep down that you couldn't change what is in your soul. Morgan, a Texan is known by his heart and it doesn't make any difference where they are born if it's there."

He pulled her into his arms and kissed her tenderly. And not nearly long enough.

"You're my Texas love," he whispered between kisses.

Alaine removed her lace hanky from the bag, and cleaned the shaving cream from first his face and then hers.

Pony Boy scrambled by hollering, "Better hurry. Shootin' contest is 'bout to start," before disappearing.

"Morgan, I can't shoot in these clothes. I have to change."

"You don't have time." He put his hands on her shoulders. "Remember, it's confidence in yourself that matters."

They hurried off toward the middle of town where the crowd had regrouped, waiting on the final exhibition event of the festivities to begin.

"Next contestant after Ty Parker is Alaine LeDoux," the announcer drawled, just about the time the couple reached the shooting area.

Morgan hugged her lightly, as Tuffy shoved her rifle in her hands.

"Good luck, Little Lady." Morgan smiled, thinking how pretty she was.

Morgan melded into the crowd that lined Main Street. His gut hit rock bottom when he realized she was the only woman shooting against all men. He believed in her—she *could* do it.

He watched Alaine prepare for her turn by squaring her shoulders and focusing on her target. He hadn't seen her do that before.

Sunlight flashed across the street like lightning on a dark night.

A gunman was on the rooftop of Slats and Fats Saloon.

Morgan raced across the street and up the saloon stairs. Making a mad dive for the rifle, he knocked the Winchester out of the gunman's hands.

"Sonofabitch, Tegeler!" Morgan threw his hat on the ground. "What in the hell do you think you're doing?"

"I have to guarantee she makes her shot, Payne. She has to win."

"No! For once, she has to do it on her own . . . without any help, or we all lose."

Morgan picked up the Stetson and brushed it off. It was too late for him to get back to the woman who meant more to him than anything, win or lose.

From the rooftop, the two men watched as Alaine leveled her Parker at her mark.

Had Morgan taught her to be the best she could be? Could she do it on her own?

The roar of the crowd drowned out the shot . . . bull's-eye!

Teg picked up his rifle from the floor and quirked a smile. "Go get her, Payne. You're what she needs."

Slapping the ol' fool on the back, Morgan said, "Alaine has truly become the best she can be and did it with all the confidence in the world."

Morgan took off to find Alaine. When he reached her, he swung her into arms and gave her a congratulatory kiss.

"I'm starving. Let's go eat, Annie Oakley."

"No, I'm Alaine Claire LeDoux and damn proud of it!"

Chapter 14

A short and busy three days later, Morgan rode away from the Slippery Elm headquarters for the last time. He had been summoned to the Jacks Bluff for supper and a poker game. He wasn't sure what was in store for him, but he couldn't resist sticking around to see what in the heck the LeDoux women had up their pretty little sleeves.

He stood in the parlor sipping fine Kentucky bourbon with Smith and Tegeler while the women bustled around in the kitchen. Every now and then he'd hear one of them give an order to the cook who seemed to overrule them each time.

"Thought Pinks didn't drink," Teg groused.

"Ex ones do." Morgan took a sip, enjoying the first drink he'd had in years.

Alaine and Tempest floated into the room dressed almost like twins in matching lilac and ivory dresses that highlighted their dark complexions and black hair.

To quote his mama, "The tree is known by its fruit." Morgan wasn't sure which lady looked happier or the prettiest, although his money was on Alaine.

Tempest accepted a glass of spirits from McKenna, smiled and turned to her guests, as if she was holding court.

"Alaine, McKenna and I have something to tell you." She sidled up to Smith.

"I know, Mama, and I'm happy for you both."

"Guess Edwinna couldn't keep her trap shut. Should've planned your weddin' in another county if you wanted to keep it quiet," Teg grumbled.

McKenna put his arms around Tempest. "Figure someone in this town will win a bet. I did ask your mama to marry me."

"And I accepted." Tempest looked up at him as though she were sixteen and going to her first cotillion. "We're getting married tomorrow and plan to split time between Montana and his ranch down in Austin." She stepped out of his arms, walked to the mantel and picked up an envelope. "And, sweetheart, I want you to run the Jacks Bluff."

"Mama, you trust me enough to do that?"

"Yes, darling." She hugged her daughter, and stuffed the envelope in her hand. "But I do have one request."

Tempest turned to Morgan. "That you hire on Mr. Payne as your manager."

Morgan was stunned, but probably no more than Alaine. Why him when Tegeler was the obvious choice?

Before he got the thought formulated enough to spit it out, Alaine piped up.

"Why him?" Then she smiled at Morgan. "Not that I'd mind working with Mr. Grouchy Trousers."

Everyone shared a laugh. Morgan didn't even mind the jab. He'd earned it.

Before Tempest could respond, Tegeler spoke up. "Because I've got too many fences to ride and don't have time for all that pencil-type work. Got cowboys to keep on their toes." He took a gulp of whiskey. "And Little Buckaroo, for your information, I've got women I ain't even danced with."

Tempest spoke up. "Plus, Mr. Payne has the finesse it takes to deal with the cattleman's association, their reps, the bank and most folks in general." She smiled at the foreman. "Something Teg is sorely lacking in."

"The hell you say!" Teg barked. "I can handle those snot-nosed greenhorns that don't know enough to not squat with their spurs on or spit downwind—"

Alaine interrupted. "Teg makes this place run, and I'd never want him behind a desk. We'd lose him in ten minutes." She raised a questioning eyebrow.

"I'm mighty pleased to accept, Miss LeDoux." Morgan took her hand and pulled her to his side.

"And you can stay in the main house," Alaine said.

"Like hell he will!" Tegeler growled.

"I've been thinking about sticking around anyway," Morgan said, looking into Alaine's violet eyes. "Thought I'd trade in my train ticket for a weddin' band."

He figured nobody was shocked by his proposal, especially Alaine who threw her arms around his neck and kissed him boldly. "Only if that ring goes on my finger," she whispered.

"Don't know for sure." He released her. "All depends if it'll interfere with your dream to be another Annie Oakley and join the Wild West show."

"Why would I do that when I can stay around here?"

Morgan tucked Alaine to his side.

"Being around you makes Wild Bill Hickok, Annie Oakley and Calamity Jane look flat-ass boring. I'd rather be your Little Lady and stay near you just to see what will happen next!" Lowering her voice, she spoke only to him, "You'll always have a place to sleep in my house."

Alaine heard the knock before anyone else. It was almost drowned out by the jubilance. She opened the door to find Pony Boy standing protectively holding a jar in his arms.

"These here are for Mister Tegeler, ma'am." He handed over the jar and scrambled away.

"Nice present, Tegeler." Morgan chuckled. "But I'd suggest you eat around the spices in those pickles."

Morgan had no doubt that every day of the rest of his life would be no less than the Wild West show. With Alaine at his side, he'd always be ropin' the wind.